3/15/89

LAUGHING DOG

LAUGHING DOG

A Leo Bloodworth and Serendipity Dahlquist Novel

Dick Lochte

ARBOR
HOUSE
MORROW

ARBOR HOUSE / WILLIAM MORROW
New York

For Judith and for Tom,
Best Gal, Best Pal

Printed in the United States of America

What follows is a work of fiction. The author acknowledges that
southern California, such as it is, actually exists. But any similarity
between this novel's characters and plot and existing people,
places, seats of higher learning, and events is totally coincidental
and unintended.

"The little dog laughed to see such sport . . ."

—M. Goose

PROLOGUE

Leo Bloodworth, whose private detective agency bore his name, dumped his 228 pounds onto his creaky swivel chair, put his size-eleven bluchers on his desktop, and picked up the manuscript. He thought briefly of opening the bottom right drawer of the desk, getting out a bottle of Irish whiskey, and sampling it. But he was not alone. A fifteen-year-old girl named Serendipity Dahlquist was in the outer office, probably watching him through the crack in the door, and he was not up to the argument that a harmless little snort or two would prompt.

He sighed, recalling a time not long ago when he did not have to worry about offending the sensibilities of a precocious teenager.

Instead of taking a drink, he read:

Manion had come to southern California expecting to stay a week or two. His first lodging was at a modest motel off of the San Diego Freeway that had been partially destroyed by one of the bigger quakes. But it was not long before he found himself being shuttled from spare room to spare bed to spare couch to spare bathtub in a series of apartments he could not remember, belonging to people he did not know.

Eventually he settled into a stark single room in a pale yellow building without electricity or running water, facing the beach near Santa Monica, where he was joined infrequently by his beloved ex-wife, Gilian. At least, he believed this was happening. Whether she was actually there or only there in his imagination was a moot question. He enjoyed her company so.

Most of his thirty-one years had been spent in the South, specifically in New Orleans, where the way of life was considerably different from that of southern California. But he felt that he had adapted admirably to this sun-kissed land where the natives, nurtured on the broadcast media, seemed to have no sense of history, no tradition, and no discernible accent. Still, his adaptability notwithstanding, he knew that he was losing his mind, slowly but surely.

Someone—it cost him too much effort to try to remember who—had offered the opinion that Los Angeles was a place where insane people could find freedom and relative happiness, lying doggo as part of a population that honored eccentricity. Manion wondered if it was mentally sound to amuse oneself with phrases like "lying doggo."

Aimless in a place where aimlessness was prized, he had drifted into an unwavering pattern dictated by the relentless good weather. That morning, as on every morning, he was awakened by the sun as it lasered through his shadeless window. Not sure if he should smile or scowl, he staggered from the bed and paused at his portal to the world, squinting out at the nearly empty beach heading south to Venice and north to Malibu, nudged by the frothy green-gray, chemically impure Pacific Ocean. He smiled; he was pretty chemically impure himself.

Thinking of which, he turned from the window and gave his sunny room a scan. The brown plastic medicine bottle resting on the edge of the chipped Formica-top table was new, and there was a fresh bottle of water beside it, but he could not remember having had any visitors. Except for Gillian, of course. But she had come with empty hands and open arms and . . .

He fumbled the child-proof cap off of the bottle and shook two black-and-white capsules onto his palm, then washed them down with water from the bottle. He could feel his blood begin to flow warmly through his veins. He staggered to the door and tried to open it. Without success. He tried to open it every morning, though in truth he didn't know why. There was nowhere else that he wanted to be.

It was too early for anyone but the increasing parade of homeless to be on the beach. The sun-worshipers would come later. There would be volleyballers and joggers and dog walkers and bicycle riders. But before that the old woman in her Hawaiian mumuu would arrive to go through a series of morning contortions. Veined hands on jutting hips, she would throw her head back and forth with a quick snapping motion that on a lesser spinal column would have resulted in at least a minor case of whiplash. Manion imagined her to be a student of Agnes de Mille. He had never seen Agnes de Mille. For all he knew, she could *be* Agnes de Mille.

She would rotate her pelvis in a circular pattern and, emitting a loud, horrific howl, would begin prancing like a show horse. At that point Manion usually became so embarrassed for the woman that he would turn away. Maybe today would be different. He would watch the old woman.

He would open the door.

He would find his way . . . to the detective Bloodworth and the enchanting girl-woman who assisted him. They would help him regain control of his mind.

But if Gil came and he was gone, would she ever come back again?

The old woman danced into view. He wanted to continue watching her. But he turned away. He stumbled back to his bed. At the end of the day Gil would come to him.

Bloodworth gathered the manuscript sheets and bounced them on his desktop. Serendipity Dahlquist arrived in his office like a shot. "What do you think?" she asked anxiously.

" 'Enchanting girl-woman,' " he said, raising his eyebrows.

"Too much, huh?" When he didn't reply, she went on, "It's just that one doesn't know exactly how much to keep oneself out of a narration. Nearly everything I wrote came directly from Terry. His background. What he was thinking. We've had several long, lovely talks."

"He told you that you were an enchanting girl-woman?"

"Not in so many words," she said. "I mean, this *is* a semifictional work. I should be able to embellish . . ."

The big detective raised his hand and grinned at her. "Relax, kid. If it's okay with Manion, it's okay with me."

"I'm sure that Terry won't mind."

"You haven't asked his permission?"

"There'll be time for that. Do you think I did him justice, so far?"

Bloodworth stood up with a little smile on his face. "Yeah. I guess. I barely know the guy. How's he doing, by the way?"

"He'll be transferring to a hospital in Louisiana in a few days."

Bloodworth walked to his filing cabinet and banged open a drawer. He dug a manila folder out of the drawer and carried it to his desk. "How much longer before you finish with the book?" he asked the girl.

"Maybe two months," she said, slumping onto the client's chair. "I just wish I knew I was doing the right thing."

"You mean about making Manion your hero?"

The girl stretched out her blue-jeaned legs and wiggled her feet. "Oh, I have no trepidation at all about Terry being my hero. I'm just not sure about my use of third-person narration. I mean, the only reason I got the book contract was because the first one did so well, and that one was in the first person, as you well know."

Bloodworth knew too well. He and the Dahlquist girl had penned separate accounts of an adventure that had brought them together. Through a quirk of fate both manuscripts had become the properties of the same publishing house and had been released as one novel, titled *Sleeping Dog.* Through an even quirkier fate the book had achieved a modicum of popularity.

Bloodworth liked what the book had done for him, both money- and business-wise: He was now getting the kinds of cases usually reserved for the larger agencies. But he was not pleased at the prospect of being joined at the hip to the Dahlquist girl on all future literary endeavors. So he had been relieved when Serendipity had decided to make Terry Manion the protagonist of her next novel. It meant that there was a chance that he would not have to share another book with her.

"The third person is working for you, Sarah. Stick with it, I say." He was using the first person for his book. "If they don't like it, you can always change it later. Who's your editor, anyway?"

"Mavis Granier. Isn't she yours, too?"

"No way! Not with her temper. I hear she was at lunch with some music conductor and jabbed a salad fork right through his mitt. And it was his baton-waving hand, too."

The little girl squinted her eyes in displeasure. "The fact is, the fellow was using his 'baton-waving hand' in a . . . well, in a manner that was sexually threatening."

Bloodworth leaned forward, showing definite interest. "You mean he was making a grab for . . . ?"

"He was behaving very boorishly."

The detective shrugged and settled back. "Well, anyway, if you're nervous about this first-person–third-person thing, ask Mavis."

"I'll make the decision myself," she said seriously. "Mavis has enough on her mind. She's marrying the conductor, you know."

Bloodworth's mouth dropped. "Jeez, Cupid must've really had to work overtime on that one."

The girl raised her eyebrows. "Perhaps so. But to return to my problem, on the one hand all my favorite novelists have used the third person. Miss Dorothy L. Sayers. Miss Ruth Rendell. Miss Martha Grimes. All of them.

"On the other hand I have achieved some success with the first-person narrative, and as Gran often says, 'If it isn't broken, don't try to fix it.' "

He gave her a perfunctory smile that was supposed to indicate that he had nothing more to say on that particular matter. His eyes dropped to the folder on his desk that he'd been tapping with a finger.

She said, "My initial thought was to focus on a character not unlike . . . you. Brave. Courageous. Dashing, if a bit sexist. But then you went jetting all around the world on some highly secretive investigation. . . ."

"It was to Italy, and at the time it was an open case, and you know I don't talk about open cases."

"Anyway, Terry Manion came along. And frankly, he has one important characteristic for a contemporary protagonist that you don't."

In spite of himself, Bloodworth was annoyed at this turn of the conversation. "What's that," he said nastily, "a drug habit?"

She glared at him. "He does not have a drug habit, and you know it. No. Terry is . . . vulnerable."

Bloodworth grunted, "I guess he is, at that." He flipped open his folder.

Inside was a spiral notebook. Bloodworth picked up a pencil and began turning pages. Serendipity watched him for a minute, then gathered up her manuscript. "I guess you've got things to do," she said.

"All this talk about books," he said.

"Oh, is that your rough draft?"

He nodded.

"I'd be glad to give you my opinion."

"It's not quite ready yet, kid. But thanks. You run along now."

"I can just about make visiting hours at the hospital if I rush."

He nodded, then began to study the scribbles in his notebook. She paused at the door, clutching her manuscript to her chest. She opened her mouth, then thought better about whatever she was going to say.

When he heard the office door click shut behind her, he removed his new reading glasses from his coat pocket. He'd had to hold the girl's neatly typed pages almost at arm's length to read them. To have worn the glasses in her presence seemed somehow out of the question. It was Manion, after all, who was the vulnerable one.

1

(Beginning: MAN FROM THE SOUTH. A mystery novel by
S. R. Dahlquist)

For Gran, again.

1. The Mandotta case had seemed so promising. A seventy-nine-year-old captain of industry, Salvadore Mandotta, mysteriously disappears at the precise moment that his import-export business is being devoured whole by a conglomerate. He had been opposed to the takeover, which will put literally millions of dollars into the pockets of his three children, two sons and a daughter. The sons are happy to be rid of the old fellow, but his loving daughter hires the Bloodworth Agency (proprietor: Mr. Leo J. Bloodworth) to find the old man. Murder? Possibly. At the very least, financial hanky panky.

In the nearly twenty-nine days since I had become a sort of junior member of the agency, performing the duties of receptionist, clerk, accountant—to be succinct, its factotum—thereby allowing the gallant Mr. Bloodworth to answer his clientele's many and diverse needs, the Mandotta file was the only case that I'd fed into my word processor that had any real potential for dramatic development.

But, alas, the ever-resourceful Mr. B. made just a few phone calls—to his sources at voter registration, the DMV (yes, the old man still operated a vehicle), and eventually Medicare—and discovered that Mr. Mandotta was alive and well in a town in Washington state named Black Diamond, halfway between Tacoma and Seattle, living in a trailer with a pleasant woman two years his junior and a black Labrador retriever. Mr. Mandotta requested that his family send him his "piece of the take" once a month, but beyond that he was not interested in hearing from any of them. Daughter included. End of report.

This was a typical case. So mundanely had the transcriptions been going, that the normally abrasive buzz of the office telephone sounded like music to my ears. Anything to escape drudgery.

"Bloodworth Agency," I answered in my most professional manner.

"Could I speak with Mr. Bloodworth?" A man's voice, offering no suggestion of age. Clear, educated, with a pleasant timbre.

"I'm sorry, but he's unavailable."

"Is this his service?"

"His associate," I replied.

"Oh. My name is Manion. Terry Manion. I tried calling him from my hotel yesterday afternoon, but there was no answer."

My grandmother had had one of her rare free afternoons, so I'd left the office early to take a little stroll down Wilshire in Beverly Hills and allow her to talk me into accepting an extravagant cashmere sweater from Neiman's in celebration of her signing a new contract at United Broadcasting Company, good old UBC. I should mention that my grandmother is Edith Van Dine, who, as you probably know, has been portraying Aunt Lil Fairchild on the soap *Look to Tomorrow* for fifteen years, which is as long as I've been on this earth. Anyway, that's why I wasn't in the office to answer the phone. And from what I've observed, Mr. Bloodworth often refuses to answer the thing and will let it ring for what seems like hours.

"We must've forgotten to turn on the answering machine. I hope you weren't terribly inconvenienced," I apologized to Mr. Manion.

"Might I set up an appointment to see him today?"

I glanced over at Mr. Bloodworth's dark office, then checked my Jane Fonda wristwatch. The bent hand with the barbell was nearing one, the outstretched arm was on six. "I expect him back within the hour."

"Good. Thank you." And Mr. Terry Manion hung up before I could say another word.

2. Mr. Bloodworth thundered in at precisely one o'clock. I rose from my computer and moved through the empty anteroom, following in his wake into his office.

He was standing beside his desk with a bottle of whiskey in one hand and a bloody handkerchief in the other. He raised the bottle to his lips, then spotted me. He quickly moved the bottle behind his back.

"Hi, kid. I thought you might be o.t.l."

"Out to lunch? No, sir. I'm a brown-bagger. Work to do." I indicated the poisonous dark brown bottle. "Isn't it a bit early for that?"

He looked at the whiskey as if he didn't quite know how it had gotten into his hand. "Oh, this? Well, I just came from Singh's, and the bastard nicked me again. This stuff is as good as any witch hazel."

He poured a little of the whiskey onto the bloody handkerchief and took a long whiff of it. Then he began rubbing the dried blood from a tiny cut on his cheek.

"I don't know why anybody'd go to a Thai barber for a shave," I told him.

"Don't be prejudiced, kid."

"Prejudiced? Thais have little or no facial hair. They rarely shave themselves. What makes you think they'd know how to shave others?"

"Some of the best barbers I've ever had shave even less often than Thais," he said. "They're women." Touché. Using feminism as a defense. He was improving. Still, his smug smile turned into a wince as the whiskey found its mark, reminding him, of course, that I was basically correct in my appraisal of Singh's skills.

He was wearing his best suit, the dark blue linen from Carroll's with the tapered waist that makes him look quite trim. "My, but we're *très élégant* today."

"Money client," he said, not putting the bottle away. I took it from his hand, capped it, and placed it into his desk drawer.

He studied his reflection in the glass sheet that covered his desktop. "How's the filing going?"

"Dullsville." I walked to the window that faced a new seven-story mural—I think they call them building-scapes—of a snake battling a mongoose. It was supposed to call attention to the main attraction of the building, the Cobra Lounge on the ground floor. "I keep expecting a good, juicy case, like that business with the banker who was the cross-dresser."

"Fedderman?"

"Right. Lucius, or as he would have it, Lucy Fedderman. Anyway, those are few and far between. Usually they're resolved by you making phone calls or canvassing locations or, worse yet, doing research."

He shrugged. "Welcome to the wonderful world of private investigations." He sat down in his chair and picked up a book that had been resting on his desk. Although I'd been trying desperately to hone my powers of observation by making mental pictures of every location I entered, I admit that I'd missed the volume completely. It was a thin library edition titled *The Architecture of Southern California.*

He said, "Just remember, kid, the stuff in those files is confidential. It goes no further than this office. I'm trusting you on this."

"I think I have proven myself trustworthy in the past." Though I had to admit the idea had crossed my mind that I might find a few incidents worth disguising and fictionalizing for my next novel.

The big detective began to peruse his architecture book. I asked, "Do they mention the fabulous Cobra Lounge Building in there?"

He looked up, then turned toward the window facing the ghastly apparition. "Next time I go into the Cobra," he said, "I'm gonna ask Wishbone how much it'd cost to have that mural changed."

"It would be worth any price if they'd scrape the building clean."

"Oh, I wouldn't want them to touch the snake. It's the mongoose. I'd like them to give it your cute little smile." Then he began to chuckle. Cackle, actually.

I shook my head. When he gets in one of those childish moods, there's nothing to be done but to ignore him completely.

At the door I stopped. "I forgot to mention that I made an appointment for you to see a potential client named Manion. He should be here at any minute."

"Damnit! I've got a *primo* appointment in Hancock Park in a little less than an hour."

"Then give him whatever time you can."

"This isn't a sandwich shop, where you walk right in. There's such a thing as calling ahead."

"He called yesterday. Nobody was here to answer. So he called back today."

"Well, I'll probably have to kiss him off." He sighed. "That's the way it is —you sit around for a week and nothing stirs but the leaves on the trees. Then, bango, all sorts of people want a piece of your action."

"The reason nothing's been stirring is that you've been turning down so many clients."

"I've been waiting for one like the lady who phoned this morning. A celebrity. Old money. Just the ticket."

"But she called only today. Mr. Manion has precedence. He's been trying to reach you since yesterday evening."

"The secret is to concentrate on the *primo* cases and make maximum use of your time. Like scanning this book to prepare for my meet—What's the guy's name? Manion? Why's that sound familiar?"

"He phoned you last month from New Orleans."

"He told you that?"

"No. But the information was on your call sheets. I've added them into the files, too. When I accessed the name *Manion*, that information became available."

He shrugged, picking up the book and flipping through its pages. "From out of town, then. All the more reason to shine him on. Your best clients are people from your own community, who will spread the all-important word of mouth . . ."

"You're beginning to sound like that guy who's on TV late at night. Paul Montclair. Mr. Success." My reference was to a creepy individual in a bad gray toupee and shiny suit who hosted an irregular TV series called *The Success Hour*. Not real shows, but half-hour commercials that attempted to cajole folks into attending his success seminars held in musty hotel meeting rooms. Gran pegged him right off as a snake-oil salesman. But his particular brand of snake oil was composed of equal parts of self-confidence, time-management, and physical regimen. None of them bad in themselves, but nothing you should have to pay hundreds of dollars to hear about.

"I take that as a compliment, kid. Montclair may talk enough to get his tongue suntanned, but he's got the right idea. Time is money. Money is strength. Strength is confidence."

"Please," I implored. "It's bad enough having to catch snatches of *The Success Hour* when I click through the channels."

"Sarah, just leave me alone for a while, huh? I've gotta psych myself up for this meeting."

I strode to the anteroom and then turned and said, "By the way, your face is bleeding again."

He scowled, put down the book, and picked up his handkerchief. "That bastard Singh," he grumbled. "He wields that razor like a goddamned machete."

"That's what I've been trying to tell you for a month," I said.

He stood up and walked to the door, which he shut in my face. I took that as a sign that I'd won another round.

3. Twenty-seven minutes later I heard the outer door open. I waited a beat, then went out from my office into the anteroom to confront a tall, thin, dreamy-eyed man with neatly clipped blond hair, dressed in tweeds, striped tie, and brown-and-white saddle oxfords. He was like a spacey college grad from another era—the fifties, if the nostalgia picture books are to be trusted. "Mr. Manion?"

His blue eyes stared at me quizzically for a moment, then softened. "You're the lady I talked to? Mr. Bloodworth's associate?"

"Does that surprise you?" I asked.

"You seem a little, uh, how do I put it, short in the tooth."

"You mean young?" He nodded and I said, "It works to my advantage. My name is Serendipity Dahlquist." I offered my hand, expecting him to shake it. He bowed and kissed it, instead.

"Pleased to make your acquaintance." He was slightly absurd, but agreeable. He continued to concentrate on my face until I could feel blood rushing to it. "Just how old *are* you, Serendipity Dahlquist?"

Enough was enough. "I don't see the relevance of such a question. And I find it patronizing and offensive. Please have a seat, Mr. Manion. I'll tell Mr. Bloodworth you've arrived."

"I didn't mean to be offensive," he said.

"It was minor offensive," I said, intending the pun.

"At the risk of making a major out of a minor, Miss Dahlquist, might I ask if Mr. Bloodworth is a little older than you?"

"He is. But I wouldn't broach the subject with him. He's much more sensitive about his age than I am."

I walked to Mr. Bloodworth's door, knocked once, and opened it. He was holding his book at arm's distance, squinting at it. As I entered, he blinked, drew the book to him, and dropped it onto the desk. "What?"

"Mr. Manion is here."

He scowled. "You didn't call him off?"

"How? He left no number."

Sighing that familiar resigned sigh, he slapped the book shut and said, "Well, shoo him in, Sarah. Shoo him in."

I indicated that Mr. Manion should join us. He came through the door, limping slightly. I said, "Mr. Bloodworth, this is Mr. Manion. From New Orleans."

Mr. Manion asked, "What makes you think I'm from New Orleans?"

"We *are* investigators," I informed him.

Mr. Bloodworth said, "Have a chair, Mr. Manion, and tell me what we can do for you."

The tall young man took the client chair and focused on the snake and mongoose outside the window. "Nice view," he said.

Mr. Bloodworth said, "Sarah, do you think you could draw the blinds?"

I crossed the room and pulled the cord. I had not been aware of the tension that grotesque vision had created until it was hidden from sight. I told the young man, "Mr. Bloodworth is presently in negotiation to put a mural of the two of us on *this* building. He'll be the one baring his fangs."

Manion looked from me to Mr. Bloodworth, vaguely bemused.

Mr. B. said, "Mr. Manion, I'm a mite pressed for time, so we'd better start the ball rolling on this."

Instead of replying, the young man stared at me.

Mr. Bloodworth picked up on it and said, "Sarah, don't you have some filing to do?"

One of the primary rules is that I am never to argue with him in front of a client or a prospective client. So I nodded and headed out of the room. As I passed Mr. Manion, I noticed that a section of hair at the back of his head had been shaved, exposing a half-dollar-size patch of scalp and a wound that had been stitched. I couldn't help but continue to stare at it until I closed the door behind me.

I skipped to my office and shut that door, too. Then, instead of sitting at my desk, where the word processor waited, humming patiently, I attached a little suction-cup device to the common wall I shared with Mr. Bloodworth's office and inserted its cord into my new Sony tape recorder. Then I slipped on the earphones that were already attached to the recorder.

"So Nadia Wells gave you my name, huh?" Mr. Bloodworth's voice sounded hollow but relatively undistorted. "How is the old dame?"

I moved closer to the wall and removed the Degas print, exposing a small bull's-eye that provided a fairly good view of Mr. Bloodworth's desk and whoever might be sitting in the client's chair. My office had once housed a fellow who had been, to use Gran's phrase, as crooked as a ram's horn—a Mr. Roy Kaspar, who blackmailed the wrong person and paid for his mistake with his life. I imagine he'd used the bull's-eye to watch Mr. Bloodworth, too, but with a much more sinister purpose than mere curiosity.

"Nadia is like the Mississippi," Mr. Manion was saying. "She keeps getting older and stronger and trickier to chart."

"What is she, about seventy?"

"Seventy-eight this year, and still cracking the whip on those security guards and skip-tracers."

"Hell, Manion," Bloodworth grumbled, "you should've dropped Nadia's name when you left that message on my machine last month. I would've gotten back to you. When somebody I don't know calls, unless they're recommended, I don't usually return the call, particularly if it's long distance. I figure if it's important enough, they'll call back."

"I guess that's what I'm doing. I'm trying to locate a runaway. Cecilia MacElroy. She likes to be called Cece. Here's a picture."

I watched Mr. Bloodworth's yellow eyes glaze a little as he took the snapshot. "How old?"

"Barely fifteen."

"You know for sure she's out here?"

Terry Manion nodded.

"Of her own volition?"

"I don't know what the situation is now. I'm fairly certain she made the trip voluntarily. Everybody tells me she fancied herself an actress."

"Oh, Jesus!" Mr. Bloodworth sighed. "I don't know what the situation is in New Orleans, Manion, but when it comes to kids, like the man says, this place can be the last curly kink of the pig's tail. Of the thirty thousand who go missing around the country every year, most of 'em seem to wind up here.

"I was just reading in a magazine that there's a Colombian gang operating in town that kidnaps little blond kids—I'm talking tykes three to ten—and smuggles 'em out to peddle to rich families in South America. The money is used to smuggle dope into the U.S. A new form of the good-neighbor policy.

"When it comes to older kids, well, L.A.'s got more runaways than Napa Valley's got grapes. And they all come out here expecting to work in movies or music."

"But she can be found, right?"

Mr. Bloodworth nodded. "Anybody can be found, assuming there's no limit on time. Or money."

"The MacElroys are well fixed."

"How long missing?"

Mr. Manion hesitated. "Four months," he said.

Mr. Bloodworth gave him a scowl. "I guess you didn't want to rush right into anything," he said sarcastically.

"I only found out about it four weeks ago. That's when Margee—Cece's mother—brought me in."

Mr. Bloodworth leaned back in his chair. "You and your client are on a first-name basis, huh?"

Mr. Manion nodded. "She's my sister-in-law. *Was* my sister-in-law."

Mr. Bloodworth waited for him to continue. When he didn't, the big sleuth asked, "So your ex-sister-in-law waited three months to do something about her missing kid? Is that the picture?"

"There's a little more to it than that."

"Let's hope so."

Mr. Manion's eyes got dreamier. They lifted to the ceiling and then descended to Mr. B. When he spoke, his voice was lower, and he enunciated every word. He reminded me of somebody reacting to a biofeedback test. "Margee and her two children have been living with her parents. Their name is Duplessix. An old New Orleans family. Socially prominent. Mrs. Duplessix is gravely ill. Margee didn't want to put her through any kind of family scandal if she didn't have to." His hand went into his coat pocket and withdrew another photograph.

Mr. Bloodworth looked at it. "Who's this bozo?"

"Cece's father, Brice MacElroy. He's missing, too."

"Oh?"

"He and Margee have been living apart for over a year. He was one of those Southern college football heroes who never quite made it into the pros. Instead, he looped a tie around his red neck and became a spokesman, originally for a soda-pop company in Houston, then for a local brewery, Southland Beer.

"He helped convince Margee not to go to the police. He was sure that they'd only muddy the water without accomplishing anything. There's some truth to that. The city of New Orleans is having money problems, and they've cut the NOPD to the bone. There's not enough cop power to handle the hard-core crimes, much less runaway kids."

"So this MacElroy went out looking on his own?"

Terry Manion nodded. "He always was a hothead and an all-around jerk. Still, I wanted to touch base with him before I did anything. Cece is his daughter, after all. The manager at the Tattersol Club, the private club where he's been living, told me he'd left town."

"Just after the girl went missing?"

Another nod. "Brice informed the club manager that he was going on a business trip and asked that his mail be held indefinitely. Since then, he hasn't called in."

"What do they say at the brewery?"

"That Brice is away on a personal leave of absence."

"What about his bank? Credit-card charges?"

"Margee MacElroy isn't all that interested in finding Brice. It's the girl she wants back."

Mr. Bloodworth said, "It wouldn't hurt to know where the father is. Maybe he's done some of the work for us. This private club, has he been paying them by mail?"

Mr. Manion shook his head. "He doesn't pay them at all. Old man Duplessix is the one with the membership. He picks up Brice's dues and rent."

"Sounds like an okay family to marry into," Mr. Bloodworth said, rather heavily.

Mr. Manion paused and his eyes literally froze. "Oh, I wouldn't recommend it," he said softly.

Mr. Bloodworth tugged at his earlobe, not the least embarrassed. "You got any objection to my talking to a friend on the force out here?"

"Not if it won't send the NOPD out to bother the Duplessixes."

Mr. Bloodworth made a note on the scratchpad on his desk. Then he looked at his watch. "I'm real sorry, Manion. But I've got this meeting mid-Wilshire." He stood up. "Tell you what. Why don't we get together tomorrow morning to hash this out over some oatmeal and coffee?"

Mr. Manion stood up, too. "I guess that'd be all right. The problem is, I'm supposed to meet a woman at six who might be able to give me a lead.

And I feel like a fish out of water here. I was hoping you would come with me."

"Who's the woman?"

"It's a little complicated. You'll be late for your appointment."

Mr. Bloodworth nodded. "I'll try to get back here by five."

They started out of the office. I dropped the Degas back into place, popped the suction cup from the wall, and tossed the whole tape-recording mess into a drawer. Then I raced around the desk and into the anteroom in time to see Mr. Bloodworth heading for the hall door.

He stopped, turned to Mr. Manion. "You said this Mrs. MacElroy told you about the missing girl four weeks ago. Since you put through a call to me about that time, you must have tracked her to the West Coast pretty fast."

Terry Manion said, "That part of it was easy."

"So what've you been doing since then?"

Mr. Manion hesitated again. "Well, when I didn't hear from you, I called another investigator who'd been recommended." He paused, then added, "Mike Kosca."

"Name's vaguely familiar. Maybe I know him."

"He was on TV yesterday," I said. "The body in San Rafael Canyon." I shut my eyes, recalling the video images of a corpse tied to a gurney being hoisted up the canyon wall. "The police officer at the scene said his throat had been cut."

"That's why I flew out yesterday," Terry Manion said. "I'm worried it might have something to do with Cece."

Mr. Bloodworth scowled at him. "And the woman we're gonna see this evening is . . . ?"

"Mrs. Kosca."

Mr. Bloodworth sighed. "Okay. Just . . . take it easy until I get back." He started forward, stopped, and asked Mr. Manion, "What makes you think your niece might be involved in Kosca's death?"

Terry Manion gestured helplessly with his hands. "A hunch."

The big sleuth relaxed a bit. "Yeah. Well, let's just put that hunch on hold until five." He turned to me. "I can give you a lift halfway home, sis."

I shook my head. "I like being here, where the action is," I told him.

He shrugged and backed out of the room awkwardly, as if he wasn't sure about leaving me with Mr. Manion. I sensed he was being protective, but which of us was he trying to protect?

His footsteps were still echoing down the hall when Terry Manion turned to me and asked where the nearest movie theater was.

"They're mainly Spanish-speaking in this neighborhood," I told him.

"That doesn't matter," he said. "As long as they sell popcorn. Care to join me?"

I thanked him but declined. He gave me a smile and a little salute, then he limped out of the office. An odd fellow, Mr. Terry Manion, and not exactly the answer to a maiden's prayer. But there was something there, all right.

2

(Beginning: POWER PLAY. A novel based on fact by Leo J. Bloodworth)

This one's for Cugie, in spite of everything.

And thanks, once again, to Jerry Flaherty of the L.A. Post *for his help in making order out of chicken-scratch chaos.*

L. J. B.
The Qualms,
Santa Barbara, California

1. Mornay House, as it is called in architecture circles, is actually three separate stone-and-glass structures built around a copse of oak trees and connected by narrow glass passages constructed to conform to the natural tree lines and the sloping of the meadow on which the whole business rests. Frank Lloyd Wright is often credited for the design, but it was actually a copy of a place he put up in the Palisades in the thirties for a minor movie mogul named Jake Berns. It burned to the ground, but before it did, Laura Mornay had grown fond of it. She was Berns's leading lady, at home and on the job. He called her his inamorata, and that's what he named the showplace, L'Inamorata.

By the time the late forties rolled around, Jake was six feet under the sod, and thanks to some nice, leggy artwork in *Life* magazine the boys overseas had taken to their hearts, Mornay had become the toast of Twentieth Century–Fox. She cajoled some slightly bent architect into duplicating Wright's blueprints and recreating L'Inamorata for her on a huge chunk of property in Hancock Park, which was then just about the most prime residential area of the city. You had your main mansion in Hancock and your casual cottage on the beach at Santa Monica for weekends, and little things like a depression or a world war didn't seem to matter much.

Today, the Hancocks, Huntingtons, Crockers, and Bannings may have moved on, but Hancock Park is still a class act, realty-wise. Beverly Hills and Bel Air and Holmby Hills are on the guided-tour route. But it's Hancock Park where much of the old money resides. Which is why, on a warm-but-smogless sunny afternoon, I eased my Chevy along the tree-lined Highland Avenue and turned into a drive inlaid with yellow and black tile that led to a black grillwork fence. There was a velvety patch of lawn to the left. It looked a bit too small for a putt-putt green, but somebody seemed to have left a deep divot near the gate.

Ten feet away from the divot, riveted to the grillwork, an inevitable Sentinel camera gave me the eye. From the squawk box beneath the camera, a feminine voice that was not Laura Mornay's asked who I might be. The magic name of Bloodworth was a synonym for Open Sesame. The gates parted noiselessly. As instructed, I drove past the tall shrubbery along a rolling landscape that was slightly smaller than the Rose Bowl but better maintained.

Before too long I caught sight of the aforementioned tripart house and parked, again as instructed, behind the first part. A tall brunette in pleated gray slacks and a white frilly blouse stood beside an open oak door, awaiting me.

"Welcome to Mornay House, Mr. Bloodworth," she said, ushering me through the door and pulling it shut after us with a minimum of effort. "My name is Holly Blissfield. I spoke to you by phone."

"Right. Miss Mornay's assistant."

She nodded and led me into one of the glass corridors. The glare from the afternoon sun was intense enough to fry a crow. "Bright," I mumbled, staggering forward.

"Amazing, isn't it?" she replied. "Solid sheets of glass attached to each other, without benefit of any molding. Mr. Wright was a genius."

"Must've owned stock in Windex," I said.

"Through here now," Miss Blissfield ordered. "Watch your head. Mr. Wright wasn't a very tall man, you know."

The room was low-ceilinged and seemed to be made completely of horizontal lines. Bookshelves, constructions, window frames, blinds. All highly polished wood. The floor was composed of slate and stone, and a slightly damp coolness rose from it and breathed on my ankles.

Miss Blissfield passed a graceful hand along a shelf. "Wright didn't like to break the clean horizontal sweep of a cabinet."

I told her, "Wright also didn't like people ripping off his designs, which I understand happened here. A book I read said that Mornay House was sort of a burr under his blanket until the day he died."

Miss Blissfield's mouth dropped, and with it her cheery-but-intense expression. A frown creased her perfect forehead. It looked as if she'd lost her place in the script. Then she recovered, took a deep breath, and said, "Well, we do not subscribe to that particular historical interpretation."

"It's your house," I said. "Or Miss Mornay's. If she wants to call it a Wright, that's aces with me."

The chair she offered rested on three legs and was about as comfortable as a sawhorse. For herself, she selected a molded plastic-and-cushion device that looked so soothingly soft and mass-manufactured, Wright would probably have thrown it through one of his self-standing glass walls. "Now, about Miss Mornay's problem . . ." she began.

"Isn't she joining us?"

That earned me a patronizing smile. "Miss Mornay is very rarely here these days. As you know, she is the star of *The Weatherbys.*"

I nodded, although it was the first I'd heard of *The Weatherbys.*

"She spends most of her time at the studio," Miss Blissfield amplified. "She has entrusted me with the daily tasks, including the handling of this . . . delicate matter. She requested that I employ you, specifically."

I shifted on the chair, trying to give my backbone a rest. I said, "I'm flattered. Did someone recommend me? Her lawyer, maybe?"

She frowned, causing another crease in that creamy forehead. "I didn't question her about it. Should I have?"

I shrugged. "It's nice to know who's sending business your way."

She picked up a little electronic gizmo that looked like a hand grenade and said into it, "Memo to myself: Ask L.M. why Bloodworth?" She put the grenade down and smiled at me. "We'll find out," she said. "Now—to business."

I smiled and gave her my most attentive look. I didn't have a thing else to do until 5:00 P.M.

She took another deep breath and began, "There's this young actor who, ah, caught Miss Mornay's fancy a few months ago. . . ."

2. As it turned out Simon Watson wasn't all that young. His agent, Joe Baskin, said he was in his twenties, which probably meant early thirties, at best. It had taken me a ten-minute phone call from a coffee shop to pry Baskin's name out of a clerk at the Screen Actors Guild, another twenty to find out that Baskin had the same address for Watson that Miss Blissfield had given me—a Santa Monica Boulevard Xerox parlor that Watson had used for a while as a mail drop.

The agent did have another address, however. It was for an industrial building on Fitzsimmons Avenue that had once housed a supermarket. The plate-glass window had been boarded up and the boards painted a flat black. There were theater posters and 8 X 10 glossies stuck to it, all concerning a production of something called *The Little Women* by Clarissa May Booth-cott.

I walked past a door posted NO ADMITTANCE and found myself at the back of a makeshift theater. Most of the space was taken up with freshly installed wooden seats, each looking about as inviting as anything Wright might have dreamed up. Nobody was trying them out, but the stage area was nearly filled with men in 1930s drag. At least I assumed they were all men. I didn't bother to check. They were struggling through a scene while a wiry, middle-aged guy in chartreuse slacks and black pullover stood in front of the first row of chairs and glared at them, as intently as a fox ogling a covey of Rhode Island Reds.

One of the actors hit the high registers with, "Well, Jo, Amy may be your sister, but, sweetheart, we're talking about your hubby, after all."

Out of pure reflex I muttered "Jesus Christ!" I didn't mean for it to carry all the way to the stage, but it did.

The middle-aged man did an about-face, squinted, and shouted, "You? Who the hell are you?"

"Name's Bloodworth. Leo Bloodworth. I'm looking for Mr. Simon Watson."

"Mis-ter Si-mon Watson. He's looking for Mis-ter Watson. Well, I'm sorry to report that Mis-ter Watson is not here."

"I understand he's one of the producers of this show, as well as an actor in it."

"You're partially correct. Mis-ter Watson is no longer an actor—here, there, or anywhere. He has, thank God, come to his senses after ten long years of self-deception."

"But he *is* the producer?"

"Precisely. Now I hope you won't think rudely of me, but we are very busy. So, please don't let the doorknob kiss your buttocks on the way out."

I strolled toward the little man. "Any idea where I might find Mr. Watson?"

He gave an exaggeratedly painful look toward heaven, then his eyes flashed back to me. "Why, I ask?"

"Oh, just because . . ." I told him.

"Get lost, Mary." He turned away.

"Just because he probably stole the money you're using to trot out this turkey."

The men on stage were interested now. So was the wiry man. "Come again?" he asked.

"You heard me, pal. The acoustics in here are dandy."

"Sandy Watson may be a lazy lout and an unreliable bastard. But he is no thief."

"Sandy?"

"Simon."

"Well, by any name, there seems to be a difference of opinion about his honesty. He *did* invest a nice chunk of dough in this production?"

The thin man nodded, scowling.

I asked, "Any idea where it came from?"

"Sandy has his sources."

"In this instance, the source was a pair of sapphire earrings that didn't belong to Sandy."

He scowled again. "This is ridiculous. Why don't you go back and tell . . ."

When he didn't continue, I asked, "Tell who?"

"Forget it. Just get a more plausible story next time."

"I'm handing you the facts, pal."

The wiry man shook his head, crossly. "Your facts are fucked, Gladys. Sandy doesn't steal, as deceitful and undependable as he may otherwise be."

"You make a mighty fine character witness for old Sandy, but I'd still like to hear all about it from him. Where is he?"

"You a cop?"

"Private. I just want the return of the earrings. No retribution."

He was quiet for a few seconds. One of his actors, a young man wearing a black cocktail dress and a cloche hat, moved to the edge of the stage and asked apprehensively, "Is there a problem, Mr. Palomar?"

The wiry man, Palomar, wheeled on him. "The only problem is your goddamn falsetto."

"Well, excuuuuse me, Peaches," the young man said, his face a stinging red.

Palomar looked back at me and nodded toward the theater exit. As I followed him out, the young man in the black dress began reciting his lines in a voice so loud and high-pitched it set my teeth on edge. Palomar didn't seem to hear it.

Outside the theater he turned to face me, "Let's see some ID."

I showed him my license. He clucked at it, then said, "I'll make sure Sandy gets the message."

"I'll deliver the message myself," I said. "As soon as you tell me where he is. You don't have any choice, Peaches. This building, the renovations. Paid for with stolen loot. You'd better hope that the fence Sandy used is still in possession of the jewels. If it's too late, you guys might not get off with a wrist slap."

"Are you sure this isn't another practical joke from Leach and that demented crowd?"

"I don't know what you're talking about."

He shook his head. "I simply can't believe Sandy . . ." He raised one eyebrow. "Sandy told me the money came from his savings. He's too bad an actor to lie. He is, however, a damn fine set designer and costumer. And lately he has been making a good buck at it. Who the hell is this client of yours, anyway?"

I just stared at him.

"Earrings, huh? Of course it would be a woman," Palomar snapped through twisted lips. "Probably an older woman. That little double-gated twit hits the jackpot every time he falls from grace. So maybe it wasn't Leach, after all . . ."

Palomar remembered I was standing there with my ear hanging out, and he shifted gears. "No! It doesn't compute. Either you're lying to me, or the bitch is feeding you a line for some reason. Sandy misses meetings. Sandy goes on political binges to save the endangered newt. Sandy spends too much time worrying and not enough time working. Sandy does not steal."

"Then neither he nor you has anything to worry about." I looked at the new Rolex on my wrist and added, "But if you don't start to cooperate, I'm bringing in the cops and the hell with it."

He smiled. "If your client had wanted police involvement, she probably would not have had to hire you."

"My instructions are to get the earrings back, preferably, but not necessarily, without raising too much dust. It's up to you."

"I haven't seen Sandy today. You can probably find him at the Green Carnation. It's a bar on Beverly."

"I've seen it."

"Well, Sandy is very well known at the Carnation. If he's not there, somebody can tell you where he is."

"If you're yanking my chain, Palomar, I'll be back."

"Promises, always promises," he said, and drifted inside the makeshift theater.

3. The Green Carnation was a middle-income gay lounge along Beverly Boulevard in a block that, almost overnight, had moved upscale around it. Nestled among button-bright little shops pitching art-deco lamps, decorative moldings, German cutlery, and other necessities of upwardly mobile life, the Green Carnation, with its fading frog-green frame and smoked-glass window, looked like a pop-art monument to barrooms past. At that time of day, 3:30, it was barely open for business. The two guys sitting at the long polished bar and the one behind it said they wouldn't know Simon "Sandy" Watson from a royal flush and I believed them.

When I got back to the theater on Fitzsimmons Avenue, the members of the cast were straggling out. They had exchanged their ladies' duds for sport shirts, tank tops, and balloon pants. They carried brightly colored duffel bags. In contrast to their splashy accoutrements, their mood seemed decidedly gray.

The young guy who'd been wearing the black dress was locking up. There was still some mascara on his eyes and a hint of rouge on his cheeks. "Where's Palomar?" I asked him.

"If *you* don't know, *I* sure as hell don't."

"What're you talking about."

"He left with you, then came back and made a phone call. It was a short conversation, but it shook him up. He looked like a ghost when he hung up. Then he stared at the phone for a while and turned to us. Naturally, all eyes were on the man. He told us, quite calmly, that the show was canceled. We all started talking at once. Palomar began to shake. Just like Regina at the end of *The Little Foxes*. We shut up and gaped at him. He regained his composure, told us he was very sorry. And he ran away. Just like that. The bastard!"

"He left you to close up?"

The young man pocketed the key. "This barn belongs to my uncle. Shit. I wanted to do this play. It was outrageous enough to get noticed. I thought Palomar was serious about making it work."

"Where'd he go?"

"He didn't confide in me." The boy looked like he was ready to cry. "We've been working on this for seven weeks, and he just fucking pulls up stakes. Just like that. Why? You tell me why?"

I shrugged. "His partner Watson is a crook. And Palomar is shady at best. You figure it out."

"Between us, the other guys and I must've put several thousands into the show. We matched Watson dollar for dollar. And that's not including the seats my uncle helped us out with."

"Where can I find him?"

He looked at me, confused. "My uncle?"

"No. Watson."

"His house, I guess. The one he shares with Palomar."

"They're roommates?"

He studied my shoes, suit, and tie and replied, "Yeah, you'd probably call them roommates."

He gave me an address on Norma Place in Hollywood. This was turning into the sort of investigation where you keep making larger circles until you bump into something. Which is okay, as long as you have a lot of free time. I didn't. I'd promised a prospective client named Manion that I would meet him at five, which was less than an hour away. Assuming I could swing by Norma Place and make it back to the office before Manion got too antsy, I worked my gray Chevy through the gathering evening traffic.

4. "They're not here," the plump woman who looked like a bumblebee informed me.

"You sure?" I asked, poking the bungalow's doorbell once more.

She was wearing yellow shorts and a yellow T-shirt over a brown body stocking. Her sunglasses had yellow plastic frames. If she'd had antennae, she could have been the queen of the hive. "Of course, I'm sure," she said in a chirpy voice. "I live right over there." She pointed to a low-slung baby-blue stucco number across the quiet street. "I saw Jerry drive up and start to go inside, but his friends were waiting and he drove off with them in their old car."

Sighing, I turned away from the Palomar-Watson bungalow with its bright orange awning. "Do you know Jerry's friends?"

"No. I don't think I've ever seen them before."

"What'd they look like?"

"One reminded me of that Don Johnson on TV."

I was glad Sarah had given me a little set for my birthday. "What, exactly? Was he wearing a pastel coat and baggy pants?"

"No. Just ordinary clothes. Khaki pants, maybe."

"Blond hair? Sunglasses?"

"No. He's, well, I don't know the name for it. Brownette? Uh, brunette?"

"Well, if it wasn't the clothes or the hair, what reminded you of the actor?"

"He needed a shave. Just like Don Johnson."

"And the others?"

"There was a black boy they called . . . ." She scrunched up her face trying to recall. It was not a pretty sight. ". . . G-man. That's it. A very strange name. Especially for a black boy. Not a boy, actually, but it seems so easy to say that, a black boy. I'm afraid that I can't tell you much about him. They all . . ."

". . . seem to look alike," I finished for her.

"Except for Prince, of course. And Michael Jackson. Oh, I modeled one of my heroes on the beautiful Michael. It was my novel about India, *Bronze Pasha*. My publisher thought it would be my breakthrough book."

"How many others were there in the car?"

"Just one more: the tight-leather guy. Bulging out in front and back. Disgusting. He was the driver."

"I don't suppose you noticed the make of the car?"

She shook her head. "They all look alike, too. A Plymouth, maybe?"

"Was Simon Watson with them?"

"I haven't seen him in quite a—" She stopped, squinting at me through her tinted glasses. "You're him, aren't you? The one who wrote that book with the little girl."

I felt a chill down my spine.

"The fact is, we didn't write it together . . ." I began.

"I saw you on cable," the bumblebee buzzed in. "On *The Denny Markle Show*. You shouldn't have gotten so mad with Denny. He has his little fun with all of his guests. What was it he called you? The middle-aged Mike Hammer."

"Ah, Miss . . ."

"Mrs. Mrs. Delium. Iris Delium. I write, too. Romances, mainly. I was voted February's Favorite by the Amour Society of America."

"Really? That's terrific, but—"

"I'm working on a new series for Heartfelt Publications. I've just been sitting around the front room, staring out of the picture window and trying to come up with ideas. I get most of my stories just by watching the people around me."

"Like Watson and Palomar?"

"Oh, I'm afraid not. I write about real romance. They're, well, you know."

"Have they been living here long?"

"Two years, maybe." She moved closer. "Sandy takes off for his little flings," she whispered. "If I were Jerry, I wouldn't stand for it. Certainly not with all the deadly diseases that are going around. I just don't understand why anyone would flirt with death that way, do you, Mr. . . . Mr. . . . I'm sorry, I've forgotten your name."

"You didn't see Sandy leave the house this morning?"

"No," she frowned. "That is odd, isn't it? Come to think of it, I haven't seen his car in several days. He has one of those little things they call bugs, painted a bright red. I used it in *Fraternity Girl*. I had my heroine deflowered in just such a car."

"With a stick shift and all?" I asked.

"What's a stick shift?"

I didn't think it was my place to tell her. Certainly not on La Mornay's time. "What kind of car does Palomar drive?"

"It's that little foreign thing parked in front of . . . Oh, my, you'll find this interesting, being a fellow writer. Dorothy Parker used to live in that very house." She pointed to a homey little shotgun.

"Do tell?" I said, trying to display the proper amount of awe. "The foreign car you're referring to, is it that pink T-bird?"

She nodded.

"Well, the Thunderbird is all-American, Mrs. Delium. Though I'm not sure they come from the factory in pink."

She frowned at the car. Then brightened. "Do you think that it's the sort of car the nymphomaniac daughter of a state senator might drive?"

"Absolutely," I said. "And I'm sure the sales figures down at Ford will bear me out."

"I must be off then, to commune with my word processor. I call it Wilma." She waved her fingers at me in a rippling motion. "You've made my day, Mr. . . . Mr. . . . Fellow Writer."

She danced into her little blue house with its sloping slate roof and slammed the door. Before she could get situated in front of her picture window, I jogged to the far side of the Watson/Palomar digs. I spent a few seconds checking for a dog or some other animal that might prove troublesome, then edged closer to the house and took a few peeks through the windows.

Eventually I approached the back door. I suppose I might have, in desperation, broken into the house. But there was no need. The lock on the rear door had already been popped. I pushed it open with my foot and listened.

Nothing stirred.

I wasn't carrying a gun. I rarely do. I took a deep breath and went in.

5. There was no immediate sign of robbery inside. The pale gray walls were decorated with framed photos, mainly of unfriendly, bearded men. One oddball exception was an oil painting in the small dining room. It was a spoof of a classic that even I recognized—one of Van Gogh's self-portraits. The painter's coat and the straw hat were the same, but they were being worn by a schnauzer—a goddamned dog! More modern-art nonsense!

The living-room furniture was in black leather. Not new, but expensive all the same. Along one wall were two speakers the size of doghouses flanking a stereo system that included one of those little gizmos that plays silver discs. Books and records filled a floor-to-ceiling set of shelves. Lots of Sondheim, the guy who writes music you can't hum.

The master bedroom had pale purple walls with soft gray accents. Neat, but not fanatically so. The furniture was dark and vaguely Oriental and included an armoire containing silk kimonos, a few sport coats, slacks, shoes. One side was devoted to European cuts, the other to traditional. Several empty hangers interrupted the traditional flow.

I moved on to a black-and-cream tile bathroom. One electric razor. One empty plug. One toothbrush. The ever-watchful Mrs. Delium said Palomar had not entered the house before going off with his friends. So the missing items probably belonged to Watson. It was beginning to look as though he'd taken a trip but expected to return. Either that, or Palomar had been tapped to send the rest of his clothes along. In either case, I did not think I would be happening upon a pair of sapphire earrings that evening.

Across a hall from the master bedroom were two smaller rooms. One was obviously Palomar's. Its walls were filled with precisely placed theater posters bearing his name, still photos of actors and actresses autographed to him, and several pictures of him while still in the flower of youth. On a black lacquer desk were two other photos in small silver frames. One was of a plump, matronly woman in a severe black dress, staring defiantly at the camera. The other was a snapshot of three young men. One, a sullen-looking fellow with light hair, was hunkered near the ground smirking at the camera. A second stood behind him, hands on his shoulder. He had a wide, open face, a good-natured, likable grin. His forehead was obscured by a thatch of dark hair. The third boy was the only one I recognized. He stood beside his open-faced buddy, a full head shorter. He was a dark, pleasant-looking young guy with large eyes and a little button nose above full lips. Watson. His agent, Baskin, had given me a slightly more recent studio photo that showed him with less hair and a wrinkle or two. I decided the older photo wasn't worth removing from the silver frame.

The other room had a temporarily abandoned look. A few papers were scattered on the floor—vestiges of junk mailings, business-reply envelopes, coupons promising all the hamburgers you can eat for only fifty dollars, a theater program that was at least five years old, a letter of thanks from the Friends of Battered Animals.

Somebody had thrown an oak door on top of two squat filing cabinets and called it a desk. In the file drawers, neatly arranged folders contained the names of plays and films with which Watson had been associated, either as an actor or a set designer dating back to his college days at UC Raven's Point. I got the impression that he was a better designer than performer.

One of the file drawers was completely vacant except for gum wrappers, a box of unused Polaroid film, staples, and Gem clips, a couple of dollar pens, and a rough sketch of a cartoon dog laughing at another dog dressed in tights.

On the door-desktop rested a lamp that looked like the product of an Erector Set, all nuts, bolts, and joints, a telephone that was still in operation, and a Rolodex filled with nothing but blank cards.

So Watson had taken a trip. And he, or somebody else, had gotten rid of a portion of his files and all of his phone numbers.

I poked around a bit more.

I was lifting the photos to check for a hidden wall safe, when I heard the floor creak somewhere in the rear of the house. I moved to a window and looked past the partially opened drape. A 1972 Mustang, painted a flat black, was blocking the drive. Iris Delium had said something about an old Plymouth, but she didn't have much of an eye for cars.

I stood still and tried to control the sound of my breathing. Footsteps moved my way down the hall. Nothing careful or furtive about them. A male voice began to sing a little ditty in which the name Hajji Baba was repeated over and over. I counted up to seven Hajjis before he appeared in profile in the doorway.

At moments like that, there's very little you can do but hitch up your pants and stonewall like hell.

The guy was about my height, six-two, but twenty or so years younger. He was Iris Delium's leather boy, cinched in shiny pale yellow trousers and a coat that I'd have called an Eisenhower jacket if old Ike had been partial to animal hides dyed a bright green. The guy looked like a Day-Glo sausage.

He started past the open door, then paused in the middle of a "Hajji Baba." He turned his greasy long-haired head my way and made a show of removing his purple aviator glasses, the better to observe me with dark, sleepy Stallone eyes.

"Hey, ho," he called out in a loud voice. "Jer-Jer didn't say anything about a new roomie."

"Where is Palomar, anyway?" I asked angrily. "The bastard was supposed to meet me here a half hour ago."

He smiled, edged into the room and, continuing to face me, slowly side-stepped along the wall. "No shit, Sherlock!"

It was not going well, but I was committed. "Is he coming or what?"

"I don't think so."

"Who the hell are you, by the way?" I demanded.

He touched his leathered chest with a manicured finger.

"*Moi?* Just an amigo of Jer-Jer's. I guess he told you to come on in and make yourself comfortable?"

"Something like that. You got a name?"

"All God's chillen's got names." He dropped an arm, and one of those damned gravity blades slid into his hand, looking particularly sharp and nasty. "Mine's short," he said, "which is to your benefit, should I decide to carve it on your chest."

"Oh, you don't want to do that," I said. "You'd get your pelts all bloody."

He looked down at his outfit and grinned. "Shit, here I thought I was being so tough and mean, and you can see right through me."

He had circled the room. His plan had been to turn me away from the door so that one of his pals could come in and put me out with a sap. It was a simple plan. And like so many simple plans, it worked.

I heard the leather lad say, "Not too hard. I like this dude."

Then there was the shock of impact. Surprise mixed with confusion. The sensation of falling. I really was getting too old for that sort of thing.

3

1. "My God, what a movie house!" Terry Manion exclaimed as he limped around my little office at ten after five. "I mean, outside on the street it's like low tide in Hong Kong. And inside, it's Shangri-La. High ceilings and statues and fantastic, elaborate chandeliers. Huge lounges with polished teak walls. This big mother of an organ. And the lobby was genuine marble. What a palace!"

In downtown L.A. there are a number of ancient motion-picture theaters that were constructed by movie moguls back in the silent-film days—in a spirit of studio one-upmanship, I suppose. My theater can beat your theater. That sort of thing. Over the years their exteriors have grown as shockingly seedy as the rest of the neighborhood. But according to reports, the interiors have been lovingly maintained in the face of disinterested patrons, vandals, and children covering the seats and the floors with soft drinks and candy. The city offers a walking tour through these now historic cinema palaces, and Gran is forever after me to take it. My answer is that I will if she will, which probably means I'll never step foot inside any of them.

"How was the film?" I asked.

"Oh. It was a Japanese flick with Spanish subtitles. About this banished Samurai father and his ten-year-old son who wander the countryside facing demonic creatures and cutting off people's heads. I've seen it before." He consulted his Cartier tank watch. "Is Mr. Bloodworth usually this prompt?"

I shrugged, mainly because I didn't want to lie to the man. He'd been wearing out the already threadbare carpeting for nearly half an hour. I'd managed to kill a portion of that by creating a client-information sheet for him, getting him to answer many of the same questions I'd already over-heard Mr. Bloodworth ask him.

To keep the Q & A session rolling along, I'd relied upon *Farnsworth's Techniques of Interrogation*, a textbook for my criminology course. But my knowledge of the text only went as far as Chapter Eight. So when that had begun to pall, I'd fallen back upon his obvious infatuation with movie houses. His enthusiasm for the topic seemed boundless, but I soon grew weary of it.

"I was wondering something, Terry," I said. (He'd already asked me to call him by his first name, and to do otherwise would indicate a certain snooti-ness on my part.) "I understand why Mrs. MacElroy didn't want to go to the police or secure the service of some unknown private investigator. But why did she wait so long to talk to you?"

He looked a bit sheepish. "I . . . wasn't really part of the family for too long. Fourteen weeks and two days, but who's counting. I suppose Margee forgot I existed. Then something happened to remind her."

"What was it?"

He paused and perched on the edge of my desk. "I was involved in a shooting and my name got into the *Picayune*—that's the local paper—and Margee came to see me in the hospital."

"How badly were you wounded?"

"Bullet hit me here," he said, tapping his right thigh.

"That explains your limp. And the . . ." I pointed to the back of my own head.

He looked puzzled, then smiled, putting a finger on his bald spot. "Right. My tonsure. I bounced it off the cement floor when I fell."

I leaned forward, trying not to seem too eager. "What kind of case were you on?"

Terry's eyes got that dreamy look again and he smiled. "No case. I just picked the wrong place to order red beans and rice to go. While I was waiting in line, this fella came in, dressed like a priest. He took a gun out of his pocket and began firing."

I can only imagine how immature I must have looked, gawking at him. "Holy moley," I said. "You were astoundingly lucky you weren't killed."

"You don't know the half of it. The guy had handled firearms before. Besides me there were three other customers, a counter girl, and a cook. He took care of them all, one shot each. I guess he thought I was dead, too. But I was just unconscious. Saved again." His eyes got that dreamy look. "For what purpose, I wonder?"

"Did they catch him?"

"Oh, sure. He waited for the cops to arrive. He was chowing down on beans and rice. He confessed to being particularly fond of the biscuits."

I shivered. "What made him do it?"

Terry Manion shrugged. "No one knows, exactly. He was just an ordinary Joe, working in a savings-and-loan, when his wife died of cancer. He went goofy at the funeral, attacked the priest, stole his clothes, and went directly to a gunshop to buy the pistol. The gunshop was only a few blocks from the fast-food place. Maybe he blamed bad food for his wife's death."

He glanced at his watch again. "It's nearly five-thirty. I'm going to have to leave. I feel bad enough bothering Mrs. Kosca at a time like this. I don't want to keep her waiting."

He was meeting the woman at her home on Fourth Street in Bay City, near the ocean. I suggested I accompany him. He did not openly embrace the idea, but I explained that I lived only a few miles up the coast in Bay Heights and would greatly appreciate a lift.

He waited impatiently while I left a note for the perpetually tardy Mr. B. and locked up the office. On the way down in the elevator, he raised an eyebrow at the roller skates I'd slung over one shoulder. "Just how old *are* you, Serendipity?"

"Older than Juliet when she took her life. Older than Cleopatra when she vamped Julius Caesar. Older than Jodie Foster when she was nominated for an Academy Award. I must remember to tell my grandmother how wrong she was."

"About what?"

"She has repeatedly said that chivalry still lives in the South. I don't consider this obsession with a woman's age very chivalrous."

The wizened old alcoholic who operates the elevator chuckled, and I wheeled on him. "This is a private conversation, if you don't mind."

His rheumy eyes bulged open; then, without warning, he jerked the brass control handle and caused the elevator to take a vicious lurch.

Terry was thrown against me, almost in an embrace. To quote my friend Sylvia Sandifer, née Leonidas, the first girl in our class to get pregnant and married, in that order, the experience was not devastating exactly, but it beat a sharp stick in the eye. He backed away, awkwardly, as the elevator door opened.

I regained my composure and exited, glaring at the inebriated elevator conductor. Terry consulted his watch again and said, "We're going to be late."

As we walked swiftly down the street to the lot where he'd parked his Ford rental, he returned to our conversation. "I don't think there's any more chivalry in the South than anywhere else," he said.

"Then it's one of Gran's few misbeliefs."

"Do you spend a lot of time with her?"

"I live with her. My parents are . . . deceased."

"Mine, too," he said, presenting his parking stub to a man in a wooden booth. "But I never knew my grandparents."

"I don't know what I would do without Gran," I said. "She's the best. Even if her profession often limits the amount of time we spend together."

"What's she do?"

"She's an actress," I said proudly. "You may have heard of her. Edith Van Dine."

Terry suddenly turned to me, open-mouthed. "Heard of her!!! Of course I've heard of her. I've seen all of her movies."

"She's been concentrating on TV for a long time now."

"I know." He stared at me even more intently. "Yes. You've got her cheekbones. And I'll bet her hair was exactly that color when she was your age."

The terrible thing about blushes is that they are absolutely uncontrollable. I felt as giddy as a silly schoolgirl. But at the moment I *was* a silly schoolgirl.

I didn't like it. I didn't like being flustered and confused. So I decided to stop this game, if game it was. "I appreciate your offer of a ride, but if you persist in your obscene obsession with my age, I may just take the bus, instead."

He gave me a strange smile. "It was the roller skates," he said.

"You have just paid eight dollars for the privilege of parking a car for less than three hours. Now, we will enter the car, burn up ten dollars worth of gas traveling twenty miles along a hot, noisy, gaseous freeway, and get less than zero percent exercise. Does this seem to you a more adult mode of transportation than roller skates?"

Instead of answering, he circled the car and opened the passenger door for me. "You know, Serendipity, if there were more gir—women like you in the South, chivalry might still be not only alive, but kicking."

2. Because of the evening traffic, it took us nearly forty minutes to reach the off-ramp leading from the Santa Monica Freeway to Bay City. At the least, Terry would be ten minutes late for his meeting. Although his mind was obsessed by his tardiness, I was still able to pry a significant amount of information out of him on the journey, as much to keep him off of the dreaded age issue as for my own personal curiosity.

It seemed that the owner of a detective agency in New Orleans, a woman named Nadia Wells, had recommended two southern California investigators—Mr. B. and the unfortunate Mike Kosca, whom Terry had hired. There were certain scraps of information that he had provided to Mr. Kosca, along with photos of Cece and her father. One was that she had run away in the company of another teen named Gretchen Leblanc, who was, according to Terry, "a year younger than Cece, but considerably more mature for her age." (Not knowing Terry that well, I could not tell if he meant physically or emotionally mature.)

Gretchen and her lover, a fellow named Gregory Desidero, had, in fact, been planning to motor west so that he could attend some sort of college reunion that he hoped would turn into a business opportunity. Cece had tagged along for the chance to give the movie capital a try. Their mode of transportation had been Desidero's bright red Porsche roadster.

"How did you come by all of this information?" I asked Terry.

"To quote someone from earlier today, we *are* investigators," he said with a smile, before frowning again at the congested freeway in front of us.

"Seriously," I pleaded. If I am ever to learn anything about this business, I must rely on proven techniques.

"Gretchen told me."

"Oh," I replied, disappointed. "Then she returned home?"

He nodded. "Sadder and not much wiser. She said that the trip out had been uneventful. But Greg's 'big deal' was not quite ready to happen. And while they were waiting and making the 'party scene' out here, Cece began to change. She emerged from her shell."

"A chrysalis," I interjected.

"Well, that's not exactly the way Gretchen put it. But that's the idea. The three of them stayed together. They had little money, but Desidero's former classmates knew people out here who helped them out. They went to parties. They got high. Some parties lasted for days, some for weeks. Eventually, Gretchen began to realize that their relationships had shifted—Greg and Cece had become a team and she was the tagalong. Finally, she phoned home for plane fare."

"Didn't she have some sort of address for Cece and Greg?"

He shook his head. "They landed at the Cahuenga Motor Inn, stayed there for three days, and after that she doesn't remember much of anything except for waking up at a house near the ocean that had large birds. 'Birds as big as horses,' she told me."

"Sounds pretty druggy," I said.

"She's not that lucid even when she's straight. She remembered a few first names of people they met, but no faces to go with the names, except for a boy with a long, wispy beard named Lorne. She remembered that because it was like the guy on *Bonanza*."

"Not exactly a wealth of material."

"No," he agreed. "But I found this"—he reached into his inside coat pocket and handed me a dog-eared postcard—"in the glove compartment of Gretchen's car."

I took the card. "A fourteen-year-old girl has her own car?" I asked.

He smiled. "A BMW convertible. Purple with yellow interior. It's about as easy to miss as a Mardi Gras float. Her father gave it to her because . . ." He stopped talking. I looked up at him. "It's not relevant. The postcard is the important thing."

According to the postmark, it had been mailed from Marina Del Rey four weeks before. On one side was the photo of a Melrose Avenue boutique, Wings 'n' Things, a depressing hole-in-the-wall that specializes in feathered fashions, the feathers probably plucked from endangered species.

The message side of the card read, in childishly neat script: "Gretch, honey, I'm strung out again, like you said. Maybe there'll be big money, but it's turning real weird. L.A. sucks, but there's nowhere else. You were hip to split. Sorry for all." It was signed "G."

I handed the card back to Terry. "We must go to this Wings 'n' Things."

"I sent Kosca the information. I'd like to find out if he followed up on it, before I just walk in there."

"You think that his going there might have caused his death?"

"Well, it makes a strange sort of sense, doesn't it? Feathers. Birds. Gretchen saw birds 'as big as horses.' "

I looked at him blankly.

"I guess it wasn't part of the TV coverage," he said. "But it was in the morning papers. Before Mike Kosca had his throat cut, his face and hands had been torn to ribbons. The police spokesman said that it looked like he'd been attacked by birds."

3. On Fourth Street in Bay City, the ocean breeze chased away most of the smog and lowered the temperature at least ten degrees. The Kosca home was a small clapboard house bordered on the north by a driveway leading to a closed garage and on the south by a new flamingo-and-green apartment building that was flying colored flags to attract tenants. Possibly to maintain its own identity, the little house had recently been painted a bright white. But its trim was so dark a blue it might as well have been black. It looked, appropriately, like a death notice.

Terry wanted to drop me off at my apartment first, but I reminded him that he was already quite late for his appointment with the widow. I was preparing for the next confrontation, involving my accompanying him inside the Kosca home, when fate intervened.

There was a clattering noise, and the front door of the Kosca house flew open and a man backed out. He was overweight and balding, wearing a brown suit, an ugly checked V-neck shirt, and scuffed gray jogging shoes. He was pointing a video camera at a tiny, skin-and-bones woman in her late fifties, whose sallow, scowling face was dominated by a strong Mediterranean nose. Her soot-gray hair was pulled back into a severe bun. Her dress was the same dark blue as the shutters, with a little scattering of white lace at the neck.

She pushed out her hands at the man, as if she were actually touching him, which she wasn't. He kept saying over and over, "I'm sorry. I don't mean to intrude. I'm sorry." But he kept his eye to the viewfinder and he continued to film her.

By the time we got out of the car, the man had lowered his camera and turned away from the woman. As he passed us, he mumbled, "So I'll go say a kaddish."

The woman moved to go inside. Terry called out, "Mrs. Kosca?"

"Please," she said. "No more."

"I'm Terry Manion. We spoke on the phone."

"Oh, Mr. Manion. I thought that man was you. He was hiding the camera behind him. I opened the door, invited him in, and he began photographing me and . . . the others."

"I'm sorry I'm late," he said. "I'm sorry you had to go through that."

"There were some TV people here this morning. Not many. Mike wasn't . . . a celebrity or anything. But I sent them away. And now this man." She unclenched one fist. There was a crumpled business card in it. She threw it at the ground as though it were dirtying her fingers.

"And who is this?" she asked, meaning me.

"I'm working for Mr. Manion," I said quickly.

Terry stared at me for a second, then turned to Mrs. Kosca. "This is a bad time, ma'am. I can come back."

"As I told you on the phone, I don't know when there will be a good time. You were a client of Mike's. Please come in."

There were several other middle-aged to downright elderly people inside —two couples and three additional women, all chattering and drinking coffee. They grew suddenly silent, staring at us with curiosity as Mrs. Kosca led us past them without introduction to a kitchen where the smell of stew was strong and pungent. "Mike's family," she said, indicating the other room with a toss of her head. "For thirty-five years we live here, and they never come. Didn't approve of his work. Now that he's dead and it don't matter, they come."

"I really am sorry to disturb you like this," Terry said.

"That's what that photo man kept saying. He didn't disturb me. He made me mad. I'm not disturbed."

She staggered a bit, and Terry moved toward her. She stepped back and steadied herself against a little shelf where a phone rested. Behind it, on the wall, was a small blackboard. On it were several telephone numbers, including one beside the notation "T. Manion." His hotel, presumably.

Mrs. Kosca said, with almost no emotion, "The thing is, the whole time he was a policeman, I expected this. Then he gets too old, and I relax finally." She looked faintly bemused, as if she suddenly recalled a joke she didn't quite understand. Then she put it behind her.

She asked me, "Are you hungry, sweetheart? We've plenty."

I thanked her but told her I'd already eaten. I don't enjoy lying, but I make it a rule never to eat in unfamiliar kitchens.

Terry said, "On the phone you mentioned Mr. Kosca's files."

She nodded and led us through a back door, across a neatly clipped lawn to the white garage that Mr. Kosca had been using as an office.

Inside were a desk, two filing cabinets, a long table on which rested one of those record players with the fat spindles. A real antique. Beside it and a stack of small records was a battery-operated portable typewriter. "Mike did this place over," Mrs. Kosca told us, "because of the tax people. Something about income taxes. I don't know. He was in the middle of several jobs. I don't know what to do about them, either. Maybe George can help."

"George?"

"He answered the phone yesterday when you called."

Terry nodded. "Oh, right. I didn't quite catch his name. George Kirk?"

"Kerby," Mrs. Kosca replied. "A fine young man, very brave."

"Brave?"

"He lost his wife not long ago. Car accident. They hadn't been married long, but they loved each other. So tragic, but you never hear him complain. Instead, he's there with a joke." She smiled suddenly, momentarily forgetting her sadness.

"He and Mike met just a while ago. Hit it off real well. I don't know why. Mike was old enough to be his father, or grandfather, even."

"Young people need fathers and grandfathers," I said, without meaning to. Both Terry and Mrs. Kosca looked at me.

She took a deep breath and nodded her head. "One of the saddest things about growing old is you got nobody you can run to with your troubles. Not that George came to Mike with his. What they spent their time talking about was silly stuff from long ago, that nostalgia stuff—old radio shows, movies, funny papers. But with that scrubbed face of his, he couldn't have been born when that stuff was going on.

"Anyway, he was good for Mike, idolized him. And he could make Mike laugh.

"When they told me about . . . what happened, I didn't know who else to call. We never was sociable people, Mr. Manion. Mike and me treasured our own company. But George is . . . well, smart about some things. And he's friendly, without being pushy, like so many. He's got the knack of knowing when to stay and when to leave. I called, and George was here within minutes.

"We both cried a little. Then he made me lie down while he took phone messages and notified Mike's relatives."

"Were he and Mike working together?"

"Oh, I don't think so. They were friends. Mike wasn't one to mix friendship with business."

While she was talking, I wandered to the white filing cabinets. One of the drawers had been pried open. The chipped paint looked fresh. "When did this happen?" I asked.

She frowned at the twisted metal. "I don't know. I never come back here much, except when Mike lets me clean up. Dove pointed it out, but I don't think his men would have done it. The whole place is in such a state."

"Dove?" Terry asked.

"Lieutenant Hilbert. Dove Hilbert. He's the one investigating the . . . murder. He said somebody broke the lock on the garage, too. But I never heard anything. I sleep pretty good, as a rule. Not lately, though."

On the drawer that had been forced, someone, the late Mr. Kosca presumably, had neatly typed "L-M-N-O." Terry opened it and found it to be totally empty.

"Dove's men took the folders," Mrs. Kosca said. "They needed them for something, I guess."

Terry opened another drawer. It was just as empty.

"I've had some experience with the Bay City PD," I said to Terry. "There's a Lieutenant Cugat who can introduce us to Lieutenant Hilbert."

Mrs. Kosca shook her head. "You won't find Dove in Bay City. He works in Beverly Hills."

Terry said, "I take it you know Lieutenant Hilbert personally?"

She almost smiled. "He and Mike go way back. They used to be partners since even before the Isla Vista days. I think that's why he's taking charge of the investigation."

I said, "I thought that it was department policy that policemen not be assigned cases in which they have a personal interest."

She shrugged. "All I know is that Dove is handling this one."

Terry began to poke around the garage. I was mildly curious about the little 45-rpm records. Mr. Bloodworth is so fond of older music that I've been trying to build up an enthusiasm for it myself. Poor Mr. Kosca's tastes seemed to be rather eclectic. There were arias, showtunes, and regular popular music like Ray McKinley's "You Came a Long Way from St. Louis," which I had heard before while in Mr. B.'s company. Apparently the albums had not been played for a while, because they were covered with dust. So was the player, actually. The only dust-free item was a box containing *Spike Jones's Greatest Hits*.

Its colorful cover featured Spike himself, holding his ears while his band, the City Slickers, played washboards and bicycle horns and other odd instruments in the background. Nestled inside the box were three little records in brown-paper covers and an odd piece of plastic, about three inches long by two inches wide. Like the records, it was black, but also smooth and shiny. It was blank except for four raised letters, "RPNP," on one side. It might have been a credit card. Or even a name card. That reminded me of something, and I excused myself and ran to the front of the house.

When I got back, Mrs. Kosca was saying, "Our girl, our only child, she lives out East. She'll be here soon. Flying out. Mike always loved her, but not as much as if she'd been a boy. It's good she wasn't. He'd have made her be a cop, like him, like his father."

Terry stood before her awkwardly. "I guess we'd better see Lieutenant Hilbert about the files."

She nodded and led us out into the yard. "I'd like to talk to George Kerby, just on the chance Mr. Kosca might have mentioned something to him about my missing niece."

"His number's inside the house. Do you need it right this minute?"

"I'll call you tomorrow," Terry said.

"Do something for me, please?" Mrs. Kosca asked. "When you see Dove, tell him to let us bury Mike. They've had him long enough. He said they needed an autopsy. He wouldn't even let me see him, my own husband I've lived with for forty years. Lying in some cold room, all by himself."

She snapped the lock shut on the garage door. There were several long gashes where the paint had been scraped away near the hasp. She said, "Maybe once he's buried, they'll leave us alone."

I thought she might have been referring to whoever'd broken into the garage, or the media scavengers, or maybe the police. But she was staring back at her house, where the relatives of the deceased were paying their first visit in thirty-five years.

4

1. The good news was that I was alone in Simon Watson's room when I came to. The bad news was that I was feeling not quite up to par. I stayed facedown on the floor for a while, trying to convince myself that I was home, asleep. In 1950. When that didn't work, I managed to roll over onto my back. My right eye was out of focus, which, to my mind, spelled "concussion." My heart was pounding too fast and missing a beat every now and then, and my head was as sore as a boil.

I stared at a little slice of pale white streetlight that snuck through the parted curtains until, gradually, the edges of the curtains lost their ghost image. All right, no concussion then. So I began the deep-breathing exercises that my doctor had given me to slow down my heartbeat. In and out. In and out.

DAMNIT! I'd missed my meeting with a potential client named Manion. He'd come to L.A. from New Orleans, looking for a missing girl, and he'd wanted me to go with him to talk to the widow of the last private detective he'd hired. How the hell did I get into these things? No, make that: Who the hell gets me into these things? Not that the kid had had anything to do with my head being dented. But I definitely would have taken a pass on Manion's problems if . . . aw, the hell with it.

I sat up, winced, and worked my arm around so that my watch might benefit from the streetlamp. Seven-oh-eight. I summoned all my forces and made it to my feet. Then I staggered over to brace myself on Simon Watson's makeshift desk.

If I still had my Rolex, just possibly . . . yes, the wallet was there, too. In my pocket. They hadn't been very curious about me. I didn't know whether to be grateful or insulted.

The room itself looked the same. They hadn't been particularly curious about it, either, apparently. Assuming they were gone. To play safe, a bit after the fact, I went to the window and looked out. The old Mustang was no longer blocking the drive.

Back at the desk, I lifted the phone. My plan was to dial the office to leave word for Manion. But then I got another, better notion. The phone was one of those Buck Rogers gizmos that have proliferated in the wake of Ma Bell's bitter defeat. A button on its base was labeled REDIAL. I pushed it.

The line clicked and buzzed and a fey voice answered, "Top Hat Travel— we'll fly you down to Rio, or anywhere else in the free world. But only during office hours—weekdays, nine to five, Saturdays, nine to noon. Bon voyage."

I filed the name away. Then, with my head throbbing, I hustled through the rooms again. Nothing that meant anything to me.

I slunk out of the place via the rear door. Behind the house, in an alley, I found the Palomar-Watson garbage cans where the sanitation experts, or somebody, had tossed them. Empty. But a small amount of trash had gathered at the sides of the alley—leaflets, torn envelopes, brown leaves. Beneath a week-old *L.A. Times* rotogravure section were several sketches, torn lengthways and sideways. I brushed them off. Hating to leave empty-handed, especially after getting my head softened, I took them to the Chevy.

I paused at my car, wondering if Iris Delium had eyeballed the boys who'd laid me low.

There was no light on at the front of her house. Only a glow at the rear. Probably at dinner. Even romance writers have to eat. Forget her! I'd already gotten her description of the friends of Jerry Palomar. The guy who conked me was either the Don Johnson look-alike or the black G-man. I doubted that it made much difference, and I didn't want the bumblebee snoop to know I'd been hanging around the neighborhood all evening. And, frankly, I just didn't want to have to talk with her again.

2. The Bloodworth Agency was unoccupied when I arrived. I like it that way. Until a year ago, for financial reasons I'd had to share the space with another P.I. named Kaspar. But Kaspar had been bent, and one of his scams sent him far beyond the need of desk, phone, and filing cabinet.

For a time it had been blessedly peaceful in the office. The phone would ring, and I'd let the answering machine field most of the scutwork calls and save myself for the assignments that were either easy or profitable, or preferably both.

That came to an abrupt end a month ago, when the kid, Serendipity Dahl-quist, conned me into letting her use the empty office. Not to put too fine a point to it, she had pulled my bacon out of the microwave on at least one occasion. So I felt I owed her. And while I was not happy to see her or the computer she'd cajoled one of her gawky male classmates into lugging up to my office, I agreed to let her come in after school for a few weeks so that she could get a taste of the business and help out in a minor way.

By the time school broke for the summer, my files were in order and up to date. She'd set up a no-nonsense billing system and created a reminder program that told me all sorts of things I didn't want to know, like when to get my teeth checked or buy birthday presents for my ex-wives.

I assumed that that would be the end of it, but as I had already discovered with Miss Dahlquist, she was harder to get rid of than carpet fleas. She was starting a pre-college course in criminology in the fall, she explained, and she hoped she might stick around the office during the summer in an intern capac-ity, getting a little on-the-job experience. It sounded like my worst fears coming true. Still, like I said, she'd been there for me when I needed her. So . . .

But that evening a miracle happened. Her office was deserted. The goddamn computer was silent. No hum. No beeps. No sign of the kid. No sign of Manion and his problems. All was right with the world. True, my head still throbbed. But there was always aspirin.

I dropped the sketches I'd lifted from Watson's trash onto the empty desk in the waiting room. Spread out, they seemed to be pencil drawings of the same skeletal structure. I jigsawed them around until I could make out what appeared to be a trellis of metal, with light bulbs spelling out the word *Circe.*

Assuming that the sketches were Watson's work, I was making progress of sorts. And there was that travel-agency he'd called. Progress, definitely. I had a smile on my face as I entered my office.

It froze when I spotted the note under my desk lamp. I hesitated before reading it. Instead, I washed down a pair of aspirin with a shot of Bushmills.

The note had been written in haste. "Terry waited for you, but anxiety to see Mrs. Kosca got the better of him. I couldn't let him go off alone in a strange city without even the most rudimentary knowledge of its mean streets. I shall turn in a complete report tomorrow. Ciao, Serendipity."

I took another drink and mentally replayed the stuff Manion had told me about the missing girl, Cece MacElroy. When I got to the part about this P.I., Kosca, getting bumped off, a rabbit ran over my grave. It wasn't that I didn't think Sarah could take care of herself, but charging around with some skiffy-looking dude from Dixie on the hunt for a runaway bimbette . . .

Damnit, she'd finally found a way to ruin my good moods even when she wasn't around.

5

1. Of course, after making his appointment with Lieutenant Hilbert of the Beverly Hills police, Terry Manion tried to deposit me at home. I explained to him that Gran would not be there—it was one of her rare late tapings; she probably would not return before ten—and that I hadn't a key to get in. I neglected to mention that the night doorman, Philippe, always walks me up to the apartment on the fourth floor and opens the door for me.

Instead, I withdrew the two items I'd husbanded while he was snooping around the office files—the curious piece of black plastic and the photographer's crumpled business card that Mrs. Kosca had thrown away in such disgust. It identified the plump man as Mark Fishburn, a self-described "Independent Video Journalist." His address was a P.O. box, and I would have bet real money that if you dialed his phone number, you'd get one of those obnoxious answering services.

I handed Terry the Fishburn card. "For the files?" he asked.

" 'The least-consequential data may assume great importance as an investigation progresses,' " I quoted from the textbook *Essentials of Evidence*. Then I pocketed both card and plastic, while we motored down Santa Monica Boulevard past the Century City shopping area and onward toward Beverly Hills.

According to our arch ape (architecture appreciation) teacher, Mrs. Wilfeen Twyne, Beverly Hills rests on an area that used to be one giant lima-bean field. A bunch of Germans tried to settle there in the middle 1800's. And then there was a half-hearted start at establishing a town named Morocco—after the one in Africa, I suppose. And finally, when these other attempts proved futile, the Rodeo Land and Water Company took charge and brought out some New York planner—I'm not sure why, since New York has never seemed to me to be so very well planned. But this Manhattan metropolis-designer figured out the boundaries and that sort of stuff (and, not incidentally, he also laid out the streets to run at weird forty-five-degree angles from Wilshire Boulevard to Santa Monica Boulevard, where they just drift off aimlessly into the hills. Some planner!).

Anyway, the little city was designed to be inhabited by the over-privileged, even in those days. And be it ever thus. The rather attractive art-deco City Hall on North Crescent Drive, with its phallic tower and shiny dome, was constructed mainly during the Great Depression, when citizens in nearby communities were so destitute they tracked down wild coyotes just to put meat on the table.

Once we'd parked the car in the BHPD visitors' lot, wandered across an expanse of splendidly landscaped lawn and brightly flowered garden, and located the Beverly Hills Police Department within the City Hall, all it took to meet with Lieutenant Dove Hilbert was an hour-and-fourteen-minute wait.

I imagine the early evening watch had just begun—it was that time—and the big, airy, brightly lit reception room seemed to be only minimally staffed. And not overly active. There was one other person waiting on the long cushioned bench along an off-white wall—a woman who looked to be nineteen or twenty, with short auburn hair that fell over one eye, and clear skin that hadn't a touch of makeup except for a demure dab of pink lipstick. She was braless under a silk T-shirt with tiny black-and-white dot patterns. Shapely and tanned bare legs were barely visible under her white linen box-pleated skirt. Her shoes were black peekaboos with that lizardy pattern. She was lost in a book titled *Somebody's Darling*.

Terry sat down a few feet away from her, pretending not to be aware of her existence. And so we stayed, staring out at mainly empty desks and cubicles. Phones rang, machines made their machine noises. Policemen and policewomen, uniformed and not, rather better dressed than any other policepersons I'd seen except for my friend Lieutenant Cugat of the Bay City PD, came and went. Fairly dull stuff, but the place was not without its amusements.

For example, there was an appearance by the recording performer Gabriel, who when he was known as Mickey Stonehead used to smash electric guitars over his bald skull. Later in his career he found God, let his hair grow shoulder length, and began devoting himself to the spread of Christianity. He arrived to complain about stray dogs swimming in his pool, which, as I recalled, had been constructed in the shape of his once-famous bald head. The problem with the dogs, he explained to an amazingly receptive officer at the front desk, was that the pool was used for baptisms and other holy ceremonies.

Then there was the actress Hildy Haines, who plays the tempestuous Avril Chantille on the nighttime soap *Key West.* She stormed in, blood in her heavily mascaraed eye, demanding freedom for her maid's son, a young man named Miguel who had been arrested for walking in a Beverly Hills residential area earlier in the day. "He was walking toward *my* home, you idiot," she screeched at the policewoman who had intercepted her.

Terry couldn't keep his eyes off of La Haines. "She's a friend of Gran's," I told him.

"She's exactly like she is on the tube," he whispered, as if we were watching a stage play. I was whispering, too, because I didn't particularly want Hildy Haines to catch sight of Edith Van Dine's granddaughter hanging out in a police department, even the Beverly Hills Police Department. My relationship with Gran, though never less than loving, had grown a bit strained the past year. I was, after all, becoming more my own woman and less dependent on her, and I think she found that unsettling or something.

"Well, of course not," Hildy Haines was railing at the unfortunate policewoman. "I told you, he's my maid's son. Of course he can't speak English."

"Perhaps if his mother or father could come down . . ."

"His father is not . . . well, who the hell knows where he is? His mother is preparing my home for a reception I'm having tonight for Senator Simcox. Perhaps you've heard of him. Paul F. Simcox. California Democrat. A very liberal California Democrat. It would give me no end of pleasure to tell him how the Beverly Hills gestapo threw a teenage boy into prison for walking on the wrong street."

"I'll get Miguel for you right away, Miss Haines."

Before the policewoman could move, Hildy Haines said throatily, "Please have him escorted to my limousine. It's the pearl-gray stretch Mercedes parked in front of this kiosk."

As the policewoman rushed away, a look of ultimate triumph crossed the actress's face. She scanned the room, inhaling deeply the scent of victory. I half expected her to take a bow. Instead, she turned and strode imperiously through the exit.

"Some performance, huh?" I asked.

Terry nodded. "Do they really arrest people for walking in Beverly Hills?"

"Depending on the circumstances, you can get arrested just for breathing in Beverly Hills." This was from the braless woman next to Terry. She'd closed her book.

"You a native?" Terry asked her, in that mocking way men have when they're expressing interest.

"Do I look like it?"

He shrugged. Then he gave her his full attention.

"Actually, you look like . . . somebody I know. Somebody I knew."

She turned away, apparently embarrassed. "I guess I have that kind of face."

Terry shook himself out of his trance and said, "It must have been the light. And that trace of a Southern accent."

"Well," she said with a half-smile, "as a matter of fact, it's a Texas accent. But the past few months I've been trying desperately to get rid of it by talking to my neighbors in Laurel Canyon."

He looked at her dopily. "Good book?"

She seemed to have forgotten it was in her hand. "This? One of the first things my roommate told me was that whenever I spend any time in Beverly Hills, I should carry a book, so that I won't be mistaken for a native."

They both sort of stared at each other in silence for a beat. "Excuse me," I said, tapping Terry on the shoulder. "We've been here over an hour. Shouldn't you ask if Lieutenant Hilbert is free now?"

"Oh, you're both waiting to see Lieutenant Hilbert?" Miss Braless asked. Terry nodded, still staring at her. I sighed and settled back on the bench.

"Why?" the brazen woman asked.

"Why are we waiting for Hilbert?" Terry replied. "Well, actually . . ."

He was interrupted by the opening of a door down the hall. A small, fiftyish man exited and started toward us. He was wearing a dark pinstriped suit with vest, polished black plain-toed shoes, starched white shirt with long, thin points, and a narrow regimental-stripe tie. His white hair was clipped close enough for pink troughs to show. He wore frame glasses, too small for Robert Redford and too large for the late John Lennon.

He stopped by the braless girl. "What the devil are you doing here?" he asked her.

"Waiting for you. Like this gentleman and his sister."

"I am not this gentleman's sister," I told her.

Lieutenant Dove Hilbert gave me a brief, unfriendly glance and then turned to Terry. "You the guy about Mike Kosca? Manion?"

Terry nodded.

"I'll see you in a minute, then." Hilbert grabbed the girl's upper arm and yanked her to her feet. She tried to pull away, but he tightened his grasp. Just before they reached the door to his office, she managed to free herself. There was the white outline of his fingers on her tanned skin. He waited for her to enter, then followed her in.

Terry looked at me and I shrugged. "Nice guy," I said.

For a few minutes all was quiet in Hilbert's office. Then voices were raised.

Then the unmistakable sound of a slap. The door flew open and the girl came through it, a red splotch high on the right side of her face. Her eyes were starting to tear. "Thanks so much for your help, Lieutenant," she shot at him, curling her lip on the word *Lieutenant.*

Hilbert took a few steps toward her and stopped, watching her move away. As she passed Terry, she said, "Watch his right hand. The pure white Dove has a mean right."

Then she was off. Hilbert glowered at Terry. A policewoman asked from her desk, "Something, Lieutenant?"

"Not from you," he snapped at her. To Terry he growled, "Okay, Manion. In here. While I'm still in a good mood."

2. Hilbert's office was obsessively neat, furnished with a dark brown two-seater and matching chair and his desk and chair, all on a pale brown carpet. The off-white-favoring-tan walls were covered with plaques, photographs, and awards that seemed to have been positioned with the aid of a T-square.

The lieutenant sat down at his desk. Through the window behind him, the streetlights of Beverly Hills suddenly snapped on, as if wired to his chair.

I perched on the edge of the couch while Terry took the stuffed leather seat directly across from Lieutenant Hilbert, whose scowl had deepened. Obviously, the braless woman was still on his mind. "She can be the sweetest little thing most of the time. Cheery. Agreeable. But give her just one afternoon with those goddamn smart-assed *friends* and . . ." He shook his head and began to fondle an odd paperweight—an antique-looking weapon consisting of a heavy metal ball with jagged points attached to a chain with a heavy wooden handle.

"She a relative?" Terry asked.

"My relatives all live in Seattle," Hilbert said slowly. "So do my ex-wife and my daughter and her cretin of a husband, and the devil can have 'em all. On toast. A relative? Christ, you don't think I'd take that lip from a relative?"

He focused his eyes on me and told Terry, "You look like you're doing a little cradle-robbing yourself."

"I would think that a man in your position would be cautious about snap judgments," Terry said, in a deadly monotone. "Miss Dahlquist is guiding me through this rather complex part of the world."

Hilbert looked from me to Terry. "What part of the world are you from, Manion?"

"New Orleans."

Hilbert glanced my way again. "Pretty decadent town, I've heard."

"Compared to what? Bangkok, Port-au-Prince, Los Angeles?"

Hilbert leaned back in his chair. "So, Mike Kosca was working for you, huh? Saw your name on one of his case folders. Something about a stray, as best I could make out."

"A New Orleans girl. Runaway."

"She got a name?"

"It's probably in the folder."

"Probably. I'll check. Mike was a thorough fellow. Slow. Some might've called him a plodder. But he was thorough. Did he have any luck finding the kid?"

"Not that he told me. I was hoping to take a look at his case folder to—"

"Oh, I don't think that'd be proper. I haven't even seen your identification."

Terry took out his wallet and placed it on Lieutenant Hilbert's desktop. The policeman studied it briefly and said, "You look older than your birth date, Manion. Hard living down there?"

Terry put away the wallet. "How about the folder?"

"So Mike got himself killed, and you rushed right out. Or did you get here before the murder?"

"I arrived yesterday on the four P.M. flight."

"Why?"

Terry hesitated. "To try and find the girl."

Hilbert looked at me. "Using her as bait?"

"Nothing like that," Terry snapped back.

"Hell, Mr. Manion from New Orleans. Don't get all huffy and indignant. Bait can work pretty well. I'll go get that folder for you."

As he rounded the desk, I asked, "Lieutenant?"

He paused.

"This isn't the operational area of the department, is it?"

"No," he said, apparently amused. "It's administration."

"Judging by the type of business going on out there, I imagine it's sort of the complaint area."

"We call it community relations."

"I was just wondering why an administrative lieutenant in Beverly Hills is overseeing a murder investigation that took place in the San Rafael Mountains."

Hilbert turned to Terry. "Nosy little brat, isn't she? Noisy, too. That's good. Noisy bait works better."

He picked up the weapon from his desk. Clasping its handle, he let the jagged-edged iron ball swing back and forth in front of my nose. "During the Watts riots and some of that hippie peace-and-freedom crap that took place way back before you were born, honey, I carried this mace with me everywhere. Mike Kosca, who was my partner in those days, used to say it made me look like a crazy. The *L.A. Times* loved to take my picture. 'This Dove Is Loaded for Bear,' that was one of the captions. But those jungle bunnies and dopers got the idea. Which is why I never had to use this on them. At least, not all that often.

"I show it to you now, honey, by way of explaining that I have a habit of doing things my way. A pattern of unorthodox behavior, bolstered by a truly amazing success record, has allowed me to do nearly anything I set my mind to. Mike Kosca was my partner and my friend. And so I assumed the authority I needed. Nobody in the system seemed to care about it one way or another, so here I am."

"Sounds like vigilante justice," I said.

He placed the mace back onto his desk carefully. "I am a law enforcement officer," he said, straightening his vest. "Your friend Manion is the vigilante. His Louisiana license doesn't mean squat in this state. If I were a by-the-book sort of cop, I'd kick both of your butts out of this office. But I have compassion. The man wants to find a missing girl. So I'll cooperate."

He nodded toward Terry. "I'm sure I can count on him keeping me filled in on his progress, particularly should it impinge upon my investigation of Mike Kosca's violent murder."

He gave us both a sudden, grim death's-head grin and left his office.

Terry was staring at me, poker-faced.

I said, "I know that when one is asking for police cooperation, one is supposed to use tact. But I had to settle this question of his authority, didn't I?"

Instead of replying, Terry Manion asked me a question. "Serendipity, do you think your grandmother might be home by now?"

6

1. I'd barely dusted off my passport and thrown some shirts and skivvies into a canvas flight bag, when a horn honked out front. I quickly went over my mental checklist. The office was locked. I'd left a note for Sarah. I'd got one of those bank machines to cough up three hundred dollars in twenties, which, together with whatever Laura Mornay's assistant would lay on me, would probably be enough to get the job done, provided that Simon Watson was where he was supposed to be.

I downed a couple of aspirin, to help with the dull ache at the back of my skull where I'd been swatted by the leather boy's pal.

The horn sounded again.

I squinted at the suitcase suspiciously. In the past I've forgotten belts. Socks. Ties. Toothbrush. Razor. In palmier days, cufflinks. I wound up in San Francisco once, wearing tennis shoes with my suit because I forgot to pack my cordovans. That's when being from L.A. comes in handy—people expect you to be a little offbeat.

In any case, I couldn't think of anything crucial I'd neglected, so I zipped up the black canvas bag, hefted it. It still seemed that something was missing. The hell with it. I slipped into my new silk and linen sport coat, grabbed the grip, and made my exit, locking the door to my coach house behind me.

Holly Blissfield was waiting out front, studying the shadowy marquee of the neighborhood playhouse that blocks my view of what was once a relatively quiet tree-lined street. My landlord and his fading-actress wife were appearing there on the weekends in a bunch of Noel Coward one-act plays that an *L.A. Times* theater critic found "wearying and pedestrian." It wouldn't have mattered much if it had been a rave. The area was in transition. The problem was not the Koreans who were buying up everything in sight. The problem was that the Koreans had kids. And some of them had formed gangs. And they were challenging the existing white gangs. What began with a spray-can marking of turf boundaries had escalated into stabbings and shootings. It was not the kind of atmosphere that attracted theatergoers. I wasn't crazy about it myself. Eventually I'd have to move on to some less-active war zone.

Miss Blissfield tore her attention away from a streetlamp-lit Xerox enlargement of a remarkably generous notice from one of the neighborhood handouts and moved a few yards to the little black Mustang convertible that was panting to go at the curb. The top was down. I threw my travel bag onto the backseat and got in just as she slipped behind the wheel.

"Thanks for the lift," I said.

"All part of the package," she said, leaving a few inches of Goodyear's best in the parking space. "Actually, I'm going to be a little late for a party I'm supposed to be co-hosting."

"Hell, I could've taken my own car."

"Now don't you be concerned. This is my job. I'm being paid very well for my time. Fun can come later."

She glanced at her digital dash clock, which had just flashed 9:01, and barely squeaked onto La Brea before the yellow light turned red. She said, "We weren't expecting you to get a line on Watson so quickly. Fortunately, Miss Mornay keeps a good supply of cash in the safe. For your airfare and other expenses, I mean."

"Uh, they only had seats in first class."

"Miss Mornay wouldn't have it any other way."

She looked different than she had earlier at the house. Less gathered and edgier. And more appealing. Her dark hair was windblown. She was wearing aviator glasses. The frilly blouse and slacks had been replaced by party duds —a loose hot-pink sweater and blue jeans that had been bleached almost white and fit her like a coating of salad oil. Some party duds.

She reached across me, punched the button on her glove compartment, and withdrew from it a tan envelope that, I discovered, contained thirty hundred-dollar bills.

Slipping the wad into my coat pocket, I mumbled that a check would have sufficed.

She gave me a superior smile while downshifting onto the Santa Monica Freeway. "Miss Mornay prefers to use cash when she can," she said.

I nodded wisely, as if I were intimately familiar with the intricacies of financial wheeling and dealing among the buried-bank-account set. "Well, I'll do my best to see the money isn't wasted."

"Wasted? You have no idea how important the earrings are. They were given to her by her true love."

"Jake Berns?" I wondered, drawing on the bits and pieces of Mornay House history I'd gleaned from the architecture book.

She shrugged vaguely. "Could be," she said. "Naturally, the jewelry is insured. But Miss Mornay doesn't really need another hundred thousand dollars. Nor is she interested in retribution."

"Not if she's willing to let this Watson creep walk, provided he cooperates. Of course, he may have unloaded the trinkets by now."

"Then you must find out where."

I nodded. "If I can get within arm's reach of our boy, I'm sure that can be arranged."

Holly Blissfield's dark hair whipped at her face. A strand lodged at the corner of her lips, and she freed it with a flick of a little finger.

"What's it like, living in a big, lonely joint like the Mornay mansion?" I asked.

She jerked her head around and stared at me. "What makes you think I live at Mornay House?" Her response was so sharp that a worm of suspicion crawled out of my subconscious carrying the thought that maybe she and La Mornay shared more than an employer-employee relationship. Not that it was any of my business.

"I just assumed it. You got back to me so quickly after I left the message tonight."

"Oh," she uttered, relaxing. "Miss Mornay arrived at her home just as you were hanging up. She relayed your message to me almost immediately at my apartment. Luckily, I had just sent my roommate out to the supermarket instead of going myself, or I don't know what Miss Mornay would have done about arranging for your money." She wiggled the Mustang in and out of four moderately congested traffic lanes while I watched with a mixture of awe and increasing terror. "She's so helpless with things like that, she depends on me totally," Holly Blissfield added.

"Well, that should make it better for you when it comes time for a raise," I told her, the words blowing back into my face. "According to this fellow Paul Montclair, who runs the Mr. Success clinics, enforced employer dependency is the key to employee success. Gives you the whip hand, so to speak."

She smiled.

"I'm not kidding," I said.

"I know. I've heard him talk about employer dependency."

"Oh. You've been to the clinics?"

"Sort of." She put the Mustang's gears to the test again as we bucked in a semicircle down onto the San Diego Freeway, where a line of cars stretched to the horizon, or at least to the LAX turnoff on Century Boulevard.

"Miss Mornay was very impressed with your speed in locating Simon Watson."

"Well," I said into the traffic din, "some days you just hit it lucky."

Actually, my luck had begun with my visit to Top Hat Travel in the South Palm Shopping Center, which at 8:30 was closed up tighter than the proverbial tick. I eyeballed the emergency number on a glass panel at the front door. Then I returned to my Chevy to consult the street directory I'd scammed with the help of a buddy at AT&T. It provides the addresses of numerically listed phone numbers. That brought me to a little bungalow in the Larchmount area where Teddy Meechum and a pal were sitting around on their tiki-lamplit patio grilling a couple of hearty-sized rib eyes.

Meechum, the proprietor of Top Hat Travel, was wearing white shorts and a bright orange pullover with what appeared to be a dead rat, toes up, in the spot usually reserved for alligators or polo players. He was tall and thin, with a long, narrow face, and he reminded me of James Stewart when he was of an age to do battle with the U.S. Senate. The pal was about 250 pounds of suntanned, muscle-bound beefcake lying on a divan in Day-Glo–green culottes and a Max Headroom T-shirt. He sipped his iced tea and watched me lazily as I told Meechum what I wanted and Meechum replied that he could not betray the confidence of a client, that Sandy Watson had specifically stipulated that his itinerary was not to be bandied about.

I moved into Phase Two, explaining to Teddy Meechum that unless he cooperated, he would no doubt be arrested as an accessory after the fact in a major theft case.

The beefcake thought the whole thing was pretty funny and asked Teddy if he should throw my ass out. Before Teddy could accept his kind offer, my already battered brain came up with Phase Three. Could I become a client, too? Could he book an itinerary for me that might, by coincidence, overlap Sandy Watson's as quickly as possible?

The beefcake apparently had been waiting all week to bounce someone like me around. But Teddy held him in check with the news that business had been slow—especially European travel since the Chernobyl meltdown—and he needed to take his bookings when and where he could. So we drove to his office, where by using the most potent weapon at my command—a new credit card (prompted by Paul Montclair's Rule 7, which states that a businessman without quickly accessible credit is like a football player without helmet and cleats)—I got my information and my plane ticket to Milan by simply signing my name. I hadn't given the Chernobyl business much consideration; and I found myself wondering if, only three months after the fact, I just might find some fallout in my pasta.

2. By 8:20 I'd left a message at Mornay House. And less than an hour later Holly Blissfield was hurtling us down Century Boulevard toward the airport so swiftly I'd have all the time in the world to deal with customs.

I purposely had not provided her with the details regarding my discovery of Watson's whereabouts or of the specifics of those whereabouts—just enough to justify the expense of the air fare. The other thing I neglected to mention was my painful encounter with the leather boy at Watson's home. Some investigators might feel that such information would indicate dedication and loyalty beyond the call of duty and therefore be worth a bump up in the price quoted. My philosophy is that a provider of service, such as myself, should always remember that the customer's primary interest is in the successful completion of the job, not in the minutiae of events that lead to that end.

I slapped my jacket pocket to make sure I'd remembered to bring the Paul Montclair paperback *Power Plan*. It was there, with my plane tickets nestled between its pages.

Holly brought the Mustang to heel behind a bus that was unloading a large group of conservatively dressed, suntanned, gray-haired people. I opened the door and climbed out of the little car, banging my left knee on a protruding section of the dash. As I jerked my canvas flight bag from the backseat, she asked hesitantly, "Mr. Bloodworth, where in Italy are you headed, exactly?"

I said, "The plane lands in Milan. After than, I'm not sure." (Montclair says, "Be as nonspecific as possible when it comes to results. Never let the client expect faster action than you can deliver.")

"But surely you know if it's Venice or Lake Como or . . ."

"I'll just have to keep you posted," I said.

She lowered her voice to a whisper. "Are you carrying a g-u-n?"

I grinned at her. "Not past the m-e-t-a-l detectors. I pull it apart and carry the pieces in the bag, which I check. To be completely honest, I wrap the pieces in my underwear."

"Oh!" She gave me a crooked smile.

"Why?"

"Miss Mornay asked. I suppose she was concerned for your welfare."

"She know something I don't?"

"Not that she mentioned," Holly Blissfield replied brusquely. Her eyes focused on the digital numbers of her dashboard clock, then moved back to me. "Well, better go, I guess. Unless there's something more you need?"

"Nope. But I hope to meet your boss one of these days. Like when I return her earrings?"

"That can probably be arranged," Holly Blissfield said, smiling. She was unwinding, freed at last from the burden of delivering me and ready to assume her role as party hostess. I couldn't remember the last time I'd been to a party, much less enjoyed one.

The only two skycaps on the horizon were struggling with the luggage from the conservative, gray-haired group, who were, according to the leader herding them onward, members of the Mater Dolorosa Church of Pismo Beach, off to spend a week visiting the churches of northern Italy. I toted my flight bag past them and entered the International Building. The nut-brown Pismo Beachniks straggled in behind me and added to the crowd around the Air Italy counter, where a harried couple in midnight-blue uniforms tried to issue some tickets and validate others.

I walked past the hubbub to the almost empty first-class counter and was on my way through customs in minutes. In all my fif—well, let's make it forty-five years ("Lie about your age," Paul Montclair says. "The younger you say you are, the younger you'll feel. The American employer has absolutely no respect for age, unless its his own."), it never occurred to me that I'd take guilt-free pleasure in money-bought class distinction. But I knew from experience that back in the coach section of the jet, the churchgoing Pismo Beachers and a bunch of other citizens were going to be jammed together, elbow to elbow, trying to carve tasteless rubber chicken with plastic knives while watching an out-of-focus video of a movie they wouldn't have wasted five minutes on at their neighborhood cinema palace. Later, while trying to beat the jet-lag rap, they'd be lulled to sleep by the music of coughs and sneezes and crying babies.

I, on the other hand, was resting comfortably in a wide, well-cushioned womb, decorated in red, white, and green like the Italian flag, a pillow behind my still-sensitive-but-no-longer-throbbing head, my shoeless heels riding high on an adjustable footrest, while two beautiful olive-skinned air hostesses ministered to my every want. Life was good. Life was easy. I would arrive in Milan by 11:00 P.M., Italian time. I would be in Verona by the following afternoon, and with any small good fortune, I'd have my mitts on Watson before the sun set on Romeo and Juliet's tomb.

I took a sip of some pretty good Chianti and gazed lazily through the window at my right.

"The only way to fly, huh?"

The well-modulated voice belonged to the guy taking his seat next to me.

About five-ten. Beige linen sport coat over a pink open-necked shirt with the collar turned up, framing his narrow, tanned face. On that were watery blue-gray eyes, lips that were a fraction too thick, and a moustache, a fierce bristle, much grayer than his lank brown hair. It was supposed to distract you from his large nose, but in fact drew your attention to it.

"It beats hanging on an eagle's back," I said, sipping a little more vino.

"Travel much?" he asked.

"Some."

He pushed back against the cushions of his seat and extended his hand. "Jimmy Bristol," he said, as if it should mean something.

I pumped his dry little mitt and said, "Leo Bloodworth."

"So, Leo, what's taking you to Italy? Business? Pleasure? A profound pasta habit?"

"A little of all three, I guess, Jimmy."

"Uh, since we're gonna be neighbors for the next twelve or so hours, Leo, I wonder if I could ask a favor?"

"Sure, Jimmy."

"Would you call me Jim?"

I waited a beat to see if I could tell what was going on behind those winter-slush eyes. Nothing apparent. "Easy enough," I said, wondering why he'd introduced himself as Jimmy. But not wondering all that hard.

I gave him a smile, then ended that particular conversation by fishing out my copy of *Power Plan*. I was finishing the chapter on power-networking and trying to apply that to my weekly poker game with my buddy Cugat and some other cops and ops at a back room at the Tin Badge, when they lowered the movie screen and began to unspool the first of two flicks that I'd already seen in the theaters. I didn't like 'em then and I certainly didn't want to see them again, transferred to blurry video images, shrunk to TV size, and butchered to make them acceptable to a group of flying nuns. Or, in this instance, flying Pismo Beachers.

My new friend, Big Jim, slipped his earphones over his ears and pieces of his upturned shirt collar and settled back, scowling at the flickering pictures and making little grunting noises. Without turning his head, he said suddenly, "Mind dousing the light, Leo? I'm getting bright spots."

I shrugged, flicked off my light, polished off my Chianti, and closed my eyes. Then I opened them again. On the screen, under the movie's title, was a scene in a Salvadoran hotel room. An American secret agent was unpacking his suitcase. From it he carefully removed a teakwood box, inside of which was an elaborate Walther with a sight and silencer and all the sort of crap I can't imagine anybody fooling with, not to mention toting around in a teakwood box.

Seeing the boxed gun reminded me, however, that I had lied to Holly Blissfield. My police Colt was not in my flight bag. It was nestled in my Blue Streak shoulder holster, hanging on a hook in my bedroom closet, which is where I usually kept it. It was the thing I had forgotten to pack.

On the screen the spy's hotel door opened and a waiter entered, wheeling a silver tray with a shiny domed lid. The waiter lifted the dome with his left hand and removed a Llama double-action automatic that was resting on a plate with a sprig of parsley. Some room service! He pumped three .45 slugs into the spy, who was getting ready to tip him. So how much good does packing a gun do you, anyway?

I didn't see any reason why I would need one. Watson was no steely-eyed terrorist or mad-dogger. He was a double-gated gigolo who grifted geegaws from old ladies.

That was settled: the hell with the gun.

I shut my eyes again, but sleep wouldn't come. My thoughts floated from Watson and guns and jewelry to the kid. Serendipity. I wasn't worried about her, exactly. But she was traipsing around L.A. with that laid-back Dixie shamus who looked about as streetwise as your average college professor. Ah, well. I figured she could keep them both out of trouble for at least the two or three days I'd need to take care of business in old Verona.

With Jim—not James or Jimmy or Jimbo—grunting and moaning at the movie beside me, I began to count sheep. I ended by counting the miles separating me from Miss Serendipity Dahlquist, whom the Fates had evidently selected to be the burden and the joy of my declining years. I hoped that I would live long enough to get to the joy part.

7

1. Lieutenant Dove Hilbert led Terry Manion and me down a back stairwell to the basement, where the late Michael Kosca's files were being kept in a caged property room. Hilbert rattled the locked door on its hinges. "By-the-book son of a bitch," he grumbled, evidently referring to a wiry, bespectacled young black man in uniform who was approaching the door.

He unlocked it, saying, "Sorry, Lieutenant Hilbert. But you know the rules. I need a request signed by Lieutenant Mallory before I . . ."

"Where's the cooze who's usually down here?" Hilbert snarled.

"Say what, Lieutenant?"

"The bimbo. You know, the redhead with the forty-four Davids." Lieutenant Hilbert cupped his hands in front of his chest and moved them back and forth. I assumed that he was not indicating that the woman had an arthritic condition.

"Oh, Salina. She went on home. Time of month, I think."

Hilbert told him not to think so much and sent him after Kosca's files. He turned to Terry. "The dame would've given me the files without batting an eyelash and saved you the walk down here. But she's gotta pick today to go on the rag, and Super Spade doesn't bend an inch."

The black cop returned with a large, lidded cardboard packing box. He placed it carefully on a solid oak library table, reexamined the tag on the box, and gestured to Lieutenant Hilbert that its contents were ready for his inspection.

Hilbert leaned in close to the black officer and whispered something in his ear. The black officer frowned. "They're not supposed to be here by theirselves, Lieutenant," he admonished.

"I'm needed elsewhere, Officer Simpson. I don't think Manion and his little girl friend will gang up on you. You're not carrying a gun, are you, Manion?"

Terry moved his head imperceptibly.

"Well, then," Hilbert said to the black cop, and started for the metal door. To Terry he added, "I'll leave you in Officer Simpson's excellent care, Manion. If you find anything interesting, I expect you to share the information." Then he gave the three of us his two-second death's-head grin and walked away. His footsteps tip-tapped down the hall and up the stairs. "Odd sort of fella," Terry said.

Simpson grunted, moved to his desk, which was about ten feet away, and picked up a book, *The Romance of Real Estate.*

Terry removed the lid to the box and began lifting out manila file folders. Some were thick with papers and carbons. Others looked empty. He flipped through them and withdrew one that had "Manion, T." typed neatly on the index tab. I moved closer to study its contents over Terry's shoulder.

Mike Kosca could have taught Mr. Bloodworth a few things about keeping files. This one began with typed notes from Terry's first phone call. Cece MacElroy's full name—Cecelia MacElroy. Age and general description. Date of disappearance. There was the shorthand story of how Cece, Gretchen Leblanc, and Gregory Desidero had driven to Los Angeles in Greg's red Porsche and how Gretchen had opted to return to New Orleans. There were two additional bits of information that Terry had neglected to mention to me—Gregory Desidero was black. And Gretchen had been carrying his child, which she aborted at her father's request in return for a new car.

There was a description of the house overlooking the ocean with the large birds, where Gretchen had last seen Cece and Desidero. The name *Lorne* stood by itself, circled in pencil.

Terry put that page aside and paused to look at a sheet of legal-sized paper filled with chicken scratches made with the same soft-edged pencil.

"Can you decipher any of this?" Terry asked.

"It looks like a bunch of lists," I said, pointing to clumps of names and addresses. "Free health clinics, shopping malls where kids hang out. Record stores. Puke parlors . . ."

"What?" he interrupted.

"Oh, fast-food places," I explained. "I guess these are locations Mr. Kosca covered, since they've been checked off by several different pens."

"Is Wings 'n' Things on the list?"

"This looks like it right here, near the top. I bet he went there first."

"Yeah," Terry said and handed me the next sheet, a carbon of Mr. Kosca's first report, which he, Terry, had received several weeks before.

It was a summation of the late detective's activity. Through friends on the force (probably Dove Hilbert) he'd managed to put Gregory Desidero's red Porsche convertible with Louisiana plates on the stolen-vehicle list. But nothing had come of it. Nor had several car trips along the coast as far as Malibu resulted in the discovery of a house with large birds.

Kosca noted that he had visited several juvenile welfare centers and known Hotel Hells (those grotty, rat-infested apartment houses where indigent young people live without heat or running water) and traveled the length and breadth of Hollywood Boulevard passing out hundreds of photos of Cece and her father—copies he'd made from the pictures Terry had provided.

Finally, he ended his report with the suggestion that Mrs. MacElroy consider offering a cash reward of five thousand dollars for information about Cece's whereabouts.

"Did she go along with the reward?" I asked Terry.

He looked up from the carbon he was reading and, after taking a beat to switch his mental gears, replied without emotion, "She agreed to twenty-five hundred."

"Oh," I said, wondering if mothers ever really understood the true value of their children.

I looked over Terry's shoulder at the onionskin carbon he was studying so carefully. It was a copy of Kosca's second and most recent report, dated two days ago. "If he got a chance to mail it," Terry said, "it'll probably hit my mailbox this week some time."

"Made a few more passes along the coast," it read. "But it's all the same: no large birds. Closest I came was a feed-and-grain store near Malibu that keeps peacocks. The owner said some of the locals had good-size birds— parrots, mainly, and cockatoos. But these were older couples. Not the kind to party it up with a bunch of kids. Inquired at a number of real estate places, and they had no suggestions. Maybe you'd better talk to that Leblanc kid again, get a better description. Could be the place is further up the coast in the Santa Barbara area.

"The newspaper ads with the reward cost $385.65 (including artwork and layout; see bill attached). Only three replies. Two were washouts, but the third had quite a yarn that I want to check out. It could mean traveling up near San Francisco.

"Meanwhile, I might be able to speed up results by using another man. With your permission, of course. I'll split my fee, and unless the action picks up so that we both will be on it full time, my rates will remain as quoted. Sincerely, Michael Kosca."

68

That was the final item in the file. Terry closed it, then began leafing through the other files. He withdrew a folder marked "Accounts Payable." Nestled among the office bills and credit-card charges were four invoices stapled together with tear sheets from weekly newspapers, the advertisement-heavy freebies that you can usually find piled up on the ground in record stores or boutiques, or littering the streets in Westwood.

One of the papers was *The Tattler*, a semi-sleazoid tabloid that had once published an article about grade-school sex, written by a boy of my acquaintance. Anyone who knew Fred Pfister would realize in a second that he is entirely too dorky to know the first thing about grade-school sex or any other kind. But *The Tattler* had featured his little fantasy on its front page, illustrated by a photograph of youngsters playing in the yard at Bay City Normal during lunch break. It was a totally innocent scene, thoroughly perverted by a headline that read: SEX BEFORE PUBERTY? So much for the journalistic integrity of *The Tattler*.

Terry riffled through other items, then replaced them in the Accounts Payable folder. He put the files back into the cardboard evidence box. Officer Simpson had stopped reading his book on real estate and was whispering into his telephone. I must admit that I had been so preoccupied, I'd heard not a peep out of him.

He replaced the receiver. "The Dove, uh, Lieutenant Hilbert would like to see you, Mr. Manion," he said. Then he added, sheepishly, "He, ah, told me to call him if you looked at any folders other than the one with your name on it."

Terry said to me, "He gets more and more interesting, the Dove does."

Officer Simpson shrugged and opened the door for us. Before we had taken three steps, he was back at his desk, once again lost in the romance of real estate. He was not planning on staying a policeman forever.

2. "Ah, Manion, there you are. Come right in. Somebody here you should meet." Lieutenant Hilbert ignored me entirely as we reentered his office, which, since I had been witness to his attitude toward women in general, I accepted as a sort of compliment.

His companion was a stocky, jowly Latin, with large circles under flat black eyes. Mini-tacos garnished with black olives. He was wearing a dark brown suit, rumpled, over a tieless, shiny synthetic dark blue shirt that was slowly sinking away from his neck.

"This be Lieutenant Perez," Hilbert told Terry, with his barracuda grin in place. "Homicide's finest. His people recovered Mike Kosca's body."

Perez didn't offer his hand or stir from his chair. The black olives rolled from Terry to me as if nothing were going on behind them.

Hilbert said, "Sorry I only got the one guest chair, Manion. Take mine, why don't you. I've been sitting all day."

Perez exhaled loudly. "Got no time for this crap, Hilbert. I came to deliver you a message. Now what's on your mind?"

"I'd like you to tell Manion what you told me earlier about the Kosca murder."

"Why should I?"

"As a favor to me, say. As a gesture of friendship for your old compadre."

Perez's face said he doubted he owed the gray-haired man any favors. He blinked, then exhaled air through his nose like a bull. "We staring at seventeen open murders, including a much-beloved ballplayer who the captain knew personally, for Chri'sake," he told Hilbert. "I got all the time in the world to sit around your office and converse with anybody who walks in."

"We're all servants of the people, Lieutenant Pee-rez," Hilbert said.

Perez grunted and shoved himself out of the chair. "Go hump a rope, Dove. The last time you served any people was when you stepped away from the action," he grumbled, heading for the door.

"Hold your *caballos*, señor," Hilbert said. "C'mon now, relax. Just run it down in your soothing Latin tones for Manion, and you can get back pronto to your seventeen slayings."

Perez gave him a look of mild contempt. The abrasiveness of their relationship was nothing new, apparently, and they were nearly immune to any insult either could imagine. "Okay," Perez said. He perched on the edge of Lieutenant Hilbert's desk, facing Terry. "Because of the condition of the body"—the words came quickly and without emotion—"we assumed that . . ."

"I'm sure Manion read the newspaper account of the death, but maybe you'd better be more specific about the body's condition."

Perez turned his head and scowled at Hilbert. "In front of the kid?"

"That's okay. She's just somebody Manion's going to use later as his staked goat."

I said, "There's only one goat in this room that I can see, Lieutenant. And he's behaving like a jackass."

Perez grinned at me. "I didn't catch your name, miss."

"Serendipity Dahlquist," I said. "I'm assisting Mr. Manion."

"You're the one," Perez nodded. "You were mixed up in that shooting out in Hermosa." He turned to Lieutenant Hilbert, who, like Terry, was staring at me. "You must remember, Dove. The guy who got put away out at that music park near Hermosa. Turned out he'd zotzed his wife and five or six others."

Hilbert squinted at me. "You're that one, huh? I saw you on TV with that tub of lard Bloodworth, plugging a book you'd written."

"Mr. Bloodworth is no more fat than you are good-natured."

Hilbert said to Terry, "I'm afraid I got on the little lady's bad side by not recognizing her like my amigo here. Celebrity temperament can be awesome to behold."

"Lieutenant Hilbert, I cannot imagine what a woman, any woman, would have to do to get you *to* recognize her as other than a plaything or a beast of burden. So I would be wasting my time to feel anger or anything else for you." I turned to the now-smiling Lieutenant Perez. "Please continue with your description of Mr. Kosca's body," I instructed him. "If you get into areas that are beyond my tolerance, I will leave the room."

He nodded, cleared his throat, and continued, pointing out parts of his own anatomy to illustrate his description. "Multiple cuts and abrasions on face, neck, wrists, hands, fingers. Hundreds of them. Short, repeated. Some cuts, some punctures. Portions of the flesh had been torn away. Coroner says this was caused by birds of prey. Hawks, primarily, judging by feather particles. Cooper's hawks. Some call them chicken hawks. The cutting of Kosca's throat may have been a merciful act to put him out of his misery."

"What do you deduce by all this, Manion?" Lieutenant Hilbert asked.

"That Kosca ruffled somebody's feathers."

"That's very witty, Manion. What about the throat wound?"

"Well, if it was made at roughly the same time as the others, it means that the killer wasn't very worried about the birds attacking *him*."

"There you go, Perez. Manion's made it easy as pie for you."

"I suppose you could try the people who worked on that Alfred Hitchcock movie," Terry said.

Perez looked from Terry to Hilbert. Hilbert snarled, "You think this is funny, Manion?"

"Something sure is, Lieutenant. Mike Kosca was a partner of yours, and presumably a friend. You had to pull strings to get a piece of his homicide investigation. But now that you're heading it up, instead of trying to nail down a few edges, you're playing some sort of screwball game when the straight, dead-on approach is clearly called for."

Lieutenant Perez said, "You told these people you're in charge of the Kosca thing?"

"I am."

The Latin stared at him, saying nothing.

Terry asked, "Mind letting us know what's going on here?"

Lieutenant Perez started for the door again.

"Hold on, Roberto," Hilbert said. "We might as well clear the air on this."

"Hey, this is southern California. You don't come here for clear air."

"Por favor, amigo. Tell them the news you just brought me."

"Why not? You got maybe five more minutes to wrap up the Kosca murder. After that, it won't be your problem any longer."

"Whose problem will it be?" I asked.

"Tell the young lady, mi amigo. Youth wants to know."

Perez shook his head sadly. "This is your craziness," he said to Hilbert.

"Tell her and Manion. Long as we're all here."

"We have this situation," the Latin said wearily. "Poachers been robbing the nests of wild birds. The peregrine falcon, the condor, the eagle. They steal the baby birds and train them to attack, to fight. Sometimes they attach spikes to the birds' claws."

Hilbert pushed his chair away from his desk. "Down along the bayou, Manion, they probably have stayed with the old traditional cockfights. Out here, where invention is our most important product, they stage these little bird fights. Very hush-hush, unless you know somebody who knows somebody. Very illegal. Very *au courant*. They have replaced the weekend A-list cocktail soirees. Money changes hands. Not literally, of course. Checks are written.

"And our towel-headed friends, who delight in possessing anything that's state-of-the-art, are finding it quite amusing to return to their native lands with a fine hunting hawk that can outperform anything their neighbors have ever seen. What's the going price for a good trained game bird, Inspector?"

"It's in the six figures, Hilbert, but that's no longer our concern." He turned to face us. "The Feds are working on it now. The wildlife people brought them in, since some of the birds are endangered species. One less can of worms for us to worry over."

"I thought you people eat worms, amigo. Bite 'em in two and swallow 'em with mescal. You ought to go into those bird sanctuaries and kick ass. Something the button-down boys'd never dream of. They'll dick around until only the crows and the goddamned jackdaws are left."

"Dove loves the stink of battle as much as he hates the Feds," Perez told us. "He would like to pick up his ball and chain and go out and bash whoever's robbing those nests. No matter it's not his territory, it's not his responsibility, it's not his war. He might even bash a few Federal skulls, too."

Hilbert said, as if he hadn't even heard Lieutenant Perez, "I think that

72

Mike, on purpose or by accident, came across these fine, upstanding poachers, who set a flock of game birds onto him, attacking him time and time
again, until his face looked like a goddamned flank steak. And then one of
those clever folks cut his throat. I also think that my friend here, Pee-rez, is
turning his wet back on the whole thing because he's too chickenshit to
enter an area that's been staked out by the almighty Feds."

"Dream on, brother," Perez said. "I came all the way here personally to
notify you to get ready to turn the Kosca material over to the Feds. You ask
me to stick around to tell this guy about Kosca's body and I do. Instead of
thanking me, you give me this shit. You're a crazyman on this. But the facts
speak for themselves."

He held up a brown hand, spatulate thumb and fingers pointing at the
ceiling. He began bending his digits in time with his countdown. "One, the
body was found down the canyon at a point that was maybe a mile beyond
my jurisdiction and that means *way, way* beyond your jurisdiction. But you
begged to get this one on your plate, so it's been yours for a day or two.
Never was it mine. I just had the misfortune to drag up the body. Two, the
Feds have come around to your way of thinking, and the murder will be part
of their ongoing investigation. But read my lips: I don't care because, three,
it ain't my business. I got enough uncomplicated, time-consuming cases to
worry about. And, four, I think you got a friggin' lot of nerve going over
department business in front of civilians off the street."

His index finger was still upright, and he leaned across the desk and
pushed it against Hilbert's chest. "You used to be a smart hombre, Hilbert.
Maybe a little loco, and a real hardnose, always. But you was also smart, so it
didn't matter. But you losing it baby, and everybody's wise. You're losing
whatever you had. Maybe you ought to retire, before they put you away."

Hilbert's face turned to stone. Perez spun on Terry. "I don't know what
the hell you think you're doing here, or where you come from. But you
better go back. This El Lay is the toughest survival course the good Lord
ever came up with. It bakes your brain with the sun, it clogs your nose with
poisons, and it robs your soul with its godless delights. It turns people into
pricks or locos. You got the loco look."

With that, he barreled through the door and slammed it hard enough to
rattle its panels. Hilbert somehow managed to work up another of his horrible grins. "Well, well," he said. "Looks like I finally hit a nerve under that
thick greaser hide."

3. Hilbert slumped back in his chair. He was pale before. Now he was
pasty. Even the pink of his scalp looked gray. "The truth of it is," he said,

then broke off laughing. "The truth of it is, I never believe anybody who starts off saying 'The truth of it is . . .'

"But the wetback is right. I *am* losing it. Mike's death has taken something out of me. Messed up my judgment. The crazy thing is, I wasn't all that close to him. I mean, I was his friend, but not that close. Mike was a very private sort. And that wife of his, Lucille, was just as withdrawn. Long as he was on the force, they never mixed with the other officers and wives. Oh, the four of us'd go out from time to time. I was still married then. Happily married. At least I thought I was happily married.

"They were hermits, except when he was working. After retirement, he didn't leave the goddamn house for a year. So I, uh, talked him into taking on little assignments. Threw some business his way. Shoehorned his license through for him. Maybe that's it. Maybe I'm feeling guilt because of what happened."

Personally, I thought he was one of Lieutenant Perez's locos, a man whose innerspring was unwinding.

Terry said, "I think we'd better be going. Thanks for . . . whatever this was."

"Wait," Hilbert said, leaping from his chair and catching Terry by the arm. "Don't you feel it, too? Isn't that why you came busting your ass out here, because you thought that you might be, indirectly, responsible for Mike's death?"

Terry didn't answer. He just stared at the smaller, older man. Hilbert said, "I thought I sensed that. You should understand my frustration in having to sit back while not a fucking thing is accomplished. Mike's just one of a hundred or so murders in this town that won't get solved this month. I want to do something."

I preferred him when he was being despicable. I said, "Mrs. Kosca would like to bury her husband. Maybe if you could get them to release the body . . ."

"Done. An hour ago, while it was still in my province. I phoned her, told her I'd make the arrangement with the funeral home. Save her a few bucks. Don't think Mike had too much dough. She's not a bad dame, Lucille isn't. She's holding up. She's strong. I didn't have it in me to warn her about the condition of the body. Maybe the undertaker can fix it up, what d'you think?"

"Tell him to keep the coffin lid closed. That worked for my father," Terry said, raising more questions about his past. Suddenly he asked, "What kind of a partner was Kosca?"

"Solid. Dependable. Trustworthy. He wasn't the world's greatest cop.

Something was missing—the drive. The spirit. Even when we were snot-nose patrolmen and the blood was still high, he just didn't have the push. But he wasn't soft. And I never saw him take shit from any man, woman, or dog. And he was a damn good, loyal partner."

"According to a notation in the files, he was thinking of bringing somebody in to help him with my problem. I imagine he was talking about George Kerby."

"Who?"

"Some guy who'd been palling around with Kosca, according to Mrs. Kosca."

"I never heard of him."

"She said he showed you through Mr. Kosca's office space yesterday."

Lieutenant Hilbert shook his head. "I was a little late getting there. Department red tape. A clean-up team had already gone through the office and the house. George Kerby, huh? That sounds familiar. Wasn't there a comic . . . ?"

"Spelled differently," Terry said. "This one's with an e."

Hilbert shrugged. "Can't help you, then. Anything else in the files worth mentioning? Something about game birds would be nice."

"Not in the ones I looked at. You ought to go through them yourself."

"I scanned a few. It's a good thing he learned to type. I never could read his writing. Nobody could. I made out the reports. That was before they had to be typed in triplicate by computer. Jesus, it's been a long day."

"It's after nine," I said.

"So it is." He circled the desk slowly, blinking his eyes. "I assume you'll be returning south now, eh, Manion? The FBI will eventually find Mike's murderer. They always get their man, I've been told. Usually by the Feds themselves."

"I didn't come here to find a murderer," Terry reminded him. "I'm looking for a runaway girl."

"Right. So you'll be around a while? How long you plan on giving yourself?"

Terry shrugged. "Till my cash runs out."

"Well, we probably won't be meeting again. I hope we won't. Some of the things . . . I'm not exactly myself tonight. I would not like to be reminded of it."

We started for the door.

"Forgive me for not recognizing you, Miss . . . ?"

"Dahlquist."

"Miss Dahlquist. I'll see if I can find your book on the newsstand. And,

Manion, let me congratulate you. You've got the one thing Mike was missing in his quest for your runaway girl. She's young. Noisy. Pretty. And at least a mini-celebrity. Miss Dahlquist's gonna make an absolutely first-rate staked goat."

8

1. My eyes flickered open as Jim ("Don't call me Jimmy") Bristol hissed, "You mealy warthog bastards" at the airline's movie screen. Curious as to the reason for his wrath, I turned my attention to the spy saga just in time to see a castle inhabited by Sandinistas blow up in a big way. The hero of the piece, a wimp who turns into a real man under pressure, dragged the half-naked brunette heroine from a secret passageway and carted her down a mountainside to safety.

"Did you ever see such horseshit?" Jim Bristol asked rhetorically. He yanked off his headset and threw it onto the cabin floor. "How in the Christ could they have made that piece of cow pucky, Leo? I ask you."

"I don't know, Jim. I guess they took a little trip down South America way, drank a lot, ate a lot, slept till noon, spent somebody's twenty million dollars, and traveled back to Hollywood land fat and happy."

He scowled at me. "What are you, pal? Some kind of asshole bliss-ninny?"

"Hey, Jim, you don't have to get insulting."

"Aw, it's just . . . hit me again, will you, sweetheart?" The last was aimed at a hostess who pranced past with a freshly uncorked wine bottle. Jim waited until she filled his glass and mine, then continued, "The fact is, Leo, and the thing that none of these young, upwardly moguled studio execs seem to realize is that the script comes first. The script means everything. Where's the script on this one? Where is the fucking script?"

"Let me guess, Jim—you're in show business."

"Of course I am," he shot back.

"And I bet, with all that talk about scripts, that you're a writer."

"Oh, I could be, I suppose. If I wanted to. Actually, I'm a personal manager. You know: take care of the kids. Make sure they don't fall off the deep end. Keep the spirits up and the fears down. My client list is pretty damned impressive, if I say so myself. And I'm getting into production too, Leo. Very shortly."

"Sounds good," I said, my mind digressing from him to my oversated body, through which the vino was rapidly flowing.

"That's why I have come to understand the value of the written word," Bristol nattered on. "You know, as the Bible tells us, 'In the beginning was the Word.'"

"The Bible never lies," I said, shifting in my seat so I could look over his seat to the lavatory door just past the galley. A little light glowed OCCUPATO.

"I remember back when I was Little Jimmy Bristol, only nine years old but I knew even then, the script was the making or the breaking of our series."

Little Jimmy Bristol. That rang some distant bell. "You were a kid actor, right?" I asked.

"What? You trying to get back for that 'bliss-ninny' zotz? I wasn't a kid actor. I was Little Jimmy Bristol." He struck a goofy, cross-eyed pose with the tongue hanging out of the side of his mouth. He reeled it in to say, in a childish, high-pitched whine, "Uh-oh, Lit-tul Jimmy's been a bad boy."

He stared at me expectantly, but I didn't know what my reaction was supposed to be. He said, rather harshly, "Jesus, you must remember *Men-About-Town*." He began to sing, "'There's Freddie, he's puttin' on his muk-luks. There's Jimmy, he's putting on his white bucks. There's Daddy, he's putting on his black tux. They're the men-about-town. Yeah!'"

"Four seasons on UBC," he went on, lapsing into his normal, everyday broadcast-industry voice. "Five Emmys. Two Peabodys. Three *TV Guide* covers. We're still running in syndication. The network wants to do an anniversary show, but Cal Bedloe, who played my dad, bailed out about five years ago. Jake Seloy, my brother Freddie, is serving time for rape. I mean, Jesus!, the guy never even liked girls when we did the show. So that leaves me and my little sweetheart, Jamie Ann Johnson, who's now the toast of fucking Broadway and doesn't have time to do what she calls 'small screen.' Big stage star. Booze, pills, the works, you know, Leo. The reason her show's SRO is that she's the *Enquirer*'s favorite cover girl. They come from miles around to see if she can still walk at eight o'clock every night."

"No anniversary show, huh?"

"No way," he said, shaking his head.

"Well, hell, Jim. You've got other fish to fry, right? Personal management. Producing."

"True enough, big guy. You know, that brings up a very good point. . . ."

"Hang onto it, Jim," I said, pushing myself upright. "While I hit the little boys' room."

He rolled into the aisle to let me pass, and I staggered the few steps to the lavatory, which was still OCCUPATO. I shifted from foot to foot and peeked into the galley where the doe-eyed hostesses chatted softly and arranged some sort of little sugar-coated cakes on a silver tray.

The end of the film had activated my fellow passengers. They were starting to mill around, and the hostesses began to look restive. I must have been looking a little restive myself.

I had just about decided to demean myself by breaking the first-class barrier and wandering through the rear of the plane in search of an empty toilet, when there was a click and the OCCUPATO was replaced by NON OC-CUPATO.

The flimsy lavatory door bounced open, and this fever dream emerged. He was a real piece of work, from the top of his aquamarine cockscomb to the soles of his pointed, egg-yolk-yellow lizard-skin boots. He was of medium height, wearing sand-colored pants baggy enough for two and a black-and-white sport coat with sleeves down to his knuckles and shoulders so padded he had to move through the door sideways. He sniffed a few times through a pale, waxy nose that resembled a parrot's beak, then rubbed his coat sleeve against it, coaxing a wink from the little zircon that was embedded over the right nostril. I backed into the galley to make way for his shoulders.

In the head, I looked for and found a faint residue of a white, powdery substance on the washbasin ledge. Which was all right with me. It meant he might not have actually used the toilet.

2. Walking back to my seat, I spotted Shoulders near the front of the plane, sitting next to a thin, pale woman whose cotton-candy-pink-hair had just a hint more frizz than Orphan Annie's. What I initially thought was a rodent coming out of her ear proved to be a bunch of feathers tacked to her lobe, a plumed earring, as it were. She was reading a magazine and sipping something brown in a plastic glass. She did it daintily, with little pinkie extended. Shoulders was slumped in his aisle seat making a half-dollar walk along the backs of his fingers.

"Nice sort of people you find in first class," Bristol snapped, following my line of sight as he stood to let me by.

"All it takes is moolah," I said.

"Rock-and-roll trash."

"You know him?" I asked.

He shook his head. "No. But I know the type. Woke up one morning and puked into a mike and made thirty million bucks. A year from now he'll wake up, do the same thing, and they'll throw him into a detox cell. And it'll be a banner day for show business."

I shrugged and pried a magazine from the seat pocket in front of me. *Notte* it was called. It was the size of the old *Life*, but there the comparison ended. The cover was a night shot of a guy in an Indianlike headdress and loincloth hoisting a nearly naked dame over his head with one hand. The dame had a figure that Raquel Welch, even with all of her fitness tapes, never quite matched. She was wearing what looked like a bikini and bra decorated with spaghetti. It was an Italian magazine, so maybe it *was* spaghetti.

I was flipping through page after page of firm flesh, when Bristol said, "You like the ladies, eh, Leo?"

"I don't make a career of it, but sure."

"I bet you prefer big mammas, like that one."

"In magazines, maybe," I said. "But in real life, I prefer women who don't shake their yams in public."

"Oh, a prude, huh?"

"Hell, Jim, I guess I am. And the more sex diseases they invent, the more prudish I'm gonna become."

"Leo, there ain't no more virgins."

I shrugged and went back to my page-turning. Bristol bounced his elbow off of my forearm. "Will you look at that?"

At first I thought he was talking about the page in front of me, on which three naked ladies were practicing their archery. But he was still staring at our green-haired fellow-passenger, who had stood to remove his coat and most of his shoulders. Underneath, his chest and back looked of normal size. But his shirt was in tatters, and in and out of the gaping slits an elaborate tattoo of a Chinese dragon wiggled across his back. When his seat obliterated the view, Bristol said, "Two thousand, eight hundred bucks for first class, and I've gotta look at some son of a bitch with holes in his shirt. I'd complain, if I knew who to complain to."

"You might try *him*," I said, pointing to the green hair.

"What is it with you, Leo?" Bristol asked, his forehead and moustache twisted in a gesture of annoyance. "I get the distinct feeling that you think I'm some sort of schmuck."

"I sure didn't mean to give you that impression, Jim," I said. "Especially since we're probably gonna be joined at the hip on this bucket for the next six or seven hours."

"Then what *do* you think about me? C'mon, man to man."

My sore head was returning. I closed the magazine, rested it on my lap, and stared at him, realizing from his now-bloodshot eyes and hint of a slur that he was running on full. "I think it's time we both take a snooze, Jim. It helps with the jet lag."

"Wait just a minute, Leo. There's a question on the floor. What . . . do . . . you . . . think . . . about . . . *moi?*"

I said, "Caucasian, five-ten, hair brown, eyes blue-gray, moustache, weight about a hundred and fifty. The sports clothes put you back maybe five hundred bucks. You let things that are beyond your control piss you off, and you hit the sauce a little too hard. You seem to be straight, but if you keep this kind of conversation going, I'll begin to wonder. Happy now?"

"That description sounded just like a cop script," Bristol said. "You wouldn't be a cop, would you, Leo?"

It didn't seem worthwhile telling him I used to be. Instead, I answered, truthfully, "I don't know any cops fly first class, Jim."

He waved a slightly uncoordinated arm. "Why not? Everybody else does." His eyes turned sly. "I asked you before and you didn't answer: What kind of work *do* you do?"

When you're on business, it makes no sense to bare your soul to every bozo who asks. "I . . . uh, I'm a writer."

He suddenly sobered.

"What?" he begged.

"What, what?"

"What have I seen?"

"Oh," I said, catching on. "No movies. Not yet."

"TV?"

"No."

"But you're a writer," he said.

I nodded.

"Hmm." He said, with some disappointment, "Like a reporter or some-thing?"

"Like that."

"Something hot in Milano? Or are you moving on?"

"I'm not sure," I said. "We can talk later. Sleep-time now."

Before he could open his mouth in protest, I leaned back cautiously against the cushion and shut my eyes. I started counting head throbs.

I think I made it into the double digits before I fell asleep.

The next thing I knew, the plane was bouncing up and down like one of those dumb cowboy-bar mechanical bulls. I awoke, gasping for air. Bristol was staring at me, ashen. We leveled off, and he ran a shaky hand over his face.

"You okay?" I asked.

"Huh? Oh, sure. Rough flight."

One of the dark-haired, olive-skinned hostesses passed by, paused, and bent down to pick something off of the floor. "Looks like this fell out of the overhead," she said, holding up the limp object.

"My sport coat," I told her.

She clucked and pointed to the hatch of the overhead compartment, which was hanging open, flapping as the plane road the airwaves. "I must tell the captain to fly more carefully," she said, folding the coat and stretching up to replace it in the compartment. "I hope there was nothing breakable in the pockets."

"Nothing at all in the pockets," I said, pulling a smile up from my socks.

She took special care to secure the compartment hatch. She started away, then paused, looked down at Bristol. "Sir, with the turbulence, the captain wishes seat belts to be fastened."

Shaking again, Jimbo managed to secure the belt. She nodded her approval and strode off.

I reached over and grabbed him by the shoulder. If it hadn't been for the belt, he would have jumped into the aisle. "Huh? What?"

"Hey, take it easy, pal," I said. "I was just going to suggest you calm down. You're acting like you've been bit by Mr. Coffee Nerves."

"It . . . it's the plane. The turbulence."

"Don't worry about that. The worst that can happen is that we crash. And we've got that covered."

"Covered? How?"

I settled back and shut my eyes again. "Hell, man, we're in first class."

3. Instead of crashing in a heap of charred and twisted metal, we touched down rather gracefully and more or less on schedule. I wound up sharing an open-sided jitney with the Pismo Beach pilgrims, and as we were whisked across the tarmac from the plane to Malpensa Airport, the air was heavier and thicker than the smog we'd left in L.A. A needle was wedged somewhere in the middle of my skull—a combination of the sapping and the Chianti—and the rest of my bones ached from the long flight. Judging by the glassy stares and slogging-through-syrup gait of my fellow travelers, religion did not let you off the jet-lag hook.

The travelers who'd taken the first jitney—Bristol, Shoulders, and his cotton-candy-haired girl friend included—were busily claiming their luggage by the time the Pismo Beach crowd and I made our entrance. I was amused to see Bristol being almost knocked on his can by the green-haired lad who'd just jerked a large metal suitcase from the moving chute.

Bristol braced himself and blocked the other's progress. Words were exchanged, but I was too far away to hear them. I moved closer, less interested in them than in reclaiming my flight bag, which had just rounded a corner on a journey away from where I was standing.

As I approached the two men, Bristol spotted me and moved back from the other awkwardly. Shoulders snarled in a voice like pebbles rattling in a tin can, "Keep your hooks off me, dude, or I'll snap 'em off at the wrist."

Shoulders turned and moved through the crowd in the direction of customs, where his girl friend waited dreamily. She was wearing a jacket that resembled several feather boas stitched together. Like her hair, eyebrows, and tight leather miniskirt, it was a soft pink color. Bristol glared at Shoulders's broad departing back. "The scum of the earth," he hissed. "The term ugly American takes on a whole new meaning."

"He's a beauty, that's for sure," I said, managing to snag my bag by one strap and rescue it from the treadmill. Before I could get started toward the customs counters, Bristol asked me to wait for him to recover two leather suitcases bearing the initials of their manufacturer. Why the hell anybody would want their luggage to have any initials other than their own, I'll never understand.

Nor do I understand why anybody'd sink a lot of loot into a suitcase that's going to bounce around inside the belly of a plane. One of Bristol's bags had a nasty gash in its side, going past leather and insulation all the way to the metal frame. His mouth dropped away from his bristly moustache as he gawked at it. "Gawdamnit," he yelped. "I paid seven hundred and fifty smacks for that bag, wholesale. And some fucking wop uses it for a bocci ball."

"I'd cool that sort of language, Jim," I said. "When in Rome, and all." He shook his head woefully. "Maybe the airline will repair it for you."

"How?" he asked, seething.

"They're pretty good with leather in this country," I said. "When they're not playing bocci ball."

"I just want to get the hell out of here," he said, clutching both suitcases with white-knuckled hands. Still seething, he followed me to the customs counters. To our left, Shoulders and his lady were just getting up to bat. A bored official in a dark green uniform opened Shoulders's passport and asked, "The purpose of your visit, signore?"

The signore grumbled, "Vacation."

The official's heavy-lidded eyes moved from him to the girl.

"Vacation," she echoed.

The official scanned their passports. "You are Signorina Hoffstattler?"

"Right. Loni Hoffstattler."

He banged a rubber stamp against her open passport, then turned his droopy eyes on Shoulders. "Your name is Port-aire?"

"Porter," Shoulders shot back. "Cole Porter."

Bristol snorted. "Right. And we're Rodgers and Hammerstein," in an aside that could be heard across the noisy terminal. The girl with cotton-candy hair turned toward us, raised one bunny-pink eyebrow, and curled her lip. Then, slowly, she lifted a thin hand partially encased in a torn black lace glove, made a fist, and raised the middle finger. All for Bristol's benefit.

His face turned red and he said to me, "The nerve of that slut."

The counter suddenly cleared in front of us, easing the tension that had been building in Bristol's skull. A fat, perspiring official waved us forward. When he grabbed Bristol's suitcase, his wet hand left its imprint on the leather. Bristol stared at it and remained silent. If nothing else, the trip was teaching Little Jimmy a few lessons in humility.

9

1. Holding the phone to my ear, I counted the irritating ringing sounds and watched a crew-cut man with a gold tooth in the front of his mouth bowl a strike and swagger back to his teammates, one of whom handed him a beer bottle. Elsewhere, other bowlers were staring intently down the alleys or doing that strange little dance that seems quite natural once the ball leaves the fingers. The phone continued to ring. Twelve . . . thirteen . . . fourteen. No one was going to answer. I gave it up and strolled past the noisy bowlers, all of whom seemed to be having a wonderful time. I smiled to myself at the thought of what Gran would say if I suggested we go bowling some evening. "Sehr," she would reply loftily, "I would rather lie facedown in a pile of Lithuanian garbage."

Or perhaps: "Why don't you ask some of your little friends?" Which little friends, I might inquire? Sylvia and George Sandifer, the newlyweds, with their four-month-old baby who was smarter and better company than both of them put together? Sally Duplainer or Randi Mumphrey, who are high 96 percent of the time? Liz Bermann, who spends most of her day eating and/ or throwing up? Lulu Pemberton and her cousin Wanda, who don't do anything unless it involves some form of sexual gratification?

There are the jocks, of course—Cora Ann Johnson, Lady Holland, and that crowd. Maybe if I could convince them that public bowling was not too plebeian (Lady's favorite word), I would have the pleasure of listening to them argue over which team would be stuck with the feeb who'd never bowled before, namely *moi*.

I wondered if Mr. Bloodworth was much of a bowler. I suspected he was, bowling being a rather manly sort of sport. Perhaps I could prevail upon him to tutor me during some off hours when nobody would be around to watch. Or if not Mr. B., then Terry Manion. Except that Terry didn't really strike me (no pun intended) as being much of an athlete of any kind.

He was sitting at a little black-topped table at the rear of the crowded fast-food place just off of the alleys. Although it looks like yet another hamburgerteria with its Formicas and plastics and lunch counter and display box full of pastries and jukebox and dimensional advertisement featuring an eternally flowing Pepsi can, the Creole Café, only blocks away from the Pacific, is something altogether unique. It's run by people from Louisiana, and their menu is filled with Cajun delicacies like red beans and rice and gumbo. Which is why I thought it an ideal spot to take Terry to dinner.

Judging by the morose look on his face as I threaded my way between tables of mildly raucous diners, it had not been one of my better plans.

"Something wrong with the Cajun meatloaf?" I asked.

He leaned back in his chair and looked at me with those pale blue eyes. "No. It's the best I can remember. Funny, but when I'm in New Orleans, I don't eat much Cajun food."

I sat down opposite him and sampled my red beans, which were large red kidney beans, seasoned with peppers, onions, sausage, and heaven knows what-all. He said, "In New Orleans they only serve those on Mondays."

"Why?"

He shrugged. "Some traditional reason, I guess. That's usually the answer as to why people do what they do in New Orleans." He paused to chew a small forkful of meatloaf, then said, "I don't suppose she's home yet, your grandmother?"

I shook my head. "I'm totally surprised," I told him, which wasn't the truth, exactly. It was just 9:40 P.M., and Gran probably wouldn't be back before ten. "But, Terry, I don't want you to feel you have to keep me company until she arrives. I could just sit here until they close and walk the twenty or thirty blocks to our apartment and hope that Gran's there by that time."

He sighed and picked up a bottle of hot sauce. The label read "Laurel Isle Red Hot." He made a wry smile and said, "When Gil left me—my wife, Gil —she took up with the guy who owns Laurel Isle."

I had no idea what to say to that, so I said, "Oh?"

"It's a real island near Fontenot. They have the cannery there. Grow their own peppers. It's quite a deal. Except that it's a little, well, confining for a woman like Gil."

"She left him, too, huh?"

"After just two weeks. Then it was a month with a hellfighter who doused oil fires in the Gulf, five months with a navy jet pilot, one of those Blue

Angel acrobats, three months with a bullfighter. How she met him I have no idea. A month and a half with . . ."

He was becoming totally depressed, so I cut in, "You must have loved her terribly."

"Did. Still do. And, yes, 'terribly' covers it. But the time we spent together was . . ." He searched for a word.

"Quality," I suggested.

"Huh?"

"Quality time."

He smiled broadly, as if I'd made a joke. "Yes, ma'am," he said. "It was quality time." He tried a bit more of the meatloaf. Then he asked, "I suppose Bloodworth is still among the missing?"

I nodded. That really *was* a mystery. "Not at the office. Not at home. I hope he's all right."

He frowned and so did I, both of our thoughts bouncing from Mike Kosca to Mr. Bloodworth. After a few seconds Terry shook his head and smiled. "No," he said, mainly to himself. "Paranoia hasn't quite consumed me yet. No one could possibly know I'd asked Bloodworth to help me."

"Unless your phone is tapped, or if the switchboard operator at your hotel was bribed, or something."

He stared at me blankly, then shook the thoughts away. "He's probably out having dinner with his wife or girl friend."

"He has neither," I shot back, too quickly. "That is to say, he has had two wives. And girl friends, too. But not precisely at this point in time."

He smiled and turned those pale blue eyes on me again, and I could feel the blush returning to my cheeks. "Eat your food before it gets cold," he said. "There's nothing worse than cold beans and rice."

I took another mouthful. It was quite exotic and wonderful. I swallowed and tried once more to cheer him. "You know, we've made enormous progress in just a few hours."

"Oh?"

"Don't you think so? There's so much of what Mr. Sherlock Holmes used to demand—data."

The dreamy look left his eyes and he leaned forward. "Such as?"

"Well"—I reached across the table for a brown-and-gold cube of cornbread—"known facts, first. Birds. For as long as I can remember, people have been robbing the nests of game birds out here. But according to Lieutenant Perez, there's now a great deal of money involved in training and selling the birds. So much so the FBI has finally become interested.

"Then there's Mike Kosca's murder. Which in its own horrible way involves game birds."

"So you subscribe to Dove Hilbert's theory that Kosca was killed by bird poachers?"

"It has a certain logic to it," I said, defensively.

He put down his fork and dabbed at his mouth with a paper napkin. "So, to continue being as logical as possible, we can probably assume that Cece MacElroy was in no way involved with Kosca's death."

The Creole Café had become a classroom, and Terry was giving me an oral exam. "We can't make that assumption," I told him. "Because her former friend, Gretchen, talked about being in a place near the ocean where there were large birds."

"Gretchen was stoned," Terry said. "I don't know as we can put much value to her big-bird story. Anything else?"

Games. Always games. "No," I said, popping a bit of cornbread into my mouth, where it literally melted. "Except for the postcard from Wings 'n' Things, the boutique that specializes in feathers. Which seems to substantiate Gretchen's story. Birds everywhere. I was wondering . . ."

"What?"

"Why you didn't mention Wings 'n' Things to Lieutenant Hilbert."

His reply was interrupted by the arrival of our waitress with a straw basket containing the specialty of the house, beignets—piping hot deep-fried rectangular doughnuts covered with powdered sugar. Just the smell alone would send a health-food faddist into cardiac arrest.

Terry waited for the waitress to fill his cup with chicory coffee, then told me, "From what Perez said, Hilbert's official involvement in the Kosca murder would be short-lived at best."

"And he would have probably gone to the boutique and behaved like the moronic martinet he is and accomplished nothing."

"That, too," Terry said, wiping powdered sugar from his lips with his napkin. "These are very good, Serendipity. Try one." It was lighter than it looked. The outer crust was almost crunchy, and the inside was tender and warm and delicious. "The secret, which they obviously know, is to use Pet milk instead of fresh cream. Makes all the difference."

"So you're a cook, too, as well as an investigator."

"Both require an amount of curiosity and patience."

I smiled, finishing the wonderful beignet. I had absolutely no aptitude for cooking or housekeeping or tasks of that ilk. I barely squeaked by homemaking with a C. But I didn't let Terry's analogy between culinary and criminological pursuits upset me, because I knew that, if anything, Mr. Bloodworth was even more hopeless in the kitchen than I was. And he is the finest sleuth I've ever known.

"So what do we do next?" I asked Terry.

"Wait for your grandmother, I suppose."

"I mean about the Kosca murder."

"Well," he said, moving his coffee cup in a circular pattern on the paper doily, "to be honest, I'm not convinced it's any of my business."

"But Cece MacElroy . . ."

"In spite of all the bird cross-references, she's not necessarily connected to Kosca's murder," he cut in. "I think it's likely that Kosca went to Wings 'n' Things to ask about Cece, and wound up being sidetracked by the bird-poaching situation that got him in trouble."

"Couldn't Cece be with these poachers?"

"Why would she? She came out here to . . . what? I don't know. Become a movie star is what Gretchen said. Bird fights seem a stretch from the silver screen."

"I think we should go to Wings 'n' Things as soon as we finish here."

He looked at his watch. "It's a little late."

"Not for Melrose Avenue," I told him.

"Maybe not for Melrose. And maybe not for you. But I'm still on eastern daylight time, ma'am. And I find myself about an hour shy of passing out."

"Tomorrow, then," I said.

"Let's discuss it with Bloodworth in the morning."

I shrugged. "We should seek his aid, of course," I said. But I was annoyed that he didn't display more confidence in my ability. Ah, well, time to switch tactics. "What about the lead Mr. Kosca mentioned in his last report to you?"

He was quite handsome when he smiled. "How could we pursue that?" He was toying with me again.

"We could check his office again. Perhaps there was an appointment book that he kept. Mrs. Kosca might have taken down a phone message. And there is that new friend of Mr. Kosca's—George Kerby. If he is the fellow Mr. Kosca was going to use to help him find Cece, he might know something. Definitely, we should try to locate George Kerby."

Terry asked, "Is that all?"

"No, as a matter of fact." I took the video journalist's card from my pocket. "I think he should be contacted, too."

"Why?"

"Maybe he knows something."

"He's just one of those grief scavengers who make a profit from other people's pain. He didn't know Kosca when he was alive, had no interest in him until he became a murder victim."

"What about this?" I shoved the black plastic rectangle across the

Formica tabletop. Terry picked it up, turned it over. "I took it from Mr. Kosca's work area."

"What is it?"

"I don't have any idea. It looks like a space-age credit card. See the letters, RPNP?"

"If you don't know what it is," Terry asked, "why'd you take it?"

"Because it was in a very dusty area, but the box that it was in had no dust on it."

He pushed the plastic object back to me and said, "You don't miss much."

"How clever of you to notice." I put the plastic and Fishburn's card into my wallet and picked up the bill before he could. "Just another customer service of the Bloodworth Agency," I said, rather boldly since the Creole Café does not accept credit cards and I, as always, was a bit short of cash. I mentally calculated the 15 percent gratuity and relaxed. I had just enough. Of course, I was certain Mr. Bloodworth would reimburse me from petty cash for what was obviously a business dinner.

2. Gran answered when next I dialed the apartment. She ordered me home, immediately. No further discussion. Terry, visibly relieved by the news, deposited me at the front of our building minutes thereafter. I hopped from the car, and a cold gust of ocean breeze raised goose bumps on my bare arms. Bay Heights, where we live, is just above the Pacific and is chilly most nights, even in summer, when the rest of L.A. swelters. My teeth were almost chattering as I said, "Since you're going down to the agency tomorrow morning, Terry, I don't suppose you could pick me up around nine?"

He seemed to be considering it, then shook his head. "I'm not sure when Bloodworth will be able to meet with me. I'll have to call him first, to set something up."

I nodded. "Well, see you whenever," I said.

"Thanks for the supper," he said. "Next time will be my treat."

"I will hold you to that," I said, turning and running toward the front door and away from the damp and chilly night breeze.

Gran was waiting for me in the living room, seated on a little French love seat recently recovered in lovely white-and-pale-green silk. She had changed into an outfit not unlike her everyday working clothes—comfortable wool skirt and cashmere sweater with one string of nearly perfect pearls. On the coffee table before her was a pile of mail, some of which she'd already read. A large portion of it was fan mail, sent to her at the network and addressed to Aunt Lil Fairchild, the character she's played on her soap for so many years. She put down the letter she was reading and said, "Please come in and sit down, Sehr-ee-nah."

I was in some sort of trouble. It wasn't just the edge in her voice. Usually, she calls me "Sehr." When she's in an especially happy mood, she calls me "Wendy," after the James M. Barrie creation who is one of my favorite childhood heroines. When she is particularly displeased with me, it's "Sehr-ee-nah."

"Hi, Gran," I said moving closer. My kiss on her cheek, which she allowed, was not rewarded with even a hint of warmth. Trouble indeed.

I looked around the room and failed to see the little black and white bullterrier puppy that should have been brushing against my legs. "Where's G-2?" His name is actually Groucho II. Mr. Bloodworth, who never seems to have time enough to use anyone's full, given name, came up with G-2. Since he had presented me with the splendid little creature for my birthday, I acceded to his wishes and G-2 it is.

"He's outside on the terrace. I think he has fleas, though how he managed it, I don't know. Where have you been, girl?" Her lavender eyes were unwavering.

"Having dinner with a client."

"A client?"

"A very good sort," I said. "One of your Southern gentlemen. We went to the Creole Café. It's too chilly for G-2 to be outside."

"A client?" she repeated.

"Yes. Well, one of Mr. Bloodworth's clients, actually. He's . . ."

She interjected, "Mr. Bloodworth asked you to accompany him and his client to dinner?"

"Mr. Bloodworth wasn't there, but . . ."

"He asked you to have dinner with a client, but he wasn't there?" From her point of view it was a rhetorical question. Which is to say she did not wait for an answer before jumping to her feet and crossing the room. She picked up the phone and began dialing, her fingernails almost piercing the little buttons.

"Gran, he . . ."

She glared at me and raised her hand, indicating a demand for total silence. I could hear an electronic click from the other end of the line, then someone talking. When the talk ended, Gran began, "This is Edith Van Dine, Mr. Bloodworth. Call me immediately, as soon as you return." She left our phone number and slammed the receiver back on its cradle.

"I have never felt it wise for you to see so much of that man," she said.

"I don't understand what's upset you so, Gran. It's only ten o'clock."

"It's ten-thirty, but that's not the point, Sehr-ee-nah."

"What is the old point, then?"

"Don't be flippant. The point is that you are much too young to . . . to be traipsing around with Mr. Bloodworth's clients. Mr. Bloodworth's profession is not a conventional one. His clients are not conventional people."

"Terry Manion seems pretty conventional to me."

"Oh?" She returned to her place on the little love seat. "Then tell me about him." Her voice was still as chilly as the ocean breeze outside, the one that was probably causing G-2's tiny teeth to chatter.

I sat down beside her. "Well, he's—" I paused.

"Yes?"

"I'm not sure I'm supposed to discuss him with you, Gran. He's a client, and client information is privileged."

"He is not *your* client. He is Mr. Bloodworth's client."

"But I work for Mr. Bloodworth."

"No, you do not. You dawdle around Mr. Bloodworth's office, instead of preparing yourself for an adult life more suitable to a young woman of your intelligence and education. Against my better judgment. Very much against my better judgment. And now that I find out that he is sending you out to—"

"To what?" I exclaimed. "What in the world do you think Terry and I were doing?"

"According to the Wicked Witch of the West Coast, Hildy Haines, who couldn't wait to phone me with the news, you and some 'blond, aesthetic type' were being arrested by the Beverly Hills police."

"We were not being arrested," I protested.

"I know. I phoned the Beverly Hills police. They'd never heard of you, they said. Once the momentary relief had passed, I began to worry that you'd given them a false name. I was about to call back when you phoned."

"I didn't think that Hildy saw me."

"With a blinding klieglight searing into her eyes, she can scan a cue card at a hundred yards. The woman has eyes like a farsighted hawk."

"Anyway," I said, "Terry Manion and I were there to talk to a policeman. We certainly weren't getting arrested. I'm rather hurt you would think that." We all play our games.

Gran softened, as I knew she would. "What was I to think, girl? Ten o'clock and no sign of you, and Hildy, strangely sober for that time of night, reveling in a detailed account of your arrest with someone she described as being too poetic-looking to be anything but a pimp."

I was shocked. "But that's ridiculous. It just proves that Hildy Haines knows nothing about pimps. Terry Manion looks less like a pimp than any man I know."

Her eyes flashed suddenly. "You still haven't explained why that Bloodworth fellow involved you with one of his raffish clients . . ."

"It wasn't like that, exactly," I explained. "Mr. Bloodworth was supposed to accompany Terry . . . uh, Mr. Manion to the home of this mur—Well, anyway, Mr. Bloodworth didn't make it back to the office. So I took it upon myself to substitute for him. Unless he has read the note I left, Mr. Bloodworth has no idea I spent the evening with Ter . . . Mr. Manion. It wasn't his idea. I'm not even sure he would have approved."

"I hope to heaven not. But we won't take that chance."

"Please, Gran . . ."

"None of that. You are not to go near that lair of Mr. Bloodworth's again."

"But—"

"Not again. Do we understand one another?"

"Yes, Gran." Really, there is no arguing with her at moments like that.

"I do not mind your seeing Mr. Bloodworth every now and again," she said. "He has been very good to us both. And I have no doubt that his heart is pure. But he is part of a milieu that is not fit for a . . . woman of your years."

"Yes, Gran," I repeated. As soon as the words escaped, I knew that I had made a mistake. I had acquiesced too quickly. I should have put up more of a fight for her to believe that I would obey her implicitly.

Her eyebrows furrowed. "You think you can get me to change my mind. But not this time, young lady. Not this time."

I nodded and looked properly chastened. "I'm sorry I caused you such concern tonight, Gran. I know how long your day was, and how tired you must be."

"I am weary," she admitted, opening her arms. I slid in and hugged her and she hugged me back. As I moved away, she kept her hands on my shoulders and looked into my eyes. "I made so many mistakes with your mother," she said. "I am not going to repeat them."

My mother, Faith Dahlquist, was not your ordinary parent. She dumped me on Gran when I was only three and ran off to follow her star. Her star led her through a series of depressing adventures that ended with her very violent death. Faith was selfish and not terribly bright or pleasant to be around, but I loved her as much as you can love someone who is incapable of returning that love.

As you may gather, Faith would never have made Mother of the Year. But she had an absolute genius for one thing: She could make you feel guilty. She would float into town with one of her rancid boyfriends, wait in their car until she saw me leave the apartment building, then go in and chat with

Gran. I, of course, would feel terrible that my mother, whom I hadn't seen in years, had made a special effort to visit and I'd been at the movies or some other dumb thing.

It was not until I began using my head that I realized that it was too much of a coincidence—her stopping by at the precise times when I was away. She simply didn't want to see me. Probably because I made *her* feel guilty.

In any case, she had Gran convinced that the reason she had matured into such a perfectly useless member of society was that Gran had taken an inactive part in her formative years—shipping her off to girls' schools and the like. My personal view is that Gran and her beloved husband, Eric, now long deceased, had not been expecting a child and didn't have the foggiest idea how to fit a daughter into lives filled to the brim with love for each other and for their profession.

And so Gran felt tremendous guilt, which Faith used whenever she grew short of funds. And which, I am not proud to admit, I also use, but for purposes other than money.

"You know, Gran, that whatever happens to us, I am not going to grow up in Faith's footsteps."

She gave me a sad smile and said nothing.

"I mean, we love each other too much for that," I said, with total honesty. Gran drew me to her again for another hug. "And," I added, "I am not a silly teenager who will be cajoled into trying drugs, or sleeping with lots of men, or even stealing stuff from the May Company that I don't need just to prove I can."

"No, Sehr, I wouldn't expect any of that from you."

"And you know that I have no intention of letting fate decide my future—that I know exactly what I want to achieve as an adult and that it includes college and hard work and eventually a home and family."

There was a flicker of suspicion in her lavender eyes, and I realized I had to get to the point quickly. "Well," I took a deep breath. "Everything—my whole future—college, career, family—everything depends on my learning as much as I can about criminology and about life from Mr. Bloodworth."

Her eyebrows began to form a frown. I hurried on, "You don't know what it's like today, Gran. Many of the girls in my class use drugs. Or they're on the road to alcoholism. They have absolutely no interest in their future. You mention the dreaded AIDS to the most promiscuous of them, and they shrug and say, 'Who wants to live without sex, anyway?'"

"I agree with you that it's difficult today for young people," Gran said. "But I don't see what that has to do with Mr. Bloodworth."

"He's very wise," I said. "Not in an academic sense, but he knows how things work. And he knows how to avoid trouble. I have no problem at all with my schoolwork. Except for math and physics, of course, but everybody has trouble with them. My shortcomings all have to do with the wisdom of life. And that's why I need to spend time with Mr. Bloodworth. You see, I don't want to wind up like Faith any more than you want me to."

She was silent for a few seconds, then she said, "I doubt very much that that would happen. You're not at all like Faith."

"Then there's no real reason why I shouldn't spend the rest of the summer interning with Mr. Bloodworth."

She sighed. "I cannot have you visiting police stations or staying out till all hours with strange men. That must stop. And I'm not at all convinced you would be able to limit your involvement with Mr. Bloodworth's business to an inactive participation."

"If that's what you want, Gran, that's the way it will be. Totally inactive. Just like a stick of old furniture. Silently observing."

"Don't test my credulity too strongly, dear. I'll settle for your being home every evening by six," she said. "No excuses. No arguments. Now go see to your dog."

I kissed her cheek again, then ran to the terrace door. I slid it open, and G-2 bounced into the sitting room. He paused suddenly and began scratching behind his ear. "Sure looks like fleas," I said.

"Take him to the groomer in the morning," Gran said.

"Before I go to the office," I agreed.

"Yes," she said, standing and walking from the room. "Before you go to the . . . office."

10

1. The hotel room was hot and smelled like some of the previous guests had mistaken the carpet for the urinal. My head ached. Other than that, the bed dipped in the middle worse than a fat man's hammock, and a bright pink neon sign just outside of the window kept flashing the words *Hotel Swank* in my face every ten seconds.

It had not been my plan to spend the night in the lovely Hotel Swank. Thousands of lire poorer for the taxi drive from the airport to the train station, I assumed I'd catch a rattler to Verona, where I had been booked into the same hotel as the elusive Sandy Watson, the Albergo Umberto. But one look at the wholesale confusion at the Stazione Centrale, where people of all sizes, shapes, and nationalities ran up and down a spider web of tracks frothing at the mouth while trains rested silent and cold, told me that I might be a bit late in making my appointment in Verona.

I approached an information cage, where a plump, gray-haired official was resting his head on the counter.

"Buona sera," I said.

He raised his head, showing me eyes that looked like mushroom caps in fresh tomato juice.

"Parla inglese?" I asked.

He shrugged. "I try."

"Good. *Bene.* Uh, when is the next train to Verona?" I asked as loudly and as precisely as if the guy were hard of hearing.

"No," he said, and yawned.

"No? There is no train to Verona?"

"Yes, there is a train. No, it is not going for a while."

"How long a while?"

He shrugged a nice Milanese shrug. "Probably tomorrow, but who can say? There is a strike. Maybe it will continue. Maybe not. I have seen it go both ways."

"How about that?" I said. "Mussolini's only been in the ground for forty years, and already his sole achievement has gone to seed. How the heck do I get to Verona?"

"It is to the west. A lovely city. A favorite city of mine. Not more than two hours by train."

"I guess I could drive," I said.

"*Una macchina?* Oh, I don't advise it, unless you know the roads." He raised his hands and began moving them up and down. He was pantomiming a man either milking a cow or trying to steady a steering wheel. "Crazy drivers," he said, clarifying that point.

"Where does that leave us?" I asked.

"The train. Tomorrow morning. Perhaps the strike will be over. Rest tonight, as I would like to. *Mio fratello,* my brother, and his voluptuous wife —her figure is like a statue—they run a fine, modern hotel that caters to Americans. Only blocks away." He removed a card from his wallet, scribbled something on its back. "Give this to Marco, the night manager. You will get their best room at a discount."

"How do I find the place?"

"It is right down there," he said, pointing to the rear of the station. "On the Via Copernico. You cannot miss it. Big pink sign blinking on and off, Hotel Swank. It means *prima* class."

It was my own fault, thinking that a place called Hotel Swank would be anything but a fleabag. But you never know what names they'll come up with in Europe. Anyway, after tossing and turning for several hours, I rolled out of the swayback bed, walked around the room trying to return my spine to its original shape, and went into the bathroom where I threw tepid water in my face.

I was dead on my feet, but sleep didn't seem to be in the game plan. Maybe there was a bar nearby. I walked to the window, where I was bathed in a bright pink glow every few seconds. The neon hissed, too, in case the light itself wasn't obnoxious enough.

I looked down on a fairly peaceful street. If there were any bars, they'd closed at midnight, a few hours before. I started to turn away, when I spotted a man crossing the street, moving away from the hotel at a fast clip. He continued down the Via Copernico to the corner, then stopped as if he were waiting for something or somebody. Within seconds he was picked up by a Fiat. The car was either tan or gray or white—it was impossible to tell at the distance, especially with the pink light going on and off.

Because of the light, I couldn't even tell the color of the night walker's hair. But I would have recognized those shoulders anywhere.

2. I never understood who was on strike, if the strike had ended or just paused momentarily, or if I was headed toward Verona on a scab train. I hadn't seen any pickets, and it seemed as if, at 11:15 A.M., the Italian railroad system was back on its famous schedule.

I'd finally nodded off at around four, after blocking out the neon sign with a blanket. That made the room hotter, of course. But heat I can take. I also flipped the mattress and figured out a way of sleeping on my side, twisted into a question-mark shape that minimized the center slope as well as the pressure on the back of my tender skull.

After six hours of sleep in that pretzeled condition and a flawless double espresso in the dining room, I felt like a relatively new *uomo*. I bid *addio* to the the fabulous Hotel Swank and took a brisk walk to the station, where things were moving right along.

I had my choice of a *dirètto*, which was leaving right away but which I was given to understand would make several stops before it would arrive in Verona, or a *rapido* that would leave in twenty minutes but, because it made no prior stops, would arrive fifteen minutes earlier.

I dawdled over another espresso and scanned a copy of the *International Herald-Tribune* for a progress report on the Chernobyl fallout. There was a little notice on a back page about cow's milk in Sweden registering radiation. Wired by both caffeine and fear of nuclear pollution, I hopped aboard the *rapido*, which was filling with travelers, some of whom were going as far as Yugoslavia, brave souls.

Lugging my flight bag, I moved down a passageway, stepping over students who were stretched out on the deck using their knapsacks for pillows. The compartments were so tightly packed with people, they were like those clown cars in the circus.

A dour conductor ungraciously accepted two thousand lire to let me park in an empty first-class sleeping car. I opened the curtain on the hyperactivity in the station, swung my flight bag onto an overhead rack, removed my wilted silk jacket and folded it neatly on the cushioned seat next to me, and settled back to wonder if the train had something resembling a club car.

Fifteen minutes later, with a jerk that would have caused Gene Kelly to miss a beat, the rattler began its nonstop journey to Verona. I looked up from the Paul Montclair opus *Power Plan*, which had just taught me how to throw the other guy off guard right before you close the deal, to watch us slice through Milan. Big industrial town, Milan, about as sprawling as L.A. Maybe that explains why Lake Como does such a big business.

We were headed away from the lakes and the cathedrals and the tombs of the Medicis and traveling through a suburb that could have been at home in New Jersey. I was shifting my attention back to the book when the compartment door opened, letting in the noise of the clattering wheels and a bespectacled brunette in a dark blue outfit, who dropped her suitcase suddenly, stumbled over it, and fell onto the seat across from me.

"Oh, I'm . . ." she began, grabbing my sport coat to stop her fall. It turned out to be a lousy anchor. She and the coat slid from the seat and hit the floor at my feet. Her dress was almost over her head, displaying very nice legs and white silk panties with little pink bows.

Awkwardly, I helped to scoop her up and sit her down facing me. "My goodness," she said, brushing off her knees, then yanking down her apparently uncontrollable skirt. Her eyeglasses were no longer on her little nose.

I retrieved them and my coat from the floor. The coat I tossed beside me, the glasses I applied to her face.

She smiled as she adjusted them and said, "I've been falling down ever since I left Cleveland. I hope you don't mind my, uh, invading your privacy like this. I don't really think I'm even supposed to be in this section of the train, but I was wedged between three ditchdiggers back there who'd obviously been working all morning and, well, they were very nice fellows and all, but I've been a little, uh, queasy ever since I ate a monster antipasto last night at this café with the bits of saints' petrified bodies behind glass. I don't remember the name, but how rude, I ask you, to have pieces of corpses, even holy ones, in the same room with food. And—oh, I am sorry. Here I am raving on like I always do, and I don't even know if you speak English."

"A little," I said. She wasn't wearing even a daub of makeup on her pale, flawless skin. Her dark hair was cut short in a modification of what they used to call a pixie sometime back in history. It picked its own spots to curl up. Maybe she clipped it herself.

"Then you're . . . what? English or Canadian or—"

"Californian," I said.

"Oooh," she said. Her eyes, which were green and seemed of normal size behind the glasses, concentrated on my face. "A West Coaster. I'm from the Midwest. Cleveland, Ohio. Lannie Doolittle."

I nodded. "Leo Bloodworth."

"Bloodworm, what an unusual name."

"It is. Mine's Bloodworth."

"Oh. Well, tell me about California. Is everybody really outrageously insane out there, like I've heard?"

"We try to encourage a few visitors from Cleveland to keep us straight," I said.

"Oh, damn. That was another of those bricks, wasn't it? Jelly says I drop enough bricks in any day to build a new courthouse."

"Jelly?"

"Just a nickname. Ann Jellicoe, my closest friend. Or she was until she married. Now, I'm not so sure. We haven't so much as had lunch together in months. But I guess newlyweds are like that."

"Like what?"

"Oh, you know. They sort of drop—well not drop, exactly, but forget to see old friends until they lose the 'newly' part of 'newlywed.' "

"I suppose so," I said, wondering if I could make her go away by opening my book again.

"Then you've been one?" she asked.

"One?"

"A newlywed."

"A few times. But not for a while." I picked up my book, found the chapter titled "Dealing from Strength," and tried to ignore the fact that she continued to stare at me, poised on the edge of her seat.

"Excuse me," she said.

I looked up.

"I know you probably want to read that book, but I was wondering: Do you have any idea if they allow jogging in Venice?"

I shrugged. "It's a question I never thought to ask."

"Then you've been there before?"

"A couple of times." I flashed on the first—honeymoon number one. Louise and Leo Bloodworth. In our mid-twenties. Me fresh from the police academy, she a brand-new assistant buyer at the May Company. Head over heels in love. Back home, a new little one-bedroom cottage temporarily anchored to the side of Benedict Canyon awaited us. We had a month all to ourselves in Italy. The world was our oyster and Venice was the pearl.

I went back twice after that. Once on business. Once not. It wasn't the same.

"So you'll be able to get around just fine," Lannie Doolittle said.

I looked at her. "What makes you think I'm going to Venice?"

"Isn't that where the train is headed?"

"Among other places," I said. I stuck my nose back in the book, certain I had not heard the last of her.

But she surprised me. She moved closer to the window and turned her attention to the passing scenery. Relaxing, I devoted myself entirely to the wisdom of Paul Montclair.

I was nearing the end of the book, skimming past the Power Diet recipes, when I noticed that Lannie Doolittle was playing with her makeup mirror, holding it between thumb and index finger. Her little finger was straight up in the air, like they might have taught her at finishing school. I found that extended digit fascinating.

I took a long look at her face, trying to convince myself that the paranoid thought that had come to roost in my skull might be justified. She saw me and grinned, daintily dropping the mirror back into her purse. "Just wondering if I needed a touch-up," she said. Except, of course, that she wasn't wearing any makeup.

I turned to stare out of the window. A highway was running parallel to the train tracks. On it bounced a beige Fiat with a driver and one passenger, neither identifiable. Suddenly the car speeded up, edging away.

I closed my book and smiled at my fellow traveler. "So tell me, Miss Doolittle, what brings you to sunny Italy?"

"Can't you tell?" she asked coyly.

"Doing a little scouting for the Indians?"

She frowned. "Indians in Italy? Now you're pulling my leg. The only Indians here are in spaghetti westerns."

Cute, but off-key. "You're on vacation," I said.

"Bravo, sirrah, bravo. But a vacation from what?"

"Let's try schoolteacher."

"But that's . . . uncanny. Although I'm not sure getting pre-schoolers to put their heads on their desks and play nap qualifies as a school-teacher. . . ."

I stared at her, wondering how she would have responded if I'd said she was a stockbroker, or steelworker, or hairdresser.

". . . the thing is, when you've got an M.Ed. there are only so many things you're really qualified to do. But I really love the little darlings. . . ."

The compartment door opened suddenly and the dour conductor entered, asking for our tickets. I fished mine from my shirt pocket and handed it to him. He punched out a rectangle from the bottom and handed it back. "We should arrive in Verona shortly, signore," he said.

He turned to La Bella Doolittle. "*Scusi, signorina, il suo biglietto?*"

She looked at him blankly, so he added, "Your ticket, please."

"Oh." She immediately began rooting in her purse. "Uh, well actually, I can't seem to . . ."

It was a pretty amusing bit. I thought so, anyway. The conductor's dour demeanor became even more dour. Finally, he said, "*Scusi, signorina*, I must ask you for a ticket."

"I must have dropped it somewhere. Mr. Bloodworm, you don't see it on the floor anywhere?"

I grinned at her, shaking my head no.

"Well," she said, resignedly. "I suppose I'll just have to buy another. How much would it be, exactly?"

"That depends on how far the signorina is going."

She paused, then replied, "Venice."

"A good choice," I said.

The conductor quoted her the price of a ticket, *prima classe, solo andata* (one way), Milan to Venice.

Her mouth opened and she put two dainty fingers into her red leather wallet, fluffing the bills. "But I don't have . . . oh, my, I seem to be a little short of money. I must visit American Express at the very next town."

"That would be Verona," the conductor said flatly.

"I'm sure there's an American Express in Verona," she said, with just a trace of uncertainty in her voice. "How much is it to Verona?"

He told her, and with a sigh of apparent relief she handed over the lire and got a few coins back along with a punched ticket. She turned to me, "Would you be so kind, Mr. Blood . . .?"

"Make it Leo," I said.

"Leo, would you be so kind as to let me share your cab to the nearest American Express office?"

"It'd be my pleasure, Lannie."

The conductor looked from her to me and cocked an eyebrow. He had lost sight of the ball somewhere on the last play. He stepped backward through the door, sliding it shut with force.

I stared at Lannie Doolittle, or whatever her real name was, as she closed her purse and dithered with her dress and hair. She looked at me and blushed, which made it a pretty amazing performance. If she'd used the blush earlier, I might have put our meeting down to chance. I'd have told myself maybe she hadn't been trying to pry my destination out of me. Maybe she hadn't signaled the beige Fiat. Maybe schoolteachers from Cleveland have never heard of their hometown baseball team, the Indians. Maybe that wasn't a fifty-thousand-lire note she palmed before searching her wallet.

Maybe finding Sandy Watson and recovering Laura Mornay's earrings were not going to be the piece of cake I'd imagined.

11

The first thing I did wrong on that impossible day was to stop to talk to Lolly the Groomer about nontoxic flea sprays when I dropped off G-2. If I hadn't, I would have arrived at the office in time to intercept Terry Manion's call. And many of the dreadful things that happened might have been forestalled. Mr. Bloodworth tells me that one should never consider might-have-beens, especially in the investigation game, and I do my best. But sometimes it is a.i. Absolutely Impossible.

According to the obnox answering machine, the call had come in at 9:30 A.M. At 10:15 I played back the message: "Leo Bloodworth, this is Terry Manion. I'm sorry we were not able to get together on this, but something has come up and I can't wait any longer. Maybe next time."

That was all. No phone number. No hint as to where he might be reached. In our whole evening together he never once mentioned the name of his hotel and, it shames me to admit, I never once thought to ask.

Feeling positively depresso and, worse yet, criminologically inept, I carried the problem into my office and flopped onto the swivel chair. Someone had used my Scotch tape to adhere a folded note to the screen of my word processor. Who else would leave a message for me in such a manner, totally oblivious to the fact that I just might have to spend hours trying to remove all of the mucilage from the monitor screen?

What was so important that Mr. B. had to go to all this trouble? I wondered, as I carefully pried up the tape. I managed to get all of it free except a small triangle that I missed in a burst of eagerness.

The note was, in a word, vexing. Mr. Bloodworth, completely mindful of

Terry Manion's predicament, had chosen to fly the country to Europe on a matter of doubtful importance. He was purposely vague, as he always is when he is feeling guilty. "Should not be more than two or three days," his scribble informed me. "Tell Manion he can have my full attention then."

Great! I would be sure to tell him—as soon as I discovered where he was.

I slumped back in the chair. Mr. Bloodworth would be no help. I was on my own. Worse yet, Terry was on *his* own. In this most difficult of cities. Whether he realized it or not, he needed my help.

All right! What information did I have?

There was the Wings 'n' Things feather boutique. Of course, Terry had probably been there and gone. How else might I connect with him?

Mrs. Kosca? His number was on that blackboard near her phone.

I picked up my phone and asked directory assistance for the residence of Michael Kosca in Bay City. As the computerized voice began to reply, I turned a fresh page of my legal pad, wrote the name "Kosca," and carefully penned the phone number next to it.

I dialed the number. Two rings and a click. "Hello," a male voice said.

"Hello," I replied. "I was wondering if—"

"I'm sorry, but there is no one available to answer your call right now," the pleasing baritone continued, unmindful of anything I had said or might say. "Please leave your name and number at the sound of the beep. Thank you."

I opened my mouth, then closed it and replaced the receiver. It is one of the rudest things you can do, to leave that maddening blank space on the tape. But there was something about the voice. And, anyway, I doubted that Mrs. Kosca would have remembered my name.

It occurred to me that her absence might mean that this was the day her husband was finally being buried. If so, wouldn't Terry be there?

At the *Los Angeles Post* I only had to get past two operators to reach Mr. Bloodworth's dreadful Irish friend, the ignoble-savage columnist Jerry Flaherty. If your average picture was really worth a thousand words, every Flaherty column for the past ten years would not add up to a blurred Polaroid.

"What d'ya need, babe?" he said wetly. I could visualize a sopping cigar wedged between his molars.

"You remember me?"

"I got a long memory, kid, and you're as easy to forget as a case of shingles. What's the Hound up to?"

"He's in Europe on business," I said.

"Hmmm. Any morsel of news in it for ole Jerry?"

"You'll have to ask him," I replied. "I need a favor."

"Oh, this is gonna be cherce. What do I get in return? Maybe some respect?"

"I'll do what I can," I said noncommittally. "I need to know where a certain person is being buried."

"Here in L.A.?"

"In the area, sure."

"Got a name?"

"The fellow who died in the San Rafael Mountains. Mike Kosca."

Flaherty didn't answer at first. Then he said, "What's this got to do with Leo hopscotching to Europe?"

"Nothing whatsoever. It's got nothing to do with Mr. Bloodworth."

"Then fill me in, kiddy-koo. What's going on?"

"Nothing, Mr. Flaherty," I lied. Gran has forbidden me to lie to anyone but the press. "Mike Kosca was a friend of my family and I wanted to pay my last respects. Only I can't find the name of the cemetery or the time."

"Why call me?"

"It's news, isn't it? Aren't you supposed to be in the news business?"

"Still the little sweetheart, huh? Well, button it for a sec."

He put me on hold. While I waited I drew a picture of Flaherty—a fat little body, a giant, veiny, pulsating head, from which sprouted eyebrows and a moustache like woolly worms.

The line was suddenly active again. In the background I could hear the bustle of the newsroom. "Tell me what you know about this Kosca's death, kid."

"Nothing that wasn't on TV."

He moaned exaggeratedly. "The bloody younger generation. They don't read, they watch instead."

"I read the *Manchester Guardian*," I said. "For local news I prefer television."

"A little darling is what you are. Give me some background on Kosca, Sarah-D. As long as he's a family friend. What kind of bloke was he?"

"Mr. Flaherty, I didn't phone you to be interviewed. I just need the details of his burial. If your paper doesn't have them, I'll try the TV stations. I'm sure they—"

"Eleven A.M., Shady Glen," he spat out. "And tell Leo he owes me one."

He hung up without another word, which was fine with me.

12

1. Call me a cynic, but I didn't really think I'd seen the last of Lannie Doolittle when I bid her *arrivederci* at the Banca Popolare Di Verona on the Via Armando Diaz. She did not, however, seem to be following my taxi. Still, I got the driver—a big, red-haired lug who looked about as Italian as Victor McLaglen but who was nonetheless the genuine article—to take me on a spin up one *via* and down the next, rounding a few *corsos* on the way. After we had crossed and recrossed the Adige River, which snakes through the whole burg, and after we'd passed the crusty-looking tombs where these ancient power brokers, the Scaligeri princes, have been residing since the fourteenth century—talk about your big sleep!—I figured we'd definitely dusted La Doolittle; and somehow I got through to Big Red behind the wheel that we could move on to the Albergo Umberto, the hotel where Sandy Watson's travel agent assured me he would be staying.

It was a small, well-kept establishment not far from the Via Mazzini, which I gathered was the main drag. Antique-looking furniture. Marble floor.

At the reservations desk a perky young woman with very white teeth and a pale yellow rose pinned to her dark hair told me in the most diplomatic way possible that I would be expected to pay for the room they had been holding for me since the night before. I replied that it was a reasonable request. While handing over my passport and signing the register, I casually asked if my friend Mr. Watson might be in his room.

A frown disturbed her placid beauty. She turned and rattled off a question in Italian to a young guy in a double-breasted suit with slicked-back hair and a pencil moustache who looked like he was waiting for Hollywood to come knocking at his door. He rattled something back.

"I am afraid your friend has left us," the lady with the flower told me. "He and several other gentlemen and ladies connected with the tour gave up their rooms several hours ago."

"With the tour?"

"The musicians. You know. In the Arena?"

I shrugged. "Any idea where they were headed?"

She shook her head. Turned to the man again. When they'd finished, she said, "We are not sure where the tour is headed next. But there are still performances here, I believe."

She reached under the desk and withdrew a flyer. She studied it and then nodded. "Yes, see? They are here for one more evening."

She handed me the sheet. One side was blank. On the other was an illustration in color that was not unfamiliar to me. It was very close to the scraps of artwork I'd rescued from Sandy Watson's garbage. Only now the illustration made more sense. It was for a rock group consisting of three guitar-toting ladies who seemed to be wearing leather diapers over Spandex tights. One was a blonde, one a redhead, one a brunette. They were snarling at an audience that consisted primarily of people wearing pig masks. Behind them, filling the performing area, was Watson's metallic trellis, on which light bulbs had been strategically placed to spell out the name *Circe* followed by *A Tour for Survival.*

Even more important, in the white area under the illustration, the play dates that had been lettered in by hand indicated that Circe was booked for one more day at the Arena. If Watson was part of the tour, he was probably just up the street.

The flower lady arranged for an arthritic little senior citizen of Verona to transport my flight bag to my room while I went out into the bustling Via Mazzini. Separated from me by two blocks, packed with small, expensive shops, the Arena towered, looking for all the world like a mini-Rose Bowl plunked down in the middle of Rodeo Drive.

The circular street and piazza surrounding it were teeming with thousands of young people, chanting, drinking from wineskins, having one hell of a time waiting for the evening rock show. The sun was high and boiling, and they were dressed in shorts and sleeveless shirts. I was melting under my suit. But I picked up their mood. I was even grinning when I approached a uniformed guard at a side entrance to the amphitheater.

Security guards are pretty much the same the world over. This one was big and surly-looking and, as much as I could understand what he was saying, officious. While he snarled Italian at me, his eyes traveled from my shoes to my tie and finally to my face. By that time he had realized I was not a kid trying to sneak in to drool on the collective feet of Circe. But he didn't know just what the hell I *was* after.

I opened my coat very slowly and removed a notepad and pen from my inside pocket. I pantomimed writing and used the work *giornale*, which I thought meant "magazine."

The guard frowned.

"Time," I said. *"Newsweek. People."* No reaction. Finally, in desperation, I shot out, *"Notte,"* the name of the sexy photo magazine I'd seen on the plane.

He nodded, grinned, and used his hands to indicate a curvy figure. I said, *"Sì. Sì."*

He raised his right hand in a "halt" gesture, then turned and walked to another guard, who was waiting just inside the entrance. Reluctantly, the second guard moved away. My friend returned and made his curvy figure again, chuckling. That was it for our conversation.

A few minutes later the second guard came back with a chunky young woman whose red hair had been tucked under a babushka. It, like her shirt, slacks, and pumps, was white. She looked like an eighties version of Rosie the Riveter.

"My name is Amy Schneider, and I'm public-relations coordinator for the Tour for Survival," she stated, with a slight edge to her voice. "Can I help you?"

"I hope so. As I was trying to explain to the officer here, my name is Novak. I'm actually in Italy on vacation, but I've been asked by my editor to file a few graphs about the tour and its progress."

"Oh. Forgive me, Mr. Novak. Your name sounds familiar, but I'm not certain what magazine you represent. The guard said you mentioned *Notte.*"

It's always best to stick with things you know. "Where the heck did he get that idea? I'm with the *Los Angeles Post.*"

"Oh? Then you work with Don Mittleman?"

"Mainly with Jerry Flaherty."

She nodded. "Well, what can I help you with? The girls are tied up with French TV right now."

"I don't think we'll have to bother them. I was thinking more of a background piece on the tour itself."

She relaxed. This was something she could knock off without any major hassle. Graciously, she led me past the guards and into the Arena.

A large platform in the center of the open-air amphitheater served as a stage supporting an intricate assortment of mikes, amplifiers, speakers, and various other sound equipment. But the main attraction was the four-story-high metal trellis.

A swarm of workers, most of them looking hungover and out of sorts, busied themselves with the wiring, the lights, and the general upkeep of the Arena. I didn't see anyone who even remotely resembled Sandy Watson.

Amy Schneider was saying, "This is the world's largest and best-preserved Roman amphitheater. It was built twenty centuries ago. Amazing, huh? Perfect acoustics. And it seats twenty-five thousand. Groups love to play here."

"That's some sign," I said, pointing to the Circe logo.

"Oh, yes. The Tour for Survival sign. As it was explained to me, the sign is a banner for a better life. At night, when the girls sing their hit, 'Survive!,' the audience takes off the pig masks and lights candles in observance of the prayer that all nuclear power be banished from Planet Earth, and the sign begins to flash—first 'Circe,' then 'the Tour,' and finally holding on the word *Survival.* I swear to Christ, I've been in this business for nearly eight years now. I've hand-held the Stones, Elton, and all the rest, but this is the first time I honestly felt I was contributing something to the culture of the world."

"Who designed the sign?" I asked, getting out my notepad.

"The girls, of course. Circe. The tour was Jessica's idea, as has been widely reported. She had this hairdresser who knew this family living within blocks of Chernobyl. He was telling Jessie all about it, and it started her thinking that nuclear power was soooo dangerous, something should be done. So she and Rini and Brooke created the Tour for Survival. I mean, the album was set and they were going to tour and all, but they decided to make the tour something really, really special and meaningful. And let me tell you, everybody—from Robert Redford to Warren Beatty to Morgan Fairchild—everybody has been soooo supportive. I've got the wire Jack Nicholson sent back at the office, if you want it. And that's true the world over. We're this close to taking the show inside the Soviet Union."

She held a purple-nailed index finger an inch away from her thumb.

I said, "Chernobyl would make it a natural. But the Russians can be hard to move on things like this."

"Oh, the Russians gave us the go-ahead. It's the girls. They're quite naturally nervous about the fallout junk. It lasts for a hundred years and it can make you go bald."

"Yeah. Well, about the sign, I realize it was the girls' idea. But there must have been a designer. I'd heard Sandy Watson was involved."

She took a step away, to give me a better look, maybe to see if my feet were on the ground. "You know Sandy?"

"No, but I was hoping to talk to him."

"I, ah, think he took off for a couple of days. We won't be needing him until we have to set up again in Rome. He's got to figure out how to adapt the sign to a slightly different situation. It's going to be wild there. We've been told the Pope has agreed to light a candle for survival."

"What happens if something goes wrong with the sign before tonight? How fast could you get Sandy Watson back here?"

"I don't think that would happen. We've got electricians, carpenters. But if we needed Sandy, I guess he could be here in what, a couple of hours. How long can it take to get here from Venice?"

"Not long. Venice is one great city, isn't it?"

"I suppose so. But it's all so damp. I have a sinus condition."

"I'd like to ask Sandy Watson a question or two about the sign. How difficult is it adapting it to other stages? Stuff like that."

"You find that interesting?"

"Well, it's all part of the background."

"I don't know if you could reach him. I mean, he probably isn't hanging around his hotel. Though maybe he is, for all I know. Or you could leave word or something. He's at the Pensione Violetta on the Grand Canal. It's one of those places that that writer wrote about. Harry James. I'll get the number for you."

I told Amy that wouldn't be necessary. I let her lead me around the Arena, chatting with the odd workman, for another half hour, then thanked her for her help. She seemed elated and relieved. She had serious work that she could be doing.

That made two of us.

2. "But you only just checked in, and now you go," the hotel clerk said with a pout. The flower in her hair was wilting. "I feel sad I must charge you for the room."

"That's the breaks," I said.

She handed me my passport with my change, a handful of thousand-lire bills. "Your taxi is waiting."

I thanked her, and ten minutes and forty thousand lire later, I thanked the taxi driver. Thirty-five minutes and ten thousand lire after that, I thanked the train conductor who stepped aside to let me board his rattler as far as Venice. Or as he would have it, Venezia.

It looked exactly like the *rapido* I'd taken from Milan to Verona, only cleaner and less populated. I was in the *carròzza ristorante*, studying the menu and trying not to salivate while a waiter poured a frosty Moretti, when there was a tapping on the window. My old travel mate, James "Little Jimmy" Bristol, stood outside on the platform, his lacerated luggage at his Gucci'd feet, waving his arms to indicate he would be joining me.

"Leo," he said as he sat down across from me, pumping my hand over the table as if I were the guy who was going to put his series back on the air, "if this isn't a fucking stroke of luck. Where you headed? Venice?"

I nodded. "See Venice and die, huh?" he asked.

"I'll settle for just seeing Venice," I told him.

The waiter wanted to know what we'd be having. I went for the veal piccata with spaghettini on the side. Jim looked at me like I was about to slip a noose around my neck and ordered a cup of minestrone, easy on the salt. He asked the waiter if there was any saltless bread. The waiter said *"Scusi?"* and went away.

Jim gave me a confused look. "Don't hold your breath for saltless bread," I told him.

"No matter. Maybe I could use a little salt, anyway. It was as hot as a nympho under glass in Verona. I must've sweated gallons."

I took a long pull at the Moretti.

"Well, Leo, what's shaking in Verona?"

"Huh?"

"You're a journalist, right? What's the big news that took you to Verona?"

My lying was consistent, if I could only remember the part I was supposed to be playing. "Oh, this rock group is having a concert to get rid of nuclear power."

"That's news?"

"Of a sort."

"To me, news would be a rock group committing suicide on stage. Now that's a story I'd like to digest slowly with my morning coffee."

The train started with a jolt, sending Jim against the table. "Jesus," he growled, "how's about a whistle, goddamnit?"

"You okay?" I asked.

"I think I bent my passport," he said, fishing it out of his jacket pocket. He fondled it and then put it back.

"What about you, Jim? What took you to Verona?"

"I always stop off there on my way to Venezia," he said. "The best shopping in the world. These shoes, this suit, the shirt. All of it comes from Verona. Usually for a goddamn song. But the way the dollar is performing, it's cheaper to shop on Rodeo Drive, for Chrissake. Still, I ordered a few items. Slacks, a beige blazer with a rainbow lining, a pair of green leather loafers that'll make their tongues hang out at the Polio. I'll spend a week strolling around the canals, hitting Harry's, taking a look-see at the Gugg, and then pick 'em up on the way back to El Lay."

"You're not at all worried about the fallout?"

"Fallout?"

"From Chernobyl. We're only a few countries away."

He shook his head. "That was months ago."

"It takes a century for nuclear particles to cool off."

He gave me a strange smile. And for a moment he looked like an entirely different person. Confused and scared. Then he tightened up again and said, "I never even gave Chernobyl a thought. Until now. Thanks a bunch, buddy."

I didn't bother to tell him about the bald part. Instead, I asked, "Where are you staying in Venice?"

"Where else but the Gritti Palace? I always get the same suite on the second-floor corner, facing the Grand Canal. The same goddamn suite where Hemingway always stayed.

"What about you, Leo? Where are you booked?"

"Oh, I'll be bunking at the Doges' Palace." He gawked at me. "You know, at the Piazza San Marco."

"I know where it is, goddamnit. But I never heard of anybody booking a room there."

"Actually," I went on with my outrageous lie, "they have a couple of bedrooms tucked up over the council chamber, hidden from the tours, that you can't book, exactly. It's more like an invite sort of thing."

"Why the fuck hasn't my travel agent told me about that?"

"Not every travel agent knows about it, Jim," I said, leaning back. "I don't even think Hemingway knew."

The waiter brought our food, which alas, wasn't much better than train food in the U.S. Jim Bristol slurped his soup, grumping about its salinity. Finally, he shoved it aside and began staring out of the window, glumly.

Just when I thought he'd decided to give his yap a much-needed rest, he snapped, "What assholes! What do they think they're gonna do with those things?"

We were crossing over a long bridge leading to the Piazzale Roma. The air was filled with smoke from oil refineries and engineering plants near Mestre. "What things?" I asked.

"The goddamn automobiles, Leo. What the hell does somebody do with an automobile in Venice?"

Beside the elevated railroad tracks was a paved bridge dotted with cars. A beige Fiat moved smoothly from lane to lane, racing to beat the train to the end of the line. I couldn't see the driver, but the passenger was Lannie Doolittle. Her short dark hair was dancing in the wind of her open window. She was wearing white wraparound sunglasses and her lips were a bright carmine red. She wasn't my little schoolteacher anymore.

13

In Shady Glen Cemetery, which a national news magazine famous for its wordplay and inaccuracies once described as a Disneyland for the dead, there were electronically controlled babbling brooks and songbirds, statues that talked, and a man-made rainbow that appeared every hour on the hour.

I personally would not have been caught dead there. But a number of film and TV celebrities have chosen to be planted under Shady Glen sod, and to my knowledge there has never been a grave-robbing or any other kind of desecration on the premises. Still, I assumed that Mike Kosca's being laid to rest there had less to do with Mrs. Kosca's wishes than Lieutenant Hilbert's. It was more his style.

Standing beside the statue of a little dwarflike creature with a sorcerer's hat who was guarding the plot inhabited by the remains of its cartoonist-creator, I watched the minister or priest or whatever he was—his black and white outfit was priestlike, but his odd-shaped flat hat definitely hinted of some Orthodoxy or other—sprinkle soil on Mike Kosca's polished coffin, now ensconced in terra firma. I was too far away to hear what he was saying.

The assembled mourners did not constitute what you would call a crowd. There was a handful of elderly folks in dark suits and dresses who would have looked more appropriate in a European movie—the relatives, no doubt. A scattering of perspiring post-middle-age men were watching Dove Hilbert instead of the priest, which made me think they were police cronies he'd recruited. Hilbert's face wore that weird death's-head grin as he stood beside a woman who was a younger, more robust version of Mrs. Kosca, obviously the daughter, lately arrived from the East Coast, who was using one hand to dab at her eyes and red nose with a lacy handkerchief and the other to cling to the policeman's arm. Next to them both, a dry-eyed, controlled Mrs. Kosca stared into the grave without expression.

Three gravediggers in dirty white jumpsuits stood beside a tree about a hundred feet away, trying to blend into the countryside. The drivers of the pearl-gray hearse and two black limousines smoked cigarettes and chatted beside one of the limos.

Funerals and burial services are necessary, I suppose, but I'm not sure why. We arrive here knowing that the grave is an inevitable end to be faced not by us—we're dead, after all—but by our loved ones. I don't think we should put them through any more agony than the world demands on a daily basis. I've discussed this with Gran, who has said that she is perfectly willing to be buried at sea, thereby providing the mourners with at least a bit of healthy salt air. I hope that this was not one of her facetious ripostes, which have become more frequent lately, because I fully plan to see that the request is carried out. Just as I hope that, should the situation be reversed, she would fulfill my desire, which is to be put to rest in a very inexpensive casket beside my unfortunate mother with no ceremony save for Gran reading some nice appropriate psalm. And I would like Mr. Bloodworth to rest there, too, though he probably has made his own plans.

The priest with the funny hat made a few more hand motions over Mr. Kosca's box, and the mourners moved closer to the edge of the grave. My eyes wandered to Shady Glen's flora and fauna, which included everything from prickly poppies with their toxic seeds to golden-beard penstemon, the tubular red flowers that hummingbirds seem to love so. I was wondering if it would be totally tacky for me to approach Mrs. Kosca as she departed her husband's gravesite to ask her about Terry Manion, when a rustling noise caught my ear.

It seemed to be coming from a dense cluster of meadow marigolds beside a small pond where ducks quacked happily. The marigolds wiggled and shook.

I wasn't the only one to be drawn to the spot. Dove Hilbert turned suddenly to glare in that direction. He carefully removed the hand of the Kosca daughter from his arm and began running toward the marigolds.

They rustled even more, and the fat, balding "video journalist" Mark Fishburn materialized from their center. Continuing to aim his camera at the advancing Lieutenant Hilbert, he backed away, then ran, circling the pond. At the gravesite, faces turned toward the two running men.

I moved closer as Hilbert caught up with the cameraman and pushed him. Mark Fishburn, whose body had been twisted in an ungainly position, trying to keep his camera aimed, fell down. Hilbert whipped the camera from the fat man's hand and, in one remarkable feat of strength, sailed it into the center of the pond, where it sank like a stone.

Fishburn's eyes were bugging out in disbelief. "Holy shit," he shouted, "you ruined my camera! You putz!"

Hilbert stood over him. His hand jutted out and grabbed Fishburn's bare throat and dug in. Fishburn was younger, much bigger, and probably stronger. But he just lay there, his face turning colors, his puffy hands ineffectually trying to break Hilbert's grip.

Finally, several of the other mourners reached them. Two men pulled Hilbert off of the fat cameraman, who was gagging and gasping. When he had regained enough air to talk, Fishburn shouted at Hilbert, "I'm gonna sue your ass off, Jack. You don't treat the press like this. You're *fershtinkina* dead meat."

Hilbert hissed, "If you ever come within a city mile of me or any of my friends, *you'll* be the dead meat. Literally. You understand, you disrespectful maggot? I shall swat you like the dung-eating insect you are."

Hilbert allowed the others to pull him away, back to the burial ceremonies that had been put on hold. Fishburn, panting and sweating, pushed himself to his feet. "That's just fucking beautiful," he said, mainly to himself.

He walked to the edge of the pond and looked out at its now-placid surface. Then he saw me. "Hey, girlchick, come over here," he ordered, not exactly endearing me to his cause.

Displaying no uncertain amount of suspicion, I approached him. He frowned and tilted his round head to one side. "The name's Fishburn. Don't I know you?"

"Not really."

"Yeah," he almost sighed, recognition dawning. "You and some blond nudnick were going into the Kosca house yesterday."

"Maybe," I said cautiously.

"I never forget a face. Which is a lucky thing, considering my business." The thought of his business made him turn again to the pond. "Uh, how'd you like to make a buck?"

"Doing what?"

"Hopping in and getting my camera back for me."

"For a dollar?"

"Okay, two dollars."

I shook my head. "I don't think so. I've heard that's how you get diseases, swimming in ponds."

"Old wives' tales. I'd go in myself, only I got bursitis. Five dollars, and that's it, kid. That's all it's worth to me. *Emes*." He was absolutely pathetic.

"You really believe that's all a video camera, even a totally waterlogged one, is worth? Five dollars?" I smiled.

"So I made a boo-boo. Okay, you got me. I don't mind admitting when I've misjudged a situation. Ten bucks. But that's it, *fershtay?*"

"I *fershtay*, all right," I said. "I might do it . . . for two hundred dollars."

His beady little eyes narrowed, and he almost grinned. "Fifteen," he said.

"Two hundred and ten."

"Wait a minute, kid. Don't you know anything about *hondling?* I come up a little, you come down."

"That's not the way I *hondle*," I told him. "Two hundred and ten. Going, going, gone. Two hundred and twenty."

"Oy, this is really my fucking day," he said, shaking his head in despair and sitting down on the ground. He began undoing the laces of his tennis shoes. He removed them, put them neatly side by side and removed his thin black socks, folded them, and tucked each into the proper shoe. Then he started rolling up the cuffs of his double-knit brown trousers. His legs were as white as a plucked chicken's.

"Being an independent is strictly *fershtinkina*, kid. A dying breed. Nobody respects you. No group insurance. No credit cards." He stuck one hairless toe into the pond, drew it back quickly, and shivered. He turned to look at me. "One hundred bucks. We're talking gelt of the realm. On the barrel."

"I have to be honest with you, Mr. Fishburn. I wouldn't do it for two hundred and fifty. For two reasons. One, I do not go wandering around in bodies of water I know nothing about. Two, once I brought you your camera, I don't really believe you'd pay me the money."

He stared at me. "Who the hell are you, kid?"

"Just a bystander," I said.

"Sure you are. And the Pope skips lunch. Stick around while I water my tokus, huh? If I get a cramp or something, you can run for help."

I wasn't going anywhere. I had a few questions to ask him.

Walking stiff-legged, he edged into the pond. Behind us, a car engine started. I turned to see the first of the funeral limos leaving the gravesite and rolling toward the main road out of Shady Glen. The burial was definitely over. Dove Hilbert was the last man to get into the second limo. Just before he stepped in, he spun around to look in our direction. I ducked behind the meadow marigolds. It was a strictly instinctive reaction. I suppose I didn't want to be seen in the company of a dung-eating maggot.

The maggot was, at the moment, only three feet into the pond, and already the water was lapping at the top of his rolled pants. "We're like the last of the cowboys, kid," he was saying, "riding the range, all alone, armed only with our . . . HOLY SHIT!, what was that? What's in here with me?"

"My guess would be goldfish."

"Great," he said sarcastically. "My luck, it's goddamn Bruce the shark." He took one more step and disappeared with a "glub." I groaned and made a silent prayer that he could swim.

His bald head broke through the water and he began flailing about, screaming. Then he got control of himself and began dog-paddling. "Shit," was all he kept saying, every time he exhaled.

It took fifteen minutes of diving down to the bottom of the pond before he staggered onto dry land with his camera. He slumped onto the grass and lay back, water and mud and slime oozing off of him and his machine, which he hugged to his chest. He began keening, or maybe singing. I wondered if I shouldn't run for help.

He sat up suddenly. One lock of muddy hair made a question mark on the top of his bald head. His shirt and pants clung like lumpy Spandex to his portly frame. There was mud in his ears and the creases of his face. He held the camera away from his body. Muddy water poured out of it. He shook it and then tossed it onto the grass. "Feh!" he snarled. "That *fercockta* fascist! He might as well have cut out my *kishkas*."

He nodded his head. "Okay, fine. That's how he wants to play. To him, I say, '*Gai in drerd arein.*'" He got to his feet, rather unsteadily, as if he'd been drinking instead of dunking. I'm afraid he also smelled of pond slime.

"You know, I could have made life easier for that *mamzer*. Well, let him try to find out about Mr. George Kerby without my help."

He picked up his camera and moved to where he'd placed his shoes and socks. He shook one hand dry and very carefully stuck two fingers into the shoes, lifting them. Then he began trekking across the grass, squishing and dripping. I followed.

He halted suddenly, and I almost bumped into him. "What the hell is that?"

An odd, unearthly multicolored glow spread over our heads. "It's the man-made rainbow," I told him. "They do it with projectors and prisms. It's Shady Glen's main attraction."

"*Narishkeit,*" he growled, and started on his way again.

Running to keep up, I said, "George Kerby is a friend of the Kosca family."

"So the old lady says. Only you didn't see him here today, did you?"

"I wouldn't know. I've no idea what he looks like."

"Fishburn never forgets a face," he said. "It's what separates the pros from the pishers."

118

"Well, what about George Kerby?"

He turned his head. "So who do I look like, Dan Rather, I should give just *anybody* the news?"

He paused beside an old, battered VW bug that was parked in an area reserved for the handicapped. He placed the camera and his shoes behind the front seat. Then, wincing, he got into the car and squished against his faded vinyl upholstery.

"I guess you want a lift somewhere, huh?" he asked, suddenly amiable.

"Sure."

"Well, you don't get everything you want," he said with a sneer, then drove off.

A wonderful human being, Mr. Mark Fishburn. Self-described independent video journalist and last of the cowboys. I was definitely leaning toward Lieutenant Hilbert's dung-eating maggot.

There was a bus stop in front of the cemetery, but I would only have to transfer three miles down the road. I sat down on a stone bench to put on my skates. Wasn't this just the pits? I was no closer to finding Terry. The one man who could help turn that situation around was thousands of miles and a continent away, probably drinking and eating himself into a coronary, having a splendid time. And there I was, alone in a cemetery.

Fudgebars! I pushed myself to my feet and began rolling out of Shady Glen. A statue of a tall, sad-eyed fellow in a robe almost scared me out of my socks by suddenly intoning: ". . . a simple child,/ That lightly draws its breath,/ And feels its life in every limb,/ What should it know of death? . . . What should it know of death? . . . What should it know of death?"

That was all I needed. Skating past, I yelled back at the statue: "So who do I look like, Dan Rather?"

14

1. I was thousands of miles and a continent away from home, in a country famous for food, wine, romance. If I had my own way, I'd be drinking and eating myself into ecstasy with a plump madonna on each knee. Instead, I was parked at the entrance to a graveyard, waiting for the rain to stop long enough for me to find a jewel thief who'd decided to picnic among the tombstones. A typical Leo Bloodworth twist of fate.

To be specific, I was on one of the several islands in the Venetian lagoon that are accessible by steamer from the north-central banks of the city. Thanks to the first Mrs. Bloodworth, I'd already visited the fishing village of Burano and bought enough of its famous lace to keep every Irish-Catholic home in L.A. in curtains for the next century. We'd run the gamut, from the Lido with its plush casinos to the slightly untended isle of Torcello with its hearty country food and Byzantine ruins.

My second island-hopping trip to the area had been on a job for a Pasadena department-store magnate who'd been sold a warehouse full of bogus Baccarat tableware. That time I'd tracked a rogue glassblower all the way to Murano, where they've been making glass since the thirteenth century and where he hoped to fit right in until the magnate cooled off.

The third visit—well, that was a combination of business and pleasure, and there was a celebrity of sorts involved, and I don't think I want to get into any of the details except to say that on that outing and the others, I never had any reason or inclination to hit the waves to the island of San Michele, the burial ground of Venice. It has the charming nickname of the Isle of the Dead, which may be why it's not exactly a tourist favorite. You know: Hey, Mom, let's go see the Grand Canal and San Marco and, oh, yeah, that Isle of the Dead place. But Sandy Watson wasn't your ordinary tourist.

The day clerk at his pensione, who looked like the ghost of Boris Karloff with a hangover, yawned and told me in broken English that, one, he had no rooms—there were no rooms anywhere—and two, Watson had inquired about the steamers to St. Michele. He quoted him as saying he was off to observe, firsthand, death in Venice. Not so amusing, as it turned out.

The clerk allowed me to park my flight bag behind the desk, but he warned that in these criminal times he could not guarantee its safety. I told him that at this point in my life I was beyond believing in guarantees anyway, and set off through the herds of tourists to the Fondamenta Nuova and the excursion steamers to the lagoon islands.

Every now and then I checked the rear, a habit I'd picked up since that Fiat began dogging my tracks. I hadn't spotted any familiar faces since leaving Jim Bristol at the Stazione Ferroviaria. But that didn't mean anything. Venice is a confined area with forward motion limited by lack of sidewalk. A good shadow man could run an invisible tail on anybody not wearing gills and fins.

Regardless, I did what I could to scan my tracks, and during a half-hour wait for the Linea 5 steamer to cast off, I searched the Fondamenta Nuova for even a hint of suspicious behavior and came up empty.

The trip was barely fifteen minutes long, but by the time we slammed against the wooden platform at San Michele, the clouds that were helping to cool off the crowds at San Marco had sprung a leak, chasing most of the gawkers and mourners away from the Isle of the Dead.

Not Watson, of course. I couldn't be that lucky. I wouldn't be following him back to his pensione, where I'd be able to brace him in his nice dry room and lead him by the nose to his luggage, where the earrings would be resting in his Dopp kit next to his toothbrush.

No, it would not be my lucky day. Unless you compared it to Watson's.

I waited under the tin-roofed platform until the departing mourners hopped aboard the steamer and arrivedercied, leaving only four of us behind—two young men in dark suits and an old man with no teeth who sat on a bench and smiled at the turbulent sky. I sighed and stared at the visible section of the island—the rain-slick cobblestones leading through ankle-high grass, around an apparently deserted red brick industrial building to open fields where flesh and bones mixed with the other elements of earth.

The platform shared the dock with a couple of open-air funeral gondolas that bobbed on the choppy water, their black ribbons and wreaths and bowls of cut flowers taking a pounding from the large, cold raindrops.

A wind whipped through the platform and rattled the windows. The old man began to giggle. If the storm really hit, he'd probably be rolling in the aisles.

One of the black suits lit a cigarette and tossed the pack to his buddy. They puffed and looked at the wet, floating hearses glumly.

The wind seemed damned cold for that time of year, especially to a guy who was wearing a short-sleeved shirt under his linen coat and pants. But at least it was nudging the rain clouds along.

Suddenly a group of very damp mourners circled the brick building and moved smartly to the black gondolas. The two dark suits reluctantly left their shelter to help them aboard. With the rain in their faces, they all looked like they were crying, especially the gondoliers.

The priest, a fat little cleric, was doing a punk job of hanging on to his temper. He ducked under a canopy that had previously covered the coffin and replaced a younger member of the funeral party, who scowled as he was forced to find a seat in the rain.

The gondoliers and the two black suits, who were acting as helmsmen, took their positions, and the long poles dipped into the mildly angry water. The boats were equipped with motors, but they weren't being used. I wondered if the family was traditional or just cheap.

The boats had barely peeled away from the dock, when a couple appeared at a corner of the brick building. The man was wearing a dark gray suit and carried an umbrella that he was using to shield himself and the woman in black beside him. I thought for a minute they'd missed the funeral boat, but as they boarded the dock, I realized that they were right where they wanted to be.

Jim Bristol lowered the umbrella, and my schoolteacher friend, Lannie Doolittle, withdrew a pistol from her smart purse.

"It's about time you got here, Leo," she said.

"Is that one of those little Sterling thirties?" I asked.

"I believe so."

"I guess I've still got an eye," I told her.

She shrugged. "Now might be the time to donate it to someone."

The old man was watching us with his happy grin. Bristol moved to him and lashed out suddenly with the umbrella, whacking the old man's head and bouncing it back against the wooden dock railing. The old fellow toppled forward onto the deck, as lifeless as a sandbag.

"Little Jimmy's been a bad boy," I said.

"Could be worse," he said, looking at the old man. "I don't think he's dead. Should he be?" he asked the girl.

"Absolutely," she snapped. "Use *his* gun."

"I don't have one," I said with a sigh.

Bristol, or whatever his name really was, moved behind me, making sure to steer clear of her line of fire. He patted me down. "Nothing," he said, confused.

"He has to be carrying it," she said. "It wasn't in his luggage."

Bristol tried again, making sure I wasn't wearing one of those really dumb, not to mention uncomfortable, crotch holsters. "Nothing. This screws it up, doesn't it?"

"Maybe," she said. "Maybe not."

She addressed me, "Where's the gun, Leo?"

"Home, last time I looked."

Bristol uttered a mild curse, then turned his attention to the old man. "Well, what do we do about Gramps?"

Lannie frowned for a few seconds and told him, "Maybe drowning. Let it go for now." She said to me, "C'mon, big boy. Let's see what trouble we *can* get you into."

Bristol pushed me forward. Lannie moved out of our path, then fell into place beside him. He opened the umbrella to keep the rain off their villainous heads.

The island was flat and green and wet, tombstones everywhere you looked. Some were plain, others so elaborate they were very nearly an excuse for death. It seemed to be a capacity crowd. I'd read somewhere that the *hoi polloi*'s remains run the risk of being dug up and transported to some less prestigious final digs to make way for the higher-born stiffs. Bum deal.

We walked along a cobblestone pathway between graves. They did not insist I put up my hands. Any detective who'd leave his gun at home was no real threat.

At the far edge of the island was a caretaker's cottage, and beyond it another, larger stone building. Gravedigger housing, probably. Lannie and Bristol led me to a lower part of the island that was hidden from the view of any occupants of the buildings. It was a burial area facing the choppy water and Venice. It made the rest of the place look like a potter's field. With its statues, gravestones with bas-reliefs and sconces, and marble crypts, it was definitely the high-rent district of the Isle of the Dead.

The sky was gray and the sea was a dark gray-green. A line of white appeared at the horizon to serve as a reminder that the rain was not going to last forever. Not far from the water, two men stood out against the island landscape like dandruff on blue serge. One was dressed in a long yellow slicker; the other was in orange pants and emerald shirt, with a pink sweater tied around his neck. They were staying dry under the portico to a particularly elaborate granite mausoleum.

As we moved closer, I saw that the wearer of the slicker was the New Age

Cole Porter. His lizard-skin boots had been regrettably soiled by the inclement weather. The other guy was Sandy Watson. Beside him was a large, soggy sketchpad. Both men watched us arrive.

Watson looked puzzled.

Cole Porter put out his hand and snapped his fingers. "The gun," he commanded.

She said, "He doesn't have it. He says he left it back in L.A."

Porter stepped forward and threw a punch at my face.

I dodged it easily and kicked him in the balls.

Unfortunately, the force of the kick was muted by the slicker, and Bristol gave me a chop at the back of the neck that sent me to the ground, reeling.

Through the mist I heard Watson screech, "More of your goddamn violence! It's wrong. The human race can't survive all this violence. You haven't been listening to me at all. You talk about saving mankind, but you're twisted."

Porter swung one of his lizard boot tips into my stomach. "This asshole leaves his gun at home. Why wasn't that checked?"

Bristol almost squeaked, "We didn't have time to do a complete prep on him."

"Whose fault?" Porter asked.

"Certainly not ours," Lannie shot back.

"It's a hell of a time to find out his gun is still in California."

"Gun? Who is this guy? Another of your idiot bully boys gone sour?" Watson's voice went up a whiny octave. "And you wonder why I took the goddamn thing?"

Porter turned to him. "That's what we have to talk about."

Watson shook his head. "Jeez, how can I take you seriously? You look so goddamned ridiculous. Still playing the same old games."

"Where is it, Sandy? I'm gonna need it, very soon. And it'd be a little messy to get hold of another."

"I'm surprised you didn't get it back. The old guy was ready to give you anything. Until I wised him up. Maybe the cops found it."

"I was hoping it was still in your possession," the green-haired freak said, curling his lip. He turned to Lannie and commanded, "Let's have your gun." She reluctantly handed it to him. Without pause, he pointed it at Watson and shot him twice in the chest.

The force of the bullets knocked him back against the mausoleum. He balanced against the granite wall for a minute, then his legs unlocked and he slid down to the ground, leaving a red trail on the gray granite.

Warily, I got to my feet. Porter pointed the gun at me. He ordered Bristol to "survey the island and see if anything's stirring. Then go to the boat. We'll be along."

"I'm glad to see you guys patched things up," I said.

"Shut up, you fucking jerk. You incompetent fucking jerk."

Lannie opened her purse and took out a flask. She handed it to Porter.

"Now it won't be as neat," he said. "But at least it'll confuse these dago jackasses." He handed me the flask. "Drink it," he said.

"I don't think so."

"We don't have any time, Jack. Either you drink it or you wind up like Sandy. It's more important for me that they find you alive, but it's not a necessity. I'm only gonna count to two."

I drank the stuff. It wasn't bad. Syrupy, but very tasty. And it hit me immediately, like a velvet hammer. I sort of floated down to the ground.

"It's called a Brompton's Cocktail." Lannie's voice was an echo heading away. "They give it to terminal patients in hospitals to make 'em feel good."

"What . . . in it?" I think I asked.

Lannie squatted down and pushed my chest. I fell over backward. The rain splashed in my face.

"The recipe calls for a little heroin, a little cocaine, ethyl alcohol, chloroform water, and cherry syrup," she said. "We gave you a double."

Porter snarled, "Did that dickhead take the goddamned umbrella? Does he want me to catch fucking pneumonia?"

He grunted and stooped over me, placing the gun in my right hand. Then he hopped back. "C'mon, love," he said to Lannie. "As Sportin' Life once said to Bess, 'let's go catch that boat.' "

They romped off in the rain. I floated off in a fog.

2. The thing that saved me was that I almost drowned. My mouth was open and it filled with rain. I coughed, and that led to consciousness, such as it was. I mean, the lights were on, but inside it was strictly "Unfurnished Cottage for Sale."

I rolled over and got to my knees and, still toting the gun, dog-walked over to where Watson was squatting against the mausoleum. The blood that had soaked through his emerald shirt was just another vivid element in his overall color scheme.

I rolled under the portico and knocked over his damp sketchpad. It was filled with pencil drawings of wraithlike figures and the word *no* written over and over.

I used the wall to push myself upright, then staggered away from the body. I was in an island graveyard. With its newest customer. I was holding the weapon that had made him eligible. What to do? What to do?

The answer: Distance yourself from the problem. I staggered into the rain and kept going until I ran out of island. I suppose the most logical step was to toss the murder weapon, covered with my fingerprints, far out into the lagoon. But I wasn't feeling all that logical. So I did the next best thing: I jumped in myself.

The potency of the Brompton's Cocktail was such that I didn't even notice the temperature of the water or the wind-chill factor.

Initially I could feel a muddy bottom about five feet deep, but that fell away quickly. I dropped the gun and began dog-paddling in the general direction of the dock.

I have no idea how long it took. My arms were heavier than a headstone, and the muscles in my legs were crying out to me to stop the nonsense. I welcomed the pain. It meant the Cocktail was losing its hold.

The dock was deserted as I paddled onward through the suddenly oily water. My eyes were burning, but through the blur I could see something that wasn't seaweed hanging on a piling directly under the platform. It was the old coot. They hadn't done a very thorough job of tossing him into the drink.

I huffed up to him. His head was out of the water, but his eyes were shut and I couldn't tell if he was ready for San Michele or not. I swung myself onto the dock and lay there like a beached whale, panting and letting the water drain off.

Then I reached over the side and dragged the old duffer up by the collar of his tattered woolen coat. He started giggling even before he cleared the deck, which was Jake with me. It meant I didn't have to try breathing life back into that toothless mouth.

We were both wheezing and panting when a steamer banged up against the dock. The only person to get off was a guy with a cap who ran over to us and began yapping at the old guy, who sat up and laughed out loud.

The cap shot a little Italian at me. I shrugged. *"Dicalo in inglese, per favore."*

He paused. "What?" he asked.

"The old man went in," I pointed to the water. "I went in and pulled him out."

He looked from me to the water and then to the old man. His face broke into a wide grin. Suddenly he hugged me. "Ok-kay," he said. "You ok-kay. *Molte grazie.*"

He stopped that and helped the old man to his feet. *"Mio zio,"* he said.

"My uncle." He made a circle near his temple. "He, ah, enjoys to sit here and watch, ah, people come and go."

He pointed at the island. "Warm clothes. Up there."

"You take your uncle," I said. "I have to get back."

"But you all wet. Catch cold."

"Don't worry about me."

He followed me onto the steamer, which had only two passengers. He shouted some instructions to the grizzled old guy running the boat. The old guy shouted back. Then my friend with the cap grinned at me. "We get you a blanket. Then Domo take you direct back to wherever you want to go."

"What about these other passengers?"

"What about them? Did they save my uncle's life?"

I wasn't going to argue. There wouldn't be much time before Cole Porter and company would be sending the law out to find Sandy Watson and his drug-crazed killer.

I mentioned the name of the area nearest Watson's pensione. My friend with the cap relayed my destination to the helmsman, and pulled a dirty blanket from behind the steering mechanism.

He tossed it to me and then hopped onto the dock. He waved. I waved back and wrapped the blanket around me. It stunk of mildew and diesel oil. It wouldn't have been more welcome had it been cashmere sprinkled with Chanel.

15

1. Terry Manion had left no further messages on Mr. Bloodworth's answering machine. Because Mr. B. had taken his remote beeper with him and because I had been unable to find the late Mr. Kasper's (could it have been buried with him?), I was forced to travel all the way to downtown Los Angeles to discover that rather disconcerting fact.

There was no word from Mr. Bloodworth, either, not that I expected him to make any transatlantic calls just to talk to me. The tape yielded only one message: An optometrist's assistant wanted to know when Mr. B. would be picking up his new glasses and if payment would be forthcoming at that time.

I scribbled the message and left it on his desk and returned to my office and the problem at hand. Well, I did have Terry's New Orleans number, so I dialed that. On the thirteenth ring I hung up. I guess they didn't bother with modern doodads like answering machines in a historic city like New Orleans. I shut my eyes and forced myself to think: What would Mr. Bloodworth do to find a missing man traveling in a strange city?

There was his rented car—a Dodge, as I recalled. But I hadn't paid any attention to the color (maroon? black?) or style (why must they use all those subsidiary identifications?) or year. Or the name of the rental agency. I tried to recall every moment we'd spent together, tried to play it back like a movie in my mind. But my memory kept drifting and deviously altering events, until I wasn't quite able to separate reality from imagination.

I was thoroughly annoyed with myself. "You are not a bunnybrain," I repeated. "You are a cognitive woman."

Eventually I arrived at only one conclusion—I had to try Mrs. Kosca again. But it being one of those *dies irae*, I was treated to the same recorded message as before.

I left no reply.

I left the office, instead.

2. As I may have mentioned, I am a fan of the Los Angeles transit system. I am well aware of its faults—the schedules are erratic, there are vast sections of the city that are simply not served, and unless you are very fortunate, you may have to transfer as many as five times to reach a particular destination. In addition, the fares are not cheap. And as Mr. Bloodworth is quick to mention, there have been altogether too many bus accidents lately, most involving drivers who have been ingesting some sort of drug or other.

Still, there are numerous simple pleasures to be enjoyed by riding the bus. At three in the afternoon it is entirely possible to locate an empty seat, where one may read while the lumbering vehicle, maintaining a 50–55-mile-an-hour pace along the Santa Monica Freeway, is able to reduce travel time between downtown L.A. and Bay City to a mere thirty-five minutes.

Ordinarily, I would not have disembarked until the bus had made the turn from the Santa Monica Freeway onto the Pacific Coast Highway, well past Bay City and a mile or so past Santa Monica. From there it is possible to climb up streets until one reaches the crest of Bay Heights, where one might employ one's skates to glide three blocks to the front of one's apartment building. That day, however, I transferred to the Big Green Machine, a lime-colored bus that goes directly from Lincoln Avenue and the freeway to Bay City. As long as I was in the neighborhood, I decided to call on Mrs. Kosca and offer my sympathy.

But there didn't appear to be anyone at home. The limousines from the cemetery were not parked in front of the little clapboard house on Fourth Street. In fact, the street was more or less car-free, except for a little sports model with a slapdash black paint job at the curb near the ugly flamingo-and-green apartment building next to Kosca's.

Feeling less than confident, I draped my skates around my neck and walked to the front door of the Kosca home. It was ajar. I gave it a little push and poked my head inside. "Mrs. Kosca?"

No answer. No sound whatsoever.

I could have walked away. But suppose in her haste and despair, she had left the door open by mistake. Perhaps I should just click it shut.

That seemed like a harmless enough choice. But there was that blackboard by the telephone. I could almost see Terry's number there scrawled in chalk. Perhaps . . .

I said again, a little louder, "Mrs. Kosca?"

Definitely no one home.

I didn't see what harm it would do if I peeked at the blackboard. So I entered the house. Illegally, I suppose, but with the best of intentions.

I was in the middle of the living room when they entered through the back door. At least two people, from the sound of them, neither Mrs. Kosca. Maybe they were police, reexamining the garage-office. Lordy. To be caught like that.

My eyes took measure of the room. Stuffed chairs. Console TV. A raised sofa. Love seat. Back to sofa.

By the time they moved into the small room off of the living room, I was behind the sofa, sharing the space with several dust balls that Mrs. Kosca must have missed in her grief. Short, stubby mahogany legs lifted the sofa about five inches off of the carpet, giving me a clear view of feet belonging to a man and a woman. Both wearing Reeboks, black for him, pink for her. Her legs were bare. His were clothed in khaki. Definitely not police.

". . . then he should have cleaned up his mess himself," the man was grousing. His voice was deep, vaguely Southern, though not at all like Terry Manion's.

"I don't think he's back yet. Anyway, it's not *his* mess, exactly. We're all in this. Equal partners." Nothing very distinguishable about her voice. Just a slight sibilance.

"Conspirators is the word. Damnit, I just don't understand why all the mumbo jumbo. What's the point?"

"Don't open your mouth about that to Arch, unless you want him to close it permanently. The mumbo jumbo, as you call it, is what he's doing all this for."

"Then I guess he don't want a share of the fifteen million?" The woman didn't reply. The man continued, "What about the phone numbers on that blackboard?"

The girl said, "That's exactly the kind of stuff we're supposed to take care of. Scrub the slate clean."

"I personally think Archie's demented," the male stated flatly.

"That's 'cause you've got a lousy memory. Christ, you saw him at full power."

"Don't start flinging that nostalgia bullshit again. The Big One-Oh and all that crap. That's how he got me out here, him and the Big One-Oh. And I surely do remember him at full power. Only lately I been seeing too much of him at half power."

My back was developing a crick, so I raised to a squat. I turned away from the two people, and what my eyes focused on chilled me to the marrow.

There was a mirror hanging on the wall just to my left, and in it I could see them perfectly. A tall, muscular man, black but very light-skinned, wearing a white knit shirt and tan khaki pants. The woman was tall, too, maybe five-nine, a brunette in white shorts and a pink cotton blouse. Both wore white cotton gloves. The thing that frightened me was the characteristic of mirrors —if you see somebody, they can see you.

I remained frozen, afraid to take a deep breath. My eardrums pounded. My heart was actually leaping in my chest.

The man left the little room and returned with a wet cloth that he used to wipe the blackboard clean. The woman went out of sight. Judging by the noise, she was puttering around in the kitchen. The man stood back from the blackboard and smiled. "Clean as a cokehound's mirror. Hey, baby, you say our man Archie's got all his brainola. But you know as well as me, he's perfectly willing to off thousands of people. Maybe even hundreds of thousands. I don't call that standing high and dry."

Her voice echoed from the kitchen, "Once you make the commitment, you have to go through with it."

"C'mon, sister, don't use that 'commitment' crap with me. This boy ain't quite ready to play in the Hitler-Ayatollah league."

She moved beside him, her eyes cold and hard. "Then you better get out of the game before it starts."

"Sure. You'd dig that, right? More mon' for the hon'?"

They both walked back into the kitchen. I decided it was time for me to leave.

I moved from behind the couch. I was a few feet from the front door, when the phone rang. Footsteps—the sound of rubber slapping wood—returned, heading for the anteroom. I flattened myself behind a stuffed chair directly beneath the mirror and hoped I was hidden well enough.

The answering machine delivered the same message I'd heard. Then there was a beep, and a female voice said breathlessly, "They've just left the restaurant. You have less than fifteen minutes to finish up." Then there was a click.

"Don't forget to erase those tapes," the brunette said.

The black man obeyed, commenting, "That egomaniac-fool, using his own voice on their goddamn machine."

The brunette snapped, "He was in character. That's the way it's done when you improvise. Anyway, that's why we're here—to get rid of the props."

"The man's a jive-ass."

"You're just pissed because your little girl friend likes Archie better'n she likes you."

"Crack is what she likes better'n me."

"I don't care one way or t'other, Sambo. But you better keep your thoughts to yourself, or you're gonna wind up a pile of spareribs."

"I'm not scared of Archie," he said.

"Then why are you sweating so much, Iceman?" she asked, snickering. "C'mon, we don't have much more time."

"We're finished, aren't we?"

"One more pass in the garage for that bloody key."

"We're never gonna find it."

I heard them move through the house and out the back.

I tiptoed to the front door and eased through it, wincing as if I were being physically squeezed.

Did ever evening air seem so fresh and comforting?

I ran past the horrible new apartment building and turned the corner. I sat down quickly on the curb and attached my Rollerballs and began skating toward the Pacific.

Before I'd gone a block, I heard the rumble of a car's engine coming up behind me.

Possibly it was they. Probably. But they didn't know me. To them I was merely a young woman skating down the sidewalk, knowing nothing of mega-murders or multimillion-dollar crimes.

The car was beside me now. From the corner of my eye I saw it, sleek and low and black. The sports car that had been parked in front of the flamingo-and-green apartments.

I dared not turn my head, but prayed for the car to speed up and drive out of my life.

It did. At least it speeded up, and I breathed a sigh of relief.

Then it pulled over and stopped.

So did I. A door opened on the driver's side, and the black man got out. He stared at me. Was he suspicious of me? Why?

I bent over, pretending to adjust my right skate.

He started toward me.

I turned and skated off in the opposite direction back toward Fourth Street. I heard him shout, "Hey!" Then he began to run after me.

I skated faster. At an uprooted piece of sidewalk I literally sailed up and through the air.

In front of me the street was deserted. I could hear the man behind me, breathing hard but closing the gap. Then, another sound: The woman must have turned the car around to follow us both.

That section of Bay City is a bit hilly, with the streets sloping down to the ocean. At the next corner I made a sharp left and began coasting, faster and faster, down the sidewalk.

My pursuers continued to dog me. But I sensed I was pulling away from the man, who was gasping for air. I dared not look. Then I heard the car brakes being applied, and a door opened and slammed shut.

He had returned to the car. Soon there would be no way I could outrace them.

I hopped the curb and cut across the street in front of the black sports car just as it was lurching forward. I could feel the air change as it neared. Then I was past and sailing down an alley filled with garbage cans and bags of leaves and the usual junk that alleys collect.

The sports car's tires squealed as it swung into the alley behind me.

Dogs began to bark. Every one of those houses seemed to have a dog in its backyard, and they heard the racket we were making or picked up the scent of my fear.

Suddenly I saw the oddest thing. A dog's head was poking through a solid concrete wall on my left. As I moved closer, I saw that a square had been routed out of the wall. Later, when I was more rational, I realized that the hole was probably to allow someone to read the electricity meter without having to enter the yard. But at the time, it was this most surreal thing: the dog's sleek brown head watching me as I raced for my life. And when I shot past it, I could see that the dog was laughing! Some dogs actually laugh. G-2 snickers. I know enough about animals to understand that no matter how smart they may be, they probably do not possess a genuine sense of humor.

And yet, this dog was laughing. Presumably at the sport of seeing a big dog, me, being chased by an automobile. I could hear him chuckle, and the sound had a calming effect on me. My brain clicked back on. I realized an alley was no place to be.

To the left was a narrow walkway between two houses, and I skated into it. The car's brakes screeched.

I was halfway between the alley and the next street, Third Street, when the man began to chase me again on foot. And directly ahead was a concrete rise beyond which I could not see.

I hit the rise at full speed and, dodging a metal handrail, sailed up and through the air. I landed on grass—part of a lawn facing Third. The skates stayed where they were, but I continued forward, taking most of the fall on my hands and knees.

I rolled over. The black man, tan man actually, was only a few feet away, at the top of the concrete rise, pulling himself along the handrail.

Still sitting down, I scurried backward, away from him.

Smiling now, he advanced slowly. He was panting. All those muscles, but with a respiratory system that had been sadly neglected.

He stood at my feet, huffing and grinning now. "Gotcha," he said.

I began to scream. Nothing too coherent. Just *"Aiiieeee."*

He reached over to stifle the sound, and I drew back my right foot and drove it and the skate as hard as I could into his groin. It was my best self-defense trick, taught to me by Gran, who I doubt ever had reason to use it.

He grabbed his privates and staggered back. I had the choice of pressing my advantage and aiming a second kick where it would do the most good, maybe his chin. But I wasn't sure of the location of the woman and the car. And I didn't know if either of them had weapons.

I clumped to the sidewalk and skated away. My legs were wobbly, but I finally arrived at a commercial area where there were people other than those chasing me. The sports car was nowhere to be seen.

With hands and knees stinging but with no skin broken that I could see, I glided to a police car parked in front of a Greaseburger and waited beside it until its occupants devoured their daily quota of mega-calories and fat. I asked them if they would be so kind as to escort me to Lieutenant Rudy Cugat of the Bay City Police Department. They asked me why. I said it was just a friendly visit. They thought this very amusing. One of them made some oblique comment about the grass stains on my jeans and sweater. But they did as I asked.

16

1. There's a limit to what your mind and body can take. Make that to what *my* mind and body can take. I'm not a totally well man to begin with: There are the heart flutters and the mild hypertension and a few other little dents in the armor. Nor am I a kid anymore. I'm not even a young, upwardly mobile adult. Hell, I only have to hold out for another fifteen years before my Medicare kicks in.

So I hope you will excuse me if my description of the trip back to Watson's pensione is a bit fuzzy, what with the punches and kicks and my witnessing a rather brutal murder followed by drugs and an impromptu dip in the freezing Venice lagoon.

I do remember sloshing up to the Pensione Violetta, a little out of control, and scaring a couple of American bird-watcher types nearly out of their tweeds. Once I made it inside the Violetta, however, events became vivid enough to be forever deposited in my memory bank.

The Italian Boris Karloff was not behind the desk. Nobody was. Nor was my flight bag.

A pinch-faced little woman with a British accent so clipped it drew blood stood at the desk, screeching at me while I searched the register for the name *Watson*. I gathered from her attitude and harangue that she had been waiting all afternoon for a clerk to help her confirm her reservations at a hotel on Lake Como.

Watson's room number was 14.

"You're a filthy disgrace," the woman announced.

I stared at her. "Beg pardon?"

"You're filthy. Your hair is unkempt. You need a bath."

"Thanks for not holding back." I started away.

"Well, aren't you going to assist me in dialing Lake Como?"

I handed her the phone. "Be my guest."

"But I can't speak Italian."

"Fake it," I said, pulling the key to number 14 from its hook on the wall.

"Well, if you aren't the rudest ruffian . . ."

I didn't wait for her to finish. I *was* a rude ruffian. After what I'd been through, St. Francis of Assisi would have been a rude ruffian.

I found number 14 at the rear of the building and up a short flight of padded stairway, next to a communal bathroom with a pebble-glass window. The heavy iron ball attached to the key banged a dull gong against the thick oak door as I worked the lock.

Inside the dark room I shut the door immediately and locked it. Then I fondled the wall for the light switch. The cut-glass chandelier positioned in the center of the high ceiling was a pale pink, bathing the room in an unnaturally rosy aura.

French windows were shuttered against what I assumed was a view of the Grand Canal. There was a fireplace built into one wall, an alcove with a washbasin, a chest of drawers, a vanity table, and a large bed. My flight bag was open on the bed, next to the body of the day clerk. In death he looked even more like Karloff, which I guess was not surprising. Either Bristol or the girl had tenderized the back of his head with a heavy metal candlestick that rested near the bed on the worn carpet.

I wondered if they'd forced him into the room to kill him, or if he'd surprised them rooting in my luggage. The point was moot. Blood had been spilled.

I pawed through my bag. No surprises. Nothing seemed to be missing. I stood back, took a deep breath. Time to roll. I removed my wet wallet with its soggy contents that included a number of hundred-dollar bills stuck together. It would be fun later prying them apart. My passport was bleeding dark blue from its cover. Quickly, I peeled off my sopping clothes and replaced them with dry duds.

I wrapped a towel around the lagoon swimwear and threw the whole mess into my flight bag.

Watson's overnight bag was in the alcove next to the basin. It contained shaving equipment, face bronzer, toothpaste and brush, comb, tweezer, nail clipper. A clean pair of Jockey shorts, a mauve sports shirt, and a freshly pressed pair of bright red pants.

There was also a small sketchpad. It contained a pencil drawing of another metallic trellis, much like the one he'd designed for Circe. On this one, the word *Mummers* substituted for *Circe* and *A Tour for Survival* had been changed to *The Armageddon Tour*.

I didn't bother hunting for the earrings I'd been hired to find. Maybe they actually existed, but I doubted it. And if they did, frankly I just didn't give a damn.

I turned off the light and left the room, making sure the door was locked. At the front desk several guests were gathered, waiting for the clerk and complaining to one another in various languages. I moved past them quickly, averting my face. Outside, on a nice little patio with a partial view of the canal, I wiped the key to Sandy Watson's room on the tail of my coat and placed it on an ashtray resting on a wrought-iron table near the water.

I ran through the narrow alleys to the dock, where a vaporetto was about to embark. I hopped aboard and didn't look back. I had been in close proximity to two murder victims. It was time for me to say arrivederci to Venezia.

2. The train ride to Milan seemed to take the better part of a lifetime. I half expected to see Porter, Bristol, and the girl sipping martinis in the *carròzza ristorante*. But the times of our "chance" meetings were past. They'd probably driven the beige Fiat back to the airport.

I spent an hour worrying that a conductor would approach, place a hand on my shoulder, and tell me my presence was requested back in Venice. But the only one there who knew of my connection to Watson was the late desk clerk. And even he had not known my name.

Then fear set in that Porter and his pals had planted some other evidence that would send the Venice police after me. But that passed, and eventually I fell into a troubled sleep. I awoke with stiff joints and an aching head, feeling very much out of sorts.

As the evening wore on, my mood grew darker. There was no direct flight available from Milan to Los Angeles that night. The best I could do was an international milk run that bounced to Paris before hopping to New York. There, I switched carriers to the West Coast. Only five more hours before I would see the blue, blue, yellow-smog-polluted skies of home.

17

1. Between sips of the best nectar soda in the world—as prepared by Scotty, the midget counterman at the Buttons and Bows Ice Cream Shoppe in Bay Heights Village—I said, "I don't think I've ever met a naturally blond Mexican before, Jorge."

He displayed a smile filled with sparkling teeth. "Our heritage is a rich and varied one, Miss Dahlquist."

The B & B was beginning to fill with the last-chance-before-dinner-to-scarf-a-scoop crowd. Lizzie Bermann, who has this absurd snobbier-than-thou attitude because her father is some sort of film producer who's on all these charity committees (Gran told me he is a sexist pig posing as a patron of liberal causes), sashayed in with her sycophantic herd and almost ruptured her eyeballs when she saw me sitting with the tall, tanned older man of twenty-four.

I selected that moment to ask to see his wedding ring, which was only six months old, and I tried it on my finger, managing to casually glance at and through Lizzie while I was doing it. Who would have thought that having a police bodyguard would be so much fun?

"Hang on to the ring while I call in," Officer Jorge Fuentes said, excusing himself from the table. I ostentatiously admired the way the yellow band looked on the third finger of my left hand. When the plainclothes policeman returned, he dropped a few bills on the tabletop and said, "Lieutenant Cugat wants us back there."

"You'd better put this where it belongs," I said, handing him the ring.

As we passed Lizzie Bermann's suddenly very silent table, I said in my sweetest voice, "Hi, Lizard, is that a Mud Pie you're gobbling? *Très beaucoup* calories. How brave of you."

When the glass door slammed shut behind us, I wheeled suddenly and caught Lizzie poking her finger into her open mouth in an "isn't-that-enough-to-make-you-gag" gesture. I stuck my head back inside the B & B and told her, "Bulimia isn't the answer, Liz. Try self-control and dieting." Then, before she could reply, I was away and into Officer Fuentes's unmarked car.

2. Police protection had been Lieutenant Cugat's idea. When I'd entered the Bay City Police Department the previous afternoon and met with him, I'd been abruptly reminded of our first encounter in that very same place the year before when we'd discussed a matter that went on to escalate horribly. It had been he who'd suggested I make the acquaintance of Mr. Bloodworth, a practical joke (on his part) that blossomed into as rewarding an association as I could have imagined.

The lieutenant had lost a little weight and put Grecian Formula 9 or something on his hair to get rid of the gray. He'd also cultivated a thin moustache. The alterations were probably because Lacey Dubin, Gran's and my agent, had been getting him walk-ons in episodic TV. Everybody out here wants to be a star.

The one thing that hadn't changed was his fondness for sharply tailored pastel suits, if the peach-colored outfit he was wearing was any indication. He seemed genuinely pleased to see me.

We went through the amenities, and then he settled down to listen to my tale of being chased and attacked. I fudged a bit on the events leading up to the chase. I said I'd gone to the Kosca home looking for a client of Mr. Bloodworth's. I did not mention that I had entered the home illegally. Instead, I told him that I was at the front door when the man and woman ran from behind the house to their car, saw me standing there staring at them, and gave chase. From that point I delivered a scrupulously honest, accurate, and complete description of what happened. I felt quite guilty about not passing on the conversation about the fifteen million dollars and the thousands of people who might die, but I didn't see how I could without admitting that I had been inside the house. What a binding web I'd woven for myself.

"Do you know the number of the Kosca home?" he asked, picking up the phone. I told him and he dialed it. No answer. Mrs. Kosca should have been there. The lookout had told the two housebreakers that the limousines were on their way. That had been hours ago.

Lieutenant Cugat depressed the telephone plunger and dialed three numbers. Then he flirted a bit with whoever answered and eventually asked her to send two policemen to the Kosca address to check for signs of entry. "Get somebody to lift a few prints out there, too."

"Uh, they were wearing gloves," I said, suddenly remembering.

"Hold it," he said into the phone.

"But," I said excitedly, "his hands were bare when he attacked me."

"You said he grabbed something. A handrail? Was that on Third?" I nodded. Into the phone again, "Okay, *muchacha,* there's a raised lawn and a handrail at the entrance to a concrete dip that leads to a passage between two houses on Third. Uh, tell 'em the east side of the street, somewhere between Delilah and Glendora . . . ?" He looked at me and I nodded agreement. "That's where they'll find prints if there are any.

"Tell 'em it's an attempted rape on a teenager and I need it yesterday. Thank you, Miss Pepper Pot."

He was still grinning lasciviously when he replaced the phone.

"Well," he said. "It could have been rape, no? That's what turns the wheels the quickest. And now, we wait." He put his feet on his desk. The soles of his pointed, highly polished black-tassel loafers were barely scuffed, as if he walked only on carpets.

"Mr. Bloodworth told me that smart policemen always used a razor to cut the leather on the soles of new shoes," I said.

He used a long finger to push his left shoe so that he could gaze at its bottom. "Why would someone destroy such excellent workmanship?" he asked.

" 'So that when you're chasing crooks, you won't fall on your butt,' to quote Mr. B."

"Ah, yes. Well, getting in foot races with the bad guys is something out of my Dark Ages, Miss Dahlquist. I let the, ah, less-experienced officers handle that end of it."

"Since you're being so nice, and since we have known each other for a while, Lieutenant, I think it would be appropriate for you to use my first name, Serendipity."

He nodded. "Well, Serendipity"—he added an intriguing trill to the "r" —"I am flattered that you've come to me to be your protector, but it makes me wonder why you did not call upon our old friend, Hound?"

"Hound," a diminutive form of "bloodhound," was his nickname for Mr. Bloodworth. "He's on the Continent," I said casually, as if he went there all the time.

"Hound is in Europe?" the lieutenant asked, amazed. "He didn't get married, did he?"

It was my turn to be amazed. "Not to my knowledge. Why?"

"He likes to honeymoon in Europe."

"No. This is business."

"So his new celebrity as an author is paying off with, ah, more interesting work."

"I suppose so."

"My very small part in the book did not harm my reputation, either. Oh, there was a certain stillness in the air concerning a few of my little moon-lighting activities, but I was definitely heroic. And that agent of ours, Lacey Dubin, she's a real pistola, that lady. She's taking offers from publishers for a book that I will write—with some help, of course. What do you think of the title 'Bay City Heat'?"

"It sounds a little like a rash," I told him, throwing him into a brief depression. He bounced out of it with, "Well, while we wait, Serendipity, why don't we do something useful?"

He escorted me out of his office and down a corridor to a smaller room where a tall young man in uniform sat at a computer hitting keys and chuckling. His red hair stuck out wildly, not punkish but just unmanageable, like a lawn that had been mowed by someone with hiccups. He was wearing large geek glasses, and a plastic penguard stuck up from the pocket of his short-sleeved brown uniform shirt. His undershirt showed in the "V" of his open neck, like that of most uniformed lawmen, but the short sleeves were about an inch longer than his outer shirt's. He was a nerd policeman.

Lieutenant Cugat had to call "Harold" twice before the young man pulled himself away from the machine.

"Serendipity, this is Officer Harold Burpee."

"Like the seed people," he said, shaking my hand.

"Harold, I'd like you to set Miss Dahlquist up with a mug file, if you're not too busy playing Pac-Man?"

"That's a very seventies reference, Lieutenant." He turned to me and made an absurd noise. It was a laugh actually, only instead of exhaling, like normal people, Officer Burpee inhaled, causing a hollow echo to emanate from his throat. After a minute of that he said, "Give me the description."

I said, "Male, black, twenties, over six feet tall, muscular."

"We don't have anybody fits that description in our files," he said and began his terrible laugh again. Hoo-rahnk. Hoo-rahnk.

Lieutenant Cugat shuddered and said, "Try not to let your sense of humor get the better of you, Harold. Serendipity, I'll be in my office when you're finished."

When the lieutenant had gone, Officer Burpee said, "Can you imagine, a man his age and in his position and he has never laid one finger on a keyboard?"

"Old dog and new tricks," I said, thinking of Mr. B.

"Yeah, well log on or drop out, is what I say. Now let's see about your black man."

He moved awkwardly, like a newborn colt, to a file cabinet with small, square drawers that slid out on rollers. They were filled with labeled floppy discs. Officer Burpee extracted one and began singing in a voice like a fingernail on a blackboard. " 'Could I, could I, could I have some of your hot, everlovin' monkey luvvvvv . . .' "

He put the floppy into his computer's "A" drive and booted up the program. Then he put a blank disc into the "B" drive.

"All right now, blondie, give me that description again."

"Are you addressing me?" I asked.

"Is there somebody else in this room?" Hoo-rahnk, hoo-rahnk.

"Then I'll thank you to call me Miss Dahlquist."

He shrugged. "Black, you said . . ." He hit a key. ". . . in his twenties. That would be between 18 and 24, or 25 and 36?"

"Could be either. But the latter, I would think."

He frowned and hit several keys.

"Okay. Over six feet? Over six-feet-two? Over six-feet-four?"

I shut my eyes and concentrated. Mr. Bloodworth is over six-two. "Over six-feet-two," I said.

"*Voilà,*" he said, and hit the RETURN key.

A graphic image began to appear on the computer monitor. The face of a black man.

"It's nothing like him," I said.

"Keep your pants on, blondie."

"Officer Burpee, why must you be such a . . . a creep?"

His smile vanished. "I was just trying to be, you know, with it."

"Fine, only do it on your own time."

"I'm sorry if you found it offensive. I just didn't want this to be dull for you."

"It's not dull, believe me. I like computers."

"Oh?" His smile returned. "Okay, then what we need to do is to create a computerized image that is most like your man. Then we'll access the mug shots, which I've got on other discs, and call up the shots most like the computer image. I'll bring them up on that monitor near the door." He pointed to a color monitor on a wooden stand.

It took about fifteen minutes of my saying things like "lighter skin color," "higher forehead," "thinner upper lip," "thinner nose," and Officer Burpee keying in the instructions. What resulted was a face that at least resembled the man who'd chased me.

Unfortunately, none of the mug shots looked familiar. Officer Burpee ran off a printed version of our computerized face and started to eject the program disc from the machine.

"There was another person," I said.

"Oh?" He began a new file.

"Woman. Caucasian. Early thirties. Brunette."

"Forget hair," he said. "Women change their hair like they change their shoes."

"Don't men?"

"Not black men, as a rule. Unless they shave and go baldie. And, in fact, male criminals don't change their hair as much as females. Men like to fool around with face hair."

The picture he brought up didn't look like anybody. It could have been Lois Lane or Tina Turner. "Eyes were larger, set further apart," I said. "Button nose, but wider at the bridge. Very full lips."

The resulting picture looked sort of like the woman. Officer Burpee frowned. "I think we'd better get more specific on body shape. Ecto, endo. Like that."

"Is ectomorph chunky?" I asked.

"That's endo. You're an ecto."

"So was she. Tall and slender."

"How tall?"

"Five-ten, maybe."

"Good. Good." Hitting keys like mad.

"Large or small feet and hands?"

I conjured up those pink Reeboks. "Large feet. Long fingers."

"You're good at this," he said. "No equivocations."

Our experiment yielded nearly twenty-five photos, eighteen of which were easily dismissed. The others, I really couldn't tell. The problem was that the photos had been taken at various times during the past two decades. Of the remaining seven, five were of women who had been arrested in their late teens in the sixties during particularly violent student protests, and two had been imprisoned for drug sales and had been users at the time the photos were snapped.

Ever the compleatist, Officer Burpee made a print-out of everything—the computer image and the seven mug shots and arrest records—that I carried with me back to Lieutenant Cugat's office.

The lieutenant was on the phone. He continued to frown when he saw me. I took a chair and waited for him to thank someone and replace the receiver.

"When's my amigo Leo gonna be back in town?" he asked.

"I'm not sure. Maybe tomorrow. But this has nothing to do with him."

He ran his long fingers through his hair. "We couldn't find any sign of a break-in at the Kosca house," he said. "If people were inside the place, they used a key."

"What does Mrs. Kosca say?"

"I gather that she and her daughter went for a long drive up the coast. They took off a couple hours ago. I left word for her to call me as soon as she gets back."

"Left word with whom?"

He smiled. "A friend of the family. I was just talking with him. A Lieutenant Hilbert."

"Oh!"

"You know him, huh?"

"Yes."

"And you and a P.I. from New Orleans named Terry Manion are somehow involved in the killing of Michael Kosca?"

"Not in the killing. I mean, I never even heard of the man until he was in the morgue. And Terry . . ."

"Yes?"

"He wasn't in town until after."

"After the murder?"

"Yes."

"Is Leo working with Manion on this?"

"Uh, not exactly. I'm sort of doing it on my own as a member of the Bloodworth Agency."

"Leo must be getting senile."

"You needn't be nasty. I was just showing Terry around town."

"The guy was using you to flush out a killer, according to Hilbert."

"Lieutenant Hilbert is a creep."

"Yeah, he is. But that don't mean he's wrong."

"What are you saying?"

"I'm assigning an officer to keep you company for a while, Serendipity."

"I still don't understand . . .?"

"We got a clear set of prints from that handrail."

"And you discovered the man's identity? That's wonderful, Lieutenant."

"Actually, his ID was not in the file," Lieutenant Cugat said, picking up the mug shots and the computer images. "The guy has never been booked for anything, I guess. But we do know one thing about him. His prints were on Mike Kosca's shoes when they found him. Your man helped to carry Kosca's body, and probably tossed him down into that canyon."

18

1. Some nineteen long, miserable hours after I left Milan, I limped from a cab and dragged my flight bag past the playhouse and down the alley to my coach house in the rear. The southern California combination of afternoon sun and glare did not brighten my disposition.

I worked the lock and stumbled into the living room, stepping on a folded note that had been slipped under the door.

I hoped it was from Holly Blissfield or her boss, Laura Mornay, two people I had a serious need to chat with.

It wasn't. I realized that as soon as I saw the embossed Bay City Police Department emblem at the top of the sheet and recognized the childish scrawl of the guy with whom I'd shared a squad car when I was on the LAPD, Rudy Cugat.

It had yesterday's date. It read:

> "Dear Hound, Call me as soon as you can. Your little Chihuahua has run into some bad hombres, I think. She tells me you jet-setting these days. It's about time you got a piece of the good life. But you better pull back long enough to talk to me about the girl. Your amigo, R.C."

A piece of the good life! Christ!

I balled the note and tossed it through the door into the kitchen, missing the trash bucket by a yard. Then I took a long, wishful look at the empty couch, which even with the lump near the middle was the most comfortable resting spot in the whole house.

Life was never fair. I knew that if I sat down I would never get up. So I stood, summoning what was left of my strength to lift the telephone and direct-dial Cugie's number. What he had to tell me pumped enough adrenaline through my veins to propel me out of the house and into the car and all the way over to Bay City.

2. Cugie rushed out of his office to meet me in the squad room. It had been a while since I'd seen him move that fast. His hand went around my shoulder as he said, "Hound, before you come into the office, there's something . . ."

I looked past him and spotted the "something" in the doorway to his office. The "something" was wearing his usual dark, tight three-piece suit and skeleton grin. "What the hell is *Hilbert* doing here?"

"He just sorta dropped in," Cugie replied as I moved toward the skinny, white-haired bastard. "Fact is, he's handling the case Serendipity's mixed up in."

"That's beautiful," I grumbled.

"Citizen Bloodworth," Hilbert greeted me. "So nice to see you in a police station as a visitor. My God, man, what's happened to you? Bloodshot eyes. Rumpled clothes. You look as though you'd seen better days."

"And better cops," I said, staring at him.

"Leo just flew in from Europa," Cugat cut in, assuming the role of buffer. "Amigo, you do look a little jet-lagged."

"Seventeen hours' worth," I said. "So excuse me if I'm not my usual diplomatic self with this asshole-bigot."

Hilbert grinned and opened his coat. "We all mature, Bloodworth. We mellow. See, my mace no longer hangs from my belt."

"What happened? Did one of Jerry's Kids take it from you?"

"As a matter of fact, I mislaid it somewhere. Been looking for it for a couple of days." He flashed a grin. "Could be I left it buried in the skull of some bleeding-heart disgrace to the uniform." He had swung his goddamn spiked ball at me once, years ago, when I was a cop. It was at the height of the Watts riots. As you may remember, that was back in '65, when about ten thousand blacks decided to burn and loot a five-hundred-square-block area of L.A. Hilbert made his mark during the riots by wading into a crowd of bodies and letting fly with a goddamned medieval mace that he hooked onto his gunbelt. The rest of us had to worry about carrying non-reg guns in our socks, but they let that psycho tote a museum piece.

Anyway, one afternoon, with the air filled with smoke from burning buildings, Hilbert and I wound up in the same alley trying to dodge the bullets zinging down the streets. There was this black kid hiding behind a dumpster, a teenager, tall, skinny, with glasses. Hilbert found him and dragged him out of the bin. He was about to give him a taste of the mace, when I blocked his hand with my nightstick. Hilbert spun around and tried to bean me with his weapon. So I laid him out with my stick.

The kid scooted from the alley to the relative safety of the bullet strewn streets. I turned in a report on Hilbert, but in those riot days, police brutality was considered on a par with bad social graces. If internal affairs ever investigated the incident, I never heard about it.

"Gentlemen, gentlemen. We have all had our differences," Cugat said. "But a whole lot of water has flowed under that bridge. Let's sit down and relax. The young lady should be with us in a minute."

I took the leather couch and hoped I wouldn't fall asleep before Sarah showed and told us her story. Hilbert prowled the room for a while, then settled on a chair near Cugie's desk. He said amiably, "What's the mood in Bay City these days, Lieutenant? The good people still think all of you boys are on the take?"

Cugat's eyes frosted over. "No," he said softly, "we have been cleaning house for over ten years, and I don't think anyone will find any dust under our rug. I understand there is some vacuuming going on at Beverly Hills, too, eh?"

I wasn't hip to Cugie's reference, but whatever it was, it shut Hilbert up like a constipated clam. For the better part of a half hour, the three of us sat there squinting at each other, like three gunfighters who had taken root. And then Sarah burst into the room, followed by one of Cugie's clean-cut new centurions.

She took a seat next to me on the couch and, staring intently at my face, said, "Did you pick up some influenza on foreign soil?"

"Nope. Just jet lag." I hoped that was the truth, but the Venice lagoon wasn't exactly on the health-spa route. And there'd been all that fallout in the air.

"Shall we be getting to business any time this day, Lieutenant Cugat?" Hilbert asked sarcastically.

"Serendipity," Cugie said, "I want you to repeat everything you told me yesterday."

"Rather than repeat it verbatim, Lieutenant Cugat, I'll use words of fewer than three syllables so that Lieutenant Hilbert can understand."

Hilbert chuckled loudly. "Brava, madame. Please begin."

By the time the kid had finished her yarn, Hilbert was feasting on the inside of his mouth. I was foaming at mine. "What the hell did you think you were doing, going to that place by yourself?"

"It was just the house of a widow-lady," she said. "What was the big deal?"

"Priceless," Hilbert exclaimed. "That Manion knew what the hell he was doing when he picked you for his staked goat, honey. Where is that rascal, anyway?"

"I don't know."

"He checked out of his hotel," Hilbert said. "No forwarding."

Sarah gave a little yip and slank back on the sofa. I asked Hilbert, "Where was he bunked, anyway?"

"I understood you were working together."

"You understood wrong. He wanted to hire me, but we never got together."

Hilbert shrugged. "He spent two days at the Miraposa Motel, just off the San Diego Freeway near Sunset. A sixty-five-dollar-a-day dump, complete with hot and cold running hookers."

"They probably weren't running until you got there," the kid said.

Hilbert sighed. "Miss Dahlquist, I fear we shall never be friends, but I can stand the loss." He stood up. "Lieutenant, I assume you've put a description of the black sports car into the hopper?" Cugie nodded. "Well," Hilbert said, "I've wasted enough time. Thanks for your meager cooperation."

Cugie didn't do anything with the hand Hilbert offered. He said, "We believe in cooperation here in Bay City."

"Yes, of course." Hilbert nodded and grinned at the three of us. Then he walked stiff-legged out of the office.

"Damnit," Cugat exclaimed, "but that man brightens a room when he leaves it."

"What the hell did you get him out here for?" I asked.

"The fingerprints tied Serendipity's attacker to the Kosca murder, which is Hilbert's case."

"How'd that happen? Sarah was attacked here in Bay City. Kosca was bumped off in the boonies."

Sarah piped up, "Mr. Kosca was an old friend of Lieutenant Hilbert's, so he made himself the investigating officer."

"Jesus, what's happening to jurisdictional boundaries, Cugie? In the old days that was the one—"

He cut me off with, "The head man at Beverly Hills—Collander, you remember him, a beachball with a crew cut—he wants Dove Hilbert out. Dove won't go. He requests a difficult murder case, and Collander pulls strings so that he gets it. Now if Dove screws it up, and knowing him he will, Collander will have one more reason to put him on early retirement."

"It's a plan," I said. "My next question is: Why are we here?"

"To figure out what we do with the young lady."

"Do?" Sarah asked.

"You seem to have run afoul of some rough hombres. But there is nothing to indicate that you are still in danger. I cannot justify the expense of assigning an officer to you indefinitely."

"From what you told me, amigo," I said, "the guy who chased Sarah is the same guy who cashed this Kosca's check."

"We have nothing positive. Serendipity's black man probably disposed of the body. But he also could have stumbled over the body after someone else did the killing. Or maybe he worked in a shoe store and took hold of Kosca's shoes while he was still alive. I don't know. In any case, we got nothing to make us think he's going to be on the prowl for her."

The kid said, "It's just as well, Mr. Bloodworth. Gran wasn't very keen on Officer Fuentes's presence at our apartment. And I don't want my relationship with her to be any more strained than it is."

I leaned forward. "Straight out, Cugie. Is she in danger?"

"She can identify the guy."

"So put her in protective custody."

"No!" the kid shouted. "I'm not going to stay holed up in some room all day with a bunch of tired old cops who are smoking cigars and playing cards."

"I couldn't do that anyway, Hound. She has no knowledge of the crime in question. The best she can do is identify a guy whose prints indicate he *might* be involved in a murder."

"But your bloody Latin heart tells you she really might be in the soup, and you want to shift the responsibility from yourself to me. Am I reading you correctly?"

"Would you gentlemen please stop fighting over who will be forced to take me to the prom? I do not wish to go with either of you. I do not wish to be in the same room with you."

With that, she leaped from the couch and ran from the office.

"I don't think you handled that so smoothly, Hound," Cugat said.

"Buzz Willie to stop her at the desk. I'll take her home."

Cugat notified the desk sergeant. "Well?" he asked, seeing me still sitting there.

"Quid pro quo?"

"Eh?"

"Tit for tat. I need you to run down some names for me. James or Jim Bristol, supposed to be a personal manager. Used to be a kid actor. Cole Porter . . ."

"The songwriter?"

"No. Guy in his late twenties. Maybe a musician. Green hair, wears a stone in his nose. Dragon tattoo covering his back. You'd like him. Uh, Lannie Doolittle, woman in her late twenties. Loni Hoffstattler—they're all around the same age, I guess. Porter and Hoffstattler have U.S. passports."

"Anything else?" he said sarcastically, jotting down the names.

"Yeah. Check out these, too—Jake Seloy, another former kid actor, possibly behind bars for rape; Jamie Ann Johnson, supposedly a Broadway actress who's a lush; Ann Jellicoe—I don't know anything about her except that she's from Cleveland, Ohio. And, finally, a Holly Blissfield of this city."

He asked me a few spellings, which I provided as best I could. Then I gave him detailed descriptions of the folks I'd eyeballed personally. "That it, then?" he inquired.

"For now," I said.

"This wouldn't have anything to do with the Kosca murder?"

I shook my head. "Another kettle of smelt entirely."

"You wouldn't lie to me?"

"Not so's you'd know it."

3. The kid pouted for part of the ride to her home. Then she said, "That I break my silence now does not mean that I am any less put out by your and Lieutenant Cugat's chauvinistic attitude, not to mention outright rudeness."

"I don't know what was rude . . ."

"I break my silence because I feel it is crucial that you know something."

"I'm all ears, kid."

"There was quite a bit about the two thieves that I did not tell Lieutenant Cugat."

"Maybe you'd better go back to being silent."

"I heard them talking about—"

"Sarah, I don't care what they were talking about. Tell it to Cugie. Don't tell it to me. Okay?"

She glared at me.

"Besides," I said, "you're home."

Edith Van Dine, who has never been my biggest fan, opened the door to their apartment with a scowl on her face. "Thank you for delivering my granddaughter, Mr. Bloodworth," she said coldly, blocking the entrance. "Did she happen to mention her six o'clock curfew?"

"Not really," I said. "Is it past six?"

"It is nearly seven."

"Well, she was at the Bay City Police Department providing information in a case . . ."

"As I told the officer who spent the evening with us, I am not in the least interested in the workings of the Bay City Police Department. I am interested in my granddaughter growing up to be a normal, refined young woman who does not spend her time in the company of men of disreputable mien. Judging by your scruffy appearance, you haven't slept in days."

"Mr. Bloodworth just flew in today, Gran. Eighteen hours in the sky."

"Then he must be anxious to return to the rest and comfort of hearth and home."

"Well, yes. But we're all a little concerned about Sarah's safety."

"The officer explained that last night. I tell you what I told him: I am quite capable of seeing to the child's welfare."

"Mrs. Van Dine, I sense a certain animosity . . ."

"Mr. Bloodworth, I have a guest coming for dinner . . ."

I realized for the first time that the old dame was really dolled up and looking great. Lipstick. Eye shadow. A pale gauzy dress that complemented her purple eyes. So what if she was in her sixties? I'd be there soon enough myself.

". . . and I don't have time to tell you how irresponsible I think you are."

"Me? Irresponsible?"

"You lure my granddaughter down to your office, where she is working for no remuneration. There is a child-labor law."

"Child-labor law? She begged me to let her hang out there. For school credits, she said."

"And then you have the colossal gall to put her in a position where she is forced to dine with older men . . ."

"*What?* I'm sorry, ma'am, but that's a barefaced lie." I spotted Serendipity tiptoeing to her room. "Hey, you!" I shouted.

Mrs. Van Dine wheeled around and added, "Come here at once, Serendipity."

The kid approached sheepishly.

"What the devil is this about dinner with some old guy?"

"I had dinner with Terry Manion," she said. "Gran's making a big deal out of it."

"Do you know this Manion?" Mrs. Van Dine asked me.

"Sure, but—"

"Mr. Bloodworth didn't know I was having dinner with him," the kid blurted out. "I told you that."

"You didn't ask her to keep your client entertained?"

"Me? Lady, give me credit for some sense, please."

She stared at me and then turned to Sarah. "I am most disappointed in you, girl."

"But I never said—"

The door buzzer sounded. Mrs. Van Dine looked at me imploringly. "My guest is downstairs. Please forgive my rude behavior, Mr. Bloodworth. I'm very appreciative of everything you've done for my granddaughter in the past. But I do not want your . . . association with her to continue. She will not be working in your office anymore."

"But there's a possible killer who—"

"Both the officer and Lieutenant Cugat have explained the situation to me. I have taken steps to make sure that no harm comes to her. And now, I'm afraid I must say good night."

The shutting door ended the conversation.

Well, I'd done my best. And I was certainly not unhappy that the kid wouldn't be underfoot at the office.

I turned away from the closed door, feeling as wrung out as a dishrag in a twenty-four-hour diner. It was definitely time for home.

On the way out I passed a guy in his late thirties or early forties. He did a double take when he eyeballed me. I guess my mien *was* pretty disreputable.

His, on the other hand, was quite reputable, indeed. He was a little young for Mrs. Van Dine, but what the hell, this *was* southern California.

19

1. "Stop playing with your food, dear."

"Snow peas are simply not my favorites," I said. "They're too big and brightly colored to be real. They're Disney vegetables."

"Taste delicious to me," Roger Thornhill said in his insufferably smug manner. "Everything does. It's a wonderful meal, Edith. And to think you slaved nine hours on the set, came home and managed to put it all together in just minutes. And you look as relaxed and beautiful as if you were just starting out." Gran gave him a smile. Lordy, what a day of castastrophes. The episode in Lieutenant Cugat's office. The confrontation between Gran and Mr. B. And now this! A sleazoid wooing my own grandmother at the dinner table.

"If you're finished, dear," Gran said to me, "you have my permission to excuse yourself."

"Oh, I'll just poke at the peas a bit more, if it's all right."

"What are you studying at school?" the Creep of the Century asked. As if he were really interested.

"She's preparing for a liberal-arts college education," Gran answered for me.

I added, "I'm going to major in criminology."

He stared at me, then smiled. "Whyever would you choose that sort of life?"

"Because there are so many mysteries that cannot be explained, I find it comforting to explore those that can."

"I have some friends in law enforcement," the yucky Mr. Thornhill said.

"I'd be glad to ask them to talk with you about it. So that you can make sure what you'd be getting into."

"I have friends in law enforcement myself, thank you very much."

"Sehr," Gran said sternly, "you and I will discuss your friends in law enforcement at some later time. Right now, I think you'd better go to your room. There must be a TV show you want to see."

"They're all reruns." She glared at me, and I could almost see a light ray shoot out from her eyes to pierce mine. "But maybe they'll be better the second time around."

I pushed my chair back from the table.

The creep hopped up and held my chair while I stood. "Thank you," I said. "Good evening, Gran. Mr. Thornhill." I did not tell him it was a pleasure to have met him. The words would have stuck in my throat.

I spent the next two hours in my bedroom in torment, with a water glass to the wall, trying to hear the conversation in the dining room. It's not as if Gran hadn't entertained men before. But they'd all been avuncular types. Actors mainly, filled with funny stories about the profession. And I'd always been encouraged to stay at the table to take part in the talk. I simply didn't like the looks of this Thornhill person. And what annoyed me even more was that he and Gran were speaking in such low tones, I could not decipher one single word.

Finally, I must have dozed. I awoke to Gran's knock at my door. I hopped out of bed and crossed the room to let her in.

"All right for me to join you?" Gran asked, neither frowning nor smiling.

"Of course."

She entered, took a seat on my only stuffed chair, and indicated that I should sit on the bed, which is where I'd nodded off on top of the summer spread.

"Is he gone?"

"Yes."

"Who was he, anyway?"

She smiled. "Roger's another of those ad men who have visions of Aunt Lil Fairchild peddling cheese spreads on billboards." Aunt Lil Fairchild is her popular soap-opera character.

"Usually you don't invite them home," I said.

"Usually they don't ask to be invited. And Roger was rather charming. And he accepted my refusal to do any endorsements with good grace."

"He's a slimeball."

"I hate it when you use words like that. I know you don't get them in school."

It was another dig at Mr. Bloodworth. I wished I could make her understand that Mr. Bloodworth's curses and oaths and negative descriptions paled by comparison with what I heard a hundred times a day at Bay Heights High. Instead of arguing, I said, "I'm sorry I caused you to have such a low opinion of Mr. Bloodworth. He's a wonderful fellow, and I wish you could see that."

"For the life of me, I don't understand what you find so appealing about him and his sordid world."

I'd been saving an answer and this seemed like the best time to deliver it. "I suppose it's the same sort of thing you found so appealing about the theater when you were my age."

She frowned. "But acting is a legitimate profession."

"Not according to Great-Grandma. You've told me again and again the stories about her unsuccessful attempts to keep you in finishing school once you'd appeared in a class production of *Tess of the D'Urbervilles*."

"It was *Trelawny of the Wells*," she said.

"Whatever," I said. "You get the point."

Her eyes started to tear. "I suppose I do, child. I'm just another old fogy. The thing that frightens me is that you're so much more determined and clever than I was. I do want all of your talents to be put to their best use."

"They will be," I said, as she left the chair and sat with me on the bed, putting her arm around me.

I asked, "Will you be seeing that Thornhill again?"

She shrugged. "That is not part of my immediate plans."

I breathed a sigh of relief. She continued, "That's what we have to discuss. Plans." And then she outlined what the near future held for us. It was quite surprising, a mixture of good and bad. I digested the information carefully; then, instead of reacting spontaneously, I said nothing.

Gran seemed a bit unnerved by my lack of emotional response. It was the ideal time for me to, as Mr. B. might put it, cut a deal.

2. "What in the hell are you doing here, kid?" Mr. Bloodworth bellowed as soon as he entered his office the following morning.

"I can see that a night's sleep did nothing to restore your good humor."

He slumped onto a chair across from my desk and his voice went up an octave in a sort of masculine whine. "What the hell are you doing here?" If I hadn't known him better, I'd have thought he was going to cry.

"Don't worry about that fellow who attacked me. I've been very careful all morning."

"Never mind him. You heard what your grandmother said last night."

"She sent me here."

156

"She sent you out? Alone? To come here?"

"She gave me money for a cab. But I didn't want to waste thirty dollars. Anyway, I came to pick up a few things. And, I guess, to say good-bye."

He relaxed noticeably. "Oh. Good-bye, huh? Well, I want to thank you for, uh, all the help you've given me around here."

"I'm going to leave the computer," I said.

"Oh, no. You go ahead and take it. I wouldn't know what to do with it, anyway."

I shook my head. "You don't understand. I'm not going forever."

He frowned. "No?"

"Gran and I made a deal, sort of."

"A deal?"

"Yes. You remember Gene Sokol, the producer of Gran's soap, *Look to Tomorrow*?" He nodded. "Well, Gran said he got this idea for perking up the show by going on location. So he worked out something called 'on-air participation' that involved a barter arrangement with an airline and a hotel and, well, Gran and I are off to London for three weeks."

"Only three weeks?"

"Right. She's ecstatic, and ordinarily I would be, too. Because London is such a wonderfully cold and aloof place, don't you think? Precisely my kind of city. And I've always dreamed of going there. Only there's this problem with Terry Manion. I fear he's in grave trouble. Not to mention his niece."

"Kid, I'm sorry, but I'm not going to go looking for Manion or anybody else. I've got my own problems. Anyway, I'm a businessman. I don't do things for free."

"I could pay you."

"No, you couldn't."

"As I tried to tell you, I didn't provide Lieutenant Cugat with the whole truth about the people who chased me."

He mumbled, "Aw, shit," under his breath, but I could hear it.

"The two of them were inside the house, wiping fingerprints and erasing a phone-message cassette made by a third party. They called him Archie, but I think the Koscas knew him under a different name. George Kerby. They talked about something called the Big One-Oh, whatever that could be."

"Big Ten? Football, maybe. Could be they were talking football."

"Anyhow, they're up to something worth fifteen million dollars, and thousands of lives are at stake. And there's a missing key . . ."

"What about a priceless black bird? There must be one of those in the story, too."

He was being purposely rude. I placed a print-out on his desk. "It's all in here: names, relationships, things that must be done, such as visiting the boutique Wings 'n' Things in an effort to retrace Terry's steps."

He held the print-out but didn't look at it. "Sarah," he said, "I've got some other, more pressing matters."

"You mean that the case that took you to Europe is still, well, ongoing?"

"You could say that. 'Ongoing' would be a good word."

"You didn't solve it, then?"

"Not exactly."

"But when you clean it up, you'll try and find Terry?"

"Maybe. No promises." He paused, frowned. "Why didn't you tell Cugie about seeing them in the house? No, wait a minute. How do you know they were wiping fingerprints? Were you inside the goddamn house?"

"Well," I shrugged, "I found the front door open."

"So you walked in? Jesus, kid. You'll be lucky if you make it to twenty. What happened? Did they spot you in there?"

I shook my head. "I'm pretty sure not. They went out the back, and I snuck out of the front. I was a block away when they drove by. Then the car stopped and the black guy started chasing me."

Mr. Bloodworth scowled again. "So they recognized you from someplace else. Where?"

"I'm sure that I've never seen *them* before in my life."

"Sit tight for a second."

He left the room and entered his private office. I heard drawers opening and slamming shut. In ten minutes he was back with a lump under his coat near his right hip.

"Are you wearing a gun?" I asked.

"Things have been a little weird lately."

"I would not want to think you were wearing a gun for my sake," I told him. I know he is not happy with a weapon on his person.

"There are a number of uncertainties in my life these days," he said. "One will be eliminated when you're on your way to London."

"For three weeks," I said.

"I know."

"After which I will be able to resume my responsibilities here at the agency. That's the deal I made with Gran. I will accompany her to London. But when I return, I shall continue to pursue my chosen field."

"That's then," he said. "This is now. When do you leave?"

"Gran was concerned that our passports would not be current, but I knew they would be. It was only five years ago when we went to Cannes for a television festival. *Très* borrr-ing, as I recall, but I was only a child of ten."

"When do you leave?" he repeated.

"Tomorrow morning," I said. "Eight-fifteen, bright and early."

"Remember Peru De Falco?" he asked.

"Of course," I said. It had only been a year ago when Peru had guarded me for several hours. He was a rather simple, pleasant fellow, who looked remarkably like the actor John Travolta. "Shall we be needing him again?"

"I think so," Mr. Bloodworth replied, picking up the phone and dialing.

"Hello, Mrs. De Falco, this is Leo Bloodworth. Is Peru there? . . . No!!! Now, Mrs. De Falco, I certainly did not tell him to put his fist through that window. It was just a natural reflex. Mrs. De Falco, if I could just speak . . . Really, Mrs. De Falco, six stitches isn't so bad. I once had fourteen down my forearm . . . Mrs. De . . . Oh, hi, Peru . . . How's the hand? Good as new? Great. Great. Listen, I've got another little . . . No, Peru. This is a piece of cake. Remember the Dahlquist girl? Yes, that's right! Peru, I am amazed. That's exactly right. Well, sure, you can watch TV with her like last time. Hang out at her apartment until morning and then drive her and her grandmother to the airport.

"The usual instructions, Peru. Nobody comes into the apartment unless the kid says yes. . . . No, that doesn't include the grandmother, Peru. She sort of has the run of the place, too."

Mr. B. reminded Peru of our address, and then he and Mrs. De Falco, who was her son's business manager, haggled over the cost of the job. When he finally replaced the receiver, I asked, "What happened to Peru's hand?"

"I used him on the Pfeiffer case, which you probably haven't put into your machine yet. It was a very standard situation involving twenty-four-hour surveillance on the Pfeiffer home in Brentwood. Well, I'd just dropped off a burger and shake Peru'd asked for and was walking back to my car to drive home, when Mrs. Pfeiffer came roaring out of her driveway and zoomed off.

"Poor old Peru, caught with one hand on the burger and the other on the shake, decided to toss the burger out of his window, so he could start his car. Only his window was rolled up, and his hand and the burger went right through the safety glass. It must've been that clunky silver ring Peru wears. Anyway, while Mrs. Pfeiffer drove off to God knows where, I was taking Peru to UCLA Emergency." He grinned suddenly. "The cut was fairly clean, but the doctor went white when he saw all the ground beef down Peru's cuff."

He moved toward the door. "Well, c'mon, kid. Time to roll. There's somebody I've got to talk to today about a dead man."

"What?" I leaped from the chair.

"Just a manner of speaking," he said. But I could tell he was annoyed with himself for telling me too much.

"Haven't you forgotten something?" I asked.

He looked at me blanky.

"The print-out with the information you'll need to find Terry."

"Oh, sure," he said. "Just leave it on the desk. I'll pick it up later."

I hoped he really would.

3. He waited with me at our apartment until Peru De Falco arrived, wearing shorts, tennis shoes, a chartreuse T-shirt, and a golden tan. The hand carrying a bright yellow jacket had a purple scar over one knuckle. My little bullterrier, G-2, eyed him suspiciously.

"Hey, everybody. Surf's up. Nice outfit, huh, Leo?" In actuality, he did look quite handsome and virile. If only his IQ had run to three figures.

Mr. Bloodworth raised an eyebrow and grumbled, "This is a bodyguard job, Peru, not beach-blanket bingo."

Peru shrugged, dropped his jacket to the floor, and suddenly there was a large gun in his hand. "The duds are, uh, you know, like the lizard that changes color so it blends in."

"Protective coloring," I said, petting G-2.

"Yeah, exactly."

Mr. Bloodworth shrugged and explained very slowly and carefully what Peru was supposed to do and what he was supposed to look out for—especially a black guy in a black sports car. Peru continued to nod his big head. "Do you want me to capture the dude, Leo?" he asked when Mr. B. stopped talking. G-2 leaped from my arms and began sniffing at Peru's legs. He rubbed up against them, evidently taking Peru for a kindred spirit.

"The important thing is that you don't let him harm Sarah or her grandmother. After that, if you think you can bag him, do. But, Peru, don't take any chances. I don't want your mother phoning me again."

"It's just she loves me, Leo."

"I know."

I said, "On the way to the airport, we'll have to drop G-2 off at the kennel."

Peru looked down at my animal and smiled. "No problem," he said.

"I'm glad to see you're getting more flexible, Peru," Mr. Bloodworth told him.

Peru made a muscle and said, "I'm using the water weights now, Leo. That's why."

Mr. Bloodworth said, "Right," and turned to me. "Have a great time in London, kid. Drop me a line, if you think of it."

"Oh, I'll write often. And I left the number of our flat on that print-out in the office. In case you need to reach me."

He headed for the front door.

"Call me when you find Terry? Please?"

He said, "If I find him, I will."

The door shut behind him without a sound. At least I could rest assured of that one thing. If there was anyone who might stand a chance of discovering the whereabouts of Terry Manion, Leo J. Bloodworth was that man.

20

1. The guy sitting on the industrial-size lawnmower was no help. Neither were the fellows manning the edgers. They were all Orientals whose knowledge of the English language was limited. Or maybe they were pulling my chain. After all, each of them was wearing an orange-and-white T-shirt reading "Haniko's Rising Sons." So somebody must have been putting somebody on.

On first impression, it didn't seem to be Haniko. The oldest Oriental, who was overseeing the replanting of a large shrub near the middle stone and glass portion of Mornay House, knew the lingo, but he didn't have any answers. Or at least none that I wanted to hear.

"I don't know any Horry Brissflierd. I hired by Grover Colpolation. Miss Land."

"What about Miss Mornay?"

"Who?"

"The woman who owns this place. The woman who lives here?"

He grinned at me, two even rows of little brown teeth. "Nobody rives here. This not a prace for riving. Prace for visits. Rots of visitors. Weekends. See sign."

I had seen the sign as I drove up. The last time I'd been to the place, I'd noticed a divot in the lawn beside the wrought-iron gate. Into that divot was now stuck a small, tasteful sign that read: DOCENT TOURS, WEEKENDS, BY APPOINTMENT ONLY, followed by a telephone number that was not the one Holly Blissfield had given me.

There was only one more question for Haniko. "Are all these men really your sons?"

"Do you believe everything you read on T-shirts?" he asked in flawless English.

I figured that was as good an exit line as I was likely to get. On the way out I snooped around a little. The tripart house had plenty of windows to peek into. But as Haniko had said, nobody was living there.

Back in my Chevy I stared moodily at the now-motionless Sentinel camera. On the seat next to me was a copy of the L.A. Times with a small article on page three about an American being shot to death in Italy. Simon "Sandy" Watson was described as a set designer who had been traveling with the rock group Circe on their European tour. If the Venice police were working on any leads, there was no mention of it. The Post would probably give the story a bigger play.

I leaned back against the imitation leather and tried to imagine why somebody had taken such elaborate steps to make me the fall guy for an execution in Venice. I couldn't see it. Not that I didn't have enemies. Everybody has. Only mine didn't happen to have that much imagination.

Ignoring motive for the moment, I took inventory of what information I did have. There was a brunette who was working with Cole Porter and the other killers. She had given them the bogus information about my carrying a gun. Holly Blissfield was surely not her real name. She drove a Mustang convertible, the license plate of which I had neglected to check. But I did have a phone number.

Make that two phone numbers. I copied the one off of the appointment sign. It was possible though not probable that Holly Blissfield actually worked for the Grover Corporation.

There was also Laura Mornay herself. I doubted that she was involved in the scam, but maybe there was a reason her name had been used. It could have been just the availability of her house. Which didn't actually seem to be *her* house. Hell, it was going to be a long day.

2. The phone number I'd used to contact Holly Blissfield was too new to be listed in my street directory, but my AT&T buddy informed me that his files had it registered to a Mr. George Kaplan in Suite C of a recently constructed three-story office building in Santa Monica. The building was so spanking new it smelled of fresh cement. The rental agent on the ground floor didn't think that Mr. Kaplan had moved in yet, and as it turned out, Kaplan hadn't.

The small office was bare. No carpet. No furniture. Just the drapes that the building provided and several telephone sockets, any one of which could have been used to take my messages. There may have been fingerprints, but

I didn't want to have to tell Cugat, or some cop I didn't know, what a donkey I'd been to get myself in this mess.

Kaplan had rented the space by telephone and made a prepayment in cash via the mail, requesting that his keys be placed in an envelope taped to the office door. Yes, this was rather unusual, but with units to fill, a live one is a live one. No, Mr. Kaplan didn't mention what business he was in. That would be on the rental agreement that was forthcoming. Was there something she should know? the rental agent finally asked.

I lied no, and smiled reassuringly. I left her a card and requested that she phone me when Mr. Kaplan finally moved in. She wondered if I might be thinking of relocating my office to a section of town where the air was cleaner. I told her that I might be sharing Mr. Kaplan's space.

3. The gardener Haniko's "Mrs. Land of the Grover Clopolation" turned out to be Mrs. Rand of the Clover Corporation. She was a gentle lady in her sixties who was extremely troubled to hear that some obviously unauthorized person had used Mornay House for a meeting with me.

She sat behind her antique desk in a small office in the bowels of a large black-glass building in the heart of the San Fernando Valley that housed the Clover Corporation, a highly conservative conglomerate that spent its time and energy eating up and spitting out little businesses from as far as Hawaii to the tip of the Alaskan pipeline.

"As I told you, Mr. Bloodworth, personnel has assured me that no one by that name works for Clover. And from your description, I'd say that, by any name, she might even be a little, well, flashy, for us."

"The tinted glasses, you mean?"

"The sports car, actually."

"The Mustang?"

"Right. Our people prefer sedans, except for Mr. Marpelli, who has a Jaguar. It's a convertible. But it's gray. Rather like Mr. Marpelli." She smiled and I made her feel it was infectious. She went on, "His is the only convertible listed with personnel. And if an automobile is not listed with personnel, then it can't be parked on our lot. Which would mean that the poor girl would have to walk miles to the office every day, and therefore . . ."

"I get your drift, Mrs. Rand. But she did have keys to open Mornay House."

"Oh, my! That is a problem. They did not come from us, I wouldn't think. I'm in charge of the docent tours. In fact, I like to be present every now and then. The home is so lovely. It's a nearly exact copy of a Frank Lloyd Wright, you know."

I nodded that I knew. "Your keys are safe?" I asked.

"The Clover Corporation keeps two sets. Kept here, in my desk." She opened the desk and pointed to a little plastic box in which two rings with numerous keys rested.

"How long ago did the Clover Corporation purchase Mornay House?" I asked.

She frowned. "But the corporation has always owned it, Mr. Bloodworth."

"I assumed that Laura Mornay was the owner."

"But she is, of course," Mrs. Rand said, smiling sweetly. "Miss Mornay owns the Clover Corporation."

So the former pinup girl was the chairwoman of the board of one of the most conservative conglomerates in the country. I tried not to snicker. "Then isn't it possible that she may have her own set of keys?"

Mrs. Rand looked puzzled. "I suppose so," she said. "I never really thought about it."

"Didn't you ever ask her?"

"Mr. Bloodworth, I've been working for the Clover Corporation for twenty-seven years, and I have never even *met* Miss Mornay."

"But you do know how to reach her."

"Of course. And I'm afraid I shall have to notify her secretary, Mr. Gollub, of what you've just told me." She frowned. "I shall also have to arrange an inventory. And get the locks changed. Oh, so much work."

"How might I reach Miss Mornay?"

"By phoning here."

"And leaving my name?"

"Precisely. And now I'm afraid I must end our conversation and begin to put Miss Mornay's house back in order." She smiled. "Thank you for taking the time to notify us."

I mumbled some lie or other about being glad to have helped and went on my way.

4. I had been saving the hardest part for last, hoping that I would not have to deal with it. I even put it off long enough to partially devour a Mongolian Beefburger. Carrying a paper plate with the few remaining mouthfuls, I left the Mad Mongol's little white franchised lunchroom and stepped onto the glaring, boiling parking lot of a mini-mall just off of the Ventura Freeway.

A pay phone had been hooked up on the other side of the wall surrounding the lot, equidistant from both entrance and exit, so that if anyone at the mall wanted to use it he'd have to walk nearly a block there and a block back to get his car.

The receiver, which had been getting the full force of the sun, was so hot I couldn't hold it without a handkerchief, and I nearly fried my ear. The phone call was already unpleasant enough, and I hadn't even dialed the number.

I had to go through an operator and two other unidentified parties before reaching Mrs. Van Dine. By then it was time to slip another quarter into the box.

"Mr. Bloodworth, has something happened to my granddaughter?"

"Not at all, ma'am," I said. "In fact, I took the liberty of assigning a very capable man to see to it that no harm befalls her."

"You did what?"

"As you know, your granddaughter was attacked two days ago."

"Yes. I spent a rather unusual night with a strange policeman in our apartment. But he was reassigned, so I assumed that any immediate danger to Sehr had passed."

"Well, it probably has, but I thought we might as well play it safe for the few hours remaining before you leave on your trip tomorrow."

"It will be most inconvenient having to put up with another stranger. Especially with all the packing that must be done."

"He's not a stranger to your granddaughter. He took care of her last year, when you were in the hospital. And he'll be no trouble, I assure you, as long as the TV set works."

"All right," she said in resignation. "How much will this guardian cost me?"

"I'll take care of it."

"You most certainly will not."

So we bounced that one back and forth for a bit before I let her win. She was about to cut me off, when I said, "But the real reason I called was to ask you about one of your, uh, fellow thespians."

"Yesss?" she asked, suspicion in every "s."

"Laura Mornay."

"What did you want to know about her? Has it something to do with Serendipity?"

"No. Not at all. I guess you might say this was personal."

"Oh? I wouldn't have thought her to be your type."

"Not that kind of personal."

"Whatever kind, do not allow yourself to be caught in the same frame with her. She will upstage at any cost. It would not surprise me to see her emulating the late Walter Brennan by performing without her teeth. Why she continues to work at her *advanced* age, with her *considerable* resources, I have no idea."

"I gather she's appearing in something called—" I thought back to what Holly Blissfield had said—"*The Weatherbys.*"

"What is it you want to know?"

"What's *The Weatherbys*?"

She laughed merrily. "Mr. Bloodworth, you are a wonder. I try to isolate myself from the outside world, but you do an infinitely better job of it by not trying. Don't you ever read *Time* or *Newsweek* or *People*?"

"Only when I get a haircut. And then I just look at the pictures."

"*The Weatherbys* is the number-one nighttime series on television. It's not original, of course. Nothing on nighttime is. This is a contemporary version of the old radio serial *One Man's Family*. Unacknowledged, of course."

"That one I remember from when I was a kid. It was on TV, too."

"Yes. It may have been the very first TV soap opera. In any case, that's what *The Weatherbys* is all about. And Laura plays the mother. She should be playing the great-grandmother." She paused, then said, "I'm sorry, but they're calling me back to the set."

"Please. One second. Where do they film it?"

There was a silence. Then she said to someone standing near her, "Please take this and assist this fellow for me."

To me she said, "Dickie will help you, Mr. Bloodworth. I'm sorry, but I must run."

"Thanks, and bon voyage."

Dickie's voice sounded like he pickled it in brine. It had timbre. I told him what I needed. He said he'd call me back within five minutes.

By then my shirt was part of my back, and perspiration had run down my legs and into my shoes. Dickie began by talking some nonsense about video-tape and film that I didn't understand and didn't want to. Then he explained that unlike the daytime soaps, which were taped on network sound-stages, the nighttime serials, with larger budgets, were filmed either on location or in studios rented by the production companies. *The Weatherbys* was produced on film at Solar Studios. Solar was on Gower, not far from the shell that used to house Columbia Pictures before it took off to become part of the Burbank Studios.

Dickie had been efficient enough to call Solar and make sure that La Mornay was on the set. He had even arranged to have a drive-on pass for me. I thanked him for his help and he replied by saying, "Any friend of our Aunt Lil's is a friend of mine."

Sad to say, Aunt Lil was no friend of Laura Mornay's, which I might have guessed by Mrs. Van Dine's comments. La Mornay sat in her air-cooled, rather plush dressing room on Stage 24B at Solar Studios being fussed over by a pretty dark-haired woman in a white uniform.

"Try not ripping out too many of my remaining hairs with that brush, Crystal." Laura Mornay had lots of hair left, and it was still honey-blond, if you believed your eyes. Her face didn't show a wrinkle, even before Crystal began dabbing at it with a makeup brush. And her blue eyes were clear and bright, if a bit frosty. I figured her for at least seventy, but she could have passed for fifty, which I suppose she did every week on the series.

"So," she said, "why did Edie send you to see me, Mr. Bloodworth?"

"She didn't actually send me. I just used her name to get in."

Crystal stopped puttering. Laura Mornay's hand went to the telephone at her side. She said, "Because you're wearing a suit and tie, I will give you one minute to explain before I have you thrown out. Begin."

Talking faster than I usually do, I told her my occupation and how the fake Holly Blissfield had arranged for me to meet her at Mornay House. When I got to the point about the missing earrings, Laura Mornay snapped, "Crystal, I wish to speak to Mr. Bloodworth alone. I'll call for you."

Crystal shrugged. Before she made her exit, she paused and stared at me. "You know," she said, touching my cheek, "with just a few moves, I could take off five pounds."

"I bet you could," I told her.

Smiling, she went through the door.

Laura Mornay, on the other hand, was not amused. She was, in fact, very annoyed, but it showed only in her eyes, not her face. She'd learned long ago that frowning causes wrinkles. "Who did this Blissfield woman say stole my earrings?"

I hedged. There were already too many people who could connect me to the late Simon "Sandy" Watson. "I don't think the fellow she named had anything to do with you or your jewelry."

"He did if the name was Ernie Mott."

I was more than mildly surprised. "Somebody *did* steal your earrings?"

"That bastard!" She pulled herself together and said, "I suppose I got off cheaply. They were only worth fifty thousand, and all but a thousand of that was covered by my insurance. He could have gotten much more. An older woman sometimes makes mistakes. Costly mistakes."

"When did it happen?"

"A little over a year ago," she said. "I met Ernie on the Fourth of July weekend at one of those crowd scenes at Wally Barclay's. I've always wondered if Wally, the son of a bitch, didn't engineer the whole thing for his own amusement. He and his crowd are great practical jokers."

"Who's Wally Barclay?"

She smiled. "I suppose that depends on who you ask. To the freeloaders and sycophants who flock to his manse in the Malibu Hills for his weekend parties, he's the reincarnation of Jay Gatsby. To the investors in his various enterprises—which change daily, I should add—he's a miracle worker. To the women who have dallied for a night in his ornate bedroom—and their number is legion—he is Casanova incarnate. To the police, he is . . . well, suspect. He has been involved in a number of dubious enterprises.

"No one knows where the hell he got his money. He just showed up on this coast in the late seventies, filthy rich and full of nice ideas on how to turn a hundred dollars into a thousand dollars. What he'd been up to before that remains a mystery. And believe me, efforts have been made to find out."

"What do you think?"

"My vote would be for Mafia front man, but I'm an incurable romantic."

"So you met this Mott character at one of Barclay's blowouts. And he stole your earrings?"

"There was a bit more to it than that," she said.

"I suppose you tried to get them back?"

"Yes, of course. I went to the police. Filled out their forms. Gave them a detailed description of Ernie. They did the usual things. Nothing came of it, of course. The earrings were never pawned or sold, at least not in their original form."

"Did you tell many people about the theft?" I asked.

"Did I tell my friends that a stray that I had taken into my home pissed on my carpet? Indeed I did not."

"How many people, precisely, knew about the theft?"

"There is Emma Burditt, my assistant. And the police." She paused and stared at me, finally getting the point. "What you're thinking is that if this Blissfield woman mentioned the theft . . ."

"She must have heard about it from someone. Maybe you."

"In this business I meet women like the one you described all the time. But as I said, I do not talk about my dirty linen to people I barely know. Present company excepted," she added with a hint of a smile.

"Maybe Emma Burditt . . . ?"

"She has been with me since *Down Caliente Way*, a 1942 Technicolor musical and one of my best. Totally loyal. Totally trustworthy."

"She couldn't have let the news slip?"

"Mr. Bloodworth, we live in an age where reporters are like hungry dogs sniffing at scraps from the table. No mention was made of the incident in the *Enquirer* or any other tabloid, so I think we can assume that no one in my employ let the news slip. If they had, they would no longer be in my employ."

"What did Barclay have to say?"

"About what?"

"About Mott."

"Oh, well, of course I called to ask him if he'd seen Ernie lately, and Wally replied in his often infuriating manner that he had seen neither hide nor hair of him since he'd left the party with me."

"How well did he know Ernie?"

"I didn't ask. As I said, I did not want to involve my friends in this sordid little nastiness."

"You mentioned the earrings were insured. Maybe your agent discussed the theft with someone."

"That's beyond our knowing. Philip Marton, who handled my insurance, passed away several months ago."

"Natural?" I asked.

"All too natural. He died of a massive coronary in a motel in Palm Springs. Though there was nothing in the papers about it, the rumor was that he died 'in the saddle,' I think the phrase is. A man in his sixties, trying to keep up with some little teen trollop, probably."

I said, "So that leaves Ernie Mott as the man most likely to have told Blissfield about the robbery. It would be neater if Mott stole the keys to Mornay House when he lifted your earrings."

She raised one eyebrow, breaking the placid exterior of her face for the first time since I'd met her. "I did have a set of keys, but I haven't thought about them for ages. I never think about Mornay House. It served its purpose for a while, but it was much too spacious for me. I couldn't bring myself to sell it. Besides, this way, my neighbors, who tried to stop my building there in the first place, now have to put up with the unwashed public parking along the street and wandering past their property to tour mine."

"Miss Mornay, I'm getting the impression you don't forget old wounds." She didn't reply, just stared at me. "So I'm sort of surprised you didn't try a little harder to find Mott."

"I left that to the police. They're supposed to be better at that game than I."

I cleared my throat and asked, "Did you consider hiring someone who could put in more time on the investigation than the police?"

She smiled at me. "Finally, the businessman emerges," she said. "Is that why you came here, to seek employment?"

"No. That just occurred to me."

"But whether I hire you or not, you're still going to try and find Mott."

I'd forgotten for a moment that she was a captain of industry. "Sure," I said. "And I will get him. If he's the guy who's making trouble for me, I'll put him away. But if he's only a small fish, I'll probably just ask him a few questions and toss him back into the pond. If I'm in your employ, I'll throw him your way."

"I would guess he is the man you want. He's arrogant, clever, and devious. The little Cockney bastard."

"Cockney? You mean British?"

"Usually they go together. And before you ask, it's Cockney and not Aussie. Actors can tell the difference."

"I don't suppose you'd have a picture of him?"

She shook her head. "Really, Mr. Bloodworth. Would you draw a revolver if you didn't plan to use it?"

I shook my head.

"I feel the same way about photographs. As an actress, it may even be good business to be seen in magazines and newspapers with younger, incredibly handsome men. But as a chairwoman of the board of a company that will soon go public, I prefer to be depicted demurely in a setting so goddamn classy it'd make Jane Russell look piss-elegant."

"You used the words 'little Cockney bastard.' Are you being literal? Is he short, skinny, what?"

"He's average height actually, and dark, and very, very handsome. Boyish, but not a boy. Just starting to lose a little muscle tone. Forties, I'd say. Dresses casually but expensively. Black curly hair. Green eyes. And virile. Very virile." She paused. "What do you charge, Mr. Bloodworth?"

I threw out a figure. She said it was too high, which was true. We finally agreed on a daily rate that was close to what I usually get. We shook hands and she said, "I'd appreciate your calling a Miss Rand at the Clover Corporation and telling her to change the locks on Mornay House." It was a nice way of establishing the employer-employee relationship. I didn't bother telling her that the mission had already been accomplished.

Just before leaving, I said, "It might help if I talked to the cops who handled the burglary."

"It was the Beverly Hills Police Department," she said. "A lieutenant with a wonderful name. Dove. Dove something."

I was sorry I'd asked.

21

1. We were to learn much later that it was the sight of his wife, the beloved Gil, that brought about Terry Manion's plight. Some men simply become enslaved to a woman. And I'm afraid that this was Terry's failing. But I am getting ahead of myself.

As I had assumed, the day after our Creole Café dinner Terry visited Wings 'n' Things, the feather boutique, searching for his niece, Cece Mac-Elroy. He learned only that the late private detective Mike Kosca had been there and left a picture of Cece. The people in the shop knew nothing more about either Kosca or the young woman, although one of the shop's suppliers chatted with him for a while.

While walking along Melrose Avenue to his rented car, Terry was stunned to see, on the other side of the street, the image of the woman he loved and had lost, his ex-wife, Gillian, parked in a Rolls Royce Silver Cloud convertible. She was talking with another young woman, who was standing beside the car.

As Terry approached, refusing to believe his eyes, the blonde started the car and drove off into the noontime traffic. Terry began to chase after the car, but it was a futile gesture. As the Rolls disappeared down Melrose, Terry saw the other woman enter a building that had no sign in front.

It was a restaurant named Angeli's, where the waiters wore T-shirts with drawings of angels' wings on their backs. It was early enough for the woman to find an empty table. Terry sat down beside her.

Her initial annoyance disappeared when he asked her if the blonde she'd just spoken to was named Gillian. She nodded. Was she from New Orleans? Then he *did* know Gil. Terry said that he did, that Gil was an old friend, and that he was surprised to see her in Los Angeles. The woman relaxed. She introduced herself as Dora. A waiter came. They ordered.

Dora explained that she had only met Gil a few weeks before. She didn't know where Gil lived actually, but there were friends who did know. Was Gil living alone? Terry asked. Dora wasn't sure, but assumed she was.

It was only when he was halfway through the meal that Terry began to notice Dora's features. She was a handsome woman, almost as tall as he, with long brunette hair and a full figure. She said she would try to find Gillian's L.A. address for him.

That night she called, suggesting that they go to a party where Gil might be. It was in the Hollywood Hills, in a large stone-and-glass home belonging to a pale little man who composed music for films. Separating the Hockneys and the Ruschas on his walls were gold records mounted on black wood.

Gil was not there. But they were informed she would be.

What Terry had not told me, and there had been no reason for him to, was that he was a recovering alcoholic. At the party he took his first drink in over two years. The results were predictable.

He awoke the next morning in a house he assumed was Dora's. His suitcase was at the foot of the bed. Someone had packed his clothes and checked him out of the Mariposa Hotel. (The clerk said Terry had done it himself, but there were reasons enough to disbelieve much of what the clerk said.) Dora arrived before he could get out of bed, arms filled with bags of groceries. She prepared his breakfast, after which he fell into a long, dreamless sleep.

When he awoke, it was evening. He was groggy and disoriented. Through the closed bedroom door he could hear other people in the house. He found his pants and shirt in a closet and threw them on, wandering out to be greeted by a crowd of unfamiliar faces and another party.

The room seemed to open into a garden where smiling people sat beside flowing water.

More cocktails.

More sleep.

This time when he awoke, he was not alone in the room. In the moonlight he saw a woman seated beside his bed. She was wearing a shimmering gown that reminded him of the gown his wife, Gillian, had worn on their honeymoon in South America. Then Gillian's beautiful face turned toward him and broke into a smile. The woman stood, glided to the bed, her arms outstretched. He felt her press against him.

With joy in his heart he fell into the abyss.

2. Of course, I knew nothing of the evil that had engulfed Terry Manion. I was with Gran in London, having a wonderful time in spite of the fact that the smarmy Mr. Thornhill had arranged to have a bouquet of pink roses waiting at our flat, with a note that read: "Have you just arrived? It seems as if you've been gone a lifetime." Barfburgers!

There had been photographers snapping away as we stepped into our limousine at Heathrow, and photographers nearly everywhere we went for the first few days. One story in a tabloid even mentioned the book that I had written with Mr. Bloodworth, labeling me "a teenage P.D. James," which I am sure Ms. James appreciated even less than I.

Gran's producer, Gene Sokol, and his staff, were spending the better part of the first week busily peparing for the location taping at Stratford Studios. That meant that Gran and I, and a friend of mine, Linda de Carlo, who, though twenty-one years of age, plays the teen vamp on the series, had oodles of free time to wander about that wonderful city. And we were having a rather giddy time, trying to do it while avoiding the ubiquitous photographers.

That day, I was able to convince Gran and Linda that a planned shopping spree would be sure to bring out all sorts of paparazzi, and so, instead, we dressed down and took a walking tour of Sherlock Holmes's London, beginning at the Baker Street Underground station, which houses ceramic tiles depicting several of the great detective's most popular cases. We also walked to the approximate location of 221b Baker Street, which never really existed, of course, either as an address or a flat for the world's greatest consulting detective. Today, the area is the headquarters of the Abbey National Building Society, whatever that is. There is supposed to be a hireling of the society who does nothing but answer tourist questions about Doyle and Holmes, but the traffic was so awful that we never actually were able to cross the street to see for ourselves. In any case, it was invigorating and inspirational just to be traveling in the footsteps of that legendary sleuth.

Finally, when the tour passed the Criterion Brasserie in Piccadilly Circus, where a plaque commemorated Dr. Watson's first hearing about a man called Sherlock Holmes, Gran suggested we call it a day and have an early dinner. I think she and Linda were both a trifle miffed because not even one person recognized them on the tour.

While we gorged ourselves on delicious roast beef—the notion that British food is somewhat lacking in flavor is a canard—I suppose that poor Terry Manion was sinking ever deeper into the black morass that had been carefully prepared for him.

22

1. "Jesus Cristo, Hound. What makes you think *I* want to talk to that *cabrón*?" Rudy Cugat asked.

"He's a fellow officer," I told him.

"Not for much longer, I hope." I had caught up with the Lothario of the Bay City Police Department at an oceanfront restaurant called the Red Head, run by a salty old dame named Lolly, whose hair, they say, was a bright, Maureen O'Hara auburn before it turned gray sometime during the Eisenhower administration. (No cause and effect there that I know of.)

Cugie sawed at his T-bone. I smiled at him and the brassy blonde sitting next to him in the curtained booth that Lolly calls the Honeymoon Express. "How'd you find me, anyway?" he asked.

"I called your home," I said innocently.

"You're as funny as a burning orphanage, you son of a bitch," he hissed.

"Actually, I spotted your car out front. I'd already cruised past most of your other, uh, haunts."

"This is really important for you? To get the report on a robbery committed a year ago?"

"Would I disturb you two police persons for anything less than crucial?"

He made a show of dabbing at his lips and new moustache, then placed the napkin just so on the table beside his half-eaten steak. He stood up, adjusted the crease in his pale pink trousers, and said, "I'll be just a minute," to whoever happened to be listening in that cubicle.

"Tell him to leave the report at the front desk and a messenger will pick it up. I'll be the messenger."

When the curtain had swished back into place behind him, I asked the blonde, "You really a cop?"

She stuck her hand into her purse and drew out a shield that she waved in front of my face.

"He used to take his meals with a fat plainclothesman named Ambersen," I said. "You're much more appetizing."

She didn't thank me for the compliment. She took another bite of her steak and said around it, "Amby got blown away on the pier couple months ago. Junkie with a popgun. Amby wasn't on duty or nothing, just putting his granddaughter on the flying horses. Tried to take the guy and the guy took him. Broke Rudy up pretty bad for a while. He and Amby'd been partners for a lot of years."

I obviously hadn't heard about it. Maybe Edith Van Dine was right: I was cutting myself off from the world around me. I rarely read a paper or listened to the news. I used the TV Sarah had given me for my birthday mainly for late movies when I couldn't sleep.

"You used to be his partner, too, right?" she asked.

I nodded. "A while back."

"I guess you could say Rudy 'n' me are partners now," she said, then chuckled to herself.

The man of the hour returned with a smile. "The bastard Hilbert wasn't there," he said. "So I got some stooge to pull the sheet. It'll be ready for you by the time you get there. Don't be in any hurry to leave."

I watched him sit, replace his napkin across his knees, and pick up his fork. "What about those names I gave you yesterday?"

He stared at me without expression. "You're starting to piss me off."

"If you don't ask, you don't get."

"How are we on favors, anyway?" he wondered.

"I think you're still down a few."

"You're gonna have to call me at work tomorrow, Hound. The only report I got back was on the three names from the passport agency."

"Should I beg for that?"

He shook his head. "I wouldn't. They didn't have nothing. The computer says no passports were issued to any of those names."

"But I saw the customs guy glom them and stamp them."

Cugie shook his head in disgust. "My people, they have trouble getting in with *real* passports."

"This was in Italy," I said.

He laughed. "Hound, you continue to amaze me. I hate to destroy a man's illusions, but there are such things as fake passports."

"Yeah, I know, but . . ."

"Please. Call tomorrow. Good evening, Hound. My steak is starting to congeal."

"I was hoping you'd offer me one."

"A steak? But of course. If you'll eat it out there."

I told him I'd take a rain check.

2. My plan was to hotfoot it into the Beverly Hills Police Department, shag the robbery report, and move out sharply. The worst fear I had was that I would bump into Hilbert.

Instead, he bumped into me. Almost. I'd picked up the report and was on my way back to my car when a polished black Ford Taurus swung into a reserved parking space and jerked to a stop about two inches shy of my knees. It was an indication of the sharpness of my reflexes that I didn't even make an attempt to jump back. I just stood there, with the adrenaline pumping through my veins, while Dove Hilbert pushed open his car door and stumbled out from behind the wheel.

My first assumption was that he'd been trying to scare me. Another example of his perverted sense of humor. But he didn't seem to realize that I or anybody else had been standing there. He turned to the girl in the passenger seat and said, "I'll be right out."

As he circled his car, I sidestepped into his path. He didn't understand I'd done it on purpose, because he tried to avoid me. "You playing games with me, Hilbert?" I snarled at him.

"Huh?" His head jerked around to look at me. "Who . . . ? Blood-worth?"

I heard the other car door open and slam. I continued watching Hilbert. His eyes were glassy behind his specs. His clothes looked rumpled. A boozer on a binge was the general overall impression.

"You got a hell of a nerve driving a car in this condition," I grumbled.

"Condition?"

"You're skunk-drunk, you son of a bitch."

"Drunk? I haven't been drinking. Tell this bastard!" His command was directed at the young woman leaning against his front fender. She said, "I never talk to bastards I haven't met, Dove. Maybe you'd better introduce us, first."

She was of average height, but that was the only average thing about her. Amber hair falling over one eye. Some tan, but not enough to make you think she worked at it. Her formidable but not overwhelming body was wrapped in a long black T-shirt with a little padding at the shoulders and a full black skirt with bright flowers on it. Her legs, which might have been carved out of a flawless block of teak by a guy who knew his business, were bare to her black pumps.

She wore just a touch of makeup and a soft pink lipstick that glistened in the rays of the setting sun.

Hilbert shook his head. "The hell I'll introduce you. I know you, dear. Just because I hate this bastard's guts, you'd have him on the backseat of my car before I could get my office door unlocked."

He staggered off in the direction of the building, paused at the entrance to look back at us, and then pushed unsteadily through the front door.

"When did he start hitting the hooch like that?" I asked the girl.

"He hasn't been drinking. At least not in the last two hours."

"Then what's the matter with him?"

She shrugged. "I don't know. He's been stressed out. They want him to retire. He's got a meeting now with Chief of Police Collander."

"He should make quite an impression," I said. I took a few steps toward the car. The setting sun had moved inside her soft brown eyes. "You're what, his daughter?"

"Do you see any family resemblance?" she asked with a smile.

I sighed and shook my head.

"Just a friend," she said.

"Sorry. I don't try to be a jerk, but sometimes it just comes naturally."

I gave a little wave and went on my way.

"Did . . . did Dove say your name was Bloodworth?"

I turned.

"He may have. That's what it is. Leo Bloodworth."

She put out her hand. I slipped the envelope containing the robbery report into my pocket. Her delicate-looking hand, when I shook it, was surprisingly strong. "Hannah Reyne," she said.

"Good meeting you, Hannah." I started backing away. "If I were you, I wouldn't let your *friend* drive tonight."

She stopped smiling and said, "How's your driving?"

"Very few complaints."

"Give a girl a lift?"

"I don't think Hilbert would like that."

"Would that upset you?"

"Not particularly."

"Maybe you're afraid of him?"

"Same answer."

"Then why mention it?"

I shrugged.

She grinned. "Oh. It was his comment about our making it on the floor of his car. You think the only reason I'm flirting with you is because he hates you? To make him mad?"

"Honey, I have about as much vanity as the next guy. If you'd spend time with an over-the-hill grade-A schmuck like Hilbert, I've gotta believe I could be in the running."

"Maybe I like older men."

"Dove's got me beat there."

"But you're cuter," she said. She stepped forward and kissed me on the lips, holding my face tightly, as if, for some absurd reason, I might want to pull away.

Finally, she stepped back. "I'm impulsive," she said.

"And I'm driving," I replied.

3. We ate at a place called the Pirate's Cove in Santa Monica, a hole-in-the-wall run by a deep-sea diver named Bill Stewall who arranged underwater stunts for the movies. His mother used to do all the cooking when there were only five tables in the joint. Then, there were about twenty, and a row of booths along one wall, and sawdust on the floor and three waitresses in tiny cutoffs and blouses and black hats with the skull and crossbones on them. Several chefs prepped the food while Mom Stewall sat all evening at the cash register making it ring like a grand piano.

Bill's bearded, demonic face greeted us at the door. He leered at Hannah and said, "How you doing, sweet thing?"

She looked from him to me.

"Bill, this is Hannah. Hannah, Bill."

"Oh, I know Hannah," he said. "Didn't we meet on that movie about the Bermuda Triangle? What was it? Yeah, *Triangle of Terror*."

She shook her head.

"Then maybe it was . . ."

"I'm not an actress," she said.

"Oh, hell, I don't believe that. Hound, is this beautiful woman really robbing the movie-going public of her radiance?"

I shrugged, hoping that he'd seat us before we starved to death.

"What do you do?" he asked her.

She smiled at him. "I'm at Midtown Clinic. We're working with the AIDS virus."

Bill's face paled slightly and he moved back from us. He said, "Uh, Hound, we're a little crowded tonight . . ."

"The back booth is empty," I said, moving around him and pulling Hannah with me.

Bill let us go. By the time we were seated, he'd sent a waitress over for our order. He didn't want us to stick around.

When the waitress had gone for our drinks, I said, "Where *do* you work?"

She raised an eyebrow. "What makes you think I was lying to your friend?"

"Your nice long fingernails. People who handle test tubes usually keep 'em clipped. Less breakage. Especially if you're playing with deadly germs."

"Try to fool a detective, huh?" She smiled, took a cigarette from her purse.

"Well?" I asked.

"I don't work," she said. "I guess you might say I'm an heiress. My father, my late father, was in oil. That makes him sound as if he were a sardine or something, but I think you know what I mean."

"From what I hear, oil isn't a good thing to be in right now."

"Just a temporary setback," she said. "Unless they can come up with something better."

Our pirate waitress was back, placing our drinks before us and scurrying away with our food order, staring at Hannah with a mixture of horror and sympathy. Bill had passed on the AIDS story.

"I suppose the lab boys will, one of these days, come up with a microchip that will send a Chevy into outer space on a gallon of gas and a quart of oil," I said, resuming our conversation. "And you'll have to get a job."

"By then I'll be too old to work."

I clinked my frosted glass of Harp against her white wine. "To science," I said.

She stopped smiling and put down her glass. "Let's try for something more positive than that," she said. "To us."

"To us," I repeated, and took my first swallow of the evening.

She looked at me over her glass of wine. "Leo, I was just wondering . . ."

"What?"

"What is it with you and Dove?"

I smiled. "Simply put: bad blood. We can't stand each other."

"But you were looking for him tonight."

I shook my head. "No, ma'am. I was not. In fact, I made a genuine effort not to meet up with him."

"Then what were you doing there?"

"I needed a copy of an accident report."

"Was it one of Dove's reports?"

"I didn't drive you all the way to the ocean to talk about Hilbert, for Chrissake," I said.

She started to say something, but our piratess was headed toward us with a tray full of seafood. Hannah stood up. "Little girls' room?"

I pointed in the direction of a poster of the old movie *The Third Man* on the side wall. "Just follow Joseph Cotten's gun," I told her.

4. Rolling away from the Pirate's Cove, three beers and a big swordfish steak under my belt and a beautiful young woman sitting closer to me than the front seat of the Chevy demanded, I was feeling dangerously relaxed. Not as dangerously relaxed as I would have felt had I had four or five beers, like the good old days of yore. But the truth was, any more than three and my driving suffered. With age had come a sense of responsibility. I didn't want either of them, but I was stuck with both.

Hannah's home was in Laurel Canyon—almost at the top—a small, one-story wooden affair up a flight of stairs from an open two-car garage that was occupied by a cream-colored Toyota convertible that I assumed was the heiress's, and a black Ford Taurus that meant trouble.

I said, "Looks like you've got company."

I parked on the road blocking the convertible. The Taurus's hood was still warm. And there was something else. The front right fender was pushed in, the head lamp cracked and jagged like an abstract jack-o'-lantern.

"He's not supposed to be here," Hannah said furiously, just before she rushed up the stairs leading to her front door.

By the time I reached the door, she was inside and storming through the house.

Twin swag lamps illuminated a living room with pale rose walls and, I suppose, antique chairs, and a rose-and-white striped sofa. I moved through it and the next—a dining room with a long, elaborate table that looked as if it might have started out in some state park before a decorator treated it to an expensive stain and created chairs to match. Finally, I caught up with her at the rear of the place, standing at the open French doors, looking out past a short wooden deck to a small, rocky waterfall that splashed into a tiny lagoon, all man-made, of course. The moonlight turned the cascading water into slivers of glass.

Dove Hilbert was in the water, his head resting against a protruding rock. The ripples caused by the waterfall broke against his chin. I pushed past Hannah and rushed to him. His shirt collar had become snagged on a gizmo that measures water temperature. I yanked it free and dragged the half-drowned son of a bitch onto the patch of grass bordering the lagoon.

Hannah stood over us while I checked his pulse and made sure he was still breathing. I said, "He's your friend, lady. If you're expecting any mouth-to-mouth resuscitation, you'd better pucker up."

She knelt down. "What do I do?"

I started to unbutton Hilbert's collar, and he turned his head and got rid of about a gallon of water and other bits of flotsam and jetsam. Hannah and I reacted naturally by leaping out of the way. Not that Hilbert minded. He rolled over on his side, moaned, and said, "Glasses."

I looked into the fake lagoon. "You can dive for them when you're feeling better," I said.

He tried to sit up. I reached out a hand, but he shook his head. "Hannah . . ." he groaned.

She moved to help him. I sat down on the deck and let my pants and shoes drain. My whole wardrobe was getting waterlogged. Maybe I'd buy my next suit at a scuba shop.

Hilbert tried to push himself off the grass, but his hand slipped and he fell back down, hard. Hannah grabbed him under his arms. He looked at her and, so help me, he started to bawl like a baby. "I need . . ." he began.

"Shhhh, honey. I know what you need," she said.

I left them there. I didn't care how his car got banged up, or why he'd wound up in the pond. I didn't care about him. I didn't care about her. I didn't care that I'd just wasted eighty-five bucks on dinner and drinks at the Pirate's Cove. Well, maybe I did care about that.

23

1. The half-mad, tormented creature placed the frail young woman in his canoe-looking boat and sailed away with her through an underground river aglow with lighted candles. The orchestra played a bone-chilling dirge, and the curtain descended. This was theater!

Eagerly, I turned to Gran. "Isn't it wondrously morbid and depraved?" I asked.

"Yes, dear," she said distractedly. She turned to Carol Taylor-Bright, the very *distingué* gentleman in the exquisitely tailored three-piece suit sitting beside her. "Sort of an oil-for-the-lamps-of-China motif, wouldn't you say, Carol?"

He chuckled. "Enough candlepower to light Piccadilly."

"Or Rockefeller Center on Christmas Eve," she said, shaking her head. "Am I wrong, or did they in their haste to create their amazing sets forget to give the actors anything to do?"

"It's a smash, Edie," Carol Taylor-Bright replied with a shrug.

"So was *Hellzapoppin,* but they didn't try to call that *theater.*"

"Can we go to the Tower of London tomorrow?"

"In a word, no, dear."

"Why not?"

"Because I'm working. We're starting to tape tomorrow."

"Then maybe if Linda's free, she and I . . ."

"Linda is going for a drive in the country with that Lord something—what is his name, Carol?"

"Lord Everett Mortmain, I believe, of the Devery-Mortmains. He's scandalized the family by going into videos."

"Directing them?"

"Selling them. Edie, would you care for a bit of grape?"

"No thank you, Carol."

"Miss Knickers?"

Carol has called me that ever since he visited us once in the States and I . . . Never mind. It's a dumb story. It's a dumb nickname, too. But Carol never seems to tire of using it. "No thanks, Kay-roll. No booze for me. I'm driving."

He shook his head good-naturedly. "Edie, can't you get the little vixen to pronounce my name correctly?"

"Blame it on her youth, Carol."

As he moved off to the bar, Gran said, "If that silly nickname annoys you, why not tell Carol? He's a perfect gentleman. He'd stop using it immediately."

"I thought I'd try a little subtlety on him first. Gran, could I possibly visit the Tower myself?"

"Dear, we've been on the Sherlock Holmes tour. We've been to Madame Tussaud's. You dragged us to that dreary seminar in which that fellow with the impossible toupee tried to prove that everyone from Disraeli to the queen mother was Jack the Ripper. I really think I have been quite patient."

"But we're going home soon and London Tower is so . . . historic."

"I know you, Sehr. You care as much about history as I do about basketball. You're only interested in visiting a place where women were beheaded."

"Not only the women," I said, "but the killing of those poor dear little princes."

She paused and drifted away for a second. "Your grandfather was a wonderful Richard the Third."

"I read a book by Josephine Tey that suggested that it may not have been Richard who had the princes killed."

She looked at me. "A book by whom?" she asked.

"Josephine Tey. A marvelous mystery writer."

"Oh," Gran said, losing interest. "Fiction."

Later that evening, in Carol's smashing mint-green Bentley, I broached the subject of the Tower again. As I thought he might, Carol offered to take me, but he would not be free for another three days. Carol is some big mucky-muck in British theatrical circles. A producer, at the very least. He and Gran have been friends for eons. And he in fact made arrangements for us to stay in a marvelous flat on Ridpath Road in Chelsea, in the same apartment where Angela Lansbury lived when she was appearing on stage there. (Needless to say, I am a great fan of Miss Lansbury's television series, she being the only female sleuth on the air and a mystery novelist to boot, talk about audience empathy.)

I said that I would not mind waiting three days at all. Carol was a good fellow and very pleasant company. I steeled myself and did not wince when he left us at the door to our flat with a "Till Thursday at noon, then, Miss Knickers."

2. There is a set at Stratford Television that supposedly is a replica of an office at old Scotland Yard—with antiquey furnishings—that was once used for a comedy series titled *Howard of the Yard*. Numbered among its contents were a comfortable if creaky wooden desk chair, a little footstool, and a rather good reading lamp with a green shade. When Gran wandered off to her location shoots, I'd hie to my office at the Yard to systematically devour by dates of publication my new collection of mysteries by British novelists such as Margery Allingham and Ngaio Marsh.

The day after our evening at the theater a rather odd thing happened. I was deeply engrossed in *The Crime at Black Dudley*, when I became aware of someone clearing her throat near the desk.

It was one of the staff girls who'd been assigned to the show. Shandee Buffin. An odd name. But so many of the women in British television seemed to have odd names. She had brightly hennaed hair and wore a mauve jumpsuit with a "StraTV" emblem on top of her right breast. I doubted that she was more than a year or two older than I. But, I realized rather wistfully, she had the breasts of a twenty-year-old.

"Been looking all over for you," she said in a slightly nasal voice.

"What's up? Has my grandmother returned?"

"Not for hours yet, luv. Busy day, today. But there is someone for you at recep."

"For me? Who?"

"A young woman named . . ." She searched her jacket pocket.

". . . Smith."

"Did she say what she wanted?"

" 'Fraid not. Should I ask?"

"No," I said, hopping to my feet. "I'll go see."

She led me down long, high-ceilinged corridors smelling of sawdust into little office warrens inhabited by men and women so busy I hoped that their activity was more meaningful than it looked.

Eventually we arrived at a door with a tiny shatterproof glass window, which Shandee unlocked.

Beyond the door was the reception area—a large oval room painted in purple and mauve, beyond which was the glass entrance to the building.

"Over there," Shandee said, indicating a woman in her thirties standing near the front door. She was rather tall—a blonde with plain glasses. Everything about her was plain. Her hair was lifeless and dropped to her shoulders without interruption. Her green-and-gray dress, though Kamalilike, hung on her ordinary frame without making any sort of statement. Her shoes were, to be blunt, sensible walkers.

She looked my way, smiled, and waited for me to cross the reception area. "Serendipity Dahlquist, am I right?" The accent was not American, but I wasn't sure that it was British.

"That's me."

"There *is* quite a bit of Edie in you, all right. I don't suppose you remember me."

She did look vaguely familiar. I said, "Who are you?"

"Ah. Of course. My name is Smith. Sally Smith."

"And we've met?"

She smiled, showing me rather nice teeth. "You were a very little girl. Your grandmother and I were appearing in a terrible Movie of the Week about people trapped in a subway, and we had dinner at La Scala and you were very picky and refused to eat your peas."

"That sounds like me, all right."

"Well, I stopped by to see if your grandmother was available for tea, and she wasn't. So I thought, why not ask Serendipity? I saw that picture of you and Edie in the *Telegraph*."

"Tea would be nice, but Gran specifically asked me to stay here and wait for her."

Sally Smith took my hand and started leading me to the front doors. A dark sedan was parked just beyond it. Sally Smith said, "Nonsense. It's high time we got to know one another better. And you can fill me in on what Edie has been up to since I saw her last."

I pulled away from her. "I . . . uh, don't think I'd better," I said. "Not without phoning Gran to tell her where I'd be."

Sally Smith paused, glanced at the car through the glass doors, and seemed to be concentrating feverishly. Then she relaxed, and said, "I'm sorry. I didn't mean to seem so . . . pushy. I hope I didn't upset you, Serendipity."

"I'm not upset."

"I suppose I didn't realize how young you were, that you needed permission for a little cup of tea."

"I'm not sure age has anything to do with it. I obey my grandmother," I told her, which was pretty nearly the truth. "And she specifically told me to wait for her here."

Sally Smith nodded. Outside, a car horn started to blare. She looked at the black sedan nervously and then back to me. "Well," she said, "this hasn't been one of my better ideas."

"Maybe tomorrow both Gran and I could join you."

"Tomorrow . . . I will be gone. Well, tell her 'hello from Sally.'"

She gave me a very faint smile and left. I watched her get into the sedan, which roared off. Angrily, it seemed to me.

That evening I gave Gran Sally Smith's "hello." She allowed as how she probably had met one or two Sally Smiths over the years, but she didn't remember having acted with one in any Movie of the Week.

"In fact, I don't recall any Movie of the Week where I was trapped in a subway. There was one where several of us were caught beneath an ice floe in a bathysphere."

"Maybe that was it," I said.

She paced a bit, asked me a few more questions, and then picked up the phone and dialed a number.

"Hello . . . Is Bernie still there? This is Edith Van Dine. Would you get him, please?" She looked at me and fluttered her eyelids to indicate that everything in the world took time, even if your name was Edith Van Dine. "Bernie? This is Mrs. Van Dine, right. Bernie, I want no more mention of me or my granddaughter in any of the British papers . . . Well, no, I understand you can't stop them from doing what they do. I just don't want to encourage them. I do not want photographers showing up unexpectedly on location shoots, or when we're out having dinner. Yes, Bernie, I realize that it's your job to get publicity for the series, but not at the expense of me or my family. Too many strange people get even stranger ideas when they see celebrity pictures in the newspaper." She stared straight at me. "No. Nothing specific. Just keep the newsmen away. Thank you, Bernie."

She replaced the receiver and said, "I'm sorry, dear. Hooray for Hollywood and all that."

24

1. "I don't know what you expect me to do for you," I was saying. "I don't know why I should do anything."

Dove Hilbert was sitting on a streamlined leather sofa that didn't seem to have any legs. We were in Century City, up seventeen stories, looking out over Avenue of the Stars at another building that probably officed just as many lawyers as ours, with just as many high-tech furnishings.

Dove didn't look like he'd slept much since the night before. I, on the other hand, had been doing just fine in that department until his barrister, T. Landrew Marr, rousted me.

"Mr. Bloodworth," he'd said. "Have you seen the *L.A. Times*?"

"Who the hell is this?"

"T. Landrew Marr. Of Morrison, Fine, Forrest, and Marr. I'm representing Dove Hilbert."

The phone had rung again a minute later. "T. Landrew Marr again, Mr. Bloodworth. I'm afraid we were cut off. As I said, I'm representing Dove Hilbert and he's in a bit of a jam, as the morning paper will explain."

"I haven't seen the paper, Mr. Marr. I was up late last night, pulling your client out of the drink. I'm beginning to realize that was a bigger mistake than I originally thought."

"He's right here with me. We were lucky enough to get a judge to post a bond. A damned excessive one, even considering the circumstances. But at least he's not behind bars. You know what a career lawman faces when he enters prison, Mr. Bloodworth?"

Instead of replying, I looked at the clock, which read ten-thirty.

"Might I outline Dove's situation for you, sir?"

"It is your quarter, Mr. Marr."

"They're saying he killed a man last night."

"Oh?"

"At first they were calling it vehicular homicide. Hit and run. A probable DWI. But now it seems even more serious."

"How could it be?"

"The D.A. has reason to think it may have been premeditated."

"You mean he ran the guy down on purpose?"

"It's slightly more complicated. Look, could you come over here to my office?"

"Why? I don't happen to live by the philosophy that if you save a guy's life, you're stuck with looking after him forever."

"Dove Hilbert would like to hire you."

"That still doesn't tell me why I should come."

"For the money, Mr. Bloodworth. That's why most of us do these things."

He'd been right, of course. Hilbert's money was as good as the next bastard's. But I hadn't rushed right over to Marr's office like a good little soldier.

I'd had breakfast. And along with the eggs and sausages, I'd digested the police report covering Laura Mornay's year-old theft. The description she'd provided of Ernie Mott—tall, dark, handsome, mid-thirties—made him sound like he should have had his own TV series. She had not told the police anything about meeting Mott at Wally Barclay's. In fact, she had not provided them with enough information to do much more than check their recovered merchandise bins.

Hilbert, the investigating officer, had stapled another sheet to the report: a Xerox of the death certificate of Philip Marton, Laura Mornay's former insurance agent. Hilbert, or somebody, had drawn a large question mark after circling the phrase "heart failure due to natural causes."

So there was one more reason for me to be sitting in the office an hour later with Marr, who was younger than he sounded on the phone and who graciously suggested I call him Drew, and with Hilbert, whom I would not call by his first name or nickname regardless of the money.

Drew sat back in a see-through plastic chair that matched his glass-top desk, and said, "According to the police report, my client, our client, Dove Hilbert, while driving erratically in his seven-month-old Ford Taurus, struck and killed a man at the corner of Venice and Hobart at approximately nine-thirty-seven last evening. He did not stop his car but continued driving east along Venice."

I frowned. "Okay. Hit and run. Manslaughter, maybe. Witnesses?"

Marr nodded. "Three. But I'm not sure they'll hold up. Barflies from a joint across the street from the accident." He consulted a notepad. "Place called Mr. Lucky's. A real dive, I gather. The three men were leaving when the accident occurred. Probably soused. Not a one of 'em could remember the number on Dove's license plate."

"What else does the D.A. have?"

"Bits of glass from a broken headlight on Dove's car were embedded in the dead man's side."

I turned to Hilbert. "You were squiffed at six, when I bumped into you. You must've been in great shape at eight."

He shook his head. "I didn't drink anything yesterday. Not a goddamn thing. Hell, I had a meeting with the chief at six. I've got enough troubles. I didn't have to show up roaring drunk."

"At six o'clock last night you were not a sober man."

"I was sick. Lightheaded. I'd been bit by some crazy flu bug or something. I walked into the chief's office and fell off the goddamn chair. Can you believe it? In front of the friggin' chief! He had a couple of suck-up weasels carry me into my office to let me sleep it off on my couch.

"I kept shouting for them to give me a Breathalyzer, anything. All they did was laugh at me. And oh, yeah. The chief left me with three little words: 'on permanent retirement.' Out on my keester."

I said, "Then you slept on your couch for a while?"

"I woke about eight. I was still very rocky. But feeling sort of . . . well, feeling off but strangely good. I don't know. I've never experienced anything like that before.

"I remember getting to the car and trying to find the keys. Searching my pockets. Then blackout. I came to in the car on Venice Boulevard. The car was stopped, but the engine was running. I was still very cloudy, but I knew where I was. I swear I didn't see anybody lying in the street.

"I heard a noise, saw these blacks staggering from a bar. They shouted at me, so I stepped on the gas and got out of there. I drove to Hannah's. I let myself in and sat down next to the pond and I guess I fell in.

"Then you were there. And Hannah."

"When did they pick you up?"

"This morning at about seven. When I drove home."

"And the premeditation?" I asked Marr.

"Well," he said. "That's where it gets tricky."

I waited. Lawyers all want to be actors.

When he felt he'd played the suspense long enough, Marr said, "The man had not been killed by the car. The back of his head had been caved in. They, uh, found Dove's antique mace a few feet away from the body, covered with his fingerprints."

I looked at Hilbert. "When this chicken came home to roost, it was a kamikaze."

"Jesus Christ, Bloodworth. I know we're not exactly drinking buddies, but give me a little credit, huh? First, I accidentally run down some poor son of a bitch. But that's not enough, I've gotta stop the car and finish the job with my famous mace that I then leave behind."

I stared at him and asked Drew, "Was the victim black?"

"No. He's reported to be a Caucasian named Jerome D. Palomar."

Hilbert groaned, "I've never heard of the bastard. I don't know what this 'premeditation' bullshit is all about."

"You did say the other day that your mace was missing."

"Exactly. Right. It has been."

"What, specifically, do you want from me?"

Hilbert stood up suddenly and moved to a window, looking out. "Somebody's slipping me a rusty nail," he said softly. "But he's playing it too cute. When you get too cute, you have to make mistakes." He turned. "Find 'im."

"And you don't have any idea who it might be?"

He shook his head.

I asked Marr, "What'd the breath test turn up?"

"There wasn't one. I spiked that."

"Why? He says he wasn't drunk."

Marr looked uncomfortable. "I . . . didn't think it was worth the risk."

"If he wasn't drunk, what was the risk?"

"The risk, as I'm sure you know, is that he may have been under the influence of something other than booze. If, for example, he'd been unknowingly drugged—a melodramatic scenario, but not an impossible one—testing would have proven only that the drug was in his system, not how it got there. He would still have been held accountable for his actions."

I nodded. "I don't suppose you thought about a private test. It may not be too late."

"No. Again it's the risk factor. Nothing remains private these days."

"Would it help if I found out if somebody slipped him a Mickey?"

"That would certainly help, yes."

I asked Hilbert, "When did you start woozing out yesterday?"

"Evening. Just before I left . . ." His brows wrinkled as if he were in pain.

"Before you left where?"

"Some crappy cocktail party or other. Hannah's always dragging me to these . . . gatherings."

"Where was this one?"

"It was in the Malibu Hills off of Corral Canyon. Big, goofy-looking place with about as much warmth as a morgue. All this modern crap on the walls. Stupid paintings. Furniture that looks like . . . hell, like that chair of Drew's. Uncomfortable and ugly as a chastity belt.

"This crooked son of a bitch lives there. Been under investigation for kiting stocks and the like. Slimy bastard who thinks of himself as a playboy type. Know what I heard, Bloodworth? This is rich. He got the word out that he had a bum ticker. Then he had one of his flacks plant an item in all of the gossip rags that he had it in his will that whoever was in the kip with him when he crossed over would automatically inherit a quick five mil. Ever since, dames of all stripes have been trying to ride him to death. His heart's probably healthier than yours or mine."

Mine gave a little leap just then. "The guy got a name?" I asked.

"Barclay. Wally Barclay. Know him?" I shook my head. "Then why are you smiling?"

"I was thinking of something funny."

"Well, do it on your own time," he snapped, returning to form.

"While you were at Barclay's party, you didn't even have one drink?"

"I told you: I had a six o'clock meeting with the chief. I knew he was going to tear off a hunk of my hide anyway. I've made zero progress on the Kosca investigation. I wasn't about to show up with so much as a whiff of booze on my breath. I got one of the waiters to get me a fruit drink from the kitchen."

"What kind was it?"

"The drink? Thick, syrupy. Very sweet. I don't know. Papaya maybe. I drank a few sips. Then I started feeling odd, like a rabbit was jumping over my grave in slow motion."

I had a hunch that if he'd sipped any more he'd have never made it out of the canyon and back to L.A. behind the wheel.

"Where was Hannah while all this was going on?"

"Off with some of her cronies."

"She's a pal of Barclay's?"

"She lived there for a while," he said in a near-mutter. "He's got a bunch of cottages up on his mountain. A lot of women have lived there," he added belligerently, as if he expected either me or Marr to make something of it.

I said, "Do you remember an insurance man named Philip Marton? Died of a heart attack in a motel along the ocean."

Hilbert scowled. "Yeah. There was a robbery investigation, and he was the insurance agent."

"Was there some question about his death?"

Hilbert shook his head. "Not really. He went out in the sack with some hippie girl."

"If he'd been Barclay, she'd have collected five big ones," I said.

"Yeah," he said absently. "Well, I'm always a little suspicious if somebody dies who's connected to an open investigation. I called the m.e. who'd signed the death certificate. He didn't convince me he'd done more than go through the motions. But the guy's family was trying to soft-pedal the sex angle, and it didn't seem worth getting them all razzed by digging Marton up again. It wasn't my beat, anyway."

"You remember if the name of the girl was mentioned?"

"No. She was a minor, I think. What the hell is all this? What's this got to do with the price of potatoes?"

"Maybe nothing," I said.

"What made you think I knew about this Marton?"

"I just assumed that all of you old goats who play around with young girls know each other."

I started to go.

"Wait a minute." He grabbed my shoulder. "I asked you a question. You're working for me, you answer me, damnit."

"If you expect me to get you off the spot, you'll remove your hand from my jacket." I turned to Marr. "I'll keep you posted, counselor. You can pass along to your client whatever you think he needs to know."

2. What had made me smile while Hilbert was going on and on about Barclay was the knowledge that I had just hit the detective's daily double. It happens only rarely to a free-lance investigator—two of your cases intersect. Parallel lines converge. Two clients are served by the same course of action.

In this case, Laura Mornay wanted me to locate her former lover, the Cockney Ernie Mott, whom she'd met at one of Wally Barclay's parties. And Dove Hilbert wanted to know who'd mixed him a Mickey at, where else, one of Wally Barclay's parties.

There was an even more intriguing convergence. Hilbert's Mickey sounded suspiciously like the Brompton's Cocktail I'd been served in Italy, where I'd been handpicked as the fall guy for Sandy Watson's murder. Hilbert was filling the same role for the murder of Watson's roommate, Jerry Palomar.

The only question remaining was: how to arrange a meeting with Wally Barclay?

3. Hannah didn't look happy to see me. "Oh, Leo, I'm afraid you caught me at a bad time."

I moved past the door anyway and stood in her living room. She was dressed to go out. Nice dress. High heels. Powdered and perfumed. "Just wondered if your pool needed cleaning," I said.

"God. Isn't it awful? They say Dove killed a man."

"Well, the irony in all this is that he probably has killed a couple. But not this one."

"Oh? What makes you so sure?" She lighted a cigarette and took a seat on her striped sofa. Without being asked, I sat down next to her.

"I think he was too stoned."

"But . . ."

"How much did he have to drink yesterday?" I asked her.

"You saw how he was behaving."

"Yeah. But I didn't see what caused it. He said he was with you at a party. Was he drinking?"

"I really . . . don't think so. But when he came to tell me we had to leave, he was staggering."

"You want to help him?"

"Of course, only . . ." She glanced at her wristwatch.

"I'm sorry. I'm keeping you from something." I stood up.

She followed me to the door. I said, "You wouldn't happen to be having lunch with Wally Barclay?"

"No," she answered quickly and emphatically. "That is, I'm meeting some friends at Trump's."

"Not Barclay?"

"No," she smiled. "Wally rarely goes anywhere for lunch. Why did you ask?"

"I'd like you to arrange for me to have a talk with him."

"I . . . I suppose I could do that. When?"

I looked at my watch. "How long would it take me to get to his place? An hour, maybe?"

"You want to see him *now*?"

"Why not? Especially if he doesn't go out for lunch."

She'd lost a good deal of her poise. "He . . . uh, is fairly busy with his business. . . ."

"He might be there all alone staring at a Swiss-cheese sandwich and wishing for someone new to talk to. If you give any kind of a damn for Hilbert, make the call."

She moved to a pale pink phone that vaguely resembled a seashell, plucked an earring from her right lobe, and picked up the receiver. She shifted so that I could not see the buttons she was punching. Then we both waited for a few rings. She whispered something, and we waited some more.

When she talked again, it was clear and precise. "Hello, Wally. This is Hannah. Sorry to disturb you, but a friend of mine is with me, a man named Leo Bloodworth. Leo Bloodworth," she repeated, turning and smiling at me. "A private investigator. He would like to meet with you . . . I'm not precisely sure . . . All right. Just a sec . . ."

She held out the phone to me.

The voice on the other end was deep but with a lilt, as if Barclay had spent time in Ireland. "Hello, Mr. Bloodworth, is it? What can I do for you?"

"I wonder if it would be possible for me to drop by, Mr. Barclay? In about an hour? There's something very important I'd like to discuss."

"I don't suppose you could give me a hint?"

"It's nothing I'd want to mention over the phone," I said.

"Well, if the lovely Hannah thinks I should see you, I shall. You know how to get here?"

"You're at your home?"

"Where else would I be?"

"Then I can find you."

"The Malibu Mountains can be tricky."

"I'm pretty tricky myself," I told him.

I pointed to the phone and raised my eyebrows, but Hannah waved it away. So I told Barclay good-bye and replaced the pink receiver onto its seashell base.

"Is Dove still with the lawyer?" she asked.

"The last I looked."

"I wonder if you know what you're doing," she said without expression.

"At least fifty percent of the time," I said.

4. Pacific Coast Highway was filled with the usual midday ebb and flow of sun- and/or surf-worshipers and campers and just plain dawdlers. I traveled north past the beach houses and junk-food stands and restaurants until the Corral Canyon Road turnoff, then headed east up that for a couple of miles until a post identified a path jutting to the right as Rudo Road.

That took me two and a half twisting miles along a hot, treeless macadam to Escandala Lane, where foliage started slowly but blossomed into towering oak and ash trees by the time the lane played out. During the whole operation I'd passed only one other vehicle, parked off the road, partially hidden in a copse of trees.

There was only one direction for me to go: right, through a separation in a thick mesquite shrub that was big enough for two cars side by side. From that point on, there was no paved road, just packed dirt forming an incline up, slowly circling the outer ridge of a mini-mountain. Every now and then the road came close enough to the edge of the ridge for you to see down into the green valley far below or spot the gray-blue ocean blinking in the misty southern California sunshine.

Eventually I arrived at a high gate emblazoned with the letter "X." Beyond it loomed a series of buildings that looked more like a small village than a man's home. The Watchbird camera zoomed in on me, and without being asked I said, "Leo Bloodworth to see Wally Barclay."

"Would you hold your driver's license next to your left ear, Mr. Bloodworth, ID portion facing out?" a transmitted voice requested. Feeling like a jerk, I did just that.

The gate clicked open before I could get my license back into the wallet.

A gravel drive took me around the main house, following a metal railing that marked the outer edge of the hilltop. The property covered about as much territory as your average city block. The buildings looked pretty subdued for a man of Wally Barclay's reputation.

There was a high-tech main structure, clean, curved, and pueblo white, going up three levels to a flat roof that also served as a deck. Trailing behind it, closer to the mountain's edge, were two long, flat buildings with windows that had been treated to reflect the sun and, perhaps not incidentally, keep the interiors safe from the prying eyes of nosy parkers such as I. Regardless, from the aromatic smoke pouring out of the nearest stack, I assumed it was a kitchen. There was no such hint offered by the other.

The rest of the edges of the mountaintop were taken up with ten small cottages, each with its own presumably incredible, unencumbered view of the sky and canyon far, far below.

An Olympic-sized swimming pool took care of some of the remaining spare footage. It was being used by several young women in and out of swimwear, most of whom didn't seem to believe all the warnings about prolonged exposure to the sun.

Closer to the main building than the others was an asphalt parking lot built to accommodate maybe a hundred cars. At the moment it served only six, all of which were clustered on a portion of the lot that was shielded from the sun by a tar roof.

I parked beside a bright blue Rolls with a license that read: XANADU4. Exiting my Chevy, I idly wondered where XANADU1 through XANADU3 were.

I was exploring the swimming pool when I heard my name being called. A pretty Spanish woman in what looked like a green silk sarong approached from the main house.

She introduced herself as Anna, then herded me to a large patio at the side of the main house where two men were seated at a white table under an umbrella the size of a department-store awning. The big, pale, moon-faced fellow perspiring in his white suit and open-neck blue silk shirt was a comedian named Philly Pontalbo. I'd met him in Las Vegas once doing warm-up for a singer who'd hired me to locate his errant business manager.

The other guy was trim and not quite tiny. His purple knit shirt with a horseman over the heart and his bright yellow slacks were, in the fashion of the times, loosely casual, hanging on his thin frame. He seemed about as relaxed as a skeleton at a dog show.

Anna asked me if I'd like something to eat or drink, and when I said no, she left us. Philly pumped my hand and told me three quick jokes, all of which I'd heard before. He did not introduce me to the not-quite-tiny man, but I gathered from their conversation that he was the top kick at one of the studios.

We sat around gawking at each other for a few minutes, when one of the girls from the pool dropped by. Her face said she couldn't have been much older than Sarah. But her body suggested a little more maturity than that. She whispered something to the not-quite-tiny man, and they went off together.

Philly said, "You know, every time I come up here, I start to worry I'm gonna break something . . . like a commandment."

I gave him a polite chuckle and asked, "You spend a lot of time here?"

"Naw. I'm in Vegas six-seven months. Then I get home to Jersey in the spring and fall. But if I'm in the neighborhood, I hang out. Wally's a hell of a guy."

"You meet him in Vegas?"

"His company bought the Desert Isle about four years ago. I headline there now, you know. Five years ago I figure the best I'm gonna do with my material is maybe become second b. on some TV show. But then Wally comes along. The guy loves comics. Has a hell of a sense of humor."

"So you don't need TV."

"Hey, I didn't say that. Everybody needs the tube, Leo. Christ, we all grew up on the tube. The tube, uh, suckled us. Uh, suckered us . . . heh, heh. I love, love, *lurve* the tube. I watch it all. That's how I used to pass the time on the road. I'm an expert on the tube.

"And I been on it a lot. *Dean Martin's Golddiggers, Flip Wilson,* and a show Carlin did during the summer once. Merv used to have me on his show couple times a year."

"I understand they don't have many comedy-variety shows anymore."

"Not since *Laugh-In.* That goddamn show killed comedy-variety. The audience wanted more jokes, faster. Hell, there are only so many jokes. You go on Carson or Letterman, whammo, your act is gone. The tube eats up the material, bubbie. Faster than my wife, my ex-wife, eats a pizza. Heh, heh. Still, when the chips are down, as they usually are in Vegas . . . heh, heh, the tube is the greatest boon to a—"

I wasn't much interested in Philly's philosophy on the subject of television, so I interrupted him with, "You remember a show that was on in the fifties called *Men-About-Town*?"

"Sure!" Philly said, his face coloring now, animated. He squinted his eyes. "United Broadcasting Company, 1958 through 1961, Wednesdays, eight to eight-thirty. That's on this coast. Sponsored by . . . ah, ah, Post Cereals."

"Who were the stars?"

"The stars. Ah, ah, Calvin Bedloe was the old man. I think he passed away, yeah. Good actor. Good goddamned actor. Jake Seloy was the older brother, and Little Jimmy Bristol was the star. How's that Leo? Mind like a steel trap. Full of dead animals, heh, heh."

"What'd Little Jimmy look like?" I asked.

"Now that's a sad story," he said, leaning in close. "Little Jimmy Bristol was this cute little towhead with a cowlick and freckles all over his face. When he'd pretend to think, he'd cross his eyes and stick his tongue out of the side of his mouth. Hell, Leo, you musta seen the show. It was a big hit."

"What's the sad story?"

"Oh, yeah. Well, this Bristol kid grows up, and maybe he's not so cute anymore. So the work stops, and he becomes a more or less average guy, maybe a little overweight. Anyway, he goes to college up north. Up at Raven's Point, which, as you may recall, Leo, was one of your hottest beds of wild-eyed radicals. Which reminds me: How many hippies does it take to screw in a light bulb?"

"Hippies? In the eighties?"

"Come on, come on. How many hippies does it take to screw in a light bulb?"

"I don't know, Philly. How many?"

"Two. Two hippies can screw in anything."

I waited for his laughter to subside and prompted him with, "The tragedy of Jimmy Bristol, take two."

"Oh, right. Well, he gets in with these hippies who are giving the university hell, and one night they're staging some kind of thing—you know, burning books and marching around and using profanity. And these cops come by and there's this scene. And some people get hurt, and Bristol winds up dead."

"Dead how? The cops hit him, or what?"

Philly scowled. "Who knows, Leo? I mean, TV is my field. How far do I have to carry my expertise? Gary Marcuse wrote the music for the show, by the way. And that Broadway dame, Jamie Ann Johnson, was the girl next door. A semi-regular."

"Is Philly keeping you amused, Mr. Bloodworth?"

The guy stepping through the archway from the house was bald as a baby's rump. He was a fleshy man, slightly under my six-foot-two, with a barrel chest and thick wrists and hands like baseball gloves. He was wearing a gray warm-up suit with dark green and purple piping, and his running shoes matched his outfit. Judging by his head and hands, booze and/or the sun had turned him the color of rare roast beef.

"Philly is never less than amusing," I said, giving him my hand to pulverize.

"Sorry to have kept you, but I've been on the horn. An overseas call I've been waiting for all day."

"I hope it was good news," I said.

Wally Barclay gave me a strange, crooked smile and tilted his head to the side. "Not what I would call good. A better word would be . . . unacceptable."

He moved closer and put his arm around my shoulders, turning his head to Philly, who was staring at him and doting on each of the master's words like Old Dog Tray. "Philly," Barclay drawled, "I want you to keep watching that snow-covered mountaintop in the far distance. See it?"

"Yes, sir."

"Well, if the snow starts to melt, you come and interrupt us. Otherwise, you just stay here and keep watching. Okay?"

"Okay, Mr. B.," Philly said, slipping back into his chair, looking neither chastened nor resentful.

Barclay led me down the path to the rear of the house, moving at a fast clip. "What do you think about Xanadu, Leo?" he asked.

"Looks pretty comfortable," I said.

"Comfortable. Yes, I'll accept that. Damned if I won't." He paused, making a sweeping gesture with his right arm. "The cleanest air in southern California. The most beautiful women. The finest food." He pointed to the nearest building. "It's better stocked than Spago's. I stole my chef from the Tour d'Argent about four years ago. We grow our own vegetables, some fruit."

"What's in the other building?"

"Ah! That, I'm afraid, must remain a secret. Unless you should decide to pony up about twenty thousand dollars to become part of a select group of investors. I can give you a hint: It's what keeps these lovely ladies spending so much time on my mountaintop. Come along, Leo."

He marched to the doors, which he threw open, bathing us in cool air. He was about to step in, when an odd, bloodcurdling cawing sound echoed through the canyon.

Barclay, shading his eyes, stared up. I followed his lead.

Out over the open canyon, a bird—a falcon or a hawk—soared gracefully, did a somersault, and shot straight down into the Valley out of our sight. Barclay smiled at me, returned his hand to my shoulder, and guided me through the doors.

We entered a carpeted hall. Along the walls were pictures of Barclay with various celebrities. "They all come to me," he said. "I don't leave my mountain unless I have to."

He led me to a large room with dark wood-paneled walls. The furnishings were painfully modern constructions of leather and plastic and chrome. Oriental carpets flanked a large parquet dance floor. A six-foot-high cabinet along a back wall housed stereo equipment and tape reels and, for all I knew, laser weaponry.

"This is the scene of our little soirees," Barclay said smugly.

On the walls were hung all sorts of modern junk—blurred Confederate soldiers, numbers, letters, and geometric shapes. A giant Dick Tracy. Marilyn Monroe with wet neon lips. Every painter in town must have seen him coming.

We went past that, down a winding stairway, past an indoor pool in which two naked girls swam like porpoises. Barclay looked at them and let out an elaborate sigh.

Beyond the pool was a small office with a desk and a computer and an additional monitor on which stock-market quotations danced across the screen. One wall was covered with purposely silly art—poodles doing the can-can, a collie dressed in a royal-blue knicker suit, a borzoi holding a ballet pose, each done in the style of a different old master.

Barclay said, "Do you like my dog art? I just got a new one."

From beside his desk he lifted a cardboard box and slid a painting from it. The dog in this one was wearing a hat with a plume and a blue satin Three Musketeers outfit. Barclay said, "It's called 'The Laughing Cocker Spaniel.' What do you think?"

"Pretty damn droll."

"Leo, I'm advising all of my friends to ride with me on this one. This painter was clever and he was prolific. And now, regrettably, he has passed on. When these start to catch on, and they will, sure as God made little Andy Warhol, there is going to be a mountain of loot for investors."

"Has he ever done one like Van Gogh? Maybe that one with the straw hat and blue smock, against a yellow background?" I was describing the painting I'd seen in the house that Watson and Palomar had shared.

Barclay shrugged. "Possibly. I could find out for you."

He opened a door off of the office, and we entered a gym filled with electronic and mechanical gizmos. Barclay said, "Usually I'd be taking a jog around the property, but I didn't think you'd want to have to work that hard while we were conversing."

"That was considerate."

He paused at a table and picked up an oblong hunk of plastic from which buttons protruded. It looked like a skinny calculator. "Let's see," he said. "Twenty minutes at four miles an hour. Through Brentwood."

He finished pressing the buttons and replaced the calculator. The lights went off in the room. A projector mounted on the ceiling began to focus an image on a curved silver screen against a wall. The camera seemed to be moving down a city street. Barclay stood in front of the screen, straddling a section of the floor that was moving. Then he jumped onto the treadmill and began jogging.

"Here I am in Brentwood," he said. "Doing my daily."

"I understand you had a party here yesterday afternoon."

"I try to have two or three a week. Keeps the staff from getting restless. You must come to the next. This Saturday."

"Hannah was here with her friend Dove Hilbert."

"The girl has no taste, Leo. What can I say? Present company excepted, of course."

"Of course, Wally. Anyway, somebody slipped Hilbert a Mickey at your party."

"Oh, really? Was that before the gent's fifth or sixth vodka?" He was jogging past the Brentwood Mart heading along San Vicente to the ocean.

"You mean he was drinking yesterday?"

"Well, I don't go around clocking my guests' cocktails. But it seemed to me I saw him with a glass in his hand."

I nodded. "He says he asked for fruit juice, and one of your waiters brought him a drink from the kitchen. It wasn't fruit juice."

"Oh, watch this," he said. On the screen, the subjective camera approached a female jogger. A hand reached out and patted her on the behind as the camera passed by. "Kerry Bartel made this tape for me. He's the producer of *Wild Boy*."

"About the drink from your kitchen . . ."

"Oh, hell, Leo. Maybe the boy made a mistake and brought Hilbert the wrong potion. That happens at parties."

"The potion the guy brought him was a Brompton's Cocktail," I said.

"What the devil's that? This year's Long Island Ice Tea?"

"It's slightly more potent. A shot of heroin, a shot of cocaine, ethyl alcohol, and chloroform water. Your man smoothed it out with papaya juice."

"That's the goddamnedest thing I've heard in years, Leo. What in the world are you talking about? Cocaine? Heroin? Here? Absolutely out of the question. Drugs are not allowed at Xanadu. There's more than enough else to take up the slack."

On the screen the camera was moving back up San Vicente, heading toward Westwood. "You're saying it would be impossible for somebody on your staff to drug a man at one of your parties?"

"Not impossible. I don't check every drink before it's served. I have twenty-five people on staff here. I try to check them out thoroughly, but in the long run you just have to see how they work out. I haven't hired anyone new in over a year. Anyway, damnit, why would anyone want to drug him?"

"I don't know."

"I wish I could be of more help," he said, "but I think it would be a waste of everyone's time if you questioned the staff. You'd need an interpreter, anyway."

I shook my head. "The police may have to do just that, Wally. It looks like Hilbert's going to be put on trial for murder, and they'll probably subpoena the whole bunch of you."

"Goddamn bother! I'm sorry for the bastard, but it is not in my best interest to get involved in anything requiring me to tell the whole truth and nothing but. Oh, nothing to do with Hilbert. But my business interests are . . . varied and complex. The idea of my being in court may not sit well with some of my partners."

All of which probably meant that Barclay really wouldn't have gone along with any plan to spike Hilbert's fruit juice. "Was there anything else, Leo?" he asked.

"Well, as a matter of fact, I was wondering if you could tell me how to find Ernie Mott?"

That one got him off the jogging wheel. He hopped to one side and said, "Ernie Mott? God, now that's an interesting segue. Or is it? Is there a connection between Ernie and Hilbert?"

There was, of course—Hilbert had investigated the theft of Laura Mornay's earrings. But she didn't want her "friends" to know about the robbery. So I said, "The only connection is that they both came to your parties."

"I haven't seen Ernie in months. He wasn't really a regular here at all. One of the girls brought him a few times. I didn't care for him. He was personable enough, but there was a distinctly creepy side to his character. Definitely not one of the regulars."

"Which one of the girls?"

"Brought him, you mean?" I nodded. He gave me what he thought was a shy smile. "You'd better ask Hannah."

"She knows Ernie Mott?"

"In every sense, including the biblical. Is this a wrap, chum?"

"I suppose so."

He put out a sweaty hand. "I really mean it about the party on Saturday. Your name's on the guest list as of now."

I hadn't seen any button being pressed, but Anna appeared at the door to lead me to my car.

As we moved across the grounds, I noticed that most of the girls had left the pool and were gathered at the metal railing, looking down into the canyon. Suddenly they emitted a universal screech, and the bird shot straight up into the ozone.

"Bird tricks," I said to Anna.

She smiled. "It takes so little to amuse them," she said.

She gave me an unemotional half-wave as I drove past on my way out. I tried not to let it go to my head.

It took me fifteen minutes to get down off of the mountain to Escandala Lane and another five to locate the car parked in the shadows of the oak trees.

"Hi, Leo," Peru De Falco said.

"You can call it a day, Peru. I'm out and I made it without a scratch."

"Great," he said. "This one really was a piece of cake."

"Any interesting cars go in or out?"

He shook his big head. "Nothing. Except a wild wagon."

"A what?"

"A camper, painted wild. You know, psychedelical. It went up after you." I hadn't seen it parked with the other cars. "It still up there?"

"Didn't come down."

"Well, you can go home now," I told him.

"Thanks, Leo. It's my mother's anniversary tonight. It'd be my dad's, too, if he was still with us."

"I didn't think people celebrated anniversaries after, you know . . ."

"No, I don't know."

"After one of the parties dies."

"My dad's not dead. He's just not with us anymore."

"Good night, Peru. Pass along my congratulations to your mom."

"Thanks, Leo," he said. "You know, you're a much better guy than the other scumbags I've gotta work for. And I'm not just saying it because you pay better."

Nice boy.

5. Even though I was traveling against the going-home traffic, it took me nearly an hour to get back to Hannah's place in Laurel Canyon. There were two prowl cars parked near her stairs. A jug-eared cop with a moustache they used to call a soup strainer stood at the side of the road, encouraging cars to move on.

"What's the trouble, Officer?" I asked.

He was wearing those black sunglasses that are supposed to intimidate you. But since I'd once stood in his boots, I was not impressed. "Just move on, mister," he said.

"Something happen?"

"Are you just being curious, sir, or do you want to stop and talk about this?"

"Just curious, Officer," I said and drove on, grinding my teeth.

Since I couldn't go back down, I headed on past Mulholland and eventually found myself in the Valley in Studio City. I didn't feel like battling the Ventura Freeway at its busiest time of day, and I needed a drink, so I stopped off at a restaurant called Laggerlough's.

Everything is a little off-center in the Valley. People used to say it was because of all the smog in the air. Whatever, folks behave in unpredictable ways. Gordie Laggerlough was no exception. He started a pretty good bar in West L.A. that he expanded to a bar and grill, specializing in seafood. Within a few years he was turning 'em away from the door, so he cut the bar back to nothing and became a seafood house.

He was making so much money and was getting so much press that he opened a branch in the Valley and let his brother, Fergus, handle the operation. Gordie's wife was his bookkeeper, and she kept telling him that Fergus's operation was dragging him down, so he sent the wife out to Studio City to keep an eye on Fergus.

Within a year the West L.A. place started to slide. Gordie couldn't understand it. It was packed every night. His prices were high enough to insure a profit, but the ink stayed red. Gordie finally figured it out when his wife and Fergus took off with all of the money they'd been skimming.

I located them for him about three months later in Montana, running the least popular bar in Butte. Fergus's expertise had used up most of the cash they'd grabbed. Gordie decided not to prosecute. He said they'd just got Valley fever.

Then he closed down his popular West L.A. place and tried to make a go of the Valley joint. The best he could do was to squeak by. The old regulars couldn't figure out why, if he had to pull the plug on one of his taverns, he didn't close the loser. One theory was that he was trying to prove to himself that he could make a success where Fergus had failed. Me, I figured he'd simply caught a case of Valley fever himself.

"What can I do you for, Hound?" he asked, looking gaunter and more pained than the last time I'd stopped by.

"Bushmills straight up."

I walked from the bar, past a dining room with two couples at separate tables, and latched onto the phone. Cugie was still at his desk. I gave him Hannah's address and asked, "Can you find out what's going on there? Two blue-and-whites standing by."

"You gonna wait?"

I gave him Laggerlough's number.

He called back within ten minutes. Dead body. Female, Caucasian. Face down, naked, in the fake pond. As yet unidentified. It had to be Hannah. They were still waiting for somebody from the coroner's office to help them sort it out.

I wondered if they'd sort it out all the way to Hilbert.

Cugie asked if I could identify the body.

I told him I didn't think so, and for him to forget I'd called.

I got through to Landrew Marr. He was in his car, and his voice faded in and out like an asthmatic's. He said our client left his offices shortly after I did, and he had no idea where Hilbert was at present. I briefly described the new development and left it up to him how to handle it.

I went back to the bar. Laggerlough had poured another Bushmills neat. Watson. Palomar. A hotel clerk in Venice. And now the beautiful Hannah. Talk to Bloodworth and kiss the world good-bye. Some racket!

I told Gordie to keep the bottle in a convenient place.

25

1. They made no pretense this time. We were strolling along Tower Hill, heading for Carol Taylor-Bright's Bentley, which he had parked illegally on Byward Street, when the woman called Sally Smith suddenly appeared in front of All Hallows Church. She had gotten rid of that lank blond wig and was recognizable now as the brunette I'd seen rummaging through Mrs. Kosca's home in Bay City. Come halfway round the world, just for me.

I backed away suddenly. Carol jerked to a halt and turned to look at me. "What's the matter, luv?"

"It's her," was all I could get out.

Sally Smith moved toward us. Carol looked from me to her and back again. "This is the same woman who was at the studio?"

I nodded, like a frightened tot. Then I panicked, turned, and ran. Right into the black man, who had been behind us all the while.

He put his arm around me and lifted me off the ground, carrying me on his hip. He took a step in the direction of a black sedan, parked at the curb with its engine idling. Then, surprisingly, Carol was standing between us and the car.

The black man said, "Get out of my way, you goofy-looking bastard."

From what I could see of Carol, standing there with one small white fist held up and the other hand grasping his guidebook, he looked not so much goofy as ineffectual. Desperately brave, but ineffectual.

The morning had started off so pleasantly, too. True to his word, Carol had arrived at Stratford TV promptly at noon to escort me on a tour through the Tower of London. His plan was for us to dine at the Savoy Grill, which, I gather, was in the same general direction as the Tower. Instead, I suggested we try to find the Grotto, near Charing Cross Station, which Margery Allingham wrote about in one of her novels.

Carol had never heard of the place. "It was started after World War I by some people named the Dominiques," I informed him. "Everybody in London goes there. It's on Adelaide Street."

Carol was game, but we just couldn't find any Grotto on Adelaide, and so we both settled on Roullard's, which was a clubroom sort of place with dark, polished booths and purple velvet cushions and waiters in livery.

I ordered a delicate shrimp omelet, and Carol decided to stoke up on various organ meats from the grill. I was trying to be polite, but the thought of eating kidneys and livers made me quite light-headed.

When the waiter brought me a fizzwater and Carol a whiskey, we clicked glasses. I decided that even though the tailoring of his sport coat and slacks made him look youthful and fit, Carol was probably a bit older than Mr. Bloodworth. He was, however, considerably more congenial.

"I can't tell you how delightful it is to be sitting here with a lovely young woman," he said.

"Gran thought I was imposing on you," I said.

"She doesn't know how happy I am to get away from business for a couple of hours. Besides, and this is the truth though I shall evermore deny it, I have never actually been inside London Tower. I'm looking forward to it as much as you are."

With that sort of charm, the least I could do was not gag when he started to nibble his kidneys. I kept my eyes on my omelet, and though we continued to hold a conversation of sorts, I did not look up again until I'd heard the clicks of his knife and fork as he placed them on his plate.

"You know," he said, dabbing at his lips with a linen napkin, "Edie is very concerned about you."

"Yes," I said. "But I do have a strong sense of how I want to spend the rest of my life. I have no desire to be an actress. Or to work in film. Or be a lady executive or somebody's happy little wife. Or any combination of those things. I want to be able to use my mind and skill to bring about changes, to right wrongs, to batter away at injustices."

"That's a lovely goal, dear heart," he said. "But life, being the cruel old bugger it is, doesn't always make it easy for us to achieve our goals as soon as we identify them. We live in a world of convention and compromise."

"Why does it have to be that way?"

"Well, in your case, there is someone you love who will be quite desolate otherwise."

"I wish she could understand."

"I have often wished that about my loved ones. But I know they won't, so I never, never press the issue."

"What issue?"

He smiled. "It's of not the slightest importance to anyone but myself," he said.

"So your suggestion is that I be what Gran wants when I'm around her and be myself when I'm not."

"That's the general idea."

It didn't sound like a good one to me. It sounded dishonest. I thought my way was better—to hold fast and assume that sooner or later Gran would come to her senses. I wondered if perhaps my way wouldn't have worked better for Carol, too, whatever his problem was.

It was nearly 1:30 when we parked the car and started toward the Tower, with its shrubs and grassed-over moat. Gray and mottled with black from the London air, it looked very much like the prison fortress it once was.

There was an enormous crowd on line, but Carol had arranged for us to move past them. I didn't have the nerve to look back at what I assumed were hot, hostile glares.

Once inside, tickets purchased and part of a gawking group, my host was as enthusiastic about the tour as I was. While our guide nattered on about British history and architectural designs, Carol followed our progress in a travel book. My mind kept leaping to novels I'd read, like John Dickson Carr's *The Mad Hatter Mystery*, which covers much of the Tower grounds.

On the Tower Green was a chained area that marked the spot where a number of famous folks—including Anne Boleyn, Lord Essex, and that sad little Lady Jane Grey, who at sixteen became queen of England for about two weeks—had been executed. While the guide quoted somebody named Macaulay who'd written there "was no sadder spot on earth," I looked with wonder as huge ravens hopped about on soil containing the remains of untold corpses. (I suppose it's a fairly well-known story, but the ravens' glistening wings have been clipped to keep them grounded. Mainly because there's a legend that if the ravens fly away, the Tower will fall. Why that would be such a tragedy in this day and age, I'm not sure.)

Everywhere was the chilly taint of death: the Wakefield Tower, where Henry VI was murdered in the 1400's, and across from it, the Bloody Tower, where the little princes met their fate. I questioned our guide about the Josephine Tey book *The Daughter of Time*, which suggests that Richard III did not smother the tykes. Like Gran, the guide had never read Miss Tey. And it seemed unlikely that she would.

We went through the White Tower, so called because it was whitewashed back in 1241, and we saw the fetters and torture devices. We visited the cavern under Waterloo Barracks where the Crown Jewels were kept, and at Carol's request we spent time at the Royal Fusiliers Museum and the Oriental Gallery, where there was this amazing collection of weaponry from Burma and China and Japan.

And nearly two hours later we emerged and started back to Carol's Bentley. He was still reading from his book. He said, "You'll enjoy this, luv. Sez here that Tower Hill and this area were the sites of the revolt of the first of the English patriot heroines, Boadicea, in the year sixty. A very tough lady, evidently. She killed everybody in her way and burned all buildings to the ground."

"What happened to her?"

"She married a nice young man and they're living a quiet, sensible life in Kent."

"Really," I said.

"Actually, she and the rest of her people were summarily dispatched by the Romans."

"Oh."

"Well, you know, luv, we British have a fondness for ghosts. And the feeling is mutual, so we can assume Boadicea is still flexing her, ah, sword around here somewhere, along with all the other specters of the Tower."

"What specters?"

He smiled. "The guide rattled off a whole rugby team of them."

"I must not have been listening."

As we continued walking, he said, "The ever-popular Anne Boleyn struts about the green, in white, with her head, head, head tucked underneath her arm. And good old Walter Raleigh takes a stroll nights, probably catching a smoke, but disappears if he spots you gawking at him. And . . ."

He stopped because that's when I saw something worse than the ghost of Boadicea—Sally Smith.

And then her partner in crime, who wasted no time in trying to get me inside their car.

Sally slipped under the wheel and shouted, "C'mon, Greg, we're drawing a crowd."

Greg? The name flew into my head. I knew who he was. "You're Gregory Desidero," I shouted at him.

He stopped and twisted me around to stare into my face. "How the hell . . . ?" he shouted.

"I know you and I know what you did with Cece MacElroy."

"Jesus Christ!" he said, and gawked at me.

And then Carol, that wonderful man, struck Gregory Desidero in the face with his book.

It drew blood. Paper can be as sharp as a razor. Desidero was so distracted, I was able to twist from his grasp and run away, back to the Tower and the other departing tourists.

I took a look back and saw that Desidero was not chasing me. He was trying to get into his sedan, but the marvelous Carol had hold of one of his legs and would not let go. Then Desidero pounded him in the face and kicked him a few times, and Carol lost his hold. He rolled away seconds before the sedan shot out into the street and roared off, Desidero's door slamming shut.

I rushed to Carol.

He was breathing hard. The skin over his right cheek was broken, and blood mixed with dirt on his face. The knuckles of both hands were scraped raw. With a grunt he stood up and got his footing. "I'd better go see my physician," he said. "I feel a little woozy."

Several people were heading toward us. A woman said, "A bobby's on his way."

"Let's get out of here," Carol said.

We made it to his car and inside just as a policeman rounded the corner. Carol smiled grimly and started up the engine. Through the back window I could see the bobby talking with some of the witnesses. Then Carol turned the corner, made a few more turns, and we wound up on Lower Thames Street, heading west.

"We should have stayed and reported it, Carol. I know who that man is. He murdered someone in the States."

"Sorry, luv, but I've had little . . . disagreements with the law before. I'm afraid their minds would have been made up about the incident, and there would have been no talking them out of it."

"I don't understand."

"You'll have to take my word."

2. Gran arrived just before Carol emerged from his doctor's office, his face and hands cleaned and bandaged. We drove with him to his flat, not talking very much. Mainly, it was Gran thanking him for protecting me. I began to tell her about Desidero, but she just held up one hand and said, "Later."

Carol was bruised and in pain, but not seriously hurt. The doctor had given him a sedative that he took while we sat in a comfortable room in his flat. The walls were filled with theatrical posters, many of them for his shows.

He tried being the congenial host for a few minutes, but eventually had to give that up. "I'm sorry, ladies, but I'm fading." At the door he waved and said, "Au revoir, Edie, dear, and to you, my lovely Miss Knickers."

I suppose he had earned the right to continue to use that awful nickname, but it didn't mean I had to like it.

Gran gave the driver the address of our flat, but I told her I didn't think it would be safe. She was convinced that the only address Desidero and the woman had for me was Stratford TV.

"But they could have followed one of us from there to our flat."

"You're convinced they're the same two people who chased you in Bay City?"

"Absolutely," I said. "I even know the man's name. It's Gregory Desidero. He's one of the people Terry Manion was trying to find. He drove Terry's missing niece to Los Angeles."

Gran leaned forward and tapped on the driver's window. "We've changed our minds, driver. Take us to the Connaught."

She settled back. "I'll make some arrangement for our luggage to be delivered to Stratford TV. And I'll get Gene to fix it so that we can head for home as quickly as possible. Why in the world are these cretins so anxious to lay their hands on you?"

"I don't know. But I'm sure they'll try again at home."

"At least there we can have police waiting."

"Shouldn't we notify the British police?" I asked. When she didn't answer, I said, "I realize that Carol has some problem and that he didn't . . ."

"Carol is gay, Sehr. And he was arrested because of it. And he feels that if we report the incident at the Tower, the police will just assume it was some gay thing and not treat it seriously."

"Arrested? People are arrested for their life-styles here?"

"This was some time ago," Gran said.

"Well, couldn't we just go to the police and say we're being bothered by . . . I guess that would sound dumb, wouldn't it?"

"I don't know how dumb it sounds. I simply would feel better about this *problem* if we, ah, could call upon people we know and trust."

I grinned at her. "You mean Mr. Bloodworth?"

She frowned. "It probably has something to do with him anyway."

"I'll call him from the hotel, tell him we're coming. He can get Lieutenant Cugat to start checking the airport for Desidero."

"It may be a little early in L.A. for you to be waking him."

"Something this important, I'm sure he won't mind."

26

1. I had fallen asleep in my clothes again. But I was improving. On the increasingly rare nights when I'd try to corner the market on Bushmills, I usually had trouble getting past the overstuffed chair next to the front door. This time I'd made it all the way across the room to the couch against the far wall.

But I had neglected to shut the door. And there was someone standing there blocking out the morning sun. At first I thought it was the morose Gordie Laggerlough returning my car. (I vaguely remembered his rolling me onto the backseat and depositing me on my doorstep. He'd performed the service before.) But Gordie wouldn't have been wearing a lime-colored suit and a dazzling smile. "Amigo," Rudy Cugat called to me. "Rise and shine. It is a brand-new beautiful day."

"What time?"

"Nearly nine."

"Nine? Are you nuts?" I groaned and rolled over, giving him my back.

He shook my shoulder. "This is . . . ah, official, Hound, mi amigo."

I sighed, rolled onto my back, and pushed myself off of the couch. I was still dizzy, and my tongue felt like it was wearing Dr. Denton's. "Why, oh, why, couldn't I have shut the damn door?"

"I would have knocked. Compadre, you aren't turning into a lush, are you?" He actually looked concerned.

I stood up and stumbled toward the kitchenette. "What's up?" I asked.

He followed and watched me put a pot on the stove. "Still fixing it with milk?"

I nodded. "Want a cup?"

"Sure," he said, and moved away from the door.

I got a jar of thick black dripped coffee from the fridge and poured some of it and a lot of milk into the pot and heated it up. Oddly enough, it didn't taste all that bad. Maybe I'd just got used to it.

While it warmed, I stepped back into the living room. Cugie was looking at a framed diploma I had on the wall, next to a portrait of my mother and father on their wedding day. The diploma was from the police academy. I'm not sure why I had it there. Probably to remind me that I had once been a cop. Maybe I kept the wedding picture there to remind me that I was of human born.

Cugie said, "Remember that crazy bastard Tucci who used to be in charge of the firing range?"

"I remember you shot part of his ear off."

"It stopped him from spooking rookies by spitting bb's at the back of their necks while all the guns were blasting."

"Yeah. All it took was a goosey Mexican. What about Tucci?"

"He's down at Parker Center. He called me this morning, asked me if I knew what my old amigo Bloodworth was up to these days."

I stepped back into the kitchenette, poured two cups, and brought one back to Cugie, who'd settled into the overstuffed chair.

"So?" I said, sitting on the sofa.

"So you were in Italy recently," he said.

"Yep," I said. "As you know."

"You didn't mention if you'd visited Venice?"

I swallowed a mouthful of coffee and asked, "What's the problem?"

"It's about an L.A. man named Watson. Simon Watson. Ever hear of him, Hound?"

Cugie and I had been partners and friends for twenty years, but I knew the way it worked. He was still a cop and he was nosing around.

I shook my head.

"What about Louis Bonfiglia?"

"Nope."

"This tastes better than I remembered," Cugie said. He placed the empty cup on the carpet and reached inside his coat. He withdrew a notebook. "Amigo, do you own a book by a guy named Paul Montclair? *Power Plan*?"

My heart hit the bottom of my stomach. I nodded. "Yeah, I had a copy with me on my trip. But I lost it."

"I gather it had your name and address on the inside cover." I hadn't written my name in the goddamn book. I hated to think of where it had been found.

I shook my head, as if in wonder. "Did somebody turn it in? I never expected to see it again. Not after that son of a gun waltzed off with it."

"How's that?"

"On the flight to Milan," I said. "There was this guy sitting next to me. Jim Bristol. He asked to borrow it and he never gave it back. Amazing," I repeated. "He's on that list I gave you. Haven't you checked them out yet?"

"You want to provide me with a few more details about Bristol and those other names?"

"What's going on?"

"Hell, amigo, that's what I'm here to ask you."

"This guy Bristol told me he was a personal manager, that he'd been an actor when he was a kid. In some show called *Men-About-Town*. I gave you a description."

"And he lives in L.A.?"

"I think so," I said.

"Was he involved with the others on your list?"

"Yes. They knew one another."

"Including the ones using the forged passports?"

"Especially them." I asked, "I don't suppose I could get the book back?"

"Maybe later," he said. "Right now the Venice police consider it evidence in a murder case."

"Murder?" I tried not to overdo it, but sometimes they expect you to be a little curious.

"Yeah. This Watson guy got dusted. As did the Italian gentleman, Bonfiglia. He was a clerk in the Venice hotel where Watson was staying. Where did you stay in Venice, amigo?"

"Like I said, I didn't go to Venice."

"No. I mean on your honeymoons. Didn't you go there twice?"

"Just one honeymoon. We stayed at the Pensione Alma. That was in the sixties. Is that when Watson caught it?"

He smiled. "Level with me, amigo. This is something big, huh?"

"How'd you wind up making this call, anyway?"

"They're shorthanded down at Parker. Tucci says they're cooperating with the Venice police, but that don't get top priority. So he was happy to let me take it off his hands, talk to you, and make the report."

"It's just July. Too early for Santa Claus. What's your angle?"

"Unlike the less-imaginative Tucci, I sense we are involved with something that is much bigger than it looks. Three dead bodies . . ."

"Whoa. Where'd the other body come from?"

"The woman in Laurel Canyon makes three. C'mon, level. What have we got here? I sense something grand. An international crime ring? Hit squads? Political intrigue?"

"What are you doing out in Bay City these days, watching too much TV, or reading too much Ludlum?"

"Don't toy with me. We can make this work for us."

"There's nothing more that I can tell you. There's nothing more that I know. If I find out anything, you'll be my main policeman. Okay? Now what's the bottom line on the Venice business?"

"Your book was found under the Italian guy's corpse."

"Oh!"

He nodded and stood up, straightening his trouser creases. "Thanks for the coffee, Hound."

"How much trouble will the book buy me, do you think?"

He shrugged. "Not too much," he said. "Assuming you work with me on this. Maybe you can point me toward a more likely suspect. That's your specialty, amigo, finding people. Bloodworth the Bloodhound. Find me a killer, and I won't have to go through the ordeal of sending your photo and prints to Italy to see if we can place you in Venice on the day the men were murdered. You want this door open?"

"Sure," I said. "Cool it off a little."

"Adiós, amigo."

I watched through the open door as he walked slowly along the brick path that led past the neighborhood theater in front of my coach house. The morning sun made a halo around that lime suit. Jesus, it was only 9:15, and I had a hangover and an ambitious Latin problem. What more could happen?

The phone rang. It was the kid, excitedly telling me that she and her grandmother were arriving in L.A. the next day. She'd had an eventful time of it in London, and there were one or two things she felt I should take care of. Then she asked for a progress report on that Manion character. I said that I'd talk to her about that when she landed. Who the devil had time for Manion? I was lucky enough to be keeping my own head above water.

2. "They'll be looking for this Gregory Desidero and his girl friend at LAX," Cugat was saying into my ear an hour later, "but don't expect any miracles, amigo. If he knows the girl has his number, he probably won't come through this way. Maybe into San Francisco. But we'll give it a try. It helps to have a name. This is it, eh, Hound?"

"It?" I asked into the phone receiver.

"The big one."

"What big one?"

"Give me a hint."

"I don't know what you're talking about," I said.

"I'm talking about the international conspiracy. Desidero is wanted in connection with Mike Kosca's murder. What with Watson and the Italian and the girl up on Laurel, that makes *four* goddamn murders. Forged passports. An international cartel of mass murderers."

"Jeez, amigo, calm down. I wouldn't count on Desidero and Kosca having anything to do with the others."

"Then you do know something you're not telling about Watson and the girl?"

"Not really." It was time to take control of this conversation. "What about that list I gave you? Little Jimmy Bristol and his pals?"

"Oh, yes." He paused because someone had come into his office and asked a question. "Are you still home, Hound?" he asked. "Can I call back?"

I gave him the number at Laggerlough's again. He made a tsk-tsk noise before he hung up.

Gordie had delivered my car, and I in return had driven him to work. At 10:30 he and I were alone in the bar, except for a fat kid with a shaved head who was playing a game of Alien Creatures on the machine at the far end of the room, making one hell of an electronic racket.

Gordie had a brownish sort of drink sitting on the counter. "Try it," he told me.

"What is it?"

"A surprise," he said.

"I haven't lived all these years by downing surprise drinks. What is it?"

"Hangover remedy."

"None of them work," I said. "Except a stomach pump. And I don't like the side effects."

"Trust me, Leo."

I sniffed at the drink. It smelled of Lea & Perrins and pepper. "Is there an egg in this?"

He nodded. "Drink it down, damnit, or never come in here again!" he growled.

The kid at the machine shouted, "Hey, keep it down, huh?"

I picked up the glass and shot it. Immediately my eyes started to water, and all sorts of taste sensations, none of them very pleasant, attacked what was left of my palate. "Holy woozers," I said through my tears. "What was in there?"

"It's the hot sauce and horseradish that's giving you the steam. One of my ex-wife's recipes."

That figured.

My voice still hadn't returned to normal by the time Cugat called back. He asked, "You hittin' the *ragù* this early, amigo?"

"No. Don't worry about me, okay? Just fill me in."

"All right. You know, it just keeps getting wilder. Like I said: Nothing on any living Cole Porter or Lannie Doolittle. A Loni Hoffstattler died in New York City on June 12, 1979. Hit-and-run. Was a runaway from Racine, Wisconsin. Hooker. Drugs. She was sixteen.

"Jake Seloy is serving the third year of a seven-year rape sentence at TI. Occupation listed was actor. Jamie Ann Johnson is appearing on Broadway in a play titled *Orchids and Ice*. Was arrested once in eighty-six for DWI. Ann Jellicoe listed in Cleveland, but that could have been a maiden name. There was a Little Jimmy Bristol who was a kid actor. I remember him, now that I see his photo. Anyway, he died on April 6, 1976, while attending University of California at Raven's Point. A chemistry lab caught fire and he was inside."

"I'd heard it had something to do with a student demonstration."

"Damnit, Hound! Are you using me to double-check your facts? According to our records, it says, and I quote: 'Accidental death in chemistry lab fire. Cause of fire, faulty wiring.' Look, lemme get to the good stuff, huh?"

"Be my guest."

"Holly Blissfield. I think we should meet and talk about her."

"I'm all the way in the Valley, amigo. Can't we just pretend we're in the same room, *mano a mano?*"

"Well, the dead woman up in Laurel . . ."

"Yeah."

"Her roommate identified her as a Dora Lasswell."

I scowled. The noise from the Alien Creatures machine was suddenly unbearable. "That's not her name."

"Oh, but it is, Hound. All verified and everything. The funny thing is, she had a driver's license and all sorts of papers in her pocket that ID'ed her as one Holly Blissfield."

The electronic noises were beeping inside my skull.

"What's the roommate's name?" I croaked.

"Just a sec. Here it is: Hannah Reyne."

So Hannah was still among the living, and Holly was dead. I had to make sure of that. Cugat derailed my train of thought with, "We must work on all this, Hound. Forget the international death squads. I went out of my head for a moment. This is the here and the now. Southern California. Turning into the murder capital of the U.S. And my amigo Leo J. Bloodworth is the hombre who is connected to at least a half-dozen."

"*Half-dozen?* Goddamnit, get hold of yourself, man. Start talking sense."

"Okay. Cool, calm, collected. The old Cugat we know and love. Hound, there are some heavy points to be made here, and I would love to leave the LAPD in the dust on this one. You know stuff, and I know you know stuff."

"Maybe we can do some business. But not right now."

"When?"

"When there's something you can work with."

"You swear this to me?"

I told him I did.

Rarely had I felt more relief from hanging up a phone.

I thanked Gordie for his help the night before. "Stomach feel okay?" he asked.

"Yeah," I said, truthfully. A good thing, too, since I was on my way to check out a stiff.

3. Hollywood's idea of a morgue assistant is a young guy with thick glasses and a five o'clock shadow, a combination sadist and ghoul who is invariably eating a submarine sandwich while describing points of interest on the corpses in his charge. Fortunately, I'd never had to deal with anybody like that.

On my way to the county morgue, I picked up a bouquet of flowers and presented them with a flourish to Lizzie McGuinn, the matronly, gray-haired, chain-smoking woman who happened to be on the day shift. She'd been doing morgue duty for as long as I could remember, and she never seemed to change.

"Well, Leo," she said, putting the flowers in a vase, "it looks like you finally got out of the habit of bringing me lilies. That's the one bloom that ain't appropriate, you horse's neck."

"That's why I popped for pink roses," I told her.

"You must be in the chips, honey. Oh, by the by, I read that book of yours. The kid sure is cute."

"Thanks, Lizzie."

"I can't ever figure out those whodunits though, and it makes me so gosh-darn mad. But I liked the book, really. So, which one of my boys and girls interests you today?"

"Lasswell, Dora," I said.

She shook her head. "The coroner's still having his way with her."

I winced. "They must have made a video of her, though. For identification."

"You don't want much for your goddamn posies," she said, and left me alone in the sterile white room. While I waited, others dressed like Lizzie in white smocks and gumshoes wandered in and out, trying to ignore me.

Finally, she got back and said, "Best I can do is a photo, but it's not wonderful."

From a thick manila folder she removed a grainy black-and-white 8 x 10 of Holly Blissfield's wet, lifeless face. I handed it back to her almost immediately.

"What else have you got in there?" I asked.

"Now, Leo, don't you put me in too much hot water."

"C'mon, Lizzie, they can't touch you," I said. "You know where all the bodies are buried."

"That's the worst joke ever to come out of your mouth," she grumbled, handing me the folder.

Inside were Xeroxes and stats of Holly's, or I should say Dora Lasswell's cards and papers that had been found in her wallet and among her effects. I supposed the originals were in a safe somewhere.

In the name of Holly Blissfield she had a fake driver's license and one credit card, several printed business cards with the phone number that she had supplied me. In her real name were passport, driver's license, SAG card —an actress, of course—charge cards, birth certificate (born August 12, 1955, in Oroville, California), and a short clipping—a biography that briefly mentioned the high points in a career that began with her graduating with honors in theater arts from UC Raven's Point in 1976 and included various productions throughout the United States.

I returned the material to Lizzie.

"Can I get back to work now, sweetheart?"

"Both of us can," I said, and kissed her on the cheek.

She said, "You're not young enough and I'm not old enough for that kind of patronizing smooch, Leo, you lout."

We both chuckled, as if she was kidding. I hoped she was.

4. Gwen Nolte must've been having a slow day. She said she was glad to hear from me. There are several operatives in the San Francisco area that I could have called, but Gwen is the smartest. Not to mention the best-looking. If she'd give up cigarettes, I'd marry her, which may be why she still smokes.

"Leo Bloodworth! The answer to a working girl's hottest dream. You coming up here to pounce on my bones?"

"Much as I would love to, no. I've got a favor that'll mean your driving out to Raven's Point."

"That's forty minutes each way. I'll have to charge my full daily rate."

"Put it on my tab," I said. "I need some yearbooks from 1973 to 1976."

"Four goddamn yearbooks? That old? How the hell do you expect me to swing that?"

"Maybe they'll let you borrow them," I said.

"Damnit, Leo, you know they won't. I'll have to tote a purse as big as a suitcase."

"Then Federal Express 'em to me right away."

"That'll cost an arm and a leg. Those yearbooks are heavy."

"If things go right, I'll bring 'em back personally and provide you with a weekend of your choice."

"Are you wiggling your goddamn eyebrows? C'mon, truth."

"No. I'm licking my chops."

"A weekend of my choice, huh? How about I spend it in Hawaii with Sean Connery?"

"I'll see what I can do," I said.

"Yeah. Well, so will I." And she hung up.

My next stop was at the Beverly Hills library, which was taking up the slack since L.A.'s main library caught fire a couple years ago.

There I settled down with several rolls of microfiche covering the *San Francisco Examiner* for the year 1976. I spooled through stories about the upstart Democratic candidate Jimmy Carter, the efforts to pass the Equal Rights Amendment, a new book titled *Roots* by Alex Haley, the banning of Red Dye No. 2, swine flu (one of my favorites), the Winter Olympics, the conviction of Patty Hearst on charges of bank robbery (handled by the *Examiner* in a manner that was understandably discreet), the Academy Awards, cheating at West Point. It was a hell of a year.

A nuclear-test pact was signed by the U.S. and the U.S.S.R. the same day that the chemistry lab at Raven's Point caught fire and took Little Jimmy Bristol's life. There were two pictures of Bristol—one during his glory days as a TV star (a posed shot with his eyes crossed and his tongue hanging out of his mouth), the other of a pouting young adult with a plump, acned face.

According to the story, a demonstration had taken place earlier in the evening on campus, commemorating the signing of the nuclear pact. The relatively peaceful event had been staged by a group calling themselves the Raven's Point Mummers. The way the article read, the Mummers were well known in the area.

One of the library assistants showed me where I could find an index to the *Examiner*. It provided the dates of at least seven other stories about the Mummers.

The first took me back to February of 1974, when they pulled their debut stunt, a reenactment of the Kent State massacre during the university's ROTC Day celebration. Suddenly two of the army ROTC officers left their ranks and began shooting into a group of somewhat anachronistic long-hair hippies.

Four of the "hippies" died very melodramatic deaths. They, like the two "officers," were the founding members of the Mummers. Their leader was a sophomore theater-arts student named Archie Leach, who was described by the reporter as, "a charismatic, darkly handsome young man" who had a lot to say about "the use of theater as agitprop."

A few days later there was a response from the university. Leach and the ten or so others would be expelled from the campus. But, as explained in a much smaller article a week later, the expulsion order was rescinded by the dean of the university. No reason given.

In 1975 the Mummers performed a "loose adaptation of George Orwell's *1984*" that went on for over a month leading to the day of the student-body elections. Leach and his merry pranksters covered the campus with Big Brother signs and staged a variety of "living theater" events in which emotionless militia dragged students out of class or beleaguered others by rapid-fire questions that left a number of them, according to a teacher named Lund, "reduced to tears."

Once again the university sought to stop the Mummers, and once again the university failed. Archie Leach was elected student president.

In his victory photo he appeared in whiteface makeup, with dark circles under his eyes, rimless glasses, and a self-deprecating smile. Beside him, ten years younger and minus a moustache, was the unmistakable phiz of my traveling companion Jimmy Bristol. The caption identified him as Tony Wharton, a cofounder of the Mummers. So Wharton had assumed the identity of a deceased classmate. Was that what actors did, mimicked people they knew?

In '76 Leach and his fellow thespians began to take their show on the road. They'd found a considerably larger target than the ROTC or campus politics. The nuclear-power controversy was in full rage, and in California a proposition wound up on the ballot that was designed to curb the operation of existing plants in the state and ban the creation of new ones.

The Mummers embraced the cause with all stops out. A photo taken just weeks before Leach's graduation showed him and a half-dozen others with ghastly makeup sitting in at one of San Francisco's toniest restaurants. The caption on that one read: "Restaurant diners get taste of the effects of toxic nuclear waste."

Regardless of their efforts, however, the proposition was voted down by the people of the state. In a final item, dated July 1, 1976, the Mummers staged a mock funeral for those who would die because of the proposition's defeat. The service, complete with a minister, a Catholic priest, and a rabbi, took place on the lawn outside of the nuclear plant at Raven's Point. It was a peaceful demonstration, attended by approximately two hundred, most of them vacationing students who had stuck around long enough to follow their leader's last political prank. After that, nothing more was heard of Leach and the Mummers.

Until now, maybe.

27

1. "Where, precisely, is the little red bag?" Gran asked me as the item in question rounded the far corner of the conveyer-belt track and disappeared into the tunnel in the terminal wall.

We had been too busy rescuing the light gray luggage as it rumbled by.

It had not been an easy flight. The rumor of a terrorist attack on Heathrow had kept us grounded for an extra hour, during which Gran kept staring out of the little round window and seeing disconcerting things—like military men carrying machine guns.

Then, once airborne, because we'd booked at the last minute, we had to put up with a cigarette smoker dead ahead of us whose fumes insisted on taking a backward swirl under Gran's nose. Finally, I was forced to approach the man to tell him how much he was upsetting my grandmother. He was a rather awful-looking fellow, with swarthy jowls and a diamond ring on his little finger, and he said in accented English that I should sit down and behave myself. That wasn't enough; he had to turn and glare at Gran defiantly, blowing more acrid smoke her way.

Bores are not to be tolerated, so I ordered a glass of water and a straw from the stewardess, and the next time the creepatolla lowered his arm, with the stench-ridden cancer stick facing the aisle, I filled the straw with water and extinguished the vile thing.

With a growl he was out of his seat and towering over me, almost rabid. "Madame," he whined at Gran. "This child has wet my Gauloise."

Gran looked from him to me and then back at him. "Sir, that is no child. That is a young woman. My granddaughter. And as for you, I suggest you sit down and behave yourself."

Oh, he was furious. But he stopped smoking for the rest of the trip. Gran's comment was, "Next time, dear, try to be more tactful."

First class or no, the remaining flight left much to be desired. The dinner was cold. Cold fettucini Alfredo doesn't quite make it, I'm afraid. And according to Gran, they did not have a white wine that could hold a candle to even an inferior California Chardonnay.

To put the capper on it, as Mr. Bloodworth says, the movie was *Benji Goes to Rio.* Which was fine for me, of course, since I could watch cute little scrappy dogs all day. But Gran is not quite so tolerant. And when Hildy Haines appeared as a villainous millionairess bent on putting the dear dog through all sorts of ghastly brain operations to discover the secret of his amazingly human intelligence, Gran said, "I am to be spared nothing," and closed her eyes and tried to sleep.

The trip took sixteen hours, I think. In resetting my watch, I may have lost count. In any case, we'd departed very early in the morning and arrived in the evening.

Gran spent the last half hour in the rest room. I was worried that she had taken ill, but when she returned, it was clear she'd been working with her little makeup kit. She looked fresh and beautiful. I wondered why she'd bothered, considering the way she felt about Mr. Bloodworth. Nor had she worried about her public image before, to my knowledge.

Once we got another chance to rescue the tiny red bag, the ordeal of customs took relatively little time. It rarely takes long. There's always some official who recognizes Gran and behaves very solicitously.

Finally, we arrived at the exit to the terminal, our luggage at our feet. The gallant Mr. Bloodworth was at the far end of the area, chatting with one of the airport-security men. He waved and, grabbing one of those pushcarts you rent for a dollar, he headed toward us quickly.

Gran was looking around the terminal, expressionless. She seemed anxious.

"Well, if it isn't the Dolly Sisters, back from their triumphant engagement in Great Britain," Mr. Bloodworth said.

Gran said, "I'm sorry, Mr. Bloodworth, but this grueling trip has just about exhausted my tolerance for whimsy. Let us simply make a hasty exit."

"Yes, ma'am," Mr. Bloodworth replied, loading our luggage onto the cart.

"Did Lieutenant Cugat supply us with police protection?"

"Not so's you'd notice," he said. "Airport security has been alerted. They've been looking for Desidero and his girl friend the past two days, without luck. Cugie thinks that if they plan on returning to the States at all, they'll probably come through some other gateway city."

"Then what we must do is to try and discover why they wish to silence me so desperately," I said.

"Yeah, that sounds like a plan."

"It must have something to do with Terry Manion. What success have you had in locating him?"

"Well, kid, I'm working on it."

"How close are we?"

"Oh," he said, leading us to the door, "I've been following a few leads."

"From the instructions I left you?"

"Right."

Gran asked Mr. B., as we passed through the door into the muggy L.A. evening, "I don't suppose you brought a limousine?"

"No, ma'am, just the old Chevy."

We were paused at a DON'T WALK sign when a limousine screeched to a sudden stop in front of us. Its back door opened and the dreaded Roger Thornhill got out, saying, "Edie, thank God I made it."

Gran's face lit up, and she gave him a beatific smile. "Roger, I was afraid you'd been held up."

"The traffic was godawful." He turned to Mr. B. "You can help Freddie put the luggage in the trunk." Freddie was a wiry, poker-faced uniformed chauffeur wearing gray Ray-Ban aviator glasses. He took control of the luggage cart.

Mr. B.'s face darkened. Roger Thornhill got out his wallet and said to Gran, "You and Serendipity hop in. I'll take care of this fellow."

"This fellow is Mr. Leo Bloodworth, a friend of the family," I said.

"Oh, hell," Roger Thornhill said, fumbling with the wallet and putting it away. "Oh, I am sorry." He put out his hand. "Roger Thornhill, Mr. Bloodworth."

Mr. B. took his time about shaking that hand. Then the advertising man said, "Edie and I and Serendipity are about to have an early dinner, if you'd care to join us . . ."

"Thanks, but I've got some things need taking care of."

I said, "I'll ride back with Mr. Bloodworth."

Roger Thornhill frowned. "Come on with us, Serendipity. You can pick the restaurant. Spago's. Citrus. You name it."

I didn't care about the restaurants. But I wasn't happy about letting Gran spend time alone with this . . . this smarmy huckster. Still, what could happen to her in just one evening? I mean, she wasn't going to elope or anything. And I was anxious to find out the progress on the Terry Manion front.

"Mr. Bloodworth and I have business to discuss," I told the hype merchant. "I'll see you later, Gran."

She bent down and I kissed her on the cheek. Then she got into the limo. Roger Thornhill stood by the door, looking at me and saying nothing. Then he turned, shook hands with Mr. B. again, and followed Gran into the limo. The chauffeur shut the door after him.

Mr. B. and I watched them drive away. Another car pulled out of the temporary parking area and followed the limousine. It was a familiar-looking battered VW bug.

As we walked across the traffic lanes to the parking area, I toyed with the reasons Mark Fishburn would be following Roger Thornhill's limo. Then it hit me: He was taping some horrible sort of exposé involving Gran and a younger man. Lordy!

Mr. Bloodworth, ever sensitive to my moods, said, "What's eating you, kid?"

"What would you do, hypothetically speaking, if you knew that some . . . some dung-eating maggot of a reporter had been collecting photographs and evidence about the private life of someone you loved?"

"Whew! That's a tough one, kid. I suppose killing the guy is out of the question?"

"This isn't funny."

"Okay. Has the guy got anything, or is he just trying to get something?"

We were at his dirty gray Chevy. As he unlocked my door, I noticed that someone had written "60-Minute Man" on the side of the car in the dust, whatever that meant. "He probably has something. Not much, I'm sure. But something."

"Then you have to find out what he wants for it."

He started the engine, and we began the descent down and out of the parking facility. "You mean pay blackmail?" I asked, astonished.

"No. I mean, you ask him what he wants. Reporters will usually settle for a better story. You know, like an exclusive interview. But I've found you can never really trust the bastards."

"So what do you do?"

"You fight fire with fire. They play dirty. You play dirtier. You find the negatives and you expose 'em and erase the cassettes."

I nodded. "You mean break into their house or office and find this stuff?"

We were on Lincoln Avenue, heading for Bay City. He turned to me and said, "Don't go putting words into my mouth, kid. I don't mean that at all. You never break into anything. You never break the law."

"I recall from your files that you broke into some guy's yacht to get his financial records."

"That was different," he said. "Look, either you get specific or we change the subject, huh?"

I said, "Are you mad because I insisted on driving with you?"

"Mad? I wouldn't have let you go off in the limo," he said.

What a wonderful thing for him to admit. Then he had to ruin it. "I mean, Thornhill and his pet monkey in uniform could have taken care of any trouble that came your way. But we would have had to explain about Desidero, and if Mrs. Van Dine'd wanted them to know she would have said something."

"Oh," I said glumly.

"What's the matter?"

"Well, I just thought that maybe the reason you didn't want me to go with them was because we hadn't seen each other for a while."

"Sure, kid," he said with a smile. "That, too, of course."

The evening traffic along Lincoln was heavy. Mr. B. turned on the radio, which was, as always, tuned to the forties music station. Some woman was singing very loudly about her boyfriend who used so many jive words, she couldn't understand what he was talking about. Lordy, but the forties were a simpler, almost childlike decade.

"Well," I said.

"Well, what?"

"What about Terry Manion?"

"Oh, that."

"How much have you actually done?"

He shook his head. "Not that much. You see, I've been kinda busy . . ."

"I know how busy you can be. Spending your evenings at the Irish Mist, cavorting with casual sexual partners, which in this age of AIDS is like playing Russian roulette."

"Kid, please. We're not gonna discuss my sex habits, okay? And I have been busy. Unusually busy, as a matter of fact."

"You had lots of free time before Terry Manion needed your help."

"I had some. Not lots, but some."

He turned off the radio and was silent for a while. Then he began to hum.

"What's the matter?"

"Nothing's the matter."

"Then why are you humming? You hum when you're worried."

"Look, Sarah, I didn't really get a chance to read that sheet you left me about Manion, but you mentioned the name Archie before, right?"

"Desidero and the girl talked about an Archie while they were searching Mrs. Kosca's house."

"Why don't you just tell me what was on that info sheet?"

So I did that. I was very complete, adding things that I may have forgotten to write down. When I'd finished, Mr. B. started pushing the Chevy through the traffic.

We snailed into Santa Monica and turned east on the Santa Monica Freeway, which was clear for a few miles, then began to snarl as it picked up traffic from the San Diego Freeway.

"Might I inquire where we're headed?" I asked.

"Well," he said, "I think we can visit that feather store on Melrose."

"Wings 'n' Things."

"Right."

"If you're sure you're not too busy."

He turned to me. "Actually, sis, there are other things I should be doing. I'm about that far," he made a U of his thumb and forefinger, "from being tossed in the slammer for at least one murder."

"That's terrible," I said.

"I'm pretty sure I know the real killer and the guy who's been making my life miserable for the past couple of weeks. And I'm gonna do something about that real soon."

"Then let's finish that up now. We can wait another day before picking up Terry's trail."

"No," he said. "It's Wings 'n' Things first."

"Why?"

"Because I promised you I'd try to find Manion," he said. "And I'm feeling guilty about it."

I gave him my fiercest look. "That's not true and you know it. I know how you act when you feel guilty, and this is not it. What's going on?"

"Maybe it's just that I need some more answers before I can clean up this other thing."

I glared at him. "This other thing, does it have anything to do with Terry? Are they connected?"

"What connection could there be?"

He was humming again.

"There's something you're not telling me."

"If you feel that way, it's your problem, kid. My conscience is clear."

2. He was moody during the whole trip down the Santa Monica Freeway, and by the time we had traveled north along La Cienega to Melrose he was mumbling to himself, which is the stage after humming.

"What's the matter?" I asked.

"Never mind," he said. "I just hope I'm wrong. Only, how many Archies can there be? Not to mention Hilbert everywhere I turn."

He started humming a song that I identified as "Accentuate the Positive." He spent an afternoon once forcing me to listen to about fifty songs by Johnny Mercer, and that was his favorite. Mine was "Moon River."

As we drove along Melrose, he hummed a bit more and then started grunting at the shoppers. Stage three. Mr. B. hates young, affluent upwardly mobiles—I'm not sure why—and he found much to raise his ire in the shops and boutiques.

Personally, I think Melrose is pretty amusing, and I can spend hours lurking in toy stores, for example, looking at the little gadgets like plastic sushi that walks or a penny bank that causes a skeleton to come out of its coffin to snatch the coin. Mr. B., however, was having none of Melrose's larkier aspects. And he was particularly offended by the coifs and clothes that were slightly moderate imitations of punker fashions. I wasn't happy about them myself, but I would never have let them affect me to the point where I was frothing at the mouth.

We were fortunate enough to find a parking space only a few doors away from Wings 'n' Things. It was a squat chalk-white building with a large picture window filled with stuffed peacocks of every color you could imagine, including Day-Glo orange.

Mr. Bloodworth took one look at the street, with its busy shoppers, lurkers, hookers, and at least one tall black pimp, did one of those rabbit-hopping-over-your-grave shudders, and said, "Wait for me."

"Why can't I go in?"

"Because I don't have time to waste, and I may have to do a little tooth-pulling in there, and it just isn't effective if there's an attractive young woman at my side. Okay?"

It was not okay, but I admit I was considerably placated by the "attractive." And I certainly did not want to interfere with his tooth-pulling. Naturally, I did not merely sit in the parked car. Instead, I poked around, looking in shop windows. The black pimp skated over. He was tall and still in his teens, I think. He was wearing hot pants and a tank top and he was carrying twin poodles under his arms.

"Hello, pretty lady," he said.

"Hi."

"You looking for merchandise or a job or what?"

I said, "I'm looking for people."

"Well, hell," he said. "You're talking at the numero-uno hombre in all the world for that. My name is Shoe. These here are Heel and Toe, my little pets. I'm in the people business."

"I'm sure you are," I said. "Do you spend a lot of time in this neighborhood?"

"Do I, Heel?" The little dog licked his chin. "I guess I do," Shoe said. "I guess I spend most of my dynamic, vibrating young life right here, T.C.B. with my ladies."

"I'm trying to find a handsome blond man who was in this neighborhood about two weeks ago. Very pale. Thirtyish. Wore glasses and probably had a summer suit on."

"Why in the ever-lovin' would you be looking for some blond dude when you got a black-haired dude standing right in front of you?"

"It's important."

"Of course it is. But could it be more important than the thing that the cosmic forces have caused to happen here, the meeting of the Ice Princess with the Black Prince of the Night?"

He did a spin on his skates and then stopped on a dime in front of me. He grabbed both dogs with one hand and reached out the other to touch my ear. "You should have a silver star right there. A beautiful silver star."

"Someday maybe I'll get one, Shoe, but right now, what can you tell me about the blond guy?"

"What can *you* tell *me* about the blond beauty that stands before me?" He spun around again and shifted a dog back to his empty arm.

This was getting me nowhere. I said, "What will it take to make you confide in me?"

He shook his head and smiled. "Shoe soothes, cajoles, cavorts. He does not confide."

He kissed the dog held in his left arm. I pointed to the little animal's eye. "What do you feed him?"

"Only the best, chérie. My creatures get only the best."

"Well, the best isn't so good for that one, I guess."

He frowned. "What the hell are you talking about?"

"Look how watery his eyes are. I bet he even sneezes when he wakes up."

"He makes a little sniffing noise, but . . ."

"He's got an allergy."

"He's fine. Nothing wrong with neither Heel nor Toe."

I shrugged. "Did they tell you that?"

"Uh. Well, what does one do about an allergy?"

I smiled. "What can you tell me about my friend?"

He stared at me for a few seconds. Then he said, "You first."

"Okay. Check your dog food and see if it contains either beef or cheese. Those are two very common causes of allergies. Try some dry food that substitutes veal for other meats. If his eyes still don't clear up, then you may have to take him to a vet and get some pills."

"Shi', I could've figured that out myself."

"Maybe. But you didn't even know the poor little fellow had a problem. And now it's your turn. Unless a promise means nothing to the Black Prince of the Night."

He shook his head. "You *are* something, Princess." He faced the little dog with the weepy eyes. "What about it, Heel, two weeks ago? White guy with a wide tie. Oh, my. He showed me the photo of a young lady who was not nearly so . . . so striking as yourself. You should have some real pearls to accentuate your lovely swan neck."

"Shoe, this is serious," I said.

"All right. All right. Except you could be my new Ice Princess. All right. Mr. Blond, he parks his car near the corner. He goes into the bird-feather place. A while later he comes out of the bird-feather place with the Bird Man."

"Who's that, the owner?"

"The Bird Man? No way. More like a supplier. Makes feather capes. What more can I say? I have had no dealings with the gentleman. I have not asked to peruse his identification."

"So the blond and the Bird Man leave together?"

"Right-o. They wander down to the corner. The blond goes into Whamm-Burger, and the Bird Man hits the corner pay phone for a beat, then follows. I assume they dine. Do not ask if they have the Whamm-Burger or the Double-Whamm or the Grand-Whamm. I do not know. I had business on the street.

"Then they're finished. The Bird Man gets into his truck and flies away. The blond passes me by, then stops and shows me the young lady's picture. And I misjudged the man, see."

"What do you mean?"

"Well, you size people up in my trade. I figure this is a dude from out of town who is seeking something special. So I tell him I can certainly come up with a young woman who resembles the lady in his picture. You see, with the magic of modern makeup and this here plastic surgery, anybody can look like anybody.

"But I called it wrong, because before I can go further, he jerks back his photo and returns to Wings 'n' Things. He spends maybe ten minutes more inside. Then he comes out. I skate over to him to apologize for my rash conclusion. But he shines me on and walks away from me. And then, sur- prise, surprise, it appears that he is, after all, in the market for some fine, firm flesh. Because he spots this pair of foxes, and once he gets his tongue tucked back in his mouth, he bee-lines after them. One gets away, in a go-to-the-ucking-fay-oon-may Silver Cloud. But he follows the brunette and eventually scores with her. End of report."

"Scores how?"

He rolled his eyes. "My dear, sweet, innocent Ice Princess. To score is to make contact, to start the process of sharing smiles and secret thoughts . . ."

"I know what it means. How specifically did he *score* with her?"

He shrugged. "I saw them walking together. Looked like a score to me."

"Thanks, Shoe," I said.

"What would you think about some *framboise* Italian ice right about now?"

"How do you suppose I could find the Bird Man or that brunette?"

He shrugged. "The Bird Man supplies Wings 'n' Things. You could ask them." I hoped that Mr. Bloodworth would gather that information in the course of his teeth-pulling. "The honey, she's not exactly street material. Her and her girl friend were strangers in my mural. All I can say is that your blond must be a mighty man. If you see him, tell him Shoe says he's lucky he gave up on that other little flower."

"What other little flower?"

"The one in his picture."

"You know her?"

Shoe gave me a large smile. "Let us put that in the proper tense. I knew her. From four or five months ago. I would have been glad to tell that to your blond friend, but since she was not in my stable, I thought he might accept a substitute. A bad judgment call."

"She's a . . . a prostitute?"

"Well, don't say it like that, beauty. It's a damn fine life for a young woman."

"I'm sure," I told him. "Where can I find her?"

"When our paths crossed, she was with a brother, and they were going double-o. But then she messed around with this dude named Devlin, and next thing I heard, Devlin had turned her out, but in an upscale way."

"I'm not sure I understand what you're saying. Who is Devlin?"

"That is a question. Devlin is a very upscale operator. The ultimate of sly. You won't find Devlin working the streets. Uh-uh. Devlin works your better hotels and restaurants and clubs."

"He's a pimp."

"At the very least," Shoe said. "He deals in women and drugs and other accou-tray-ments of power. The man is a pro. Not that I have ever laid eyes on him. But I know of him. He calls himself Devlin, the Secret Agent. He's secret all right."

"So Cece MacElroy works for this Devlin," I said, almost to myself.

"She did."

"You wouldn't know where he is?"

He shook his head and the smile left his face. "You don't want to know, Princess. When you run with Devlin, sometimes you wind up barefoot. Like the young woman you call Cece. Her career is probably going to be short and sweet."

"What do you mean?"

"Most of us, we allow our women to remain with us even though their allure gets tarnished. Not Devlin. His turnover is quite high."

"What happens when he's finished with them?"

"I don't want to put ideas like that in your head, beauty. But if it'll keep you away from Devlin . . . his ladies wind up in a hotel where you don't check out until you check out."

"He keeps them in a hotel where they can't get out?"

"Something like that. Gives the profession a bad name."

"Wh . . . where is this hotel?"

He smiled. "That would take some . . . investigating. Whyn't you come along with me and I'll find out for you. We can have ourselves a pizza, too. How's that sound?"

"Where do we have to go to find out?"

"Over to Sunset and east a bit, talk with my friend Slide. He knows a little more about Devlin's operations than me."

"Where specifically is Slide?"

"Usually he's by the Greaseburger stand on Sunset, near the school." By the school he meant Hollywood High.

"Okay," I said. "Just a minute."

"Hey, wait . . ."

I walked away from him and entered Wings 'n' Things.

3. Inside, Mr. B. was pulling the teeth of a henna-haired plump woman in hot pants. He turned, saw me, and gave me a signal for me to go back to the car.

I glared at him for a few seconds, then arrived at a decision. Let him pull all the bloody teeth he wanted. There was important work to do.

Outside, I tore a section from one of the brown bags littering the rear of

Mr. B.'s car and scribbled a note on it. I draped the note on his steering wheel.

Then I went off to see whether Shoe was serious or just another time-wasting idiot.

28

1. L.A. wouldn't be L.A. without its weirdo factions. The hordes of hot-eyed and mind-blown young rebels who claimed the Sunset Strip in the sixties were replaced by the single-minded, shaved-head Buddhists and Jesus freaks of the seventies. In the eighties the flower peddlers were being pushed aside by the latest, and in my opinion the worst, breed of southern California street freakos—the Terrible Trendies.

They prowl the oddball boutiques of the city, throwing money away faster than their parents or spouses can make it, on fashions with a life-span of twenty minutes, one-joke geegaws and food less appetizing than pork tartare —in short, the least necessary items of consumer merchandise that the fevered mercenary mind of man could devise.

Melrose Avenue was the new mecca for the upwardly mobile, and its effect had been so devastating on the shops along Rodeo and Brighton that Beverly Hills had begun to provide free parking for its customers' Rollses and Benzes. The thought of anything free in Beverly Hills made me suspect the Millennium was at hand. And there was nothing along Melrose to suggest otherwise.

Wings 'n' Things was a whitewashed cinderblock building with an entry like the opened beak of a bird. There was a display window filled with pink feathers and beach balls. A thousand flamingos had probably been denuded just to satisfy the whim of some fever-brain decorator.

The store was in the middle of a particularly active block. To its left was Monster Mash, a black building with a garish red sign that was shaped to resemble a four-foot bloodstain. Its display window was padded with broken plastic baby dolls. A stream of customers, young and old, poured in and out of the place. Sarah informed me that it was common knowledge that Monster Mash had "the most disgustingly horrific" T-shirts, temporary tattoos, trading cards, and windup toys one could find this side of the Orient.

To the right of Wings 'n' Things was something called High Priest and Postulant. That display window featured two mannequins with fifties-style hairdos, both wearing starched white blouses and short, pleated skirts. The blond one was standing beside a broken goldfish bowl and a little plastic goldfish that lay peacefully on its side. The other mannequin wore glasses and a stern expression and was shaking a finger at the blond while using the other hand to brandish a straitjacket constructed of white leather. Further down the street was a health-food restaurant with the mouth-watering name of Earthgrub and a fast-food joint named Whamm-Burger.

I sighed and started to get out. Before the kid could push down on her handle, I said, "Just sit tight, Sarah. This will go better and faster if I don't have an attractive young woman with me." Sometimes, I can be diplomatic.

"But . . . ," she said.

"I may have to pull a few teeth in there, and I need elbow room. Okay?" She shrugged, defused by the "attractive young woman."

Waltzing through the Wings 'n' Things bird beak was like journeying into a dust mop. There were feathers on the walls and ceilings. Nightmare time for hay-fever victims. A clear plastic covering separated my shoes from the white feathers on the floor.

The room was not quite barn size, with feathered fashions draped on racks and on displays. Preening mannequins stood beside stuffed peacocks and egrets. Other plumed creatures dangled from the ceiling on black wires, their button-bright eyes catching the glitter of the passing parade along Melrose.

Soft-rock music mixed with bird noises as it floated from speakers in four corners of the room. Only one of the fifteen or twenty people present seemed to notice the insipid music—a black guy in cutoffs and a pink full-dress coat with tails who stood in front of the suede-jacket display with his eyes shut, rocking back and forth in his baby-blue basketball shoes to the undernourished beat.

A sad-faced young woman with tan hair that had been shaved high above her ears was behind the only sales counter, studying the *L.A. Times*'s comic section as if her life depended on Doonesbury's punch line. Her bright yellow fingernails were long enough to rescue nickels from sewer gratings, and dirty enough to have been used for that purpose. She gnawed on one of them while she read.

I gave the place a once-over. My problem was, I couldn't tell the customers from the clerks. Since nobody rushed forward to see what they could sell me, I toured the joint myself.

In an alcove leading to rest rooms and a pay phone, I found a bulletin board. On it, among the scattered hiring notices, roommate requests, and mug shots of missing kids, I glommed a card containing the same photo of Cece MacElroy that Manion had shown me the day I'd met him. The instructions were for anyone who'd seen the girl to phone a number. Somebody had drawn a line through the original number and written in a new one (that, I later discovered, was answered by Manion's former L.A. home, the Mariposa Hotel).

I carried the card to the tan-haired girl at the counter. "Excuse me, miss," I said.

No reply.

"Miss?"

Nothing.

I rapped a knuckle against the counter next to her comic page. She looked up at me, expressionless. I got the feeling she was putting price tags on my suit, shirt, tie. Evidently she found the total wanting, because without a word she returned to her comics.

There was a standing display for Circe on the counter. It consisted of a color cut-out of the three women who made up the group and a plastic bubble where you could deposit your "Bucks for the Nuclear Ban." It was packed with folding money. I placed the photo of Cece MacElroy next to it and slapped the counter.

"I'd like to talk to you about this picture," I told the tan-haired girl.

She continued to ignore me. I felt a flush working up from my neck. A hand touched my shoulder. I was so tense, I jerked to one side and spun around. I was staring at a girl of Sarah's age. "Take it easy," she said. "I didn't mean to push your button."

There was a little scar near her right eye that made an "x" when she smiled. She said, "Tuli's deaf."

"Huh?"

She pointed to the girl behind the counter. "Tuli, she's deaf. She used to be with the Satanic Sluts. Female heavy metal. Played sax. Blew her ears to hell. She has to be looking directly at you to see what you're saying, and even then she can't always tell, because she can't see very well, either."

"How's her memory?" I asked.

The young girl shrugged.

"How's yours?"

"Excellent."

I passed her the card. While she studied it, I asked, "Do you work here?"

"My mom does. Over there." She pointed to a beefy dame in a halter and hot pants spilling over a chair while she yakked with some other dame, who was made up to go dancing with Dracula.

The redheaded mother spun around, as if her antennae had picked up an alien siren. "Dan-ee, c'mere, hon."

"Gotta go," the kid said. And went.

As I crossed the floor, the redhead's eyes did not waver. "Excuse me," I began, but was cut off by her flat query, "That prick Chester send you?"

I shook my head. "Don't bullshit me," she said. "You can tell Chester the place is mine now, he's out of it. And out of my life. I don't give a fuck how many cops he sends around."

I said I was no cop.

"Then who the hell are you?"

I fought to keep a friendly smile on my face and said, "Just a guy trying to locate a few people. This girl, for one."

The redhead glanced at the card. "Don't look familiar to me. Frumpy little kid, huh?"

"Maybe your daughter has seen her?" I asked.

"You know anything about this, Dan-ee?" she asked the kid.

Dani shyly nodded yes.

The redhead turned back to me. "What's the deal on the reward?"

I looked at the card. It mentioned a reward would be forthcoming.

"If your daughter can lead us to the girl, she might qualify for the reward." I hadn't any idea if I was telling the truth or a lie.

Dani said, "I ain't never seen the girl."

The redhead looked at her as if she were ready to disown her.

"I already told the other guy," Dani said.

"What other guy?"

The redhead said, "Hold it! I don't know what this is all about. But Dani don't say word one until we see some cash."

I gave her a disappointed look.

Dani said, "He was a blond guy with glasses. Talked funny."

The redhead rubbed her fingers together.

I peeled a ten from my wallet and handed it to her. She wasn't impressed. "You can't get a loaf of bread for that anymore."

"You want the tenspot for about five minutes of your time, fine. If not, hand it back and we forget it."

Somehow she managed to get the folded bill into her tight pants pocket without a shoe horn. "Ask your questions."

"Thanks. Dani, what can you tell me about the blond man?"

"Nothing. He came in, saw the card, and took it down. He wrote on it and put it back up."

The redhead smiled. "The blond hunk, yeah. Hunky, but square." She turned to the woman with the vampire makeup job sitting next to her. "You remember, the guy with the Randolph Scott accent. He and Low Rent hit it off and went out for burgers."

"Who's Low Rent?" I asked.

"The Bird Man of Melrose."

"Where can I find him?"

The redhead's eyes narrowed. "We're doing a lot of giving here, dude."

For another ten she got up off of her duff and did a quick strut over to the sales counter, where she reached around Tuli and found her Rolodex. She used a blood-red fingernail to flip through the entries, paused, and jotted down something on a business card.

Then she strutted back and handed me the card. It contained the name Low Rent Lacotta and a telephone number.

"No address?"

"What do you expect for loose change, the key to his front door?"

I took out my wallet again, but she waved it away. "Don't bother. We don't have his address. That's all we got. All our business we do in cash. Makes it easier on the bookkeepers."

I started to leave, but I paused at a full-length jacket that seemed to be made of feather boas stitched together. I turned to the redhead. "You sell many of these?"

"Can't give 'em away," she said. "Too hippy-dip for current trends. That's Low Rent's problem: He thinks just because it's from a bird, it's fucking great. I'm giving 'em another two weeks, then he gets 'em back. Full refund."

"He manufactures these?"

"Manufacture? Oh, sweetie. These are o-riginals. Made by hand by that tweety bird he lives with."

Low Rent Lacotta was definitely next on my list.

Outside, Sarah was not in the car. I looked up and down the block before I spotted the note stuck to the steering wheel. It was on brown wrapping paper. It read: "Have gone away with a fellow named Shoe to find Cece MacElroy. I'll catch the bus home. If they didn't mention the Bird Man in Wings 'n' Things, go back and pull more teeth. Serendipity."

A fellow named Shoe! Terrific. There's a gunman who hops the Atlantic following the kid, and I, in my wisdom, let her wander off with a fellow named Shoe. I should have known better. She collects weirdos like closets collect dust.

I drove around the block. No sign of her. Damnit!

Well, it would take at least an hour for her to get home by bus. I might as well do something useful. I pulled the phone-address registry from the back-seat and looked up Low Rent's number. Again, a strikeout.

So, I needed a phone. There was one just down the street on Melrose, but I started up the Chevy. I wanted a pay phone where I wouldn't have to worry about some street freak with hair like a tuning fork biting me on the ankle while I was dialing.

2. The number rang eight, nine, ten times. Then a tiny, very Southern feminine voice asked, "Is somebody there?"

The accent gave me an idea. "Cece?" I asked.

"Huh?"

"Is this Cece?"

"Oh," the tiny voice said, "that's somebody's name. I thought you was speaking Mexican. We get lots of Mexican wrong numbers on this line."

"Let me speak to Low Rent."

She hesitated. "He . . . uh, he's out right now. Is there something . . . some kind of a message?"

I wondered if she'd been asleep. Her voice had a dreamland, thick-tongue quality that went beyond a Dixie accent.

"Where is he? It's important."

"Uh . . . he's just out. That's all he tole me." There was an odd flapping noise, then a squawk. "You stop that," the girl shouted away from the receiver.

"Are you okay?" I asked.

"Sure. It was Jerry. Nasty old thing just shit on the sofa."

"Really?"

"She does it all the time."

"Right. Look, I've got an order for a dozen—naw, two dozen of those great plume capes that are on display at Wings 'n' Things. I've got a check all made out, only I don't know where to mail it."

"I'll get the post-office box number for you," she drawled.

"No. Wait! I don't send money to P.O. boxes. What's your address?"

"Low Rent'll be here in an hour. You all'd better call back then. But he's going back out real soon."

"I'm catching a plane in an hour. I've got a check here for"—I stopped to think—"for five thousand dollars."

"But he didn't say nothing to me about any check. I'm not supposed to give out our home address to nobody."

"Suit yourself, lady. The longer the money stays in my bank, the better I like it. But Low Rent isn't going to be happy about the way you're holding up this payment."

"Darn it. Any way it goes, I'll be wrong. . . ."

"It might be better if you're wrong with a check for five grand in your hand. It'll be a week before I get back here, and I'll have to tell him what caused the delay."

So she gave me the address. She also told me her name was Georgia. I told her mine was Homer and that the check was all but in the mail. "You and Jerry have yourselves a nice evening," I said.

"We always do," she said sadly. "Me and Jerry and Mick. Low Rent'll come in, eat, and then rush off, and me, Jerry, and Mick'll just have ourselves another nice old evening."

"Stay off the sofa," I said.

"Huh? Oh, yeah. I see what you mean."

3. To my surprise, the address she gave me was in Beverly Hills, on Rexroth just off of Wilshire. An old apartment building guarded by a stone centurion. Both of them had recently been painted an ivy green. The centurion looked properly indignant.

The front door, though loaded with locks, stood ajar, leading to a vestibule with pale purple walls and dark purple carpet, decorated further by mirrors in silver-leaf frames and elephant-ear plants in big red tubs that were anchored to the floor by chains.

Apartment 6 was on the second-level rear, overlooking a small swimming pool filled with algae, end-of-summer leaves, and an elderly woman the color of an acorn in a tank suit, exercising her wrinkles by flopping around in the deeper end. She paused long enough to point to the apartment and tell me I couldn't reach it from there. It was accessible only by traveling through the vestibule, down a hallway, up a stairwell, then out onto a balcony leading around the rear of the building. You either had to have the instincts of a Mohawk Indian or you had to find someone to ask. My assistance came from a dapper old fellow in a three-piece flannel suit, with an Esky moustache and an armful of sample cases containing his photos under glassine. His instruction was simple and his accent upper-class Brit. "Go through that door and follow your nose. When the odor gets rank enough, you'll be there."

There *was* a vaguely ripe smell coming from apartment 6, where a small brass plaque screwed to the door read: MORITOURI.

I knocked and heard the flapping of wings, then something a little more human scuffling about.

I knocked again and the door opened a crack, letting me see part of a tiny feminine face with large, worried eyes. Scratches showed on a bare shoulder above a leather halter. "Uh . . . yes?" she asked.

There was another flutter of wings, and the girl ducked and started to shiver. A green object flashed by the partially opened door. "Jee-sus," the girl shrilled. "Mick almost got out, and that would have ended it." She looked at me fearfully. " 'Scuse me, mister, but I gotta close the damn door."

She tried to push it shut, but something was blocking it. My foot. "Please. C'mon now," she begged, struggling with the door. "Don't let the birds get out."

"I'd like to see Low Rent."

"He's not here. Please . . ."

"I'll come in and wait."

That worried her more than the possibility of a bird escaping. "NO! Please. Jus' go 'way!"

I was tired of it. I shoved the door open and entered the room.

It had been turned into one huge bird cage for two parrots. They'd torn off the leatherette tops of chairs, chewed and clawed the cloth off of the sofa, and crapped all over everything, including hardwood floors that looked mottled for life. The room smelled as nice as it looked.

Three pairs of eyes were turned on me. Georgia's were about to cry. The two parrots watched me suspiciously. One was perched on a lamp, the other on the back of a chair. They looked mean and nasty. If there's one thing that turns my blood to ice water, it's the idea of something flying into my face. I backed against the front door, shutting it.

Suddenly the chair parrot took off, headed for the high ceiling, and then dive-bombed to mid-room, where it fluttered to a landing on Georgia's bare shoulder.

It drew blood, but she barely flinched. "Mick needs a . . . a manicure or something."

She pointed to the bird on the lamp. "That's Jerry and I'm Georgia. You're the man who just phoned. I remember your voice. But I'm not terribly clear on what we talked about."

I scanned the room. There was a glass and a bottle of Mescal on the floor next to the couch. The bottle was almost down to the worm. Maybe she was saving that for the birds.

"What we talked about wasn't important," I told her.

"That's what I thought," she said, suddenly proud of herself. "You must know Low Rent real well for him to give you this address. He doesn't give nobody this address."

"You gave me the address," I said.

She tensed suddenly, and Mick took flight from her shoulder.

"I couldn't have done that," she whined. "'Cause he'd hit me if I did that."

"He hit you often?"

"No. Not often. Sometimes when I forget to feed the birds. I don't always remember so good. I try to put out their food when I eat, but sometimes I forget to eat myself."

She was only five feet tall. Sarah was bigger and certainly healthier. She looked to be in her late teens, but tiny girls tend to look younger than they are. Her halter didn't have much to hide, and her trousers were too big, as if they'd been hand-me-downs from an older sister or brother.

"Have you and Low Rent been together long?" I asked.

She cocked her head to one side. I wondered if Low Rent had picked her because she reminded him of a bird. "It must have been four-five months now. I know, 'cause J. C., that's my husband, got busted down in Mexico in February. A dope thing, but he was set up, I'm certain. Only they say he may never get out, because they're kinda tough down there. I was hoping to pay him a visit, but the way I am now, I'd probably get thrown right in there with him. Let me show you something."

She left the room. When she returned, she was carrying a new, almost-finished plumed cape, intricately patterned by a rainbow of colored feathers. It was quite beautiful, but I had no idea what anybody would do with the damn thing. Hang it on a wall, maybe.

"What do you think?" she said.

"Lovely work," I said. "Have you ever made a cape out of pink feathers?"

"Pro-bab-ly."

"For a girl with blond hair like little Orphan Annie's?"

"You mean Afro'd?"

"I guess."

She frowned and then shook her head. "Nope. Don't remember anybody like that." I wasn't surprised. She hadn't remembered our phone call from ten minutes before.

"But Low Rent said he gave one like that to Mr. Devlin a couple weeks ago."

"Who . . . ?"

The two birds grew suddenly restless and lunged from their perches. I back-stepped to a wall as they began their noisy dive bombs.

"Oh, hell," Georgia said. "I better get this back before these birds mess on it." She lifted the cape carefully and edged out of the room backward.

Just outside the front door, rubber squeaked on cement. The birds heard it at the same time I did. They swooped to the front door, then zoomed away. A key clicked in the lock.

The door opened and a boy entered. He looked about as young as Georgia, maybe younger—a sullen teenager with short dark brown hair that had been severely chopped by a barber with no style and less time. He made up for the bad crew cut with a droopy, wispy beard that looked like it would float away the next time he washed his face. He was wearing khaki trousers with at least four sets of pockets and a striped T-shirt. He took me in. Then he sniffed, drawing up one side of his lip in a sneer that reminded me of Presley. Slowly and deliberately, he pocketed his keys and closed the door behind him.

I wasn't sure that he was Low Rent. A kid brother, maybe. Then the birds flew toward him, each taking a shoulder, twittering merrily as he reached into his pocket and brought out a handful of seed. He stuck out his lower lip and placed a few grains on it. One by one, unhurriedly, the parrots fed from his mouth. He was either brave or stupid or both. There were thin white scars and fresh scratches on his neck and jaw and on his hands and arms. Maybe he'd reached the point where he didn't feel the pain from his beloved pets. Maybe they hadn't made the scratches. When those grains were gone, he opened his bony hand and let them go to town on the remaining grains.

Georgia returned during the feeding. She stared at the boy and the birds, transfixed yet anxious for him to acknowledge her. Finally, when the parrots had filled their bills, he asked her without emotion, "You cattin' around on me, bitch? With fat old men?"

"I . . . he . . ."

"I told her I'd set your birds free if she didn't let me in."

He snickered, still not looking away from Georgia. "You don't have an ounce of brain in that head, do you?" He touched her shoulder, then walked his fingers up to her neck. He grabbed a fistful of hair and tugged at it slightly, smiling.

"Please . . ." she begged, and he withdrew his hand, using it to pat the hair back in place.

"Georgia, my Bird Girl." He turned to me. "What was it you wanted?"

"You met a guy in Wings 'n' Things about two weeks ago."

He sprinkled birdseed in Georgia's hair and stepped back when the parrots landed on her shoulders to peck. "Description," he demanded.

"Early twenties," I said. "Blond. Glasses. Coat and tie."

"What do you want with him?"

I said, "He's been missing since the day you saw him. He's involved in a murder case."

I was trying to watch both his and Georgia's reactions, but I was wasting my time. She was too involved in keeping the birds from getting tangled in her hair, and his face held less expression than his parrots'.

He asked me, "You a cop? Or are we talking money here?"

"Maybe I could scrape something together."

He smiled. "Why don't you do that and get back to me."

I asked him, "How old are you?"

"What the fuck's that got to do with anything?"

"Eighteen?"

"Okay, so I'm eighteen."

I said, "I was just trying to figure out exactly where they'd put you in the slams. You'll be with the big boys."

"Don't get wicked," he said.

"Tell me where my friend is and I'll keep the cops out. At least for a while."

"Keep 'em out of what, jagoff?"

"Out of your face, boy. They're looking for the murderer of a man named Kosca. Their theory is that while searching for a young girl named Cece MacElroy, he stumbled into a scene involving fighting birds. They came up with the theory because his face had been worked over by beaks and talons. His cuts were a little deeper than yours."

"Jam it, Jack. I don't know anything about any murder."

"What about a woman who calls herself Loni Hoffstattler? I saw her boyfriend kill a man."

"Why tell me about it?"

"She was wearing one of your feather capes."

"Lots of people do. I ain't responsible for the lives they lead."

"Who's Devlin?"

He took a step backward and shrugged.

"Ever hear of a guy named Archie Leach?"

"Never."

"What about Wally Barclay?"

"What's a Wally Barclay?" He guffawed, but he wasn't really amused. He turned to Georgia and began to brush the remaining seeds from her hair onto the birdcrap-encrusted floor. "You're a fucking insult to my intelligence, old man. One thou and I'll tell you about the blond guy."

"Too much."

He glared at me. "Screw around and see what you turn up. Maybe he'll croak. It's your play."

I decided it might be fun to plant a fist right at the corner of his jawline. His eyes turned flinty, as if he could read my thought. I said, "That statement buys you a piece of his death. Knowledge of a crime; accessory to murder."

"Prove it, Dick Tracy. But right now, get the fuck out. You decide to do business, come back with the grand. But move on it. Georgia and me ain't going to be sticking around here too much longer. This city's rapidly turning to shit."

I looked at his floor, his furniture, his apartment. I said, "I can see where you might get that idea."

29

To my great surprise Slide was a thin milk-white boy of not more than seventeen, with a bleach-blond flattop that had black roots and a love-slave dog tail hanging over the collar of his shiny black shirt. He had a little piece of teak dangling from a chain attached to his left earlobe. His forehead was high and rounded and damp with perspiration. His eyebrows were a dark black that matched the mascara around his large dark eyes. He had a permanently surprised expression because of the arched eyebrows, and a little pug nose above a rather long upper lip that, regardless of its length, or perhaps because of it, kept creeping up over his huge, glistening white teeth.

Slide was dressed all in black, as one might have guessed. Runty would-be hoodlums always think they look more frightening in black. The truth was, Slide was about as fierce-looking as Bugs Bunny, whom he vaguely resembled.

He was sitting at an orange Formica table in the Sunset Strip Greasyburger, with a cigarette in one hand and a Greasydog in the other. He was wearing those awful leather gloves with the fingers cut off. He shoved what was left of the Greasydog past his large teeth and began munching, watching us as we approached.

A middle-aged Mexican wearing an apron and a chef's hat with the Greasyburger emblem on it shouted at Shoe to take his dogs elsewhere. Shoe ignored him, shifted Heel to his other arm beside Toe, and put out his now-empty hand for Slide to slap and do all those silly recognition movements.

Slide pointed at me and said, "New mamma?"

"Hardly," I said.

247

"Just a friend, man. A good chick."

Slide eyed me as if he didn't believe such a thing existed. Then he offered his gloved hand. I didn't want to touch it, but this was a time for diplomacy. I put my hand out tentatively, and to my surprise he took it by the fingertips and raised it to his lips. The gesture reminded me of my first meeting with Terry Manion, who had kissed my hand, too. It's not often that a woman gets her hand kissed these days. Especially by such disparate types.

"My name's Slide, señorita," he said, mispronouncing the Spanish. With the utmost control I managed not to wipe my hand on my trouser leg.

"Hello," I said. "My name's Serendipity."

"Sweet name. Sweet frame."

Shoe shifted Heel back, and in one continuous motion did a little pirouette on his skates and slid into a chair. I took the seat next to him.

"So?" Slide wanted to know.

Shoe answered the question with, "Serendipity's looking for a guy who might be one of Devlin's people."

Slide wrinkled his forehead and stubbed out his cigarette on his plate. "Voluntary or not?"

"I don't know," I said. I described Terry and added, "He was searching for a girl my age, named Cece MacElroy."

"The little blonde who used to be with G-man," Shoe explained. "You know. Gregory."

Slide nodded. "Yeah. I know him. I ratted for him for a while."

"I don't understand."

"I did the street rat. The scurry." I didn't know what he was talking about, and I guess it showed. He shook his head, as if I were pathetic. Then he looked away.

Shoe said, "If a guy comes in with even a little power, he needs somebody to suss things out on the street, to get him a place to stay, spare food, information, or to run errands. Like that. He needs a street rat. That's what Slide is—the best goddamn street rat in Hollywood."

"I'm branching out," he said with a smile. "Working my way to the ocean. Do some surf scurry."

"If you were Gregory's street rat, you must know a lot about him."

"I know a lot of shit," Slide said. "But the deal is, I don't say what I know. Are you the one he's after?"

The question took me aback. "What?"

"I heard he was after some kid, that he and Devlin are involved in something advanced."

"Advanced?"

Slide got his disgusted look again. "You got your *basic* and you got your *advanced*. They're into *advanced*."

"What is it?" I asked.

"Just like that, huh? Where'd you find this one, Shoe, off a game show?"

I resented him and his attitude. I said to Shoe, "I thought you said this fellow knew his way around. The only thing he seems to know is how to eat a hot dog with his gloves on."

"Don't term on me, honey. I know when I'm being fogged."

"You don't even speak English."

"Sometimes that puts you one up. Especially in what is rapidly becoming a Third World outpost. What do you want from me, frill?"

"What I think she wants—" Shoe began, but I cut him off.

"I can speak for myself. I want to find Terry Manion. To do that, I will probably have to first find Cece MacElroy. So that's what I want: her where-abouts."

The man in the Greasyburger hat shouted once again for Shoe to take his dogs outside. Slide gave the man the finger.

"Hell, honey. I could use the Tel-Bell and have G-man Desidero here in a minute. He'd pay me and you'd be able to ask him about his chick. How's that sound?"

"About as worthless as everything else about you." I stood up, turning to Shoe. "Thanks for all your help. This . . . this *street rat* is not someone I'd care to trust."

"Sit it down, sweets," Slide said, patting my hand with his germ-infested leather glove. "I'm not going to phone G-man. I'm not about to do nothing to make life easier for him."

I sat down. "Why not?"

"Because he's an A-number-one badios, that's why." He stared at Shoe. "You must've heard about the trouble at the Stork?"

Shoe shook his head. He hadn't heard.

"Well, I been bunkin' with that fairy director, Winkermann, a very unde-manding old fart, for nearly a year. And it was a good scene. Copacetic. No hassle, as long as I'm around Sundays for the Wink's big soirees.

"You shoulda seen me, dressed in all this gear the Wink laid out. Polo, man. Very Robert Redford. White pants, like that. He just wanted me to hang out so's he could point me out to his queen pals as his 'ward.'

"Actually, I dug being his ward. He's not a bad old duff, Winkermann, and I think the son of a bitch really cared for me. And for somebody out of Boyle Heights Foster, having somebody care for you is not a commonplace experience."

"So what about the Stork?" Shoe asked.

"Hey! Let those crotch-squeezers out a notch and relax. I'm coming to it. Anyway, I'm going out one night and the Winker is moping around and he asks me where I'm headed and I tell him Galaxy, Moebus Trip, and the Stork. And he wants to know could he string, see what the places are like, meet my friends.

"Now this sounds like a real weevil of an idea, but the old guy doesn't spray or scatter sand or anything, so I figure why the fuck not? And we hit a few spots, him being his usual laid-back self. Then G-man and some Wiffleball catch up with us at the Stork Klub . . ."

"Wiffleball?" I asked.

"Dorkus. Snook. Asshole, okay? Anyhow, G-man wants me to do the scurry for him, but I tell him I put away my ears and tail for the night. So he gets all frosty, and maybe a little physical in his demands. And poor old sweet Winky comes to my defense. Jeez. Like your granddad taking on Godzilla.

"G-man's got him up against the bar, with a broken beer bottle about an inch from his chin whiskers. And the poor son of a bitch is so woofed he voids. G-man sees what's happening and he gets Rambo-mad and he kicks Winky's legs out from under him and Wink slips down and flops in his own mess. And the Stork being the kind of place it is, everybody's laughing. Wink, who's weeping like a baby, sees me garping at him. I move to help him up, but he pulls away from me and gets up by himself.

"So I follow him out, but he keeps shouting at me and cursing me and telling me it's all my fault, that I associate with psycho-sludge like G-man. Then he tells me he never wants to orb me again."

"So what happened?" I asked.

"Another romance ended. I went back inside and told G-man I'd do the scurry," he said, trying to be hard and cynical. But his mascara looked moist.

"Could you describe the guy with G-man?"

"The yotz? Strictly a yuppatola. Thirties. Little friggin' lipbrush. Hair combed just so. Wearing the white slacks, the Sy Devore pink shirt. Screw him."

"When was all this?"

He shrugged. "A couple weeks ago."

"You said you could phone G-man?"

"Maybe."

"Do you know where he lives?"

He gave me an enigmatic smile. "Like I said, I know a lot of shit."

"I don't have much money, but maybe I could get some more."

"How much you got?"

I took out my pink wallet, undid the Velcro snap and, drawing away from the table and Slide's prying eyes, took a peek inside. Oh, Lordy! Nothing but a few pounds. Not even dollars. I hadn't bothered to exchange my British money. I didn't even know if I could make it home. Maybe Mr. Bloodworth was still . . . No. He would have pulled any teeth that were there to be pulled by now.

The point was to keep Slide in the dark about my financial condition. "I have ten dollars," I said.

"For the phone number I need twenty. For the address it goes up to fifty."

"Let's say you give me the number," I told him. "And I'll decide what it's worth."

Shoe shook his head. "You're too much, Princess." He chuckled. "Anyway, Slide don't know that man's address."

"Oh, yeah?"

"Yeah, brother." He leaned over and whispered in my ear, "You see that vein above Slide's right eyebrow that's bouncing like a Mex jumping bean? That's his lie detector. If it's beatin', he's cheatin'."

It certainly was beating. Slide didn't like us staring at him. "Cut that shit out!" he ordered.

"And you know Desidero's phone number?"

"I said I did."

The vein continued to jump.

"Is Slide your real name?"

"Of course not, dwat! But don't bother asking what my real name is." I didn't really care. The question had been a test, and it worked. The eyebrow twitch was now quiet. No phone number, no address. I wondered if this absurd little boy could help me at all.

"What was it that Desidero wanted you to scurry for him?"

"You don't scurry. Scurry is like a . . . a thing. You do *the* scurry."

"Excuse me," I said. Who'd he think he was, Edwin Newman or somebody? "What'd he want you to do?"

"Errand of mercy. St. Bernard bit."

Shoe whispered "dope run" in my ear.

"And you did it?" I asked.

"Why not? What else did I have going that night? It was only a few blocks away."

I said, "So Gregory Desidero is a drug addict on top of everything else."

He raised his eyes heavenward. He said in a stage whisper, "Drug addict? Honey, if you must use the word, it's 'rugs,' not 'drugs,' okay?" He reverted to his nasal whine. "G-man doesn't use rugs himself. Not this year. Oh, he takes a toot now and then, but he's no addict. He had other use for this dust."

Shoe said, "You're a dramatic bugger, Slide. But will you tell your story and be done?"

"I picked up the goodies from Fred the Fender on Ivar and brought 'em back to G-man and his scumbag friend."

I asked, "What was it about this friend that rubbed you the wrong way?"

"He had that actor look. You know, full profile, half profile, and out. And I didn't like his attitude. He kept mocking me. I'd say something and he'd repeat it, like he was trying to get inside my head or something. He even sounded like me."

"Maybe he's planning a *Slide* TV show," Shoe said. "With him playing a debonair street rat."

Slide glared at him. "You wanna hear this fucking story or not?"

We both nodded.

"Well, the Q. was: What were the rugs for? To get the A., I waited for them to take off from the Stork. Then I did my own scurry. Hopped my chop and was on their taillights all the way downtown past Little Tokyo.

"It was beautiful, Shoe. I cut through alleys, wound up in front of 'em twice. They never had any fucking idea I was stringing 'em."

"So, where did they go, man? Is this leading to something?"

Slide shrugged. "You tell me. They go into this flea-pit. Up to the third floor and into a room. There's this wasted guy in there."

I sat forward. "Wasted how?"

"Stoned to the hairline. He's raving about romance and his little girl friend. Babble. The rugs are for him. G-man is keeping him triple-blissed."

"What did this man look like?"

"Well, it ain't like I followed 'em into the goddamn room. I didn't see the guy. Only heard him. Sounded like a cracker to me."

"A cracker? You mean Southern?"

"The man pronounced love like luuuuv. A cracker."

"What's the address?"

"Who knows addresses downtown? It's by Little Tokyo, like I said."

"Take me there!"

"Just like that, huh?"

I had no idea how to bargain with him, but then I remembered his twitch. "If you do, I'll tell you how people know when you're lying."

Shoe scowled. "Hey, that was told you in utmost confidence."

"It's worth a man's life," I said.

Slide squinted at me. "More," he said.

"More what?"

"More information. Why is G-man trying to find you?"

"Because I know something that can make trouble for him."

Shoe stood up suddenly. He spun once on his wheels and said, "Time to move on and make my livelihood. I don't like the direction this is heading."

"What're you mouthing about, man?" Slide asked.

"There are things it makes sense to know, and things it don't. It makes no sense to know if anybody's doing something that might eventually make Devlin mad enough to come looking for somebody who knows what anybody's been doing.

"Serendipity, my Ice Princess, you know where to find me."

I said, "Thanks for everything, Shoe."

"Good luck to you both," he said, skating to the door. There, he paused and faced the counterman. "Hey, Cholo!"

The counterman glared at him. Shoe let his poodles leap from his arms. He commanded, "Shine on."

The dogs lifted their legs and began to urinate on opposite sides of the open doorway. The counterman stared at this for a second, then began to scream.

Shoe told him, "You have now seen Shoe's dogs whiz in stereo." He lowered his arms, and the poodles leaped into them.

The counterman picked up a plastic bottle of catsup and threw it, but by the time it landed, splattering catsup all over the entryway, Shoe, Heel, and Toe had sailed away down Hollywood Boulevard.

"Are you going to take me?" I asked Slide.

"There's no way you can tell if I'm lying or not. But if there was, I wouldn't give a damn."

I smiled at him. I said, "I can tell you're lying now."

30

1. Personalized license plates have maintained their popularity in L.A., though I'd never seen one of them that wasn't so cute it'd set your teeth on edge. I seem to recall a TV detective who had his name, MANNIX, on his plates, front and back, as if it weren't hard enough to tail a suspect. Still, the extra bucks they cost supposedly go to an antipollution fund. And for many of the car owners, it's the most creative thing they do all year, so who am I to complain?

Even without the LO RENT plates, there would have been no difficulty in spotting the Bird Man's vehicle. It was the only sky-blue van with giant birds painted all over it parked on Rexford. The Mercedes and the Beamers seemed to shy away from it. I was pretty sure it was the same "psychedelical" van that Peru De Falco had eyeballed on its way up the mountain to Wally Barclay's Xanadu. And I was even more certain that every woe that had befallen me since Manion made his call to my office had been designed to keep me from helping the poor bastard, wherever he was. Maybe that nasty little weasel Low Rent would lead me to him.

I moved the Chevy around so that I would be facing Wilshire, half a block away from the birdmobile. I was anxious to find out Sarah's whereabouts, but I didn't want to risk losing the Bird Man. Georgia had said earlier that his plan was to move out quickly.

It took him about fifteen minutes. He was in a hurry. We barreled through the late-evening traffic. Most of the nine-to-fivers were already into their first martini or white wine or whatever the hell nine-to-fivers were drinking those days. And we were headed downtown, which is the place most of the cars were escaping.

Low Rent drove as wildly and as confidently as a man sitting in one of Uncle Sam's tanks. The van was big, but it wasn't invincible. A little Japanese bug might get the worst of a fender-bender, but a semi could have cleaned the Bird Man's cage for him.

Regardless, we cannonballed down Third and didn't stop until we hit the heart of downtown L.A., maybe twenty blocks west of my office. We were in the warehouse district. Quiet streets. Lots of chain-link fences and squat, unpainted structures. Low Rent stopped his van behind a battered sports car and beside the only tree in the defoliated area. Gnarled and cracked, it sat in an ugly patch of yellow weed and did little to improve the property value.

By the time I drove past him, Low Rent had circled the tree and was headed for a plain red-brick apartment-hotel. The name identified it as La Casa Dolce, but diabetics had nothing to fear from it. There didn't seem to be a window along the street level that hadn't been broken and boarded up.

I continued on until I saw the last of him in the rearview, then pulled against the curb.

I considered removing my rotor and locking it in the trunk—it was that kind of neighborhood. But I might have needed to get out of there in a hurry, and that's tough to do when your rotor is sharing space with your jack.

I strolled back to La Casa Dolce, paying special attention to the car parked in front of the van. It was a Porsche with a paint job so lousy, it looked like the black had been slopped on with a roller. Streaks of red showed through the black. California plates of no particular distinction. I patted the gun at my waist and felt mildly reassured.

There was a family of flies in the foyer of La Casa Dolce, but no humans. The dark green carpet was turning a dull gray in the center. Spiders and other industrious insects had established squatter's rights.

Once I entered the lobby, whatever light the setting sun provided the foyer was gone completely. I could barely see three feet in front of me. I felt roaches crunch as I trod the carpet.

"Something?"

The question had come from my right. Through the gloom, I could make out the vague outlines of a figure seated on a chair. "I'm looking for Robert Westermann," I lied.

"No Westermann here," the male voice replied.

I moved closer to it. It belonged to a tall figure in a suit and tie. "That's far enough," he said, menacingly.

"I was supposed to meet him at this address."

"You must have made a mistake, friend."

"I guess so. Must be North instead of South." I began backing away.

I didn't get far. Something was in the way. Something solid that smelled of cheap cologne. The something sang a melody welcoming me into the arms of love, the arms of Hajji Baba.

I tried to spin away from him, but he was right smack in the entryway. Big. Leathery. The last time I'd seen him had been in the house once owned by Sandy Watson and Jerry Palomar. He was crooning the two words at the top of his own private hit parade, "Hajji" and "Baba." He couldn't get enough of them.

"Nice song," I said. "Kinda grows on you." I moved my hand slowly until I could feel the handle of my gun.

He continued to sing.

"You're not going to hit me again, are you?" I asked. My fingers wrapped around the grip.

"Me? I never hit you before."

That was right. He'd kept me busy while his friend hit me. I heard a few roaches crunch behind me, and then, just as my gun cleared its holster, history repeated itself.

2. "She was so bu-full . . . li'l bu-full girl. Mos' bu-full thing I ever saw. He'pless. So bu-full . . ."

I returned to stark reality in a room brightly lit by a bare bulb. I was lying on a metal bedframe. My hands and feet were secured to it with wire.

There was no other furniture in the room. No carpet. No window shade. No nothing. Just a yahoo, sitting in the corner, going on and on about his "bu-full li'l girl." I twisted around to take a gander at him.

He was big but slack, like somebody had removed a major portion of his skeletal structure. His head rolled around on his big chest. His eyes had stopped focusing a long time ago. He had a beard that was neither neat nor clean. He smelled as ripe as week-old calamari.

"Hey!" I shouted to him.

He didn't even blink. "Cece," he said. "My li'l Cece. They destroyed my bu-full li'l girl."

This sorry sumpheap was Cece MacElroy's father. I shut my eyes to see if I could squeeze out the memory of his first name. Nothing. Maybe Manion never bothered to tell me. All I remember him saying was that the guy had come out here looking for his daughter. That wasn't a smart thing to do, evidently. Looking for Cece MacElroy, was, on the scale of dangerous occupations, somewhere between tightrope-walking and manning the American Embassy in Beirut.

Mike Kosca, the old sleuth, had been the first to try and find her, and he'd wound up filleted at the bottom of a canyon. Terry Manion seemed to have been taken out of the picture. The guy sitting across from me, drooling into his beard, was another casualty. And of course there was me—the newest member of the suicide squadron.

"Hey, MacElroy!" I shouted. And for the first time there seemed to be some life behind his eyes.

"Huh? Oh, no . . . bodies glowing . . . melting."

"MacElroy! Cut the crap!"

He smiled. "Coach?" he asked.

That clicked. Manion had said that this guy had been a college ballplayer. And his name . . . ? His name? Brent? Brick? Hell with it. "Hey, MacElroy, get on your fucking feet, man!"

"Feet?"

"I'm sending you in, damnit. Get ready."

The big man shook his head. Then he tried to get his feet under him. But he was too far gone. He fell over on his side. "They destroyed mah li'l girl."

"Destroyed her how?"

"She's not there any more. Pfffft. Gone. No more. Bad men. Faces masks. They do terrible things . . . melting . . ."

"Damnit, man, straighten up. I'm counting on you!"

Suddenly the sole door was thrown open, and a big light-skinned black man charged in, eyes glittering. He was carrying a small Gladstone bag, like a country doctor's. "What's all the goddamn shouting?" he asked me.

"I was just trying to chat with my friend here."

MacElroy continued to babble on. The black yelled at him to shut up. It was like yelling at the wall.

The black took a hypodermic needle from the Gladstone, jammed it through the cap of a small bottle of liquid. When he'd siphoned off enough of the fluid, he moved to MacElroy, who was into a litany of "li'l girl" 's.

In barely a second, MacElroy stopped talking and fell asleep. The black placed the needle back into his bag.

Low Rent appeared in the doorway. Behind him Hajji Baba, resplendent in pale blue leather pants and a bright red undershirt, winked at me and blew me a kiss.

He was with another familiar face, minus one moustache. "Hey, Little Jimmy," I said. "My old traveling companion."

A fourth man in the other room muttered something, and Jimmy replied, "I'll find out."

He shouted to the black, "G-man, Mr. Devlin's curious about how Bloodworth got here."

"You heard the man," the black growled at me.

Mr. Devlin? What about Leach? Or even Barclay? Who the hell was Devlin, and why was he being so coy? I tried to shift on the bed so that I could sit upright. "If you could loosen the wire a little . . ."

"Yeah, right. Hey, man, we're not bargaining here. You talk to me."

"What was the question again?"

The black slapped my face. Hajji moved closer. "C'mon, G-man, chill out, huh? This dude'll talk. He's okay." He looked at me. "Right?"

"Sure. What do you want to know?"

"How'd you find this place?"

"I followed Low Rent."

Low Rent jumped. G-man edged toward him. "Whoa, now. Look, this turkey shows up at my place talking about Manion and the girl. I don't know him from a blue jay. I kick him out. How the hell do I know he's gonna hang around and . . . Look, I'm not used to this kind of setup."

The mysterious Devlin must have said something, because Low Rent went into the other room and started to whine something about his not understanding the full implication of what Devlin and his pals were up to. "I just mess around," he said. "I don't off nobody." I didn't catch Devlin's reply, but Low Rent moaned, "He was already dead meat. I had a hell of a time getting the birds to . . ."

Hajji asked me, "You got any idea where you fit into all this?"

"Some."

"Yeah?"

"I've been hoping against hope that my being hired to find Sandy Watson had nothing to do with Terry Manion and his search for Cece MacElroy. But I come here to get a lead on Manion and the girl, and who do I find? You and the nasty Little Jimmy. I'm a guy who believes in coincidence, but not that big a coincidence."

Hajji shouted into the other room, "Is that enough, Mr. D.?"

"Turn out the light!"

Hajji frowned at G-man, who said, "Check those wires, first."

Hajji bent over and tugged at my hands and feet. "Tight and twangy," he said.

The black man reached out a hand and switched off the light.

Little Jimmy came back into the dark room. I could make out his outline. Devlin stayed at the door. His voice was hoarse, as if he'd been smoking too much. He said, "Where's the Dahlquist girl?"

It was a question I had not expected. "At her home, I guess," I said.

"Hit him. Hard enough to make an impression. And the pun is intended."

Hajji buried his fist in my stomach.

"Where is the girl?" Devlin asked again.

My eyes filled with tears from the punch. I blinked them away, took a deep breath, and said, "I left her with a friend of mine. He's a cop."

"That's a possibility," he said. "In that case, you will phone her."

With the light off in our room, the view through the window was much clearer. The moonlight illuminated a warehouse some twenty feet away. And peering at us through the warehouse window was the last face in the world I wanted to see.

I looked away from it and tried to push it from my mind. I'm not sure I believe that people can pick up your thoughts and fears, but I didn't want to take the chance.

"What do I say when I call her?" I asked.

"Then you'll cooperate?"

"What choice do I have?"

"Excellent."

I heard rather than saw someone leave the room. Suddenly a flashlight shone in my eyes. Devlin. He chuckled. "That should set back your night sight for another few minutes."

"Is he going to get wire cutters?" I asked.

"Why?"

"So that I can get to a phone."

"Bloodworth, you're like some hermit from the Dark Ages. They've got phones now that come to you. Makes the job twice as easy when you're holding prisoners."

There were footsteps and Hajji said, "Here it is, Mr. D."

Devlin asked, "What's the number?"

I gave him Cugat's phone number.

While Devlin punched the buttons, he said, "Tell your friend you're coming to pick up the girl." Hajji placed the phone between the metal bedsprings and my ear. Maybe if Cugie was there and he answered the phone . . . The connection was made and I heard the voice of his wife, Estella. I licked my lips and said, "Hi, Estella, this is Leo. Let me speak to that old man of yours."

She told me he wasn't home. I should have known. It was still early evening and he had a new female partner. "Good," I said. Then, while she rattled on about what a feckless bastard she'd married, I said, "Cugie, I'll be coming by for Serendipity."

Estella, for whom English was a second language, seemed to be having difficulty understanding my end of the conversation. "Hope she hasn't been

too much of a burden. . . ." My mind was zipping along at about 150 mph.
Maybe by the time we drove there, Cugie would have returned and . . .

Suddenly Devlin reached over and yanked the phone away. I saw him put
it to his ear.

He placed it onto its cradle and stood up. "He's no use to us," he said to
the others. "What a pathetic, ineffectual asshole. We just can't count on
him for anything. I doubt that he has any idea where the girl is. Help Low
Rent to set up in here."

I looked over to the warehouse. Its window was empty now.

"Shit, do I have to handle this again?" G-man grumbled.

"Let's consider it a wrist slap for losing the girl. More than once."

"Don't bust my hump about that kid."

"Look, mister. I sent you all the way to London to perform a relatively
simple task, and you fucked up. I don't forget that, and you don't forget it."

"I'm not the only one who fucks up," G-man said.

Devlin replied softly, "There's something else for you to remember, G-
man. In the game of terrorism, life is cheap. And your life is growing less
valuable with each syllable. Now if you think you can handle your end, I'm
out of here. There's a lady I've been keeping waiting too long."

When Devlin and Little Jimmy had gone, G-man turned to Low Rent
and said, "That man's turned into a true-blue honky prick."

Low Rent said, "You go to your church and I'll go to mine. Leave me out
of this discussion."

"Let's put a little light on the subject, huh?" Hajji said, hitting the switch.

He bent over MacElroy and gave a little chuckle. "Dreamland. I could use
a short dose of that shit myself. I got the sleepless days and sleepless nights."
He began singing a song, twanging an imaginary guitar.

Low Rent said, "I'll go get the bird. But I gotta tell you, I don't find this
shit amusing."

"None of us finds it amusing," G-man said. "But we do it for the massa."

Hajji joined me on the bed. "A word to the wise, buddy," he told G-man.
"You better chill it around Devlin. That sucker's got a mean temper."

"I know all about him and his temper. I've known him longer than you.
Hell, I knew him before there was a Mis-tah Devlin."

"When was that?" I asked.

G-man stared at me. "Just shut up, Jim. You're a dead man. Behave like
one."

"As long as I'm dead, satisfy my curiosity. What are you guys up to?" It
was a ploy that always worked in movies and books.

G-man shook his head. "You're so uncool, it's sad. You're dead, man. I don't waste time talking to the dead."

"What about you, Hajji?"

"Hajji? I like that. Yeah, Hajji." He grinned and said, "Matter of fact, I like you, Bloodworth. But when the man's right, he's right."

MacElroy coughed and woke long enough to begin his "bu-full li'l girl" nonsense all over again.

G-man took two steps and backhanded MacElroy across the face.

Hajji said, "What's your problem?"

G-man snapped, "Him with his 'bu-full li'l girl.' If he hadn't slipped it to his 'bu-full li'l girl' when she was just a kid, neither of us'd got caught up in this crazy man's scheme. That's my problem. You want a piece of it?"

"You got a woman with Devlin, fine. Just don't try hopping on my ass, spade. I'm not old and I'm not stoned."

G-man stared at him, and Hajji stood slowly and stared back. Great! A fight would be welcome at this point.

G-man took a step forward. Protective hands went up. And Low Rent entered the room with a covered bird cage.

Hajji shrugged off the tension, and G-man backed away. Both men kept their eyes on the cage.

"What about the veg?" Low Rent asked, indicating MacElroy.

"We're taking him out to breathe some of that clean ocean air," Hajji said. "Maybe give him a swim to wash him off."

Low Rent asked, "We gonna play this out, huh?"

"Just do what you're told," G-man ordered. "But let us get clear."

"What the hell's in that cage?" I asked.

Low Rent sneered at me. "You won't know till it's too late, jagoff."

Hajji gave me another wink as he and G-man maneuvered MacElroy out of the room. G-man said to Low Rent, "Don't forget my medicine bag."

Low Rent nodded, then reached over and flicked off the light.

"Wait a minute now . . ." I said.

I heard the rustle of the cage cover being removed, then a slight metallic clatter. The cage door being opened.

Then I heard Low Rent grunt, and I felt drops of some kind of liquid across my face and hands. "What the hell . . . ?"

"You can't smell it, but the bird can. He's crazy for it."

Then there were footsteps to the door and the door closing.

I strained my eyes for the bird. Nothing. Christ, it would have to be a bird. Snakes are slimy and terrible. Spiders make your hair stand on end. But birds! Flying rats!

What the hell was it—a falcon, a hawk, a buzzard? What? The cage was gigantic. I remembered the kid telling me that Kosca's face had been turned to hamburger by a bird.

There was the flutter of wings. I ducked my head under my arm to protect my face and eyes.

That's when I felt something touch my neck!

31

1. Had I but known that Slide's method of transportation, his so-called "chop," was what appeared to be a homemade motorcycle, with bare wheels that shot gravel into your hair and no cushions to speak of, I might not have pressed so hard to get him to drive me to the place where Gregory Desidero and his friend had taken the narcotics.

Once I had signed on and straddled the seat behind him, however, there was no stopping us, literally, as we zoomed down streets, darting between cars and dodging startled pedestrians, with me being forced to not only touch the filthy jacket that was wrapped around his emaciated chest, but to hang on to it for dear life.

As we soared pell-mell down Third Street, Slide said, "Tell me this isn't as good as flying."

I could think of a few retorts, but with my being slightly downwind of him, I was afraid to open my mouth.

Just as the sun was setting, we arrived at a dismal warehouse district. Slide relaxed and slowed his patchwork cycle to a dull rumble. The street was dusty, and the cars parked along the curb looked as though they had been there for decades.

"This is the ugliest area of the city that I have ever seen," I said.

"It sure is the deadest," Slide said. "Doomsday plus one."

I shivered.

He halted the machine and told me to hop off. Then he cut the engine and rolled the cycle into an alley between an apparently deserted warehouse and an apartment hotel.

I watched curiously as he pushed the cycle behind a large dumpster, almost wedging it in. Then he poked around in the dumpster until he found an old newspaper, which he draped over the bike. "Camouflage," he said. "There's no way to lock it."

I pointed to the apartment hotel. "Is that the place?"

He nodded. "One of Devlin's shooting galleries. He has these pits all over town—burnt-out-looking places where he sets up little parties for people with bucks looking for new and exotic kicks."

"Sort of like the degenerates' Elsa Maxwell."

"Who?"

"This woman I read about who used to throw parties for royalty and the like."

"How do I meet her?"

"I'm afraid that's an opportunity missed," I said. "Are we just going to walk in there?"

"Hell, no. Only an ultimate feeb would walk into a place like that. There's always a watchbird on the ground floor. What we're gonna do is orb a little."

I looked up at the brick hotel. There were no fire escapes. At least not off of this alley. "How do we do that?"

He tapped his nose with his forefinger and ran silently to the front sidewalk. Then he turned away from the hotel. "Where are we going?" I asked.

"Cool your jets, Serendip. You'll see."

What I saw, eventually, was the alley on the other side of the warehouse. Slide ran down it, hopped over rusted barbed wire, and beelined for a boarded-up cellar window. Using one finger, he pulled the board away from the window frame and it swung down on one remaining nail, exposing more than enough space for a thin body to enter.

"I found it the other night."

"Why'd you leave your bike way on the other side?" I asked.

"Follow me on this and learn something. Let's say some watchbird happens along and orbs the bike. He susses its owner must be around. So he starts checking windows on the alley. By the time he gets around to thinking about heading to a new alley, I'm out of here."

There was some sort of logic at work, but I didn't think it significant enough to merit too much scrutiny. Instead, I followed Slide into the bowels of the warehouse.

It was, in two words, dark and dirty. I couldn't see a thing, but Slide took my hand and drew me swiftly past crates that banged my knees and cobwebs that brushed my face. "How can you tell where we're going?" I asked him.

"Maybe I'm part rat," he said, adding a "he-he-he" rodent noise that I found singularly unamusing.

2. By the time we arrived at the stairs, I had developed my night eyes and could progress without his help. But at the second flight, while pausing to catch my breath, I demanded, "Are you sure you know what we're doing?"

"Never have I experienced such a lack of faith. Slide does not do mistakes. Remember that."

It was too dark to see if his eyebrow was twitching. So I followed him to the third level, where he made a right face and left the stairwell. As I stepped after him, I felt his hand grab my arm. At the same time, the floor disappeared. Slide yanked me back, and we both stumbled onto what appeared to be a catwalk. "I forgot to mention that this building has no guts." Then he began laughing again. It was not a particularly healthy sound, and it did not bolster my confidence in him.

He moved gingerly along the catwalk until we arrived at a spot where moonlight outlined a large frosted window. He sat down on the catwalk and, gripping the metal handrail that separated the catwalk from the wall, extended his right leg directly out until the toe of his boot connected with the latch of the window. He gave a little kick, and the window came loose from its frame and flopped down on chains, like the drawbridges I'd just seen in London.

Suddenly we were looking into a room across the alley. The hotel's window was grimy, but the light was very bright, and our slight elevation made it possible for us to see literally everything in the room. Not that there was much to see. Only a bedframe and, on the floor, a pathetic bearded man, crying and shouting. The grimy window barely muffled his words. He was saying something about a beautiful girl who no longer existed. Then he began to shout about something "melting," over and over.

"That the duffer on your dance card?"

"No, thank heaven," I said, surprised that I was now beginning to understand his odd patois. "That poor fellow. Perhaps we could—"

I stopped talking because the door to the hotel room opened and three men walked in. I heard Slide inhale sharply. One of the men was Gregory Desidero. The others were strangers to me—a tall, dark, thick fellow togged in tight, bright leathers and a relatively bland-looking man with brown hair and a moustache. Slide hissed, "There they are, Superfly and Mighty Mouth. I don't know who the leather teddy is."

Desidero leaned over the sick man and looked at his eyes, then he shook his head and they all left the room.

I stood up. "Help me find my way out of here," I said.

"Why? You sure as hell don't want to bump into them outside."

"What I want to do is notify the police. They're torturing that unfortunate fellow. And Gregory Desidero is wanted for murder."

"Look, you're not bad for a layover. But I won't have any truck with the Blues."

"You can do what you want—"

He put his awful semigloved hand over my mouth and said, "Shhhh."

I wiped my lips on my shoulder and watched as Desidero and the man with the moustache and a thin, nasty-looking specimen with a downy beard entered the room.

"That's the Bird Man," Slide said.

"Shoe told me about him. He was one of the last people to see Terry Manion."

"Whatever, he works for Devlin, performs at his circuses."

"Performs?"

"He handles birds, gets 'em to do things."

I remembered reading about burlesque queens who used birds to remove their clothes. I asked Slide if that was what he meant.

"Maybe that, too. Only I never heard of it. What he usually does is get the birds to fight."

I stared at the little weasel across the way and wished I could hear what he and the others were saying. But the only sound to reach our ears was the railing of the sick man on the floor.

The three men stopped talking and turned toward the door. I had the feeling that someone else was about to enter, but no one did. Instead, the man with the brown hair, whom Slide had labeled Mighty Mouth, did a very strange thing. He nodded twice and then reached up and peeled off his moustache. Then he placed it into the pocket of his jacket and ran his hands through his hair until it was fluffed up. Finally, with a grin for Desidero, he took a deep bow and left the room.

"I knew the wiffle was an actor. Wearing fuckin' disguises! What do you think?"

I told him honestly that I didn't know what to think. But I was remembering some of the things I'd heard Desidero say the day I lay in hiding at the Kosca home. He and the girl had talked about staying in character and being able to improvise. And the reason they were there, the girl had said, was to get rid of Archie's props. One need not possess the incomparable Sherlock's powers of deduction to realize they were, or had been, in show business.

"Could this Devlin's first name be Archie?"

Slide shrugged. "I never heard of anybody who knew him on a first-name basis."

He looked over into the room. "What the hell is going down now?"

I stared across in horror as the man in leather backed into the room carrying the top half of an unconscious Mr. Bloodworth. The bottom half was being kept aloft by a man in a dark suit who didn't quite enter the room. Instead, he dropped Mr. Bloodworth's legs, and the leather man had to struggle to drag the big detective across the floor and dump him onto the bed's bare springs.

Then the dark suit left the room, and the leather man ran after him. A minute later the leather man returned with wire that he used to tie Mr. Bloodworth to the bedframe.

Slide said, "Is that the Manion guy you been talking about?"

"No. That's Leo Bloodworth. He . . . he's my partner."

"Partner? Partner in what?"

I stared him straight in the face and said, "We're private investigators."

He said, "You're shitting me, right?"

I didn't bother to reply. Across the alley the men cleared out of the room, leaving Mr. Bloodworth and the sick man alone.

Slide said, "Well, I hope you don't have too much stationery with your partner's name on it."

"Nothing will happen to him if I summon the police now."

"Cops come, making all their noise, those guys'll either use your friend Bloodworth for a hostage, or they'll scratch him and scatter like dry leaves."

"Then what can we do?"

"Accept the fact that they've got control. What we do is check for signs of weakness."

"But . . ."

"Stay here. I'll do the scurry out front."

I started to object, but he was gone.

Leaving me to stare mournfully across the alley at the fallen Mr. Bloodworth.

I watched, heartsick, as he awoke and began shouting at the ill man. He called him MacElroy. Cece's father!

Then Desidero and the other villains returned. The black man slapped Mr. Bloodworth, and for some reason the lights were extinguished. I moved closer to try to see what was going on. Where was Slide?

Eventually the lights returned. Mr. Bloodworth was talking with the leather man and Desidero. The Bird Man left the room and returned with a large covered bird cage. Oh, Lordy.

I got up and moved toward the stairwell.

Then I began the climb downward.

As I worked my way through the ground floor toward where I thought the broken window might be, someone grabbed my shoulder.

"Didn't I tell you to stay planted?" Slide asked.

"They're plotting something with a giant bird up there. We have to help."

"Take it easy. Devlin just left in a goddamn rolling town house that was parked behind the building. I think the rest are moving out, too."

I said frantically, "But they've got some sort of bird up there. A man named Kosca was torn apart by birds. Mr. Bloodworth is at their mercy. . . ."

"Relax," Slide said. "I watched the Bird Man get the thing from his van. I think it's okay."

"How can it be okay?" I shouted, pulling away from him. I bumped into a crate.

"Don't confetti on me," he said firmly. "Hold together. We'll probe. But we'll do it on the wise." Whatever that meant.

He led me to the open window and through it, pausing to carefully return the wooden board to its former position.

When we reached the front sidewalk. Slide pulled me back into the alley. Gregory Desidero and the leather man were leaving the hotel, carrying the unmoving Mr. MacElroy between them.

"This guy smells like a bad dream. Where the hell do we put him? In the boot?" the leather man asked.

"It's him or you."

They opened the car's boot. "This isn't gonna work. Why didn't you get a real car, like a Jag?"

There were more footsteps leaving the hotel, then the sound of a door lock snapping. "Hey, Low Rent," Desidero called. "You gotta take this guy to the Hell at the beach."

"Me? Shit, I'm supposed to be getting ready for the big blowout."

"You can do this on the way."

"I . . . I can't even lift the guy."

"Nicky'll go with you and help."

"Hey, c'mon . . ." the leather guy whined.

Desidero was adamant. "It's gotta be done, Nicky. And it's easier if you use the van. I'll pick you up at the beach."

"If you're going out there, too, then let me drive with you. Low Rent drives like a schoolgirl on poppers."

They loaded the unfortunate Mr. MacElroy into the van. Then Nicky and Desidero walked to the sports car.

Nicky asked, "How long before somebody finds Bloodworth?"

Desidero shrugged. "Long enough."

As soon as the van and sports car drove away, I started for the hotel. But

Slide stopped me. "Trust me on this," he said. "There's time for us to be careful." His brow remained placid.

We circled the hotel. At the rear door Slide found the pane of glass he was looking for. He pulled a knife from his boot and began cutting away the dried putty until the pane was free. He removed it carefully, holding his breath.

Then he reached his arm through the open hole and fiddled with the lock. He smiled at me as the door creaked open. Quietly, we moved through the building. It was deserted by everything except vermin and dust.

As we approached the door to Mr. Bloodworth's room, I wanted to rush forward, but Slide, ever cautious, held me back. No light showed around the door. They'd left him alone in a darkened room with some kind of winged creature.

I pushed past Slide and opened the door. He stepped in behind me, turning on the lights.

I was momentarily blinded, and I hoped the bird would be too. And then I saw it, in the middle of the floor, looking around goofily. It was a little white turtledove. I turned to Slide. He shrugged.

Mr. Bloodworth was on the bed, his arm and shoulder covering his face and eyes.

I went over to him and touched his back. If it hadn't been for his wire bindings, he would have leaped from the bed.

Then he opened his eyes, saw me and Slide. Perspiration was dripping from his face. Slide pointed to the dove and said, "Coo, pops."

Mr. Bloodworth took a deep breath and let it out. "It was a joke, a bloody prank," he said.

"At least you're still alive to hear 'em laugh," Slide said, getting out his knife again and using a metal notch on it to pop the wire around Mr. Bloodworth's hands and ankles.

"This is Slide, Mr. Bloodworth."

"Slide, huh? Well, thanks for cutting me loose."

Slide nodded and picked up the bird on his finger. He moved to the window, opened it, and sent the bird out into the night. He watched it fly away. He sighed, then closed the window and turned to us. "I've heard about Devlin doing this kind of goof before. There was this layover who'd defaulted on the icing from one of his uptown sprawl-bangers."

"Son, I'm sorry, but I don't understand a goddamned word you're saying." Mr. B. sat up and began massaging his wrists and ankles.

I interpreted, "A girl didn't pay Devlin his cut from whatever she made at an upper-class sex party."

Mr. Bloodworth looked from me to Slide. Slide said, "Right. So he scooped her off the strasse . . ."

"He kidnapped her."

". . . and while his ganoons adjusted her blinders and hogged her, he started moving a toad-sticker across her upper mask, down her headwalls, and criss-crossing her chicken wings . . ."

"While his thugs covered her eyes and tied her, he started touching her body with a knife . . ."

"Then he tossed her out on Holly Bully . . ."

"Hollywood Boulevard," I translated.

"Yeah. At around ten P.M. Top of the grand tour. Cruisers are cruising. Hookers are hooking. Walkers are walking. Stringers are stringing. Everybody screaming. And she takes off her blindfold and she sees red. Red on her arms, hands. Her reflection in the rent-a-car window tells her she's bleeding to death. And there are five kinds of cops rushing to her.

"Now here's the deal. The medics arrive and they start sponging away to find the wounds. Only there aren't any! Then one of the whitecoats gets brave and takes a taste of the red and says, 'Things go great with V-8.'

"So the layover, who's still so scared she's left it all on the bus, takes a little fall for disturbing the peace and whatever."

"That's a fine story," Mr. Bloodworth said, standing and testing his feet. Evidently the feet passed muster, because he began walking away.

"Then," Slide continued, turning off the light and following behind us, "a few weeks later another layover tried to bust free of Devlin and join another head's stable. This time Devlin didn't hold back. It was Shish-kebab City.

"The way I suss it, the first one only annoyed him a little, but the second one tried to do him real damage.

"So consider it four-leaf-cloversville, Blood-man, that Devlin figures you for a schmuck who can't do him any harm."

Mr. Bloodworth turned to him. "You've built up a little goodwill with me, son. Don't blow it by calling me Blood-man. Don't ever call me Blood-man." He turned to me. "Where'd you get this poor man's Road Warrior?"

"Hey, that's not bad. I dig the ref. Poor man's Road Warrior. You're a groove, all right. But do me a favor, Blood-worthy, let's go out through the rear, huh?"

Mr. Bloodworth glared at me. Then he said, "I have to check the lobby first."

He lumbered away. Slide said, "He's not a bad old duffer. Reminds me of this duff used to live in the Montecito. Doc Larkin. His grift was weight loss. Used to peddle these pills he got from Tijuana. I think they was tapeworms, something like that. They worked great for a while, but then it was time for a trip to Cedars."

"What could Mr. Bloodworth have in common with that fellow?"

"They're both old and fat and moved like they had lead in their shoes, but you could tell there was still some danger left inside. Devlin was stupid not to chalk him."

"Mr. Bloodworth is neither old nor fat nor slow. But you're right about the danger. I have seen him at his fiercest."

Slide asked, "Is he your old man?"

"My father?"

"No, not your father. Your old man. Your stud. Your man."

I stared at him. "Uh . . . why do you ask?"

"I thought I sensed something there, between you. You know, the needle pushing past the friendship mark."

"I . . . I may be a bit young . . ." I could feel myself blushing, and I hated it.

"Hey, Serendip. Age is just a state of mind. And as is well known, California is the mindless state."

I was still trying to unravel that when Mr. Bloodworth joined us. He was holding a revolver with his fingertips, studying it.

"Where'd you cop the bang?" Slide asked.

"It's mine. I just don't know what those joyboys did to it. I got a feeling they rigged it."

"Don't get paranoid, Blood-worthy. Especially not in front of your main squeeze." He pointed his half-gloved thumb at me. "You lose points that way."

Mr. Bloodworth raised an eyebrow and looked at me questioningly. I shrugged as Slide led us out the way he and I had come in. As he replaced the glass pane and tried to reapply bits of putty, he said, "One of my little ways: I like to leave a place the way I found it."

"Why?" I asked.

"A street rat never knows when he might want to return to a familiar hole."

"Street rat sorta sums it up," Mr. Bloodworth said, and went off down the alley. I ran to keep up.

"What now?" I asked him.

"Cece MacElroy's father was up there tonight. They said they were taking him to the beach. I don't know if he's worth the effort, but I'm going to try and find him."

"Why wouldn't he be worth it?"

"Never mind," Mr. Bloodworth said.

"Maybe we'll find Terry Manion there, too."

"That thought crossed my mind," the big detective grumbled.

"I can't wait."

"You're going home, and I'm gonna try to set up some police protection for you. This Devlin character is out to grab you."

"Do you suppose his first name is Archie?" I asked. "That's the name Desidero and the girl used at Kosca's."

Mr. Bloodworth got a strange little smile on his face and said, "Yeah. His name might be Archie, all right."

"Don't mind me," Slide, who had been trailing us, said suddenly. "You two make a right nice couple. Three's a crowd and all that."

"What the hell does he want?" Mr. Bloodworth whispered to me in a voice loud enough, I'm afraid, for Slide to hear.

"Well, he did get me here, and we were able to set you free."

We were on the sidewalk, not far from Mr. Bloodworth's Chevy. The detective turned, took out his wallet, and said, "You did good work, Slide. But thanks don't buy groceries, so . . ." He handed him two twenties.

Slide started to put out his hand, then looked at me and back to Mr. Bloodworth. "Well, Blood-worthy, it's a most bodacious push, but it was my notion that you still needed the poor man's Road Warrior to lead you to the Promised Land."

"Meaning?" Mr. Bloodworth said, suspiciously.

"Meaning this little Junebug and me heard G-man talking about toting the human jellyfish out to the beach Hell. I assume that would be Devlin's Hotel Hell along the boardwalk between Santa Monica and Bay City."

"You know where it is?"

"I've a rough approx."

I looked at him carefully. No twitch near the eyebrow. "He's telling the truth," I said.

"Thank you, ma'am. So, Blood-worthy, if you'll give me a mo' to get my chop, Serendipity and I shall lead the way."

I said, "Would you mind if I drove with Mr. Bloodworth, Slide? There's a lot we have to talk over."

Slide nodded. "Right. Partners. I scope."

Mr. Bloodworth watched him retrieve his cycle and asked, "What exactly does he *scope* about us being partners?"

"He's such a strange young man," I said. "Full of strange ideas."

Within seconds Slide met us on the street astride his curious cycle. Mr. Bloodworth told him, "I'll drop Sarah at her home, first. I'm not taking her anywhere near Desidero."

"But he'll be gone by the time we get there," I said. "We heard him say he was just going to pick up Nicky and be off."

"That's what he woofed," Slide said.

I whispered, "Besides, I don't really want ide-Slay to know where I ive-lay."

Mr. Bloodworth looked from me to Slide and he shook his head. "Okay, kid, into the car."

3. We trailed Slide to the Santa Monica Freeway, with Mr. Bloodworth mumbling to himself every time Slide made some extravagant move, like darting in and out of cars.

"That's some piece of work you tied in with, kid," he said. "He looks like he weighs about ninety pounds and ten of that's dirt. I wouldn't be surprised if he was raised by wild animals."

"He is a bit feral," I said. "Probably because he has lived by his wiles for most of his life. He knows a lot about this Devlin fellow."

"So do I," Mr. Bloodworth said. "The son of a buck made a jackass out of me, and he's gonna live to regret it."

More macho nonsense! "Would you have preferred it if instead of wounding your pride, he had killed you?"

"No, but he's going to wish he had."

Slide cut across three lanes and pointed to the Bay City off-ramp. Mr. Bloodworth put on his blinkers. "Who is Devlin?" I asked.

"I think his real name is Archie Leach. He was a top dog in college, had his little clique. They were all theater students, and they used theatrics to make political statements. Sometimes they used comedy, sometimes heavy drama. All that was about ten years ago. I don't know what's started 'em off again now. Maybe they were just bored. I knew guys on the force who got a little fame and glory and had a hard time living with it afterward."

"Fame is a heady, dangerous brew," I said.

"I guess you could say that. Anyway, this Leach, after being a big man on campus, wound up pimping and engaging in a number of other unsavory occupations. No wonder he gave himself a new name."

"More than one," I said. "Assuming I'm right that he enacted the role of Mr. Kosca's supposed friend George Kerby."

Slide drifted down an incline onto Main Street.

"How did you get onto Archie Leach?" I asked.

"You talk to enough people, certain facts begin to stand out like lint on a dark suit. Then, once you realize how the guy operates, all sorts of things begin to make sense. A famous actress meets a guy at a party, one of Leach's crew, and she falls for him and he steals her earrings. Her insurance man investigates and he dies, uh, while romantically occupied with a very young girl. A mean and hard-bitten cop gets involved with a young woman and starts acting like a grade-school idiot."

"Are you talking about Lieutenant Hilbert?"

He nodded. Then he exclaimed, "What the hell?"

Slide seemed to have gone off the road. Mr. Bloodworth parked, waited. With a roar Slide's bike reappeared. He had a Sno-Kone in his hand. He must have zipped to the beach, grabbed one, and zipped back.

Mr. Bloodworth said, "I just thought of something. The dean of Leach's college was going to expel him, but he suddenly changed his mind. Probably at the request of some sweet little co-ed. I think Leach learned a lot in college."

"So this guy has a history of using sex to gain money and power," I said. "What's he up to now that could be worth fifteen million dollars and put hundreds of thousands of lives in peril?"

"Devlin did mention terrorism back there."

I shivered. "How did Terry Manion ever get mixed up in this?"

"He tried to find Cece MacElroy, who happens to be Leach's girl friend. What I want to know is how did *we* ever get mixed up in it?"

We both knew that. I said, "I guess I should never have told Terry to come to the office, huh?"

"I've been running through that," he said. "And I don't think it would have made any difference. Leach started setting me up before Manion actually arrived at the office. Manion must've had my name written down somewhere. In his hotel room. Or he mentioned it to the Kosca woman. I don't know exactly, but somehow Leach found out Manion was going to come to me for help. He wanted me out of the way, and he also was trying to locate a man named Simon Watson. So he concocted one of his famous pranks. Through one of the actresses in his group, now deceased, he hired me to find Watson. And he put a few more of his actors on my tail. When I finally ran Watson to ground in Venice, they bumped him off and then had the gall to blame it on me."

"What an astonishing story! And you escaped that trap," I said, excitedly.

"You're damned right." He spun the wheel hard and followed Slide into a darkened and empty parking lot.

"And you must know why they wanted Simon Watson killed."

He scowled. "That part I haven't quite figured out yet."

"Maybe he had the key."

"What key?" he asked, as Slide left his cycle and walked back to us.

"The one Gregory Desidero and the girl were looking for at the Kosca home."

Mr. Bloodworth stared at me. "They tried to get something from Watson before they plugged him. He told them he'd given it to 'the old man.' Let's say that was Kosca. Kosca, looking for Cece MacElroy, stumbles across Leach and Company. He convinces one of them, Watson, to help him. Watson gets something for him. Bango. Good-bye Kosca. But where's the gizmo? The key?"

"Leach sends Desidero and a girl to search Kosca's. They don't find it, but they see you. Somehow—through Leach, probably—they knew you and Manion had snooped around the Kosca house earlier. They've got Manion, and they know by now that he doesn't have their key."

That prompted a king-size grin. He asked, "Have you got their key, kid?"

"Of course not," I said. "I'd know it, if I had something like that."

"Well, they think you've got it, which might be just as helpful."

"A-hem." It was Slide, standing at my window. "You two gonna take the show up on Mulholland, where the lights below look like diamonds? Or do we hit the hotel?"

We got out of the car. Then we had to wait for Slide to bury his cycle beside a dump, under newspapers and rubbish. Mr. Bloodworth said, "I don't know why you bother covering it, Slide. It looks like it belongs there, anyway."

Slide smiled. "It helps me keep my low profile. Try to picture Slide strad-dling an Intruder 700, chrome-on-chrome, down Holly Bully. I'd last six–seven minutes before some muscle took it away or some Blue hauled me in for grand theft, almost-auto."

"Where's this hotel of Devlin's?" Mr. Bloodworth asked.

Slide tossed his head in a northerly direction. "You gonna use your gun?"

Mr. Bloodworth tossed it to Slide. "How much moonlight do you see through the barrel?"

Slide pressed something on the gun, and the cylinder popped open. He held the gun up to the moon and squinted through the barrel. Then he clicked the cylinder back into place and tossed the gun back. "Wonder what they plugged it with?"

"Something that'd make it blow up in my fist. Funny boys."

"Ah, Blood-worthy, before we make our presence known," Slide said, "maybe you could pass some of those green men my way? In case our paths break apart."

The detective got his wallet out and handed Slide three twenty-dollar bills. Slide folded them once, twice, three times, and put the little squares into a pocket of his jacket, which he then zipped.

"Okay," he said. "Tour bus leaving. Next stop, Hotel Hell."

32

1. The Gull Wing Apartments looked like it should have been condemned years ago. Instead, it was sitting on a choice piece of beachfront property in the as-yet-unincorporated area between Santa Monica and Bay City. That I was standing on the brightly lit boardwalk observing the eyesore, and not still tied to a bed halfway across town with a bird of prey turning me into chuck steak, was due to a stroke of luck. After Devlin and his mob took off, Sarah, who'd been following her own lead with this weird street kid named Slide, broke in and freed me. Together we managed to maneuver the bird through an open window without losing an ounce of blood. A miracle.

Now, we were following a trail to Cece MacElroy's father, a trail we hoped would lead to Terry Manion.

Behind a five-foot concrete wall topped by beer cans and pizza boxes and ratty swimwear left to dry, the Gull Wing sat in darkness. Like the wall, the three-story plaster building had been white once, but now, thanks to sand, surf, and sun, it was a mottled sickly yellow in the glow of the halogens along the boardwalk.

Noises escaped its murky, barred windows—idiot laughter and snores and sobs. The place worked hard to live up to its nickname, Hotel Hell.

Slide said, "Give me a sec to suss."

He waited for a break in the late-evening boardwalk strollers and hopped onto the wall, rolling over silently to the other side, taking a few dirty towels with him. I looked at Sarah. "Don't get your hopes too high, kid," I told her.

The last time she'd sent me looking for something near and dear, things hadn't worked out so well.

I turned my back on the Gull Wing and peered out over the dark beach.

At its edge phosphorescent breakers rolled in off of an inky, mysterious ocean. You could taste the salt on the breeze. Overhead, a large, heavy moon looked a little bit old-fashioned in a sky shot with high-tech summer lightning.

"I wish you had a gun," she said.

I smiled. "If I'd had one in Italy, I'd probably be in jail right now."

There was the sound of metal grating against metal, and the iron gate in the concrete wall swung open. Slide waved us in. "The Bird Man just flew. No sign of G-man's black Porsche."

I said, "We oughta let the police clean this up."

"It looks like there's just one moke inside to cause trouble," Slide said. "But if MacElroy and Manion are considered mystery guests, there may be another skullcracker near them, ready to cut their cords. If any of the kids have been troublemakers, they'll be taken out, too. That'll happen if the cops come wailing. Assuming you can get any cops to move at all. Jurisdiction ain't so clear in this particular location. That's why Devlin picked it."

I sighed. "What's our best way in?"

He pointed to the barred windows. "Through there. The rooms on the ground floor are for the young stuff. They're too stoned or scared to make any moves, so their doors are left unlocked. If we shinny up to the first floor, we'd have to bust through the inside door."

"How do you know so much about this place, Slide?" Sarah asked.

"You been in one of 'em," he said, poker-faced, "you been in 'em all."

I looked into the window nearest us. In the light from the boardwalk I could make out seven or eight kids, none of them looking any older than Sarah, huddled on the floor in dirty underwear. A little redhead girl had a tiny plastic radio pressed to her ear, but there didn't seem to be any sound coming from it. The room was littered with pizza bones, pop bottles, empty bags, food, boxes, broken toys, and clothes in piles.

Slide reached up, wiggled a bar, and removed it from the window. He looked at us with a sheepish grin. "So maybe I been inside this particular crib once before," he said.

"You mean you snuck in?" Sarah asked, a bit awed.

"Naw, I snuck out."

Slide poked his head inside and whispered, "We're comin' in. Okay?"

A boy raised his shaved head. "Don't step on Mousy."

I stuck my head inside. Directly under the window was a tiny black boy, hunkering.

Slide hopped over him. I said to Sarah, "If there's any trouble, run like hell and get help."

"I'm not staying out here all alone. Trouble could come from outside as well as in. I'll be safer with you."

I lifted her by the waist and sat her on the sill. She swung her legs in and joined Slide.

Slide asked me, "Need anything? Like a forklift?"

I ignored him and put my back to the building, arms bent, hands on the sill. I hoisted myself up, and with barely a groan swung inside, being careful not to step on Mousy.

The other awake inhabitants of the room watched us with eyes that were almost the size of the kids' in those creepy damned paintings from the sixties.

"What's the matter with them?" Sarah asked.

Slide said, "They're hungry, thirsty, sleepy, and afraid. And they don't know what the hell to do about it. If they leave here, they probably will get thrown into some child-welfare dustbin that won't be much better. And their brothers and sisters and friends won't be in there with 'em."

"We better get this done," I told him.

"Look," he said. "There's this guy sitting at a desk down the hall. His name's Mal. Got these tattoos of skeleton heads all over his body. He's not gonna let you find your friends without a rustle. I . . . I'd rather not have him see me here. Okay?"

"What's the problem?" I asked.

"He gave me this." Slide pushed up the sleeve of his jacket, exposing an arm to the outside halogens that was so white and lean it looked like it had been carved from a block of balsa. Except for a ragged pink scar that ran down it from wrist to elbow. "From when I put in my time here. I guess you could say I was one of the troublemakers."

I nodded. "How's he positioned, exactly?"

"At a desk facing the front door. We're to his right." He added, "Mal keeps the knife strapped to his left calf. He's got a battery-operated TV he watches."

I said, "It'd help if his attention was focused on that front door."

Slide sighed. "Maybe I can do something, but don't count on much. If you can't handle him, I don't want him cutting on me again."

"Stay as clear as you can," I told him.

He nodded and moved back through the room and out of the window.

I opened the door a crack. The hall was dark, but there was light and sound coming from a TV set on a desk. I could barely see Mal's tattooed arm resting on the desktop. It looked like something used to stun elephants.

I searched the room we were in. In a corner, near a half-eaten sandwich covered with ants, I found a Day-Glo-pink child's baseball bat. It was light, but there was some heft to it.

I carried it back to the door. I told Sarah, "If this doesn't work, take off out of that window and bring back some police before that monster beats me to death with my own club."

In the distance, over the tinny sound of the monster's TV set, a thin voice cried out, "Hey, Mal, you sorry sack of shit. It's time to pay your dues."

The TV set went quiet. I heard the chair being pushed back, then sighing as if a great weight had been lifted from it. Mal, wearing swim trunks and a scowl, rounded the desk slowly and headed for the front door. He wasn't as tall as he'd looked sitting down, but he was built like a lumpy pylon. One that had been spray-painted by the best graffiti artists in town. He'd changed the carrying place for his knife from his calf. It was strapped to his left forearm.

I took a deep breath and moved quickly and quietly down the hall. I got to within four feet of his back, when the wooden floor creaked under me. One more step and I'd have been on a quiet knit rug, but I didn't get that step.

Illuminated by the TV glow, Mal turned slowly, moving like King Kong in awkward but invincible little jerks. He unsheathed his knife. I rushed him with my baby bat and put my whole body into a swing at his head. The bat shattered like kindling, showering us both with pink and white splinters. Mal staggered backward and dropped the knife. Then he threw out his right arm, catching me across the neck and chest and sending me into the desk and TV set.

I jabbed the jagged edge of the bat handle at his face, and he brushed it aside with his left hand. His right swung back and caught me on the ear, spinning me away from the desk and onto the floor.

I landed on my back, with my head hitting the hardwood. Blinking, I saw Mal lift something from the desktop. A typewriter. Not one of your wimp electronic keyboards. This was one of the old pre-electric warhorses. What the hell was a Neanderthal like Mal doing with a typewriter? Using it for a murder weapon, that's what.

With a snarl Mal hoisted it over his head and took a step toward me.

He poised to toss it to me like a medicine ball, when a little voice called, "Over here, you despicable cretin."

Both Mal and I stared through the gray gloom at Sarah, standing in the room with a few of the frightened children behind her. She held the edge of the rug in her hands, and before Mal could move, with all of her strength she gave it a yank.

Mal did a short, wobbly ballet, then his knees folded. He hit the floor a second before the typewriter landed on his surprised mug.

I scrambled to my feet.

Mal's body was still wiggling, but it was reflex action.

I lifted the machine off of his head. He was alive, but not by much. It looked like a broken cheekbone and a broken nose and maybe a concussion. He was breathing raggedly through an open bloody mouth. I put the typewriter on the floor beside him.

Slide entered the room and moved beside Mal, smiling down at him. "You're looking good, Mal," he said. "Serendipity, you do nice work."

"I doubt he'll be moving, Slide," I said. "If he tries, keep him quiet but don't hurt him too much, huh?"

Slide picked up Mal's knife from the floor. He said, "I wouldn't rush upstairs just yet."

He ran to the desk and reached into the kneehole. He found a pistol taped to the underside of the work surface. He threw it to me. I peeled the remnants of the tape away from the barrel and handle. It was a Walther PP seven-shot.

"Like I said, sometimes they got more muscle upstairs." He opened another drawer and found a key ring. "Your best shot's the third floor. Second floor is mainly a storeroom."

Sarah circled Mal and Slide and followed me to the stairs. "Wait down here with Slide," I told her. I started up the stairs, then turned back to her. "And before I forget, thanks."

There were no more goons in the building. I located MacElroy and Manion in rooms side by side on the third floor. MacElroy was still yapping about his "bu-full li'l girl." Manion was mainly quiet, except for an occasional mention of the word "Gil," according to Sarah, the name of his ex-wife.

He didn't look much like the same guy who'd been in my office only a few weeks before. Matted hair, bearded, filthy, lying in a bed he'd soiled many times. And very ill.

Neither man was capable of self-propulsion.

Sarah was waiting downstairs eagerly. "Is Terry here?"

I nodded.

"Well, where is he?" She started up the stairs, but I grabbed her arm. "No sense your seeing him like this, sis. Wait until they get him cleaned up."

"*Who* gets him cleaned up?"

I didn't answer. Instead, I bent down and started wiping the typewriter with my handkerchief. Then I worked on the bat handle.

"What's going on?" Sarah asked.

I ignored the question. Instead, I asked one of Slide: "Is there a phone here?"

He shook his head. "No water, no electricity, no phone. The nearest is down on Pacific about a quarter of a mile."

"Okay," I said. "Let's go."

"Go?" Sarah glared at me.

"Yeah, go. You, me, and Slide here."

"But Terry . . ."

"You let me worry about Terry."

She started to argue, and I grabbed her arm and dragged her out of the place. Slide was on my heels.

At the phone I dialed 911 and gave a detailed report of the condition of the three adults and uncounted children at the Gull Wing. I told them my name was Devlin, and I said that I would wait for the medics and the cops and whoever else they wanted to send.

It took them nearly half an hour, probably because of the jurisdiction thing. While we waited, Sarah explained to Slide how it was that people knew when he was lying.

Then the sirens headed for us and we moved out. Slide gave us a salute and cycled off. Just after we hit the Pacific Coast Highway, an emergency wagon sped by carrying paramedics. A Bay City prowl car had just pulled up to the entrance to the Gull Wing.

Sarah twisted her head to watch the building. Then she faced forward and said, "I feel absolutely crummy."

"Why? Manion'll be fine."

"Not about Terry. I know he's in good hands. I was not honest with Slide about his telltale sign of prevarication."

"Why?"

"I guess it's for the same reason that he likes to leave things as they are. Maybe a time will come when once again I'll need to know if he's lying or not."

I stared at her for a beat, wondering if they were born like that.

2. Peru De Falco was just leaving Le Sportique, an upscale exercise parlor on Santa Monica Boulevard. He was wearing a flowered Hawaiian shirt and white neatly pressed pants and was carrying a red leather overnight bag.

I gave the horn a toot.

He looked over, squinted, and then his face broke into a Campbell's Kids' smile. "Hi, guys, what's doing?"

"I just talked to your mom," I said.

"Oh, yeah? How's she doing?"

"Fine. She told us you were here."

"She's usually right about those things. What are you guys up to?"

"Well," I said, trying to remain patient, "I was hoping to hire you."

"Oh!"

"I need you to stay with Sarah and Mrs. Van Dine again tonight."

"Oh!" He glanced at the small automobile tire he calls a wristwatch.

"Was there something else you had to do tonight?" the kid asked him.

"Yeah. It's my night for giving this girl, Jane, her workout. I don't know if I mentioned it, Leo, but I'm making a good buck doing a little one-on-one physical-fitness work."

If it had been anyone but Peru, I'd have thought it was a double entendre. "You didn't mention it," I said.

"Then you can't come?" Sarah asked.

"Your mom said you were free," I informed him.

"Like I said, she's usually right. I am free. I just finished with Jane. That's why I checked my watch, to make sure."

Sarah rolled her eyes heavenward. "Uh, Peru," I asked, "I don't suppose you're carrying a gun?"

He grinned. "To the gym? Jane's not that kind of girl."

"I mean, you might need it tonight. I'd like you to take Sarah home and make sure nobody disturbs her tonight. But get your gun first. Okay?"

"Sure, Leo." He opened the car door and helped Sarah out.

She looked at me. "Is this necessary?"

"Yeah. These guys play rough. And even if you don't believe it, so does Peru. Right?"

"If you say so, Leo."

The door to Le Sportique opened and an astounding blonde glided out. She spied Peru and shouted at him. "Per-uuuu, you beautiful hunk. When are we going to do it again?"

"Soon," he shouted, and she blew him a kiss.

"Was that Jane?" the kid asked.

"No," he said. "I don't remember what *her* name is. It's tough enough remembering my clients."

I felt like Jack Benny talking to Dennis Day. "Now cut that out," I said.

"Huh?"

Slowly, I described Desidero, Hajji, Little Jimmy, and Low Rent, and I conveyed as much as I'd picked up from the newspaper picture of Archie Leach in makeup. Then I told him about the old Mustang, the black Porsche, and the bird van, and warned him that should any of those vehicles be in the vicinity of Serendipity's apartment, he was to drive immediately to the Bay City Police Department and call me from there.

"I got it, Leo. One question, though."

"Sure, Peru."

"Can I pick up a change of clothes when I get my gun? For tomorrow, I mean?"

"Sure. And your shaving stuff, too, if you need it. I'll spell you tomorrow morning."

He put out his arm and Sarah took it. She said, "When will I be able to see Terry?"

"I'll let you know tomorrow."

They walked to his car, a BMW that he'd picked up a year ago. I told him it was a good choice. There were as many of them in L.A. as there were Chevys. And they were a hell of a lot more comfortable. Maybe I'd trade the gray ghost in on a Beamer before too long. Assuming I'd get paid from somebody—Laura Mornay or Dove Hilbert—for taking this mutt Leach out of the game.

I followed Peru's BMW as far as La Cienega, where he and the kid took a right, heading for his apartment off Burton Way. I continued eastward for another twenty minutes, then spent five more finding a parking spot near my coach house.

The problem was that, this being the weekend, my landlord's theater was in full swing and, even though it was half empty, there were enough parked cars to use up the curb space.

As I passed under the dimly lit marquee, a plump woman with bright red hair and an electric-blue evening dress called my name. She was either my landlord's sister or sister-in-law. I was never quite sure which. She acted as cashier for them, sitting right inside the front door at a kitchen table with a little black tackle box to hold the receipts.

"Mr. Bloodworth," she said, her eyelashes batting so fast they almost caught fire. "I bet you're planning on burning the midnight oil with a good book."

"Huh?"

"This came for you," she said, trying to drag a large Federal Express box from under her table. "It says on the waybill that it contains books."

"Oh, right. Thanks," I said, trying not to throw out my back as I picked up the box.

"I'm quite a reader myself," she said. "Perhaps we should compare authors sometime."

"That'd be swell," I said, backing away and rushing down the alley to my digs.

Using my free hand, I unlocked the door and then grabbed a fistful of mail from the box. It was a banner day for deliveries.

I dumped the books and the mail onto the kitchen counter. Then, before

I even took off my coat, I scooped a Harp out of the fridge and popped the cap. One swallow and I started moving the envelopes around. Bills, bills, notices, flyers. And a pale gray envelope bordered in white with my name in script on the front.

It was an invitation to a party that Wally Barclay was tossing that same night. I looked at the Rolex. It had already begun. According to the invite, it was his Annual Hounds and Hares Gala, with fun and food and drinks for all.

I studied the envelope. It had been hand-delivered. Probably before Devlin/Leach left me in that La Casa Dolce, trussed up like a turkey and waiting for a vulture to tenderize me the hard way. Or was it possible that Barclay wasn't involved with Leach? Not likely. The final question: Should I go to the party?

I postponed that decision by prying off the lid of the Federal Express carton and discovering four college yearbooks and a note from Gwen Nolte. "Leo, you lout. Not that you care, but I had to make two trips to that goddamned UCRP library. There is just so much you can stuff into your panty hose. Speaking of which, when do we get our weekend? G.N."

UC Raven's Point called its yearbooks *The Goldenrod* for no immediately apparent reason. I leafed through the 1973 edition and eventually came to the two pages devoted to the Raven's Point University Theater, or, as it was designated, RUT. There were three photos from campus productions, and a fourth, of a group of young RUT thespians, and a tall, thin chap with a moustache and tweedy clothes who I assumed was the fellow listed as "director," Dr. Waldemir Bernstein. With or without a magnifying glass, there would have been no way to tell if any of the faces in the grainy photo were familiar. An accompanying text, unsigned, indicated that the simple task RUT had chosen for itself was the elevation of the quality and content of world theater. Unfortunately, the RUT influence had not yet spread to my landlord's operation out front.

I took the three remaining *Goldenrods* and what was left of my Harp into the living room and settled back onto the couch. The first thing I discovered was that in 1974 RUT underwent a major change. Instead of the previous year's performers in togas or tights or tuxedoes, that year they were wearing garbage cans or diapers or dog suits. And there was a snap of "dead" hippies and victorious National Guardsmen, reminding one and all of the infamous reenactment of the Kent State massacre. Once again the photography was so poor that none of the faces registered. The clearest snapshot was the one of the dogs. A male dog in black tights looked on as a female dog in a white floor-length gown contemplated the floor. The set was a makeshift castle made of cardboard stone.

Under RUT officers the name Archie Leach was listed as president, with

Simon Watson as vice-president. Dr. Bernstein was not only director but faculty adviser. The text had taken a new turn, also. Now it talked of street theater and guerrilla theater and theater of outrage and anger. RUT was dedicated to not only entertaining or educating audiences but to moving them to action.

In 1975 the heading of the theater section was "RUT/ MUMMERS." According to the text, the Mummers was a sub-organization within RUT comprised of a chosen few of the university's more advanced thespians.

It had emerged the year before, under the leadership of student activist Archie Leach, a theatrical genius who while still only a junior had captured the hearts and minds of the campus and become its student-body president.

It described Leach as a junior dedicated to shaking up the establishment with his theatricality. He had gained campus-wide recognition in 1974 with his "Cafeteria Capers," satiric and often brutal skits improvised during the luncheon hour that sharply underlined deficiencies in faculty performance. And he had masterminded the highly controversial *Kent State Revisited* tableau, as well as designing, with his close friend Simon "Sandy" Watson, their production of *Hamlet: The Melancholy Great Dane*, a raucous and ribald version of the classic, performed "in dog face," which "caused a monumental furor throughout our own English department and the entire world of Shakespearean scholarship." Right. Olivier and Gielgud had probably been rocked back on their heels.

The rather breathless text closed with the thought that Leach was unquestionably destined to become as famous as his namesake, the British actor who went on to international fame as the film star Cary Grant.

Considering that he was also student-body president, it seemed odd, even purposeful, that there were so few pictures of Leach in the yearbook and none in which his features were clearly defined. But there were shots of Simon Watson, who took over as president of RUT when Leach embraced campus-wide politics, of Tony Wharton (aka Little Jimmy), RUT's v.p., and of Sharon Whittiker, its secretary. She was my favorite schoolteacher-murderess, Lannie Doolittle. Another co-ed, Suze Stillwell, shared some of the photos as the organization's treasurer. She didn't seem to be anyone I'd bumped into thus far. Maybe she'd found something more constructive to do with her diploma than her co-officers.

The main illustration for RUT/Mummers was a full-page photograph of the university's auditorium, filled with students facing a huge poster of a man's face, a man with mesmerizing eyes. The poster was captioned: "Big Brother Is Watching You." He certainly was. I looked closely at Big Brother's mug. Then I went back and checked the 1973 *Goldenrod*.

Finally, I cracked the 1976 edition. The Mummers had their own section, no longer a part of RUT but an entity all their own—"a sociopolitical performance group whose stage goes beyond the confines of any theater."

Dr. Bernstein went with the Mummers, and someone else became faculty director of RUT. There was a nice picture of the doctor and several of his charges—Watson, Wharton, Greg Desidero among them—picketing the Raven's Point nuclear base. In another they were heckling the telephone company for reason or reasons unspecified, but for my money probably justified.

I slammed the books shut, drained the last drops from the beer bottle, and stood up to grab another brew. It looked as if I'd be going to good old Wally Barclay's shindig, and I didn't think I'd want to be drinking anything there.

33

1. "Knock knock," Peru De Falco said.

"Who's there?" I answered dutifully.

"Catgut."

"Catgut who?"

"Cat got your tongue?"

Neither of us laughed.

"You sure been quiet over there," he said.

We were driving toward my apartment in Peru's splendid little BMW, which, unlike Mr. Bloodworth's auto, was spotless and smelled new and fresh. My mind was filled with the dire image of Terry being whisked to some terrible detox ward at Bay City General. Mr. Bloodworth promised to check on him and find out when I might visit.

Then there was Gran. I called the apartment on Peru's miraculous cellular car phone, hoping to at least start the soothing process for my being so late. But the phone rang and rang, meaning, of course, that she was still with the ever-awful Roger Thornhill. I did not want to be totally negative, but the thought flitted through my head that they might be in Reno at that very moment, getting married! Is it any wonder why the cat had got my tongue?

"Problem?" Peru asked.

"Several," I said. "Peru, have you ever been attracted to an older woman?"

"Attracted? You mean have I wanted to score with one? I don't think so. You see, I've only got a limited amount of time, what with working as a P.I. and the phys. ed. stuff. And doing my own thing. So I narrowed down the field to in-shape blondes between the age of nineteen and twenty-five. That way I don't have to make a big decision every time a girl calls. I just think: How old is she, what color hair? Like that."

"Great answer," I said.

Then, in the depths of my despair, I remembered the horrible fact that the dung beetle, Mark Fishburn, had followed Gran from the airport. I got out my wallet and removed his card. "Can I try the phone again?"

"Sure. That's what it's there for."

The number connected me with an answering service. An overbearing woman told me that Mr. Fishburn was not available but that she would take the message.

I hung up.

"You're not clicking tonight, are you?"

"Not at all," I said. "What do you do when you want to find somebody and all you have is a phone number?"

"I call my mom."

He picked up the phone, dialed. I handed him the card. "Hi, Mom. This is Peru. Yeah, I know I'm your only son and if I say 'Hi, Mom' I don't have to identify myself, but I don't know why it bugs you. . . . Oh, yeah, well, I need an address. The guy's name is Mark Fisher . . ."

"Fishburn."

"Fishburn. And his phone number is . . ."

He gave his mom the information and replaced the receiver. Within minutes, the phone was ringing. "She's great, isn't she?" he asked as he lifted the receiver.

He listened for a bit, frowning. Then he asked, "Is that just off La Brea? Yeah, right. Okay. Thanks, Mom. No, ma'am. I can't Monday 'cause that's my Silva Mind Control night. Later." He hung up.

"She had a tougher time than usual because the number you've got is to an answering service that's not hooked up to his phone."

"How'd she get the address then?"

"I never ask. I think it has something to do with the computer I bought her about five years ago. She can make it sing 'Volare.' "

"Well, where does this Fishburn live?"

"Oh, sure." And he gave me an address on Orange Drive.

"Ah, Peru, would you do me a favor?"

"I guess so."

"Would you take me by there for a minute?"

"I don't think I can, Serendipity. Leo gave me my instructions. And it's way the hell the other side of town."

I said, "Mr. Bloodworth specifically said that you were to make sure that nobody disturbed me."

"Yes. He said that."

"Well, Mark Fishburn is definitely disturbing me. So I'd like to visit him and get him to stop."

He shook his big head. "It doesn't seem right. Leo said that I was to take you home and—"

"That's just it. Once we get home, I realize that we can't go out again. But we're not home yet. So I thought, on our way home, even though it means going across town, we could stop by Mark Fishburn's address . . ."

He pulled the car over to the curb and put it into park. Then he turned to me. "Look, we both know Leo doesn't want us driving all around. And he didn't say a word about any Mark Fishburn."

"I'll be honest with you, Peru. I think this Fishburn fellow is trying to harm my grandmother. I'd like you to help me convince him to stop."

He faced forward and remained immobile for at least a minute. Then he put the car in drive and made a sharp U-turn. "Consider him stopped," he said as we hit the Santa Monica Freeway and sped east.

2. Since there was a "1/2" on Fishburn's address, I'd assumed we would have to hunt for his apartment and/or office. Sure enough, it was at the rear of a triplex masquerading from the front as a duplex.

The neighbors in the front lower unit were having a noisy dinner party that Peru and I did nothing to disturb as we strolled down a car-crowded driveway to the back of the building. "I'm glad there's no fence," Peru whispered. "Fences mean dogs."

Fishburn's apartment was up a flight of unpainted wooden stairs. There were no lights on inside. His wreck of a VW bug was parked just off the alley on a patch of dried grass. I pointed it out to Peru.

"Good, the scumbag's home," Peru said. "Let's go put the fear of God into him."

"But there are no lights on."

"I guess we'll just have to wake him up."

But as we started up the stairs, there was a flash of light inside Fishburn's apartment, followed by a loud crack.

Peru swung round and, lifting me by the waist, carried me away from the building. He stopped in the alley, with Fishburn's VW between us and the yard.

"You can put me down now," I whispered.

"Right." He eased me to the ground. "That was a gunshot," he said.

The dinner party had turned very quiet. A side door opened and two men staggered to the back and called up, "What the hell's going on up there, Fishhead?"

"Hey, you okay up there?"

"That was a goddamn shot. You think we should go up and see?"

"Maybe ole Fishhead's being robbed."

"We ought to go up."

"What for? Screw ole Fishhead and the boat that brought him. Let's go back to the party."

"Okay. But I'm phoning the cops."

"Yeah. That might be good for a laugh. But stash the blow, first."

They staggered back indoors.

Peru must have excellent hearing. Even before Mark Fishburn's screen door swung open, he'd pushed me down so that both of us were concealed by the VW.

Peeking through the windows, I saw G-man and the fellow Slide called Mighty Mouth move stealthily from the apartment and work their way carefully down the stairs. They circled the building, ducking beneath the windows of the party apartment.

I leaped up and ran toward the building. I heard Peru say, "No. Wait!" behind me, but I didn't want to wait. The police might be on their way.

I opened the screen door and entered the dark apartment seconds before Peru followed. "Serendipity, damnit . . ." He had drawn his very contemporary-looking pistol, but I was in no mood to really appreciate it. By the light of the moon I could see Mark Fishburn draped across a rumpled bed with bright red blood flooding his chest.

Peru didn't stop to study Mark Fishburn. He continued on through the messy apartment, making sure no one else was there.

As I crossed to the bed, I realized that the floor was covered with something slippery and slimy. Not blood. Videotape. Unspooled, ruined. I saw that one whole wall was filled with shelves of boxed videotapes. Another was taken up with monitors and machines. In that rundown little apartment Mark Fishburn had thousands and thousands of dollars worth of electronic equipment.

Then the photojournalist startled me by not being dead. He coughed and held up a hand. I moved to him. Lordy, but he was ghastly looking. *"Scarlett O' Harlot,"* he said with almost his last breath. "In machine . . . *Scarlett O' Harlot."* Then the dreadful man cried out *"Gevalt!"* and expired.

The wail of a siren sounded the leaving of his spirit. Peru looked at me anxiously. "Time to move, Serendipity."

I crossed the room to the only video machine that I recognized as such. A tape was indeed in it. Trying to remove it, I turned on the monitor by mistake. The room was filled with its glow.

"Come on," Peru called anxiously.

I finally got the tape free. In the light of the screen I read the title, *Scarlett O' Harlot.*

"That siren's almost here."

The tape was important enough for Mark Fishburn to use up his last words talking about it. Would it tell me his killer? Would it contain photos of Gran? "I'm taking this," I said. But as I started to go, my eye caught sight of a row of tapes along one wall, all garishly labeled—Mark Fishburn's porno collection. Under "S" was the box for *Scarlett O' Harlot,* and it was not empty.

The siren sounded as if it were right in front of the building. Peru screamed, "Now!"

With a tape in each fist I raced through the apartment and out the screen door. Peru waited until I was past, then followed me out.

The members of the dinner party were starting to mill about the driveway and move toward the rear. I had no idea if they saw us or not.

Peru and I raced down the alley, then circled the block and waited for our breathing to return to normal. It took me twice as long as it did him. He offered to start me on an aerobics program when I had the time.

We continued to discuss aerobics as we strolled to the BMW, past police vehicles and the hubbub of the discovery of Mark Fishburn's body. I held tight to the two videotapes. No one seemed to give us a second glance, except for a stoned lady from the party who told Peru she thought he looked enough like John Travolta to be his twin brother.

3. At 9:45 Gran was still out on the town. Which was just as well, since we were using her video player to screen a porno movie.

It was a silly thing that was supposed to be a parody of *Gone With the Wind,* but it was really just an excuse to show every sexual possibility the filmmakers could think of. Lordy, in the age of AIDS, such indiscriminate promiscuity just seemed suicidal, not sensual.

Peru wouldn't even watch it. He sat in a chair beside the front door, shaking his head.

"What's the matter?"

"It just sort of clicked in," he said. "That dead guy, Fishburn. All the blood. I guess I got a flashback from the marines."

"You were in Vietnam?"

"Nope. I missed that. But you don't have to go to Vietnam to see blood. I went through marine boot camp. You gonna watch that junk much longer?"

"Might as well see what's on the second cassette."

I ejected *Scarlett* and removed the other tape from the box. I hoped it wasn't *Scarlett II*.

There was no identification whatsoever on the outside of the cassette. I fed it into the machine.

There were blips on the screen, then the color bars and a sort of whistle, and then the most fascinating footage began.

Fishburn must have held his camera on his shoulder as he drove his car, because it seemed as if we were driving up a steep mountain road on a lovely summer day. The sounds were sharp, almost harsh, of the car springs, twigs snapping, Fishburn humming to himself.

Peru moved away from the door and took a seat beside me.

The camera rounded a curve and got a breathtaking view down a valley, and as the car leveled we could see the glistening Pacific.

Peru said, "I know that place. I was just there with Leo."

On the screen the rear of a large cream-colored car appeared, raising dust. It paused for a few seconds by a high iron gate. The gate opened. The cream car went in.

The gate closed as we approached. A large filigreed "X" was part of its grillwork.

A tinny voice asked, "Yes?"

"I'd like to see Mr. Barclay."

"Please place your invitation beside your left ear."

"I have no invitation."

"Just a minute, sir."

Fishburn hummed.

"I'm sorry, sir, but Mr. Barclay is not available. Is that a camera you have?"

"You bet it is, pal. Tell that to Barclay."

"Sir, you are on private property. I am dispatching security guards to assist you in leaving the premises."

"Fuck you, too, yotz."

The scene changed to another view. In the distance one could see a hilltop and houses and a swimming pool. The camera zoomed in on a party in progress. People in outfits ranging from dinner wear to bikinis. The camera shifted and we saw a flag carrying the same elaborate "X" as the gate. This was a view of the estate, taken by Fishburn from another mountaintop. He was going to the party, invitation or no invitation.

A large bald man in a white dinner jacket, looking for all the world like

Daddy Warbucks sans moustache, moved to the wall surrounding the estate and pointed down. The other partygoers took their places at the wall.

The camera followed Daddy Warbucks's suggestion and moved down the canyon. Suddenly it picked up a blurred object. A bird. I think it was a hawk.

I tried to remember what I'd learned about birds of prey. Hawks have short, rounded wings and long tails, which make for bursts of speed, quick stops, and rapid swoops. Birds with long wings, like eagles, soar.

This one zoomed up, then did an abrupt twist and zoomed back down, a brown blur. Another, more reddish hawk streaked into the sky without warning and, talons outstretched, buzzed the brown hawk, sending it into a free fall.

Until then, the soundtrack was nothing more than wind and static and possibly Fishburn's heavy breathing. But the red hawk screeched as it damaged its prey, and from across the canyon came the shrieks of the partygoers' surprise and/or pleasure at the violent sight.

The red hawk was showing off its aerodynamic prowess, looping the loop, when a brown dart hit it full, ripping and tearing and then zooming away. The red hawk fell lifelessly out of the sky, and the camera followed it down.

"What's that?" Peru asked.

I paused the picture.

"Back it up."

I did as he requested. Lower on our mountain was a man, looking across the canyon with binoculars. I had been too busy concentrating on the fallen hawk to notice. But Fishburn must have seen him, because the camera focused on the fellow.

He was elderly, wearing a rumpled suit and a straw snap-brim hat. I didn't think I'd ever seen him before.

Fishburn moved his camera back to the party. The victorious hawk now rested on the arm of that boyish-looking creep with the cottonlike beard, the one they called the Bird Man. He was grinning at the hawk, but the other partygoers seemed to have lost interest.

Fishburn's camera went back to the elderly man, who was slowly and carefully crawling up the side of the mountain.

The next sequence involved cars leaving the estate. It was dusk and the picture was quite muddy. But that did not stop Fishburn from zooming in on every driver. Music and garbled conversations drifted through the evening air.

None of the faces seemed in any way remarkable. Though there was one young man with long hair, driving an old dull-gray car, who reminded me of someone. I just couldn't place the vaguely familiar face.

Peru said, "This is pretty dull stuff." And I had to agree with him.

I speeded up the tape. Finally, Fishburn aborted his fascination for autos and concentrated on the front of a house that I knew quite well. The Kosca residence. The elderly man from the mountainside appeared at the front door with Mrs. Kosca, kissed her, and left the house.

Mike Kosca, for it must have been he, got into a brown, fairly new car and drove away.

The next scene had Mike Kosca standing in front of a neat little bungalow with a mandarin-colored awning. A dark-haired man answered the door. Their conversation was too faint to understand. They both entered the bungalow.

There was a black flutter, and the camera was peering past the blinds of a half-opened window. Mike Kosca and the dark-haired man were in a room, sitting at a desk constructed from a board and filing cabinets. The two men were frowning.

". . . serious goddamn business," the dark-haired man was saying.

"You bet your butt it is, Sy. With luck, though, I can pull you out of it. And you've got your twenty-five-hundred-buck reward."

"Call me Sandy. Nobody calls me Sy. Okay. I'm gonna take a big chance with you. Hell, I don't know what else to do. I've got something they need. I took it."

He reached under the desk and slid something out. An envelope. Kosca's big hand opened it and withdrew . . . the little piece of plastic I took from his office! "What the hell is this?" he asked.

"Archie says it's his key out of the place."

"Oh, yeah. I guess they do use these things." Mr. Kosca stood up, slipping the piece of plastic into his pocket. "Until I pull the plug on this bastard, you take care, Sandy."

"Don't worry about me. I've got it worked out. I'll be out of the country for the next two months."

"He'll be poundin' rock by then. Sorry about the MacElroy kid, though."

The black-haired man shook his head. "I don't want to sound callous, but she should have known better than to fool around with a guy like Archie."

Mike Kosca said, "Just fifteen. Christ, I'm glad I won't be the one to have to tell her folks." They walked out of the room.

"It was just getting good," Peru said. Then he exclaimed, "Jesus!"

On the screen was a shot of Mike Kosca's body being lifted up on the gurney, but an angle not seen on TV news. The rain or something had washed the blood from his wounds. His gray face was in shreds, his puffy tongue protruding . . .

"C'mon, fast-forward past this!"

But that was all there was of Mark Fishburn's apparent documentary on the killing of Mike Kosca. Anything else must have been in the camera when Lieutenant Hilbert hurled it into the water. Could the lieutenant have known what he was doing when he destroyed footage that might have aided in apprehending Mike Kosca's murderer? And why was Mark Fishburn photographing Gran?

I did not have the luxury of time to speculate. I now realized that I did possess the key, though I had no idea what its significance might be. I had to report to Mr. Bloodworth.

His line was busy.

Ten minutes later it was still busy. I dialed the operator and informed her I had to make an emergency call. Peru shook his head. "Leo's not gonna like this."

"That's where you're wrong. . . . Oh, well, that's odd."

I replaced the receiver.

"What's the matter?"

"His phone's off the hook," I said.

"I guess he doesn't want to be disturbed."

"Peru," I said. "I have another favor to ask of you."

He looked worried.

34

1. "Mr. Bloodworth? Just a second. Yes, here's your name. Welcome to Xanadu's Annual Hare and Hounds Gala. An attendant will take care of your automobile."

The iron gate with the big "X" glided open, and I drove the Chevy onto the sacred ground. Behind me another car took my place at the talking gatepost. I'd spent barely thirty minutes making it to Barclay's estate and another thirty getting up the hill. The ID at the gate was the bottleneck; but to keep tempers from fraying beyond redemption, Barclay had arranged for liveried servants to wheel portable bars up and down the hill, so that you could get well oiled while you waited.

Once or twice a helicopter clattered overhead to land somewhere on the hilltop. I thought at the time that it was a mode of transport reserved for special guests. But our host was using it for something else entirely.

Cugie was on the narrow road behind me somewhere. It'd been a while since he'd done any fieldwork, I guess, and he'd grown sloppy. I hadn't driven more than three blocks when I spotted him, hanging back, trying to keep at least two cars between us.

I wasn't sure why he had decided to stake out my apartment and follow me around. Probably because he believed I would lead him to a meeting of this year's Black September, or a criminal conclave equally monumental. The sort of thing to cap a cop's career.

From time to time along the Santa Monica Freeway I had switched lanes and made a few moves just to keep him awake. I didn't mind him tagging along. In fact, I was glad to have him in the vicinity, in case the party got rough.

I was amusing myself with the thought of Cugie trying to crash the gate when a man in a white jumpsuit used his flashlight to aim me toward the parking area. There, another jumpsuit took my car and handed me a numbered ticket in exchange.

An airport metal detector had been set up along the path to the main compound. I passed right through with flying colors. I was carrying a better weapon than a gun.

As I approached the landscaped area, where the party had spilled over from the main house, I began to realize the full significance of the Hare and Hounds Gala. In the pool were the usual assortment of pretty girls in bikinis and a few men huffing and puffing to keep up with them. But the high-and-dry fun-seekers were all togged out either in dog suits or bunny costumes.

Near the poolhouse several long tables were being manned by uniformed servants who were providing new arrivals with the proper party garb.

"Your name, sir?" a bright young man in a cutaway asked.

"Bloodworth, but I don't think I'll need one of those."

"Oh, yes, sir. You will. House rule. Unless you'd prefer a swimsuit. What'll it be: trunks, hare, or hound?"

"Oh, hound, I guess." Cugie would be amused.

"We've got a few large ones left."

He ducked into the poolhouse and returned almost immediately with a neatly folded costume that looked like a bearskin coat. "You can slip it on right over your suit," he said.

Feeling only slightly less a jackass because of the other hares and hounds, I donned my dog suit. I guess I was supposed to be a sheepdog. White with black spots. The doghead fit like a hat. Judging by the others, the impression was of a rather large, lumpy animal with a long neck and a human face peering out of a large, round hole located under its jaw.

I strolled through a crowd of movie and TV stars, politicians and power brokers, dogs and rabbits to a man (or woman). They seemed to be having a barking good time.

A pretty redheaded bimbette bounced from the pool and ran to me, throwing her wet arms around me. "Well, hello, Tramp," she said, continuing to run her hands over my chest.

"I beg your pardon?"

"Tramp. You look like Tramp. You know, the big, fuzzy dog. My three sons. I loved that dog when I was growing up. I mean, I really loved that dog."

"Yeah, right," I said, backing away from her. Three kids! She looked like a kid herself.

With a great whoosh, a helicopter ascended until it was able to look down on the mountaintop. Then it edged over us, whipping the pool water to a frenzy, hovering for a minute or so before touching down on a large, brightly painted circular patch of cement in the center of an empty expanse of lawn.

It was a medium-sized chopper, built to hold four or five passengers. There were only three. Barclay, that sly dog, leaped to the lawn, followed by a little lady bunny. Last man out was a stocky, floppy-eared young basset holding a camera.

Barclay was wearing a specially tailored dog suit with flowing yellow threads that shimmered in the light. I assumed he was supposed to be a golden retriever. Instead of wearing a doghead, he had used makeup to transform his bald pate into a gilded crown, with nose and upper lip extended by putty.

He gave a nice authentic howl at the moon. Then he proclaimed, "Mission accomplished. And you shall see the results"—he consulted his watch—"fourteen minutes before the eleven o'clock news covers it."

He clasped his bunny's mitten, and they raced inside the house. What scamps!

A waiter passed with a tray containing champagne. I told him, "No, thanks," and followed the gang inside.

TV monitors had been set at various key spots. Barclay grabbed a glass of bubbly and announced, "We came, we barked, we conquered."

The screens blinked, and a picture jiggled and then settled in, carrying with it the harsh sounds of the helicopter's wings and wind and static.

The chopper seemed to be hovering as through its window we got a view of the Hollywood Hills near the spot of the famous sign. We heard Barclay's voice: "You sure this thing's safe?"

Then we saw him being lowered by cable to the ground, where three giant white letters rested: "R," "I," and "E."

Barclay, aground in his dog suit, which was now heavily belted, unsnapped the cable's hook from his belt and carried it to the Hollywood sign.

Then the screens went dark.

Barclay explained to his audience, "With several city officials present, we thought it politic to edit out the repetitious—and possibly illegal—footage. But in just a few seconds, we should see . . . yes."

The screens were filled with a shot of Barclay affixing the cable to his belt and being hauled aboard.

Then the chopper swung wide of the hill and came back to give us a lingering view of the sign. It now read:

H-O-L-L-Y-W-E-I-R-D

A cheer went up in the room.

Barclay held his champagne glass high and shouted, "To the weirdest little city in the world, and one that we all love."

He drained his glass.

"Now, eat, drink, and be merry. For tomorrow we eat more, drink more, and be merrier."

As I worked my way toward him, his little bunny put her lips to his ear and said something that he found hilarious.

He was still laughing heartily when I reached him.

He saw me and stopped laughing.

"Ah, Bloodworth," he said. "Welcome again to Xanadu. Hell of a show, eh?"

"Beats the Big Top," I said.

His bunny turned to me, her cute little face surrounded by pink bunny fur. "Wally comes up with the most hilarious stunts."

"He's very good with makeup, too," I said, pointing a doggy finger at his snoot.

Barclay stared at me for a beat, then smiled and said, "A little hobby of mine."

"Do you suppose we could have a very short chat, dog to dog?"

"Of course. Don't go away, Andrea. I'll be right back."

He led me through the party animals like a saint strolling through a leper colony, pausing to stop and bless each and every one.

"What's on your mind, Bloodworth?" he asked just before we left the big room.

"School days," I said.

He paused with a slightly puzzled frown on his puttied face. Then his eyes shifted past me, and he breathed a relieved sigh and shouted, "Paul! Come here a minute. Someone wants to meet you."

A middle-sized black cur reluctantly withdrew from a crowd and pranced in our direction. A narrow white face wearing pince nez smiled politely at Barclay.

Barclay said, "Paul, this is Leo Bloodworth. Leo is a big fan of yours, I understand. Leo, meet Paul Montclair."

Damned if it wasn't him! Paul Montclair! Mr. Success! I was almost speechless. I said, "I've never seen you with glasses."

"I only wear 'em to see with. Mr. Bloodwilly, is it?"

"Bloodworth. Listen, I can't tell you what a privilege it is to meet you . . ."

"Yes, yes. C'mon over here, Bloodworth. I want you to observe the old master in operation. See the famous Success Power work its magic."

Barclay had slipped away somewhere. I craned my neck, but he was no longer in the room. Well, he wasn't going anywhere. I followed Montclair to the group he'd been chatting with before his host had summoned him.

"As I was saying, the idea is to soft-pedal productivity," he told a middle-aged beagle, while the other mongrels and bunnies lent an attentive assortment of long ears. "Productivity is equated with profit in the worker's mind. The more productivity, the more product, the more pay. You fall into the union-baited trap. Ix-nay on the productivity. Give 'em incentive, instead. Fire that foreman with his sour-lemon face. Hire a couple of dames with legs to bring the guys soft drinks when they get thirsty and, not incidentally, make fun of 'em when their production is off. In short, get rid of the stick and buy yourself some carrots."

The beagle wasn't convinced. "But, Paul, won't it cause problems, having attractive young women behaving provocatively in the work areas?"

"Charlie," Montclair said, "what kind of problems would it cause?"

"Well, these are not exactly Stanford graduates down there. I imagine they might . . . try taking liberties."

Montclair grinned. "But that's the beauty part, Charlie. The only guys who will try to take liberties, to use your own quaint phrase, will be the most aggressive workers. The girls should encourage them to take whatever liberties they want. Think of it, man, on one fifteen-minute break you'll gain the total loyalty of the cream of your work force. They're not going to be thinking about unions or job security or bigger paychecks. The only thing they'll be thinking of is nookie, and what they'll have to do to get some. And what they'll have to do is work at full tilt."

Montclair and I left the beagle and his pals to chew over those bones. I told him, "I don't recall your putting that kind of stuff in your books."

"You haven't been reading carefully enough. There's the mind," he pointed a dog finger at his head, "and there's the body. I don't believe you can achieve anything without considering both. If you're physically tuned and mentally tuned, you can move through the business world like a snake on wheels."

"Excuse me, but didn't you just tell that geezer to hire hookers to keep his workers happy?"

"So?"

"Well, I don't know. It seems a little Old World or something."

"Old World? Of course it is. Don't you get it, Bloodworth? The real secret is that modern times and its technologies and psychologies just muddy the water. You have to keep your goals clear. You want power. You want control. You want your ashes hauled.

"Look at our host, Barclay. He lives here like a feudal lord whose subjects gather to serve him. He wants a ham sandwich or a Dr. Brown's or a broad, does he have to put on his pants, get out the car, and go out and get 'em? Hell, no! He doesn't even have to pick up a phone. All he has to do is raise his voice."

"That part's true, but—"

"No buts, Bloodworth. The guy is the personification of everything I write about. He read a book of mine and he was amused by it. That's why we met. What amused him was that the things I had to think about and analyze, they came to him naturally. He is the real Mr. Success, not me."

"There are things about him you may not know," I said.

He smiled. "I guess you mean the clinic. I admit that that may be a bit extreme. But he has the power to bring it off."

It was, of course, the first I'd heard of any clinic. I asked if he'd been through it.

"Not for a while. I assume Childress is still in charge?"

"Last I heard."

"Can you imagine, a private individual having the imagination and the power to buy the exclusive services of the acknowledged greatest cosmetic surgeon in the world and then to use him solely for keeping the people around him beautiful?"

So that was what the secret building behind the kitchen was, a face-lift clinic. "More theater and makeup," I said, mainly to myself.

If Montclair heard me, he didn't indicate it. He was rattling on about Barclay's many and wondrous achievements.

I stemmed that with, "Let me try out a hypothetical question on you, Montclair. What happens when your man of power decides to use it against society?"

"What do you mean?"

"You've heard of antisocial acts?"

"Of course. But in this case, they don't apply. The man of power creates his own societal rules. He changes rules, he doesn't break them. Law and order is for the masses, not the elite."

Jeez, my former guru was going to start telling me how wrong we were about Hitler in another minute. So one more bright balloon bites the dust. I grumbled, "What a load of sewer gas!"

"Huh? What's the matter, Bloodworth? Don't have the heart to fly with eagles?"

"You fly with who you want to, Montclair," I said, leaving him. I raised my fist. "Power to the people."

He gave me a disgusted look. It made me feel I was on the right track.

2. "Where Monsieur Barclay is . . . I don't know," a woman in a maid's uniform informed me, avec accent.

"That makes two of us."

I wandered on.

Among the hounds and hares in the vicinity of the elaborate buffet, I spotted a familiar-looking Doberman with a full plate of steak-kabobs and rice standing at the patio door, looking wistfully at the water nymphs cavorting in the pool.

I snuck up behind him and whispered, "That way lies heartburn, amigo."

He jumped, startled, juggling the plate. "Damnit, Hound, I almost dropped my dinner."

"This is a pleasant surprise. You and Barclay old buds?"

He gave me a vague nod of the head, causing his Doberman ears to wiggle.

"How'd you get in?" I asked. "Rush the gate?"

He grinned. "I spotted Ed Valesquez a few cars behind mine."

"And the liberal Congressman Valesquez let you ride on his coattails? I'm surprised, considering the way he feels about cops."

"Actually," Cugie said, pausing for a mouthful of rice, "I figured whoever was manning the monitor wouldn't know one Chicano from another. So I told 'em I was Valesquez and I'd forgotten my invite, but that he certainly knew me by sight."

I laughed. "When they get it all sorted out, they may be able to identify your car."

"Do I look worried?"

"Why are you here, amigo?"

"Because you are, Hound. Simple as that. This is the night we catch the bad guys, no?"

"I'm not sure what we're going to catch."

"Right. Play it close to the vest, Hound. I know this is the place. Even Hilbert must think something's up."

"Hilbert?"

"I saw him a minute ago. Wearing a terrier dog costume. He was with a real mind-bending Chihuahua."

"A terrier and a Chihuahua," I said.

"This Chihuahua was wearing about an inch and a half of bikini. I don't know how Hilbert does it."

"Where were they headed?" I asked.

He shrugged and began to nibble on his rice. "¿Qué sé yo?" He frowned and said, "You and me are the closest of amigos. Why do you refuse to tell me what's going on? You know damn well this is something big. And I need to be a part of it."

"Why? It won't mean any more money in your sock come retirement day."

"Retirement day?" he spat haughtily. "You think I sit around waiting to retire? I am a vital man. I have many untapped talents. I want in on this because I want my first book to be a smash."

He stopped a waiter and asked him to hold the plate while he removed the skewer from his kabob. *"Gracias,"* he told the waiter.

"You're writing a book?" I asked him.

"Don't you think I'm capable? Because I am Latin, you feel I am illiterate? Have you not heard of Borges? Of Marquez?"

"You're writing a book. The kid's writing a book. It's like a goddamn land rush. Everywhere you look, somebody's trying to jump your claim."

"Ah. So you *were* going to cut me out."

"Cut you out? I didn't even know you were in."

"This is my big chance, Hound."

I shook my head and said, "Cugie, last I knew, you couldn't even write an accident report."

"That's grammar you're talking about. Somebody else takes care of that."

"Sure," I said sarcastically.

"So you wrote your book all by yourself?" he asked.

"Damn right."

"And fat-ass Flaherty didn't contribute nothing?"

"I guess he helped me a little."

Cugie said, "Ha!" triumphantly, and then developed a sudden interest in his food. I started away from him.

"Hound, wait for me."

"Find your own international conspiracies," I told him over my shoulder.

"But this is happening right here. I know it. Why would you be here? Why would Hilbert?"

"Maybe he's writing a book, too." Christ! Maybe he was!

Cugie paused to put his plate on a table, and I tried to lose him in the crowd. The last I saw of his Doberman head, it was twisting right and left trying to pick up my trail.

I moved quickly from the dining hall into the large living room. Since Barclay didn't seem to be in the midst of his own party, I thought he might have retreated to his small office. I cut through a pack of dancing dogs and made it to the stairwell leading to the indoor pool.

The smell of chlorine attacked my sinuses as I entered the steamy room.

The pool's surface was being churned by a state senator who was showing two bikinied ladies the Potomac breast stroke. As I passed them, I felt something like Cugie's hot paw against the center of my back.

I turned around, saying, "You're behaving like a jer—"

But it wasn't Cugie. It was Little Jimmy in a collie suit that had gotten all frizzed from the humidity in the room. His right paw seemed quite hard and metallic under the fake fur. He pointed it at my bay window. "Keep moving," he repeated.

I nodded, turned, and continued on to Barclay's office.

Jimmy knocked once on the closed door. "It's Tony," he said. "I've got Bloodworth with me."

There was the click of a lock, and the door was opened by Gregory Desidero. He vaguely resembled a Lab retriever. Barclay was seated at his desk.

Dove Hilbert, wearing his terrier togs, and a bikinied Hannah Reyne occupied the couch. And rounding out the room, Hajji stood beside them, in a dark outfit that made him look more like a bear than a dog.

Barclay said, "We were just talking about you, Bloodworth."

Hilbert looked away.

"I gather it wasn't anything real complimentary."

Barclay smiled. "Quite the contrary. I was just explaining to Lieutenant Hilbert how truly clever you were. He didn't think you were capable of murdering four or five people and trying to blame him for at least two of your kills. But I think we've offered him enough proof for him to realize how much he has underestimated you."

"If you think I've killed somebody, you ought to tell it to the police," I said.

"That's why we turned our facts over to Lieutenant Hilbert."

"He's no longer active," I said.

"So we've discovered. But this may be just what he needs to get back in harness. Right, Lieutenant?"

Hilbert didn't answer. He stared at the floor.

"All right," I said. "Let's hear your proof."

"It would be simpler if you confessed," Barclay said.

"Simpler how?"

"Well, maybe not simpler. But it would make some of us"—he looked at Hilbert—"feel better after your execution."

"Execution? In this state? You'd have to kill the governor to get executed. Mayors aren't even enough."

Barclay smiled. "You're being purposely obtuse. There won't be any arrest or trial. I dispense the justice here, and I have a feeling you're going to die right around the time that my last guest leaves the party."

I asked Hannah to move over on the couch and flopped next to her. I said, "Let's hope this is one of those clambakes that never ends."

35

1. Peru De Falco is a very sweet young man, and I truly like him. But I sensed that Mr. Bloodworth was in trouble and I could feel time running out. "If you don't do it, Peru," I said sternly, "I shall be forced to tell your mother."

"Tell her *what?* That I wouldn't help you break into Leo's house?"

"That you stood in the way of saving Mr. Bloodworth's life."

He looked remarkably handsome even with his brows furrowed and his mouth hanging open. He said, "We don't know for sure that he's in any trouble."

"His phone is off the hook. Look through that window. You can see the phone on the carpet, with its receiver knocked off of the cradle."

"He could have just kicked the cord on his way out."

"Why are you fighting me, Peru? I can sense these things. He needs us to help him."

Peru looked back down the alley to the street. "His car's not even out front. He just drove off somewhere."

I spotted a loose brick in the walk, bent, and picked it up. "It's up to you, Peru. You said you carry a lock pick. Either show me that you can use it, or I'm going to smash in a window and get in that way."

"They'll hear you at the theater."

"Then use the pick."

He hesitated. I drew back the brick. "I'm tired of this argument," I said. "Wait. I'll open the lock."

He removed from his pocket an object that resembled a very narrow knife. It contained an assortment of loose metal sticks (some round, some with sharp edges) with a circumference of less than a sixteenth of an inch, and others that were ultra-thin and flat.

He began poking the sticks into Mr. Bloodworth's locks. "This is a terrible thing," he said. "Breaking into my employer's house. Leo'll never understand. My mom won't understand."

The lock clicked and I threw open the door and rushed in. Peru stood at the door. He said, "You see. There's no sign of a struggle or anything. Just the phone. And the way the cord is stretched across the floor, he probably tripped over it on the way out."

I purposely did not replace the receiver, since it might have contained useful fingerprints. But I did notice that on the counter where Mr. B. usually kept the phone were several yearbooks. From UC Raven's Point. I knew that Mr. Bloodworth had matriculated from UCLA. And considerably before the 1970's. Which, naturally, made me curious.

One book was open to a page devoted to a theater group called RUT. I was studying the photos in total fascination when Peru shouted, "You see! I was right! He's gone to a party!"

He waved an invitation that I snatched from his hand. I read it, then paused to consider its significance. "Where did you find this?" I asked him.

"On the floor. I guess he dropped it on his way out. Hell, he's partying. I should never have—"

"Peru, Peru, please try to think. Is Mr. Bloodworth totally irresponsible?"

"He never has been while I was around."

"You know that he is in the middle of a very serious investigation. Have I not described to you, in vivid terms, exactly what we both have endured this day?"

"Yes," he said.

"Then do you think he would come home and turn right around and go off to a party?"

"He might want to unload. Forget his troubles. According to that tape you've got, they know how to have a blast at this Xanadu place."

"This party is at the same location as the party on Mark Fishburn's tape?"

"Sure. Like I said, Leo and I drove out there a couple days ago. He was a little nervous about going in without some backup." He paused. Frowned. "You might just have something, Serendipity. If Leo was nervous about going in there during the day, why would he go back by himself at night?"

"Exactly," I said, starting for the front door.

Peru closed the door carefully and made sure it was locked. "On the other hand," he said, "nothing happened to him that first time. And the guy did send him an invitation to a party. . . ."

"The more you think about these things, Peru, the more complicated life becomes. Just go by your . . ."

We were passing the little theater, when this round-faced woman with nervous eyelashes rushed to greet us. She was wearing the most amazing bright blue dress. She said, "Little girl, haven't I seen you with Mr. Bloodworth?"

"Yes," I said warily.

"Oh. I'm just so worried. I've been sitting by that door since we opened this evening. And early on I spotted a man parked in a car across the street, watching and watching this building. Well, I wasn't too concerned. I mean, we've had trouble with Korean teenagers. And while he obviously wasn't one of those, he did have some sort of Third World ancestry. And when the play began and he still stayed there, watching, I got a little uneasy."

"Excuse me, but what does this have to do with Mr. Bloodworth?"

"When Mr. Bloodworth left his home an hour or so ago, this man started up his car and he drove away, and it looked to me like he was following Mr. Bloodworth. So if you see him, tell him about it, will you? And tell him Marie was worried about him."

I told her I would. And when Peru and I were safely inside his car, I said to him, "No more nonsense, now. You know exactly where we're headed."

"I guess so," he said glumly. "Only, how are we going to get in?"

I took the invitation out of my pocket and waved it under his nose. I said, "You let me worry about that."

2. About twenty or twenty-five cars were waiting to pass the gate with the large "X." I hopped out of the BMW and raced up to the front of the line and observed the procedure, then I ran back to Peru. "The invitation won't help. They're checking names."

"Then what do we do?"

"I'm thinking."

There was a knock at Peru's side window. I looked over and one of the liveried butlers was there with a portable bar on wheels. He was a clean-cut young man with remarkably perfect teeth. "You and your lady friend care for a drink while you wait, Mr. Travolta?"

"I'm not . . . ouch."

"He's not much of a drinker," I said. "But we do have a problem. It has to do with him finding a bathroom very quickly."

"Oh." He was concerned for a second, then he grinned. "Well, there're about five miles of woods out there."

"Please," I said. "Try to think how that would look in the *Enquirer.*

Unless you can assure us that there are no paparazzi lurking around one of the biggest parties of the year."

"I see what you mean. That's basically why security is so tight at Xanadu, the paparazzi. Well, why not just park off to the side and walk ahead of these cars and tell them at the gate about . . . your problem."

"And make all these people in line hate us forever? Isn't there an entrance you use for your carts?"

"Yes, but that's not supposed to be for the guests."

"Mr. Travolta would be eternally grateful. Maybe he'd even want to hear about some script you're writing. . . ."

"Oh, well, I'm not really much of a writer," the young butler said. "But I am studying acting with Charles—"

"Great," I said. I poked Peru again and said, "Just pull the car over to the right, *Johnny.*"

Peru did as I asked, but he was behaving very strangely, keeping his face rigidly straight ahead. "Relax," I whispered, "the hard part is over."

"You don't understand," he said out of the right corner of his mouth, "I only look like Travolta from the left."

"That'll probably be enough," I told him.

36

1. "If anybody's going to be executed," I said, "I'd like to cast my vote for Archie Leach."

Desidero frowned. Little Jimmy (his name may have been Tony, but he would always be Little Jimmy to me) straightened in his collie suit.

Barclay said slowly, "Leach? I don't know anyone by that name."

"That's surprising, Barclay. . . . Excuse me, but I'm going to have to stand up for a second." I struggled to my feet in the costume. Then, carefully, I unzipped its side.

Jimmy moved closer, his swollen paw extended.

I said, "Down, Fido. I just want to get a piece of paper from my coat."

Barclay was leaning forward on his chair, curious now.

I worked my arm out of the costume and deliberately put just two fingers into my coat pocket, pulling out a folded sheet of slick paper. I handed it to Hilbert.

Hannah leaned over to take a peek as he unfolded it. "What the hell is this, Bloodworth?" he grumbled. "It looks like a page from a goddamn school yearbook."

He glared at it more carefully, then he looked up at Barclay. "I'll be damned!" he exploded. "This is you, Barclay. A little skinnier, with a moustache and some hair and . . ." He laughed. "You had a nose job. But the eyes are the same. Hell, yes."

Barclay leaped from his desk and circled it, snatching the sheet from Hilbert's hand.

"You made a damn good Big Brother, Barclay." I smiled at Hilbert. "The guy who just said he'd never heard of Archie Leach taught him for four years at UC Raven's Point. The mysterious Wally Barclay used to be a theater professor named Waldemir Bernstein at a little college upstate. Not exactly a secret to rival Jay Gatsby's. But he's made up for that."

Hilbert leaned back against the sofa. "I'm not sure I see the significance . . ."

So I started to point that out to him. "He had several pupils, including Tony here and Mr. Desidero and maybe even this gent." I indicated Hajji. "But he also had a star pupil: a dynamic born leader named Archie Leach."

Until that point Barclay had been staring at the page from *The Goldenrod* with an intense concentration. Suddenly he relaxed and interrupted me. "We all want to hear what you have to say, Bloodworth, but I'd prefer it if Hannah could run a short errand for me." He turned to her. "Dear?"

I moved forward, but Jimmy's paw pressed against my back.

Barclay whispered something in Hannah's ear. She smiled. Hilbert didn't like any of it. He said, "What the hell's going on, honey?"

She said, "Sorry, Dovesy, but this is very important." She bent down before him and, as she had done once with me, took his face in her hands and kissed him. "I'll be just a few minutes," she said, standing. He looked pretty much the same as he had when he was near-dead from drowning.

At the door Hannah paused and pointed a finger at Hajji. "You'd better come with me, in case I need a strong back."

Hajji turned to Barclay, who said, "It's okay, Nicky."

Hajji looked unhappy, but he did as requested. He unlocked the door and held it open. Hannah pivoted on her bare heel and left. Hajji, like a bear reluctant to leave his cave, followed her out, slamming the door behind him.

"What the hell is going on?" Hilbert demanded.

"Bloodworth here is telling us a story. Please continue."

I was as confused as Hilbert, but I had come to confront Barclay and I was going to, even if he seemed to be encouraging it.

"Well, like I said, Archie Leach was Barclay's prize—an actor, a man of imagination, possibly even a genius. And he was a prankster, at least as fond of jokes as his professor was. They planned little, impractical ones at first, then gradually the jokes got more and more practical. And more political. Barclay and his charismatic puppet took over the whole school.

"But, Hilbert, you know what the man says: 'Today Raven's Point, Tomorrow the World.' Barclay realized that if the props were right, you could prank anyone, and if you carried that formula into the real world, such as it is, and upped the stakes all around, your punch line could be money and power. So he and Leach created a role for Barclay to play—a mysterious financier and kingmaker wheeling and dealing from the one spot in the country where no one cares a hoot about histories or credentials, where the only thing that counts is what people think you can do for them—southern California.

"Barclay, in his flamboyant way, got results for his investors and women for his friends. Along the way he may have jiggered a few stocks or sold a little flesh or even bumped off a few minor characters. But, hey, nobody's perfect."

Barclay yawned. "Did I kill Sal Mineo, too?"

"I wouldn't say no without checking. You definitely killed Mike Kosca, or you ordered him killed. And you sent a hit man who called himself Cole Porter to get rid of another of your students, Simon Watson."

"That's two, so far. Any more?"

"Watson's roommate, Jerry Palomar. Does that name sound familiar, Hilbert? They set up one of their elaborate pieces of street theater to make sure *you* took the heat for Palomar's death."

Hilbert looked from me to Barclay and back to me again. "Barclay just told me almost that same story, Bloodworth. The difference was, he said you were the guy pulling the strings."

I stared at Barclay. He looked smug and very self-satisfied. I took a deep breath and said to Hilbert, "As you know damn well, I'm a little more straightforward than that. Besides, I'm not the guy controlling the gun in this room, Hilbert. And I'm not the guy in the Big Brother photo who's trying to protect a new name and a new life. I'm just another mark the Mummers roped into one of their not-so-funny gags."

The door to the room suddenly swung open, and a figure in a dog suit stepped into the room.

"I'm sorry," Barclay began, "but we're having a very private chat just now. . . ."

The figure grabbed Little Jimmy by his swollen paw and the scruff of his costume's neck and smashed him into the bulkhead. He had to do it twice before Jimmy folded.

Desidero jumped toward the newcomer, and I stopped him with a right to the stomach and a left to the side of the head.

Barclay's bald scalp was taking on a purple hue. He growled at the newcomer, "Who the hell do you think you are?"

"He thinks he's a writer, but he makes a much better cop," I said, watching Cugat rip open Jimmy's costume to get at the pistol in his limp hand.

2. There were another three guns in the room. I took one from Desidero. And two from Barclay's desk drawer. I didn't think to check Hilbert. Instead, Cugie and I used Desidero's and Little Jimmy's belts to hogtie them to the legs of the desk.

Hilbert said, "I want to go see about Hannah."

"She's probably flown," I said.

Barclay shook his head. "She's only swimming. I sent her from the room because I didn't want her to hear too much of our conversation. She has nothing at stake here, and she might have felt compelled to tell tales."

He looked at the two bound men on the floor. "I do think you have acted in haste . . . Lieutenant Cugat, is it? At least five of my guests upstairs outrank you enough to not only rip your badge from your chest but make you happily eat it for supper. I just have to lift a finger."

Cugat was on the phone, on the verge of ordering in a platoon of policemen. He looked at me. "What do you think, amigo?"

I pointed to Desidero. "His prints were on Kosca's shoes when they hauled him up. And he's attacked Sarah, twice. The other weasel was an accessory to murder: the Watson guy in Venice."

Cugie's face broke into a wolfish grin. He put down the phone. "I can make my call anytime," he said, sitting down on the sofa, putting his dogfoot on Jimmy's neck. "Spin me a yarn, Hound."

I sighed. I knew when I was licked.

They were all looking at me—Cugie, Hilbert, and Barclay. I sat on the edge of the desk and spun them a yarn.

3. To fill Cugie in, I repeated the business about Archie Leach and the formation of the Mummers and how after graduation Leach and his old prof, Dr. Bernstein, created Wally Barclay and lived happily ever after for ten years.

"At that time," I continued, "they decided to have a graduation-day reunion of the Mummers—Desidero had referred to it as the 'Big One-Oh'—and to mark the event with some sort of elaborate stunt. You saw tonight how elaborate their stunts can be.

"Desidero had gotten the call while he was in New Orleans. So he and his girl friend and her girl friend, Cece MacElroy, a fifteen-year-old runaway, motored west. As these things happen, Desidero and Cece got together, and the odd-girl-out went home. Lucky her.

"Cece's parent's were at least mildly upset about her run-out. The father, who was probably the reason she left in the first place, followed her here. My guess is he was tipped to her whereabouts by the jilted dame. A while later Cece's mother got Terry Manion, a New Orleans P.I., to see what he could do about tracing the girl. He hired Mike Kosca.

314

"By then Cece had moved from Desidero to the charismatic Archie
Leach; and Kosca, the poor bastard, must have stumbled on the setup out
here. So they bumped him off with the help of a little rodent of a poacher
and bird trainer named Low Rent Lacotta. Is he here tonight?"

Barclay nodded his huge head.

"Kosca's death moved Manion to come to L.A. himself. He tried calling
me for help. But by the time we connected, Barclay had discovered enough
of Manion's plans to improvise a little scenario to get me out of the picture.
This is a good one, Cugie. One of the Mummers, Simon Watson, didn't go
for whatever they were planning to pull. My guess is that he threatened to
blow the whistle on Barclay. . . ." I paused, as a few loose ends connected.
The smile didn't leave Barclay's face.

Hilbert stood up impatiently and began pacing the room.

I said, "Watson may even have spilled to Kosca. In any case, he packed his
bags and split. Barclay wanted him out of the way permanently, and me out
of the way at least temporarily. So, using another 'student,' a woman calling
herself Holly Blissfield, he hired me to find Watson. And I love this touch—
to enhance Blissfield's con job, they used a mansion that another protégé, a
gigolo named Ernie Mott, had secured for them months before they even
thought they'd be needing it.

"Like a stalking-horse, I led them to Watson in Venice, where this creep"
—I shoved Little Jimmy with my foot—"and a woman named Lannie Doolittle stood by and watched a nasty bastard named Cole Porter shoot him
down in an appropriately named spot called the Isle of the Dead."

"*Madre de Dios!*" Cugie yelled joyously. "What drama."

"Would you like me to provide you with a printed outline?" I asked him.

"Please continue, Hound. This is good stuff."

"They drugged me and left me with the stiff. But I got out of there before
the Venice police arrived.

"With a good deal of luck I made it back here in time to stop these
bastards from killing both Terry Manion and Cece MacElroy's father with
drugs. And . . ." I turned to Hilbert, who was my client, ". . . and to
throw a monkey wrench into their plan to discredit you."

Hilbert shook his head. "It doesn't make sense. What the hell did they
have against me? I wasn't any threat to them. I didn't even know any of 'em
until Hannah took me out here."

"About a year ago the gigolo Mott stole some jewelry. You were the
investigating officer."

"Yeah, you asked me about that before. It was nothing. I was twiddling
my thumbs that day. The call came in and I . . . I was sorta curious about

what the dame who lost the stones looked like in the flesh, so I took a ride out . . ."

"Who was the lady?" Cugat asked.

"That's not important," I said quickly. "The point is, Hilbert, you did investigate. You filled out a report. That was fine. But a few weeks later you scribbled a note on the report, about the death of the woman's insurance agent, Philip Marton."

"Yeah." Hilbert stopped pacing. "We've been over this. There was nothing suspicious about his death. He was just too damned old to be playing around with teeny-boppers."

"The same could be said about you," I told him.

"You son of a bitch!" He took a step forward, and I pushed off of the desk to meet him. But instead of taking a swing, he wilted. "Shit. I guess it does look like that."

"I think Barclay engineered the insurance agent's death. Consciously or not, you did something to make him nervous. And so you had to be neutralized. That's the way he operates. He uses young women. He was doing it back at the college."

Cugie said, "Hound, I do not wish to stem your flow of rhetoric, but I wonder: What was the big thing Barclay and Leach had planned for the reunion that led them to kill so many?"

I looked at Barclay. "How about it?"

"It's your story, Bloodworth."

I shrugged. "I don't see that it matters any longer. Whatever it is, it's done for now."

"Another thing, Hound. You say your friend Manion and Kosca were both looking for a runaway. What happened to her?"

I opened my mouth, but Barclay beat me to it. "Archie Leach killed her," he said. He moved to the chair behind his desk and sank onto it. "Bloodworth's little tale is essentially correct except for one tiny detail. I'm not pulling Archie's strings. He's pulling mine."

4. I passed my hand over his head and around his back. "No strings," I said.

He picked up the sheet I'd torn from *The Goldenrod.* "This was his string. Archie was a brilliant young man, brilliant enough to make me understand that all of this was within my grasp. It was a case of the student instructing the teacher." Barclay smiled, but he seemed to be in pain.

"So I took the plunge. Gave up my position and my tenure. Archie led me by the hand. He was an astonishing con man. You should have seen his performance at the Golden Pacific Bank. We drove to Beverly Hills in a rented Bentley, wearing six-hundred-dollar suits, seventy-five-dollar haircuts, and less than a hundred dollars between us. I walked away with a credit line of a quarter of a million dollars. Before the day was out, we had parlayed that into an account topping a million."

"What was his cut?"

"That was the point," Barclay said. "He set me up and then he drifted off with just a few thousand. I kept expecting to see him heading a film company or becoming baseball commissioner or running for governor. But nothing. Then, two years ago, he showed up at my gate, demanding . . . certain things."

Hilbert began pacing again. "Spell 'em out. We're all adults."

"He needed sanctuary, actually. Just as he had created a new life for me, he'd stepped into a new persona—Devlin, a shadowy figure engaged in narcotics, prostitution, and Lord knows what-all. And he'd run afoul of some of the other fellows engaged in those same businesses. I arranged for him to meet with . . . well, I don't think we need mention names, but with some rather important gentlemen in the Italian community. They wound up agreeing to let Devlin take care of some of the smarmier sections of their portfolio, in return for seventy cents on the dollar.

"So Devlin was back in business. But since he was operating on only thirty percent, to maintain his former life-style, he had to broaden his base. And he did this by blackmailing me."

"So you're telling us that the murders, the crap Hilbert and Manion and I have been through, Leach is to blame for all that. Not you."

He nodded.

"And these soldiers"—I prodded Desidero with my foot—"they're working for him, not for you."

"Precisely."

"Why the hell should we believe you?" I asked.

"Because it's the truth. Archie is the master criminal here. The prime manipulator. The chameleon who takes on a hundred guises. I'm afraid he must have been greatly influenced by those Dr. Mabuse movies they used to show at the art house off campus.

"You gentlemen have all met him, more than once. He is Devlin, Ernie Mott, George Kerby. He followed you to Italy, Bloodworth, in the outrageous guise of a rock composer named Cole Porter, of all things. He worked in your office for a while, Hilbert, as Detective Danny Barr. He's a brilliant actor."

"Oh, man, I love this kinda stuff," Cugat said joyously.

"I'll sign any statement you want," Barclay said. "I readily admit to having played a little fast and loose with my financial manipulations. But I have not been a part of Archie's hard-core criminal activity, and even these poor souls will tell you that.

"I suppose I'll have to spend a few years at Chino. But it'll be soft time. And it'll be worth it to get Archie off of my back. His genius is starting to fray around the edges."

"Then you won't mind telling us how to find him," I said.

Barclay looked at Hilbert, who was trying to struggle out of his dog suit. "Probably with his true love," he said, "entwined, wrapped in romance," he grinned. "Appropriate to our gala, like two dogs in heat."

"He's here?" I asked.

"He just left this room a little while ago with his woman."

Hilbert, only half out of his costume, rushed the desk. His hands grabbed Barclay's throat and began to squeeze. "You lying son-of-a-bitch!" he screamed.

Barclay had spent the last ten years working out and beefing up. He pried Hilbert's white fingers away with ease. He said, "Archie didn't mind sharing her with you, Hilbert, as long as you didn't damage the merchandise. From what she told us, you barely touched it."

Hilbert looked shell-shocked. His eyes were glassy.

Cugat was on the phone, calling out the troops. That done, he handed the receiver to Barclay. "Get your people on the gate to keep it shut until the officers arrive. I don't want this *master criminal* to escape."

Barclay shrugged and did as he was told. Hilbert was muttering to himself. Then, suddenly, he pulled a gun from his costume. He pointed it at Barclay and said in a chillingly soft voice, "Where are they?"

Barclay backed away. "Archie has a suite at the rear of the clinic. Just don't . . . do anything . . ."

Hilbert waved us back with the gun and marched to the door.

Barclay said, "They'll be making love. They can't seem to get enough of each other. They spend hours . . ."

Hilbert screamed and rushed through the door, slamming it shut behind him.

Cugie got it open and ran after him.

Barclay looked at me. "You don't want to be in on the kill, Bloodworth?"

I shook my head. "I'd rather make sure you don't do something crazy, like hop the next helicopter for Mexico. Because I think that 'soft time' may be a little harder than you realize."

The gunshots sounded muffled and quite distant, but they were definitely gunshots. Three of them. Barclay said, "That Hilbert fellow just couldn't take a joke."

A security guard rushed through the door, saw me with a gun on his boss, and reached for his holster. Barclay patted the air. "Relax, young man. The problem is out there. Not here. Mr. Bloodworth has quite properly placed me under arrest."

The guard's eyes bugged when he spotted the two tied dogs on the floor. Desidero was wiggling around.

"What happened upstairs?" I asked the guard.

He still wasn't sure what was happening right there. "This, uh, guy, uh, shot, uh . . ."

"Take your time and spit it out," I said.

"He shot a guy by the swimming pool. It was Nicky, Mr. Barclay. He shot him twice."

"What was the third shot?" I asked.

"Th-that's the worst thing, Mr. Barclay. He also shot one of your guests. That crazy bastard shot John Travolta."

37

1. "He was protecting me, of course," I told Mr. Bloodworth as we sat in the emergency waiting room of St. John's Hospital.

It had been an astonishing thing. Peru in some sort of woolly costume and I in a rather sweet little blue bunny suit were wandering through a crowd rather remarkable for its celebrity content when suddenly there was a disturbance by the pool. Lieutenant Hilbert stood there, the bottom part of him in a dog costume the top of which was flapping like a flag behind him. He pointed a gun at some oily-looking fellow in shaggy black mufti who was standing near the pool.

The fellow tried to put up his hand, but Lieutenant Hilbert fired at him point-blank, and the man was thrown back into the water. The lieutenant went to the pool's edge, reached down and grabbed the dying man's face. AND THE MAN'S EYEBROWS AND NOSE CAME OFF IN HIS HAND! The lieutenant fired once again, and the man, weighed down by his costume, sank to the bottom of the pool.

The whole area was in chaos. Security guards, guns drawn, raced onto the scene, but they didn't know what to do, really. Guests, looking absolutely absurd under the circumstances in their dog suits, began pointing at the unfortunate lieutenant.

He was screaming the name "Hannah" over and over and looking around frantically. He spotted my face sticking out of my bunny costume and, squinting, he drew closer. "Where is she?" he yelled. "Where has the deceitful bitch run to?"

I couldn't think of anything to tell him. Then Peru grabbed the lieutenant's gun hand, and the gun went off. Peru flew back and someone yelled, "He's killed John Travolta."

By then a bunch of security guards were wrestling with the lieutenant. And Lieutenant Cugat appeared as if by magic to take charge. I tore off my bunny costume and rolled it into a pillow, which I placed under Peru's bloody head.

Mr. Bloodworth, who as it turned out *had* kicked his phone while he was leaving home, and who had not needed or welcomed our assistance at Xanadu, followed our ambulance as we sped to St. John's.

Peru's mother was there before us. She was a solid woman in her middle years whose hair was still dark and whose emotions were quite volatile.

While the doctor examined Peru, she sat across from us in the waiting room, mumbling prayers while fingering a rosary. Every time Mr. Bloodworth tried to open his mouth, she shook her head and crossed herself and went back to her beads.

When the doctor on duty—a bleached, bloodless sort of fellow—came out to see us, it was impossible to read his blank face. The man was a cipher.

He said, "Mrs. De Falco?"

"Yes?" She looked up at him fearfully.

"I'd say another couple of hours . . ."

"Oh, my God! Jesus, Mary, and Joseph!"

". . . and he can go home."

She stopped wailing and looked at him. "What are you saying?"

"Your son's okay. He's had a close one. The bullet creased the side of his head about four inches above the ear. There was some bleeding. There's still a very slight possibility of a mild concussion and/or very minor sight problems. We'll know definitely within the next two hours.

"But he seems to have a remarkably thick skull, and with the exception of a scar and very minimal hair loss, he'll be as good as new before you know it."

"Saints be praised," she said.

"You can go back and see him. He's sitting up. He has a headache, but we've given him something to help that."

"Nothing too strong?"

"No. Don't worry. I'll check him again in a couple hours, but I'm pretty sure there'll be no problems. He can leave then."

As we walked down the hospital corridor through the flapping doors, Mrs. De Falco swung on Mr. Bloodworth. "Where's Peru's car?"

He looked at me.

"In Malibu," I said. "Near Xanadu."

"I'll get it back to you," Mr. Bloodworth said.

"You're damn right you will. With a full tank of gas. And you're damn well paying for *this*, too."

It was pretty embarrassing, because Mr. Bloodworth began to argue with Mrs. De Falco, exclaiming that Peru had disobeyed his orders and therefore he felt no obligation to pay the hospital bill and didn't Peru have insurance, anyway.

Mrs. De Falco countered that, yes, Peru did have insurance, but the rates would hit the moon if he used it, and it was the employer's responsibility to take care of that sort of thing, and that Mr. Bloodworth was a penny-pinching son of a bitch who had needlessly endangered her only son's life for the last time.

The other patients and guests and even the staff were frowning at this heated discussion, and the bloodless doctor was turning pink and trying to distance himself from us.

Finally, however, he pulled back a curtain to present Peru, sitting up in bed with a bandage on the side of his head and circles around his eyes. He was sipping some liquid through a straw stuck into a plastic cup. He grinned at us, and both Mr. Bloodworth and Mrs. De Falco shut up.

She moved forward and threw herself on the bed, hugging him.

He said, "Aw, Ma. C'mon. I'm okay."

"We're happy you're not seriously hurt," Mr. Bloodworth said.

"Not hurt? Look at my boy's head, you ingrate."

"Hey, Ma. Don't talk to Leo like that."

I took his hand and squeezed it. "Thanks for protecting me, Peru."

"That's what I do," he said. He moved his head very slowly and carefully. "Did that guy with the gun get put away, Leo?"

"Him and a whole bunch of others," Mr. Bloodworth said.

Peru smiled suddenly. "He's gonna have a lot of explaining to do."

"Lieutenant Hilbert?" I asked.

"No," Peru said. "John Travolta's publicity guy."

2. It was nearly 2:00 A.M. when Mr. Bloodworth dropped me off at the apartment. "Don't you feel like coming in?" I asked him.

"It's a little late," he said, reaching over and opening the door.

"But you should take a look at the tape I got from Mark Fishburn."

He shook his head. "That's none of my business anymore. Give it to Cugie and tell him about Fishburn. He's the guy writing the book."

"What?"

"Nothing. I'm just tired."

"Gran wasn't home at midnight when I called. Maybe she's still out."

He yawned as I got out of the car. "She's probably unplugged the phones so that she could sleep."

"With me still out?" I shook my head. "I'm worried about her."

"What do you think happened to her?" he asked as he reached over to close the door behind me.

"My worst fear is that she and the creepy Roger Thornhill have eloped."

He coughed. At first I thought he was laughing, but then he began coughing. "Something in my throat," he said. "Look, I don't think she'd do anything like that without telling you."

"She knows I despise him."

"She's probably upstairs waiting for you."

"Maybe." I remembered something and reached into my pocket. I took out my wallet and handed him the piece of plastic, the "key" that Gregory Desidero had tried so hard to get his hands on.

He turned it over in his big hand. Then he held it out to me. "Something else for you to give to Cugie."

"You'll probably see him before I do," I told him, backing away.

"Okay," he said, tossing it into his glove compartment with his scarves and crumpled hat. "Okay, Sarah, into the house, now."

"Apartment," I said.

"Okay. Into the apartment."

I waved and turned away.

He waited until I'd unlocked the front door. As I shut it behind me, I could hear his Chevy driving off.

Oh, Gran, please be home, I said to myself as I unlocked the door to our apartment. I waited for G-2 to rush up to welcome me, an indication that Gran had been able to pick him up at the kennel and would herself be home. But there was no happy dog, nor any human to greet me.

Glumly, I shut the door behind me.

"Sehr?"

It was Gran. In the living room. Thank heaven! Now, all I had to do was sit through a brief scolding for coming in so late.

I ran into the living room and stopped cold.

Gran was sitting on the sofa, stiffly. She looked as if she had been crying. Worse yet, sitting across the room from her, on a silver-and-gray tufted chair, was the dreaded Roger Thornhill.

"Hello, Serendipity," he said. "Your grandmother and I have been waiting for you to come home. We've something very important to talk to you about."

I looked at my grandmother, then I rushed to her. "Oh, Gran, you haven't done something absolutely silly, have you?"

She put her arms around me and said, "Now, now, child. I'm sorry, so very sorry."

I heard the chair creak and I turned my head. Roger Thornhill was walking toward us. He had a gun in his hand. He said, "Fun is fun, Serendipity, but I want that key. And I want it now."

38

1. Yes, sir-ee! Now that was what I called a good night's sleep! The clock by the bed read 9:30. I pried the wax plugs out of my ears, stretched maybe three or four times, and rolled out of bed.

I felt great!

As I sipped my hot-milk-coffee and passed a razor over my throat, I tried to focus in on business—specifically, how much I could get away with billing both Laura Mornay and Hilbert for my services. True, Hilbert wasn't in such a hot position to be signing big checks. But his lawyer, T. Landrew Marr, would see I got paid. After all, I had proved that Hilbert hadn't killed Palomar, which was all that I had been hired to prove.

Mornay would be a trickier collection. I hadn't really made it possible for her to get in touch with Mott, unless she had a Ouija board (which in southern California you don't rule out). I had, however, kept her name out of the whole mess, which should have been worth an extra zero or two.

I wiped off the shaving cream, hopped into the shower for a quick one, broke out a clean pair of slacks and a relatively fresh sport coat, and got ready to greet a brand-new beautiful day.

Just before I walked out of the door, my mind set on an afternoon of fresh air, sun, the smell of the turf, and the sound of pari-mutuel machines grinding out my winning tickets, I noticed that my phone was still off of its hook from the night before. That was no doubt the reason why my sleep had been undisturbed by either police or reporters.

No sooner did the receiver kiss the cradle than the damn thing started to squeal. I hesitated, then answered it.

Cugie's anxious voice sounded oddly shrill in my ear. "Hound," he said. "I been trying to get you for hours."

"Why so uptight, amigo? You should be sitting back and basking in the limelight."

"Bask, hell. We got to talk. I'm over at Bay City General. It looks like MacElroy may never come out of it, but Manion's sorta lucid. He's calling your name and Serendipity's."

"Then bring her in, find out what he wants. I'm surprised she didn't hit the hospital first thing this morning."

"Nobody answers at her place."

"Then tell Manion you're me and see what he has to say. It's a beauty of a day, amigo. I was gonna hop a rattler to that sunny spot where the turf meets the surf."

"Manion won't say anything to anybody but you or the kid. He's just this side of loco. C'mon, Hound. You've got time to come in here and still make it down to Del Mar before Crosby sings."

"Come out with me, Cugie! Forget about your goddamn book. We'll tote along a jug of margaritas. I got a feeling that I'm gonna be a winner. I just don't know how big."

"Hound, the guy Hilbert shot wasn't Archie Leach. His real name was Howard Pope. He was an undercover Fed trying to drop the lid on Leach and Barclay. Leach is still out there somewhere."

The image of Del Mar wavered and faded in the distance.

"Squeeze Barclay," I said.

"The Feds have taken over. They did all they could, but they couldn't unlock his lips. The other two *cabrónes*—Desidero and Wharton—they ain't worried at all. They say that by this time tomorrow Archie's going to set them free."

"How's he gonna do that, on a white horse, or what?"

"This is serious, Hound. I . . . make that *we* are in kind of a spot. I'm surprised the Federals haven't been to your place by now."

"My place? Maybe they were. I was passed out in the bedroom with the phone off the hook and plugs in my ears. A cannon couldn't have changed that. What do they want with me?"

"You and me, amigo. They say we screwed up an operation that they'd been working on for nearly two years. Not only that, we just stood by while their man in position got killed. Hell, they're trying to make the pieces fit so that *we* got him killed. They're in with Manion now, but he ain't saying anything they can understand. If you can get him to talk straight, maybe we can walk out of this backward with our *testiculos* still attached."

"I'll be there," I said.

2. Bay City detox was depressing. And it smelled of powerful disinfectant. And it was filled with the cries and screams of poor bastards who'd lost it all to drugs or booze. But at least it was clean and freshly painted in bright colors. And the personnel seemed caring and concerned and not overly cynical.

The Feds had scooted Manion off of the ward and stuck him in a room at the rear of the hospital. It was small and sterile with pea-green walls and barred windows and two guys in suits and striped ties sitting on foldout chairs.

A heavily starched nurse stood beside the narrow bed where Terry Manion was propped up, his bare arms strapped to the rails. One catheter was dripping a liquid substance into his wrist, while a second was removing a liquid substance from somewhere under the bed linen.

His face had been shaved, but not very carefully. Patches of pale beard stood out against his chalky skin. His pale blue eyes darted nervously around the room. "Gil?" he asked. "Have you found my wife, Gil?"

The nurse said, "We're trying to locate her for you, Mr. Manion."

One of the dark suits stood up. He was a shade under six feet, trim and bland as a boiled potato. "This Bloodworth?" he asked Cugie.

"Leo Bloodworth," I said, offering my hand.

He looked at it as if I'd been using it to empty Manion's wastebag.

"This is Agent Quayle," Cugie said. "And Agent . . . ?" He waited for the other agent to introduce himself, but that didn't happen. The guy just looked blankly at us both.

Quayle pointed to Manion and addressed me, "See if you can get him to kick in, then we'll tell you what to ask him."

I opened my mouth to tell Quayle what a fine Federal agent I thought he was, but Cugie shook his head.

So I stepped closer to the bed. Manion tried to focus his eyes. I asked, "Where are his glasses?"

"Don't worry about 'em," Quayle snapped.

"Bloodworth?"

"Yeah, Manion."

"You find her for me?"

"Find who?"

"My wife. Gil."

Quayle said, "Ask him about the 'Big One-Oh.' "

I frowned.

"You don't have to understand it. Just ask."

"Terry, what can you tell me about the 'Big One-Oh'?"

Manion shook his head. "That's it. That's it, exactly. Find my wife. She'll tell you."

Quayle was as impatient as he was arrogant. "The wife's shacked up with Jerry Telamarco, the car jockey, in Japan. Supposed to be visiting automobile manufacturers."

"NO! She's here!" Manion began to scream. "I SAW HER LAST NIGHT!"

"Okay, Terry," I said. "Only you were here last night."

He was shaking now. He pushed back against the pillows, trying to wrest his arms free. The nurse was beginning to look anxious.

Terry said, more quietly, "Last night before I . . . came here. She was there. In my room. I saw her. I see her every night."

"Get him back on track, Bloodworth," Quayle ordered.

I moved away from the bed. "Why don't you try it yourself, Quayle? Charm him, the way you're charming me."

Quayle asked, "Uh, Manion, what can you tell us about Archie Leach?"

Manion closed his eyes and started to cry. "Cary Grant," he said through the tears. "Cary Grant names."

Quayle said, "What?"

I pushed him aside. I said, "Terry, what about the Cary Grant names?"

He nodded his head. "Grant's real name was Archie Leach. I remembered. Any fan knows. Leach uses Grant's names for his disguises. George Kerby. *Topper.* You know, about the ghosts. Funny flick. I could use a few grins."

I said, mainly to myself, "Grant played Cole Porter in a movie. I can't recall the name . . ."

"Night and Day," Manion answered eagerly.

"What the hell is he babbling about?" Quayle wanted to know.

Cugie was staring at me, too. I said, "Something Barclay forgot to mention. Leach evidently has this thing about Cary Grant. When he creates a character for himself, he uses the name of one of Grant's screen rolls. I'll bet . . . Manion, what about Devlin?"

Manion happily replied, "Alfred Hitchcock's *Notorious.* Grant is a secret agent. Has to stand by while the woman he loves marries a Nazi."

I said to Cugie, "Leach's Devlin stood by while his woman, Hannah Reyne, slept with Hilbert. Pretty droll, huh?"

Cugie didn't answer.

Quayle wheeled on the other Fed. "Hatcher, rustle up a list of Grant's movie names. Maybe they'll tell us something."

"Uh, where should I start on something like that?"

328

"Hell, I don't know. The library or a bookstore. There must be books on Grant."

Quayle focused back on Manion. "Look, son, did Leach say anything about the 'Big One-Oh'?"

"No," Terry said. He licked his lips. "Dry," he complained. While the nurse poured water into a plastic cup, he shook his head. "Gil told me. She told me. 'It will dry up, melt. Nevermore for Nevermore.'"

Quayle turned away from the bed. "Great. The wife again." He hummed the opening notes of the *Twilight Zone* theme.

"You sure he couldn't have been with her?" I asked him.

"I told you. We've tracked her to Tokyo."

"But nobody's actually seen her there?"

Quayle said, "No. We haven't seen Nancy Reagan for the past three days either, but we know where she is. And I got a flash for you, Bloodworth, she hasn't been in this dopehead's bedroom quoting 'Nevermore,' either."

"Find her for me, Bloodworth," Manion said. "You said anybody could be found. Even Cece."

"I was wrong about that," I said.

"No," he said. "Not Cece. Gone forever. Gil told me." He tried to lean forward, knocking the cup of water from the nurse's fingers. It spilled on his chest, but he didn't seem to notice. "Don't let it happen, okay?"

"Don't let what happen?"

"China sin."

He began crying again. The nurse, annoyed with herself for getting her patient wet, turned on us. It was time that Manion rested, she stated unequivocally.

Quayle refused to leave the room.

Cugie and I left them to argue it out. Quayle shouted after us, "You guys find a hole out of our way somewhere, and crawl in there until we need you."

The door swished shut behind us.

I asked Cugie, "Where's MacElroy?"

"One flight up. Why?"

"I've got something to ask him. I've got a hunch."

"You sure, Hound? Quayle just said . . ."

"Even if I didn't have an obligation—to Manion, and in a weird way, to Hilbert—I would do just the opposite of whatever that meathead Quayle told me to."

He shrugged. "How much worse can it get, huh?"

"Exactly."

The agent bed-sitting MacElroy had a ferretlike face, but his haircut was nice. And he was wearing a fresh white shirt and a subdued striped tie. He stood up when we entered the room, which was, if anything, smaller than Manion's downstairs.

Cugie flashed his badge, but the agent still looked a bit dubious about letting us talk to his charge, who was at that moment staring goofily at the ceiling and continuing his old refrain about "bu-full li'l girl."

I let Cugie argue with the agent while I barked, "MacElroy! I'm sending you in!"

"Yes, Coach," he answered.

The agent stopped quoting his rulebook to Cugie, and both of them looked at the puffy man sitting up in his bed, catheters dangling.

"You ready for anything, MacElroy?"

"Yes, Coach."

"Tell me about the melting."

MacElroy froze. His lips quivered. "No. No. People die."

"Do they melt?"

"No. The ground. The ground melts. People get sick. Die. Poison. Rot and die."

I turned to the agent and gave him a big smile. "Thanks for your cooperation."

I went out of the room. The agent yelled, "Wait a minute! What the hell was that all about?" He all but pushed Cugie out of the way to grab my shoulder.

I turned easily and shook off his hand. "It's a bet the lieutenant and I had. I told him I could get the agent on guard in that room to leave his post within five minutes." I turned to Cugie, "Pay up."

Cugie was grinning at me.

The agent looked from me back to MacElroy's empty room. His right foot moved to go back, his left foot moved to follow us. Finally, the right foot won and he rushed back into the room.

Cugie said, "Sometimes, Hound, you can be one humorous son of a bitch."

On the way out of the hospital, we passed Hatcher chugging in, a pack of Xeroxed pages in his hot little hand. I gave Cugat my elbow and pointed to the fast-stepping Fed.

"Agent Hatcher," Cugat called.

Reluctantly, Hatcher stopped and did a half about-face. "What do you want?"

"Did you find the Cary Grant information?"

"As a matter of fact, I did. I made a bunch of copies of Grant's roles and the pictures."

Cugat said, "I'd like one of those for our files."

"Quayle didn't say anything about giving you one."

I said, "Are Grant's movies classified info these days?"

"No. Hell, I guess it's okay." He peeled off a Xeroxed page, and Cugie snatched it from his fingers.

"Thanks," he said. "It'll give us something to do this evening in our holes away from the action."

Hatcher gave him a blank look and continued on his way.

I scanned the list over Cugie's shoulders. I spotted *Mr. Lucky,* which also happened to be the name of the bar near the spot where Hilbert was supposed to have murdered Jerry Palomar. Ernie Mott from *None But the Lonely Heart.*

And then a name flashed off the page and made my knees a little weak. The movie was a favorite of mine, Hitchcock's *North By Northwest.* I must have seen it three or four times. But I still hadn't remembered that in it Grant had played an advertising executive named Roger Thornhill.

39

1. "Too much wind on you, Edith? Freddie, put up the rear window and turn on the a.c. Yeah, that's great. Well, here we are. Archie Leach and his girls."

To have one's opinion vindicated in such a forceful way is, I suppose, worth something. But Gran and I were paying a rather high price for my having the privilege of saying I told her so.

She was sitting opposite me on the backseat of the evil and obviously psychotic Mr. Leach's limousine. He lounged next to her, viciously handsome with eyes so cold they almost made me ill. His sculptured, nearly pretty face showed at least a five o'clock shadow, and he had pulled his silk tie with small polka dots away from his throat and opened the top button of his shirt. His ultra-expensive suit coat was tossed casually on the front seat next to the driver. He had kept my grandmother locked in her own closet, hands and feet painfully tied for nearly three hours while he'd terrorized Mr. Bloodworth.

Leach yawned, stretched, and kicked off his shoes. He lifted his feet and placed them on the lap of Hannah Reyne, another rotten apple that I had correctly identified at first meeting.

Occupying a jump seat like myself, she had changed her look rather dramatically. Her hair was blonder and fuller, surrounding her face like a lioness's mane. Expertly applied makeup had brought out her cheekbones and made her blue eyes seem quite dazzling. But she was still as braless as she was that day that Terry Manion and I first met her while waiting for the hapless Lieutenant Hilbert.

I asked Leach, "Who exactly was it that Lieutenant Hilbert shot, thinking it was you?"

"A player of no consequence," he said. His speech was affected, like that of several of Gran's classical actor cronies. Sort of a half-American, half-British accent that did neither country justice.

"Why was he wearing a fake nose?"

"You'd have to ask his superiors at the FBI. Maybe they thought we'd recognize him. Maybe a disguise is s.o.p. for their undercover s.o.b.'s."

What irony! Lieutenant Hilbert had finally killed one of his hated FBI agents! I said, "So the FBI is on to you."

"In a manner of speaking. In this instance, we were on to him."

"They'll hunt you down. They always get their man."

"You're thinking of the Mounties. The FBI rarely gets its man. Look at all of those wanted lists in the post offices. Some of them are ten years old."

He was so smug and arrogant. "Well," I said, "one of them actually penetrated your organization."

Leach shrugged. "It was clever of them. They sent an actor to catch an actor. But they weren't clever enough to pull him out when they should have. You see, we discovered that, of our little close-knit group, two members had fallen from grace. Poor Dora was happy enough to accept my offer of wealth and beauty, but when it came time for her to live up to her end of the bargain, she hesitated, grew nervous. So we watched her very carefully. And to whom did she run, when we applied the least amount of pressure? To one of our newer recruits—leather-clad Nicky, or, as the Feds knew him, Howie Pope. He should have realized that once we'd rid ourselves of Dora, he would be next."

"When one of their men is murdered, the FBI never rests until his killer is brought to justice."

Leach shook his head sadly. "Serendipity, your brain is full of hopelessly outdated rumors and folktales. But even if what you say were true, the FBI has its killer in storm-trooper Hilbert, and will no doubt extract swift justice."

Gran turned her head and looked out of her window. She seemed to have aged twenty years in just a few hours. Of course, we were both feeling jet lag combined with a lack of sleep.

"You said there were two defectors from your group," I said.

"Yes." There was a wistfulness in his reply that was not acting. "My best friend in all the world, my collaborator on so many of my early dramas, Sandy Watson, had, in just a very short decade, embraced the faggot lifestyle and become so gutless that he turned against me. Defied me, actually.

"It wasn't that he'd come out of the closet. When you're connected with the theater, homosexuality goes with the territory. I always suspected he was 'that way' in college, though he certainly never made a play for me. But he'd become a preening fruiter. Even so, I expected him to understand the importance of my plan. Regrettably, his head was filled with all that save-the-forests-and-beaches crap. I was talking about all humanity, and he was concerned with a patch of land, for Christ's sake."

"So you took his life?"

He nodded. "He left me no choice. I trusted him, and he stole the goddamned key. Not that the key was terribly crucial to my plan. There are, after all, other keys. It's just that now we have to make a slight detour."

Gran shifted and stared at him. She was definitely worn down. "Where are you taking us, Mr. Leach?"

"Please call me Archie, Edith." He grinned. *All in the Family.* Archie and Edith."

"Where are we going?"

"To save the world," he said.

"How?" I asked.

"By proving a point," he replied. "By improving a point. And I know we shall be victorious."

I said, "The same way you knew that your pal Sandy Watson would be happy to take part in your scheme, whatever it is?"

He frowned. "You're right, Serendipity. We don't know everything, though God knows we try. We didn't know, for example, that Sandy would give the key to that oaf Kosca, or that you would entrust it to the equally oafish Bloodworth!" His temper was rising, and with it rose the pitch of his voice. "And we didn't know that Bloodworth would suddenly become . . . unavailable. Unreachable by phone! Unreachable at his home! Where the hell does a man go when he's dead on his feet? He should go home. But not Bloodworth!"

"You should have tried busting in," Hannah said. "He could have been in there."

"Of course. He forgot to take in his evening paper or turn off his outdoor night light, but he was home. Freddie made enough noise pounding on the door to wake up the neighborhood, but Bloodworth probably was in there, sleeping through it. That's what you think?"

"You know why you didn't bust in. Because you got scared by the little boys."

Leach leaned forward. His arm shot out with astonishing speed, snakelike, and he grabbed Hannah by the throat and squeezed.

She gasped for air. He said between clenched teeth, "Those little slant-eyed bastards had zip guns and worse. Did you want me to start a minor war with a teenage gang just for the privilege of breaking into the house of a man who wasn't home?"

He relaxed his grip and pushed her back against the jump seat. Her throat was blotchy red. She began coughing.

"I let that . . . that government pig talk me out of killing Bloodworth. Twice. 'Why bother killing somebody that stupid? Somebody that big a bungler?' Because bunglers do not behave predictably! That's why we should kill bunglers. Otherwise, they forget their guns when you need them, or aren't home when they're supposed to be, or . . ."

He leaned his head back against the leather seat and closed his eyes. Gran stared forward at me, not saying a word. I could tell from the whiteness of her lips the helpless fury that was building up inside her. I hoped she would not do something that would push Leach over the edge.

"Archie," Hannah said in a hoarse voice, "if you ever manhandle me again, I'll walk out on you. Depending on the situation, I may kill you first."

He opened his eyes and smiled at her. "My own true love," he said, and opened his arms. She moved over onto his lap, and they began to kiss and fondle each other.

Gran edged even further into her corner to avoid any contact from the tacky pair. She closed her eyes.

I stared out of the window.

2. We'd been driving since four in the morning, which is when the street gang threw the Coke can at the window of the limousine, and Leach and his chauffeur, Freddie, rushed from Mr. Bloodworth's alley to confront all twenty or twenty-five young Asians. Freddie had drawn his gun, and the boys simultaneously displayed their unique weapons—two-edged knives, zip guns, chains with wooden handles. They began hissing and grunting fiercely like Bruce Lee. Pasty-faced and cursing, Leach and Freddie slowly backed into the limousine, and as we drove away suffered the humiliation of having garbage heaped upon the vehicle, while the gang members laughed and called out insults.

So Leach had not succeeded in his plan to recover his precious key. I hadn't wanted to put Mr. B. on the spot, but the vile one had threatened to do awful things to Gran unless I told him the truth. Fortunately, he had been unable to find Mr. Bloodworth.

After that failure we began our journey. Gran had slept fitfully, but the rest of us had remained fully awake. Most of our six-plus hours' driving time had been spent on Route 5. But a short while back, we'd turned west onto

152. And as I glanced through the smoke-gray windows, I saw that we were turning onto Route 1, and heading around Monterey Bay toward Santa Cruz.

I reached over and jiggled the door handle. Suddenly Leach tossed Hannah from his lap and grabbed my arm in a steel grip.

He realized I wasn't trying to go anywhere and he turned me loose. Hannah picked herself off the floor. "You're one little bitch, you know it?" she said.

Leach was grinning. "Serendipity's just having her little joke. I can appreciate that."

He turned his head quickly to look out of the window. A signpost read: RAVEN'S POINT, 7 MILES.

Leach smiled broadly, "Ah, home again after all these years."

"Are you from Raven's Point?" I asked.

"Only spiritually," he said. "It's where I came alive."

3. Raven's Point was on a bluff overlooking the Pacific Ocean. Driving up to it, we passed close enough to the edge of the narrow winding road to look down on the sparkling water with its dramatic waves breaking against the mossy rocks.

Freddie slowed the limousine as we joined the traffic along Raven's Point Drive, the main boulevard of what seemed a typical college town—clean and cheery but rather without personality, probably because of the transient quality of the bulk of its population.

Though the neat little bookshops and restaurants and lunch counters and shopping malls looked brand new, they must have been there at least a decade, because Archie Leach remembered them from his college days. He grew more and more delighted with each passing block.

The car eventually turned down a side street and glided easily through a residential section of town. Pleasant middle-class homes in a pleasant middle-class neighborhood. We stopped at 2135 Lark Street, in front of a gray two-story home with white trim, separated from the quiet, tree-shaded street by a tidy lawn and brick walkway.

Even before Freddie had a chance to tap the horn, the front door to the house opened and a brunette in pleated dress and white blouse rushed out to the car. It was the same woman who had been with Gregory Desidero in Bay City and in London.

Archie Leach lowered his window. "Hello, Suze. You forgot to shut the front door."

She smiled nervously, "I just couldn't get him to part with it. You'll have to talk to him."

Archie Leach sighed. "If I must, I must."

He nodded to Freddie, who pressed a button that unlocked the back door. Then he opened it and made an exaggerated grunting noise as he hopped out. He remained bending over slightly. "What do you think, Suze? Maybe a bit of a stoop?"

She grinned. "Arthritis, from sitting too long in front of a test tube?"

He nodded. "Take my place in the car now. Keep our guests happy. Have you a gun?"

She patted a lump on her thigh. "Good," Leach told her. "Try not to shoot anybody unless you have to.

"Freddie, leave my coat, but I must get into the trunk."

Through the rear window I saw the trunk pop open. When Leach shut it, he was carrying a leather satchel rather like a doctor's bag. He walked jauntily to the gray house.

The woman called Suze replaced Leach in the limo and pulled the door shut after her. Freddie locked it from the front seat. I watched Suze give Hannah a nasty look and get an equally nasty one in return. Then I said, as innocently as I could, "He certainly is a rather dashing, handsome man, isn't he?"

Gran frowned at me. The others scowled.

"I mean, it's a wonder he chose not to become a film actor. He would have made a great star. He has this irresistible . . ."

"Can it, sweetie," Suze snapped. She said to Hannah, "Have you got a cigarette?"

Hannah shook her head. "Don't smoke."

"Men don't like the way a smoker's breath smells," I said. "I was reading the other day that nearly ten percent of the divorces in America—"

"I told you to shut up," Suze said. "Freddie? Cigarettes, s'il vous plaît?"

The window behind me lowered. I didn't bother to turn my head. I kept staring at Suze as a pack of cigarettes flew through the air. She caught it, shook one free, and tossed the pack back. The window whooshed up.

Suze nervously lit her prize with a lighter from a panel in the door. Gran turned her face away from the smoke. "Is that your house?" I asked Suze.

"I moved out a long time ago," she said.

"Then your family lives there?"

"Sort of. Just sit still and keep quiet, huh."

"But I'm only—"

"I'm not going to tell you again. Force me and I'll start making it very

uncomfortable for Grandma here. I'm fed up with you, kid. It's because of
you that—" She looked at the house and then looked away. "Just . . . keep
quiet."

Leach returned to the limo after fifteen or twenty minutes. His sleeves
were rolled up and he had been sweating. He pushed in beside Suze and
smiled across at Hannah. "Miss me?" he asked, placing his satchel on his
knees.

"Well?" Suze asked.

He reached into the pocket of his shirt and removed a thin piece of plastic
similar to the one I'd had.

"What did it take?" she asked.

"Some bloody do-gooders have been trying to dry him out, which is why
we had this little glitch. But I have him back on course again."

"He was a bastard, but still . . ."

"I did have to break two of his fingers," Archie Leach said casually. "But
the good news is: For the moment he's feeling no pain."

4. In just the very short time it took for us to reach our ultimate destination, Archie Leach had withdrawn from his all-purpose satchel a stick to put
streaks of gray in his hair and another to cause wrinkle lines to appear on his
face. Gran watched him very carefully as he applied the makeup. He even
made his five o'clock shadow gray.

He turned to her and said, across Suze, "What do you think, Edith?
Fiftyish?" He flicked a lock of hair down over his forehead. "A touch wool-
gathered? Or is it too much?"

Gran did not reply.

Suze said, "You look perfect."

He shook his head. "Not yet."

He pulled off his silk tie and replaced it with a thinner, duller tie that he
had in his bag. Then he got out a spray can and began coating the backs of
both hands with its contents. "Ah, the miracles of modern science," he said
as his hands coarsened and wrinkled. "I always feel cheated when actors
forget to do their hands. It's so slapdash, isn't it, Edith?"

"Why are my granddaughter and I here, Mr. Leach?"

"In a word, publicity. You'll see."

The limo approached a chain-link fence, where an armed security guard in
gray flagged us to a halt.

Archie Leach ran his hand under Suze's skirt. She didn't react at all,
which made me suspect she was used to his hands. In this case, however, he

was going for her pistol, which he withdrew and pointed at Gran. He looked me in the eyes and put his other finger to his lips. Then he replaced the gun in the woman's leg holster, letting his hand linger there. More as a threat than a caress, though Suze may have thought otherwise.

Freddie lowered his window and told the guard, "Professor Barnaby Fulton and party."

"Just a minute."

The guard moved back to a little wooden hut, relayed the message to a woman security guard who was seated at a desk. She nodded and made a check on a big board that was partially visible through the limo window.

The male guard returned. He squinted through the dark window at us. "The pass is for four," he said. "You folks seem to have multiplied."

Archie Leach lowered his window. When he spoke, his voice was high-pitched and dithery. "Oh, I'm dreadfully sorry, but when the university arranged for my little tour, I just didn't know that I would be playing host to a celebrity. You must recognize the noted actress Edith Van Dine, and that's her lovely granddaughter. It was a last-minute thing. . . ."

The guard poked his head half into the car. "Sure, I recognize Miss Van Dine. My wife's been hooked on your show since before I knew her. I don't suppose . . ."

He began slapping his pockets and found a piece of folded paper and a fountain pen. He handed them across Leach and the girl to Gran, who, frowning in discomfort, leaned forward and took them.

"If you would just sign it and put on it 'To Long, Tall Sally.'"

Leach was staring at Gran and trying not to laugh.

She scribbled on the folded paper, then handed it and the pen out to the guard.

Leach intercepted it, glanced at the scrawled words, and smiled. He pushed paper and pen through the window, where the guard accepted them happily. "This is super," he said. "You folks go right on in."

The car window snicked shut, and Freddie aimed the limousine through the now-opened gate. "Brilliant!" Archie Leach said sarcastically. "No request for IDs, no search of the limo. I knew it! I knew it would be easier to get into this place than it is to get into Disneyland. These people are like children playing in a science lab. They have no idea what they're doing, or how much havoc their work can cause. Well, it's time to educate them. Suze, you'd better put your little weapon into my bag. No sense sending their metal detectors into a frenzy."

The chauffeur parked in an area marked VISITORS, turned off the engine, and leaped from the car to open the rear door, just as Suze's pistol was being put into the infamous satchel.

Leach smiled at the open car door and said, "All right, kiddies, magic time."

And that, in a nutshell, is how Gran and I became part of a gang of radicals calling themselves the New Mummers when they took possession of and held for ransom the nuclear power plant at Raven's Point.

40

1. The Air California jet touched down in San Francisco at about 11:30. My favorite Frisco P.I. and the best-looking and meanest redhead in town, Gwen Nolte, was waiting for us beside a parked Saab, tapping her foot impatiently.

She looked terrific in a silk blouse and slacks that may have been gaberdine. Cugie started in on her right away. He took her hand and fondled it and said, "Even if the Hound is completely wrong in his surmise, this trip will not have been wasted, señorita."

Gwen removed her hand from his. "This must be your cop buddy, huh, Leo?"

"Lieutenant Rudy Cugat, at your service."

"No heel clicks, please."

Cugie opened the Saab's door and pushed the seat forward, indicating that I should get in. Gwen said, "You take the rear, señor. Your purple suit clashes with my hair. And I want Leo where we can play kneesies, should I be so inclined."

Cugat got into the car looking slightly miffed. I figured it'd only be a matter of time before the complaints and the questions would begin again.

That's about all I'd heard from him ever since we'd left L.A. Was I sure that Leach really had Sarah and her grandmother? How could I have deduced from the word *nevermore*, mentioned casually to a drugged man by the ghost of his wife, that something was about to happen in the town of Raven's Point? Couldn't "China sin" have a drug meaning and not be Manion's attempt to say *China Syndrome?*

Carefully, I'd explained that Philippe, the night watchman at Sarah's building, had seen her and her grandmother leave with "a well-dressed young guy" at around four in the morning. That it wasn't just Manion's ex-wife's mention of "nevermore," but also Cece MacElroy's father's ranting about "ground melting and people dying" that had made me think of the Raven's Point Nuclear Power facility.

As Gwen maneuvered her Saab through the airport traffic, I filled her in as well as I could. When I was finished, Cugie said glumly, "Jesus Cristo! I am of a mixed mind. I hope you are wrong about the nuclear plant, but I also hope we have not just flown four hundred miles for a bad guess."

Gwen said, "Bad guess? Leo never makes bad guesses. Now, if you're talking about colossal mistakes . . ."

"It's no mistake," I said, admiring her freckled-nose profile as she studied the traffic pattern. "Because Leach and the others left college a decade ago, I'd assumed that the 'Big One-Oh' referred to some sort of graduation-day celebration. But that date passed a month ago. After graduation, however, the Mummers gathered for one last stunt, to aid the proposed state ban on nuclear-power plants. On this very date, July 1, ten years ago."

Gwen turned on the car radio. "I didn't hear any panic reports on the way to the airport."

"I doubt that anybody at the plant will be calling in the news. A panic would put them out of business just as fast as, well, a disaster like Chernobyl."

"Maybe he's just going to march around the plant, Hound. Wave a few signs."

I shook my head. "That was for when he was a college kid. Now, he's a dangerous killer. He'll be upping the stakes."

Cugie didn't want to believe it. "Hell, those places must have security up to their eyeballs."

"Let's hope so," I said.

"And all those fancy gadgets that require fingerprints and eyeball prints and 3-D ID cards."

"You mean something like this?" I held up the plastic rectangle that Sarah had given me.

"What are those letters?" Gwen asked.

"RPNP. My guess would be Raven's Point Nuclear Power."

She let out a long whistle, then swung the Saab onto Highway 280, moving south to San Mateo.

"What the hell do you do with it?" she asked.

"It's been referred to as a key, so I guess it opens doors."

"You know," Cugat said with a slight smile, "this will make one magnificent book."

"If either of us is around to write it."

Gwen said, "Judging by Chernobyl, the fallout could be so deadly that nobody'd be around to read it."

"That, too," I said.

2. Before we could complete the twenty-five miles to Raven's Point, Leach must have made his move. Suddenly Highway Patrol vehicles, their sirens wailing and dome lights flashing, rushed past us, scattering the traffic. They were followed by equally noisy prowl cars from an assortment of cities, and at least one helicopter, all heading in the same direction. The all-news radio station didn't seem to be aware of any calamity. It was too busy broadcasting an interview with a guy who'd crossbred a groundhog with a beaver. The rest of the dial was filled with music, recipes, Bible-thumpers, or call-in psychologists, certified or not.

By the time we'd left the highway and zipped past Redwood City, there was a traffic jam that spread for nearly a mile in all directions from the nuclear plant.

Gwen watched a black-and-white police car use a narrow, dusty road shoulder as an emergency lane and turned to me. "What'd'ya think, big boy?"

"It's pretty narrow, and this nice foreign car of yours could wind up in the ditch," I said, toying with her. "Besides, that cop could drive rings around you and you know it."

She spun the wheel savagely, and we hopped the curb to the shoulder. Cugie had been reloading his pistol. After going over his ID with a microscope, the airline security guards had made him unload and break the piece, bag it, and leave it with the senior flight officer. He leaned forward. "¿Qué pasa?"

"Better move to the right of the car, amigo, or we could topple over into a twenty-foot gulley."

He hopped to the right and buckled himself in. Gwen grinned and shook her head, never moving her eyes from the road for a second. She followed the cop car's dust all the way to the main gate, where two gun-toting security guards flagged us down.

I told them, "We've got information about the people inside."

The nearest guard said, "Okay, tell your driver to park over there, next to the police car. Got to clear this road."

I said to Gwen, "Hear that, driver?"

"Yes, sir. Was that next to the car, or behind it, or on top of it, or what?" She pulled the Saab beside the cop car. The guards watched us get out.

Cugie opened his orchid-colored coat slowly. The guard made note of the gun on his hip. Cugie pulled out his badge with his fingertips and showed it to the guard.

"Bay City? Down south?"

Cugie nodded.

"You're a little off your beat, aren't you, Lieutenant?"

"So's the guy inside your plant," I said.

That, of course, led to a conversation about who *I* was. And by the time the guard had figured out he was dealing with a police lieutenant and two private investigators, a khaki-haired man with a whiskey nose moved his dark suit in our direction to join the fun.

He ordered the security guards to keep sending the "tinhorn yokel cops" on their way. Then he identified himself as Jay Tobak, an FBI agent whose superior was inside the building *hondling* with the plant's honchos.

"You say you know this Professor Fulton?" Tobak asked.

I asked Cugie for the Cary Grant list. I scanned it and told Tobak, "Yeah, we know him."

He grabbed the sheet from my hands. "It says, 'Professor Barnaby Fulton, *Monkey Business.*' What the hell is that: some kind of code?"

"You know an agent named Quayle, out of your L.A. office?"

"I know him."

"We got this list from him."

"And all these other names?"

I ran that one through my head. Would it be better for Sarah and Mrs. Van Dine for the law to know precisely whom they were dealing with? I decided to let Leach play whatever game he had in mind.

I said, "I don't know. Ask Quayle."

"So Quayle has already been onto this guy?"

I shrugged. "I wouldn't want to speak for him. I suppose you guys can work out your own jurisdictions without any help from an outsider."

"I better go check with somebody," Tobak said. He started away.

"Hey," I shouted. "How's about the list back?"

"Just relax, mister." He pointed a finger at one of the security guards and ordered, "Take these people over to where the chief's waiting, and make sure they sit tight until we're ready for 'em."

Cugat watched Tobak kick up dust to the front door to the plant. He said, "Ah, the quest for glory. He'll be conniving with his partner over how to keep Quayle out of this."

Gwen snickered. "Don't bet on it. This one could be a real worm can. My guess is that they'll try to hand it over to your friend Quayle, then run like hell."

I winced. If I'd thought that, I wouldn't have even brought up Quayle's name. I'd assumed, like Cugie, that they'd want to hog the action and that Quayle would be the last guy they'd contact.

The security guard led us to a bench that had been placed next to the fence. A man in a brown police uniform sat there cooling his bootheels while his blood boiled. He was young, with the rugged, Hollywood-handsome sort of face that casting directors and beautiful redheaded private eyes find attractive. "I got things I ought to be doing," he snapped at the guard.

"Sorry, Chief. They know you're here."

Cugat removed his display handkerchief, dusted off a section of the bench, and sat on it. I sat next to him, and Gwen took a spot between me and the chief.

She put out her hand, introduced herself, and then got around to us. His name was Chance Gillory. He'd been chief of police in Raven's Point for nearly three years, he told us, as he lit Gwen's first cigarette of the hour. In all that time he'd cooperated with the FBI on a number of small matters. Now that something big had come up, they were keeping him on the bench for the whole game.

"You a Raven's Point native?" I asked him.

He nodded, eyeing me suspiciously.

"And you went to the college?"

Another nod, and even more suspicion.

"I don't suppose you remember a group in the theater department there who called themselves the Mummers?"

His suspicion faded and his face broke into an easy grin. "Sure. They graduated the year before me."

"And Archie Leach?"

"Archie? He was some kind of BMOC. Had every damn co-ed in the university eating out of his lunchpail. The guys all liked him, too. He was our student president. You know him?"

"Yeah. Sort of."

"What ever happened to that old boy?"

Both Cugie and Gwen were staring at me. I said, "Oh, he did a little of this and a little of that."

"I sure thought we'd be seeing him on the tube. Something."

"The day's still young," I said. "I don't guess Archie's returned to town since he graduated, huh?"

"Why would he? I don't even know why I stayed, and I sure didn't have the potential he did. A bunch of his classmates did come back for their ten-year reunion last month. There was a big party over at the Rec. That's this place where we used to hang out back in those days . . . . Anyway, I dropped by there on my rounds, to say hello and see who'd showed. Archie didn't, of course. But Suze Stillwell did, funny enough."

The name rang a distant gong. "Who's she?" I asked.

"Used to be Archie's main lady, the BWOC to his BMOC."

Right! Suze Stillwell had been in the yearbook—the Mummers' treasurer.

The chief was wading a little deeper into his reverie. "I always had this thing for Suze. Guess a lot of us did. Hadn't seen her in ten years, but she still looks pretty damn good. I asked her if she and Archie had, you know, tied the knot after college. She said no."

"Where's she been living?" I asked.

"New York and L.A., I guess. She says she's been doing okay, acting, but I don't recall having seen her on the tube." He checked his watch. "Screw this. I'm gonna try to get hold of that jerk Tobak."

"He'll be back soon. Tell me some more about the reunion. Who else from the Mummers showed up?"

"Lemme think. I didn't know many of 'em. Just the ones who, you know, were the achievers. There was this guy who was a hell of an artist. Sandy Watson. He and Archie were real tight in school. I think he might have been with Suze, because I saw them both coming out of her old man's house the next day."

"So she's got family here."

"Father. Mother's dead."

"She hadn't visited her father in ten years?" Gwen asked.

He closed down a little. "She and old man Stillwell had a falling-out a long time ago. Back when she was still in school."

"Over Archie?" I wondered.

He ducked his head. "In a way, I guess. I mean, Mr. Stillwell didn't have anything against Archie. It was just all the bad feelings about this plant and all. Archie got Suze an up-front spot on the protest line. And there was that thing in the restaurant, with Suze covered with fake sores and everything. She wore the makeup home, and her old man really blew a gasket.

"You see, none of us who live in town have ever wanted the damn plant in our backyards. And we sort of felt that George Stillwell turned some kind of traitor when he went to work for the company that runs it. He was a real pariah. And when his own daughter went against him, well . . .

"I heard he wasn't in such good health these days. I guess that's maybe the main reason why Suze came home."

The door to the plant opened, and Agent Tobak and another dark suit started across the yard to us. I asked Chief Gillory, "Is Stillwell still working here?"

He stood up to greet the Feds. "Not for a while," he said. "The old guy's too sick to do much more than putter around his lawn."

"Was he an engineer, or what?"

"Stillwell? Naw. He was an ex-cop from New Jersey. The owners of the plant got him out of retirement."

"To do what?"

"To head up their security force. George probably knows more about this place than anybody else in town, except the new security head, of course. 'Scuse me now. I want to find out where I fit into this situation."

He crossed the yard and met the two agents. They weren't terribly interested in him, but if they'd phoned Quayle in L.A., they probably were very curious about us.

"Time to go," I told Gwen and Cugie.

"But . . ." Cugie began. By that time both Gwen and I were heading for the car. He double-timed to catch us.

Tobak called out for us to wait.

We got into the car.

A security guard was poised in front of us. I could hear Tobak's shoes hitting the cement.

"Time to go," I repeated, and Gwen started the engine and turned the steering wheel in what seemed to be a single motion.

As we shot by him, going from zero to seventy in about forty seconds, the Saab literally brushed the arm of the security guard. He goggled at us as if he wasn't sure why he was still alive and standing.

Behind us Tobak waved his arms and tried not to eat too much of our dust.

"That'll teach him to keep us waiting," I said.

"Oh, Hound. I think the thin ice we were on has now cracked."

"You have to crack a little ice to make a margarita," I told him.

"What the hell is that supposed to mean, Leo?" Gwen asked.

"Just writer talk," I told her. "Drive on, honey, drive on."

3. Twenty-one, thirty-five Lark Street, the phone directory had said. It was a clean-looking gray house with white shutters and a lawn that somebody had spent time cultivating. "Maybe he's not home," Cugie said after our third ring.

Gwen snapped, "Didn't you hear what the man said, Lieutenant? George Stillwell is a sickly man."

"Maybe he's gone to the hospital?" Cugie persisted in his not-at-home theory.

I hopped off the steps and wandered around the house.

By trampling on some shrubs near the rear I was able to get a view into a room, possibly a den, where an old guy lay motionless on a cot.

I tapped on the window. Nothing.

I moved to the back door.

Gwen and Cugie joined me just as I had the lock picked.

Only after we'd entered the Stillwell kitchen did I remember that the guy was a security expert. Of course there was a little gray box where a red light was blinking angrily.

I pointed to it. "We don't have much time," I said.

Gwen shrugged. "That hunky police chief is sure as hell gonna lead the Feds here anyway. No big deal."

Stillwell lay on his cot with his eyes open. His face was gray and covered with sweat. "Look at his arm," Cugie said.

Stillwell's right sleeve was rolled up, exposing innumerable needle scars along the vein line. "A junkie," I said.

". . . with broken fingers," Gwen added.

"Jesus. Call Emergency."

Tears formed at the corner of the old guy's eyes. "You have key," he said. "Leave me alone."

Gwen picked up the phone and got the operator. I asked Stillwell, "Key to what?"

He groaned. "Dump."

"What dump?"

He moved his good hand to the broken fingers, brushed them, and cried out. "Dump, goddamnit. Waste into ocean. Never used."

"Hospital's sending an ambulance," Gwen said.

"They dumped nuclear waste into the ocean?" I almost shouted.

"No. No. Not needed. Got water? Thirst."

Gwen went for the water. Stillwell gulped it, wincing.

"What about the dump?" I asked.

"Not used. Built but not used. Tunnel to ocean."

"And the key opens the tunnel?"

"Don't know. Supposed to. Never used."

"Who knows about the tunnel?" Cugie asked.

Stillwell shook his head. "You. Me. Nobody else. Forget. Dead. Me. You."

"And Leach?"

He moaned. "Take key. Anything. No more hurt."

The ambulance was wailing down Lark Street. But before it reached the house, the back door was thrown open and Chance Gillory was standing there, pointing a Magnum at the three of us. Four of us, counting Stillwell.

41

1. It wasn't that Archie Leach was so brilliant. It was that security at the Raven's Point nuclear plant was so lame.

A seemingly pleasant but utterly witless young woman named Lydia Dorland was waiting for us as we exited the car. She was a frumpy-looking lady who was dressed much too old for her age, in a baggy jacket and an even baggier skirt that brushed her shoetops. For some, the Annie Hall look would forever be in vogue. She was carrying a clipboard and a pen that went well with her eager expression.

"Professor Fulton?"

Archie Leach was the picture of an addled man of science. Bent, doddering, clutching his Gladstone bag, he bowed to Lydia Dorland and nodded. I toyed with the idea of doing something to get the attention of the security guards. But I didn't trust them to be able to handle the situation. And I knew that one of Leach's first actions would be to kill me or Gran or both.

My grandmother seemed to be aging before my eyes. The strain and the lack of sleep were taking their toll. When the Dorland woman began to gush over having Edith Van Dine as a mystery guest, Gran couldn't even manage a false smile. Walking beside her into the plant, I was conscious of her slightly labored breathing. As was Leach.

"Edith, my dear," he croaked in his old man's voice, "what's the matter?"

She waved her hand airily, and continued along the long, pale blue corridor with its highly polished floor that was painted a very impractical light gray with a bright red stripe down its center.

Miss Dorland tapped Leach on the shoulder and said, "I'm sorry, Professor, but around the bend we're going to have to subject you and your party to a metal detector."

"Ah, I understand. Security is of paramount importance," Leach said. Then he stopped, rocked his head a bit, and added querulously, "But I've audio tapes in my bag. My notes. I use a tape recorder. I hope there are no X-rays that would destroy . . ."

Miss Dorland smiled. "Well, ordinarily, we do X-ray all bags and packages, but in this case, I'll carry your bag through."

Leach allowed himself to go a bit out of character and shot me a totally menacing glance.

We approached the metal detector, which might have been purchased from a defunct airline. It was manned by two security guards—a man and a woman—who appeared to be very bored by the process. The purpose of the red dividing line on the floor was now apparent. We were to continue on, walking through the detector's archway. The other side of the hall was used by employees leaving the building, and was therefore not monitored by the machine.

Hannah went past the detector first, then Suze, whose bracelet set off an alarm. Then me. And finally, Leach "helped" Gran through, keeping his hand on her shoulder, near her neck. I had witnessed the speed and power of that hand.

Freddie the chauffeur had not accompanied us into the plant. One of Leach's last instructions to him was to "return for us at the appointed time." Which was obviously some sort of code for whatever evil was to take place that day.

That idiot Dorland woman was certainly making it easy for Leach. She walked around the detectors with his weaponry bag. She was simultaneously simpering and officious to the security personnel.

Leach didn't seem too anxious to get his hands on the bag. He seemed more interested in me. I stared right back at him.

Dorland, still clutching the bag and her clipboard, said, "I've arranged for you to meet briefly with Mr. Gladiolus, our plant manager."

"Wonderful."

She led us down another corridor, this one painted dark green with a pale green tile flooring. She paused by an unmarked wooden door. Her intention was to turn the doorknob, but her arms were filled. She said to Leach, "Professor, could you help me with your bag?"

"Oh, of course," he said, taking his deadly satchel.

She opened the door and led us into a neat waiting room, where a plump young woman in a summer dress was poking a pen into a wall vent just over her head. "Oh, excuse me," she said as we traipsed in. "Lydia, just a minute."

Casting one last troubled look at the vent, she returned to her desk and pressed an intercom. She conveyed the information that "Lydia is here with Professor . . . Professor . . . Professor Fulton and his party."

Mr. Gladiolus said for her to send us in. And she did.

His office was a bit uncomfortable—bone-white with a dark green carpet and almost-matching dark green accessories. Green is such a difficult color to match. His desk was squeezed against one wall, allowing the rest of the room to be filled with a small conference table and chairs. A bank of windows exposed what seemed to be miles of untended greenery.

Mr. Gladiolus was a rather ordinary-looking man in an ordinary-looking brown suit. If I had not known his occupation, I would have picked him to be a talent agent with a mediocre client roster. He had a little piece of tissue stuck to a razor nick on his jaw.

Lydia Dorland introduced us all round. Mr. Gladiolus seemed particularly impressed by Gran, no surprise. And he asked her to please call him Lou, but I'm afraid that Gran was past the cordial stage and she just sat there, looking pale and wan.

"Could we get you something, Miss Van Dine?"

"Perhaps some water."

Mr. Gladiolus relayed that order and finally redirected his attention to Leach. He said, "Professor, I understand from Lydia that the university is preparing some sort of study concerning the untapped potential of nuclear power and that you have a few questions to ask."

Leach opened his black bag and reached in.

What he removed was not a pistol but a little cassette recorder that he handed to Hannah. "My assistant will record your answers and transcribe them later."

"What exactly is it that you want to know? I'm all yours for about thirty minutes, then Lydia can show you through the plant."

"We hate to be a bother," Leach said in his quavering professor's voice.

"No bother at all," Lydia Dorland replied. "It will be a good opportunity for me to get a better fix on the plant. I've only been here a few weeks."

"Then we shall learn together," Leach said. "Mr. Gladiolus, my questions, quite naturally, concern your reactor and the safety of the town and the surrounding area. I suppose our main theme is to prove that Chernobyl can't happen here."

"There is no way that a nuclear accident of that scope could ever happen in this country. We're too safety-conscious. But in any case, as horrible as

Chernobyl was, there were not the tens of thousands of deaths that the doomsters had predicted."

Leach nodded his head. "Thankfully not. Of course, if the wind had been blowing toward Kiev with its half-million people, instead of away, the predictions might have been more accurate."

Mr. Gladiolus leaned back in his chair. "Maybe," he said.

Leach scratched his head. "But let us talk of the here and the now, eh? You mentioned safety. Could you be more specific?"

"The Nuclear Regulatory Commission is the place for you to get the full story on safety, Professor. They set the standards and the rules. What we do is abide by them. They come and inspect us, as they do every plant, on a regular basis. If they don't like what they see, they have the power to yank our license."

Leach gave him a brief smile. "But not close you down."

"No."

"The existing regulations allow them a rather broad leeway, I understand, but the truth is, you could be violating a number of basic safety rules and the NRC would likely do nothing more than slap your wrist or pat you on the head."

Mr. Gladiolus was frowning now, very conscious of the tape recorder. "I don't know as I'd put it in those words, exactly." His secretary came into the room and he wheeled on her, saw the glass of water she was holding for Gran, and relaxed.

After the secretary had delivered the water and exited, Leach continued to put Mr. Gladiolus on edge.

"Not long ago, when questioned by Congress, the NRC stated that there were at least eighteen nuclear plants with ongoing histories of safety violations. The Raven's Point plant was on that list, I believe."

Mr. Gladiolus said nothing. He merely glared at Leach, who continued, using his avuncular accent, "These were not just little glitches in the system but, and I quote, 'repeated, flagrant, willful violations of federal safety rules, presenting a clear and present danger to the community and to the country as a whole.' "

Mr. Gladiolus's head began bobbing up and down. "We have complied with all requests from the NRC. One of our emergency cooling pumps, which was the main source of the complaints, has been replaced. We're off their goddamn list now."

"Congratulations," Leach said dryly. "And no problems from the Nuclear Safety Oversight Committee?"

Mr. Gladiolus smiled ruefully. "Not much."

Leach matched his smile. "Especially since President Reagan did away with that committee, right?"

Mr. Gladiolus shrugged. "He didn't do it to make me happy, but it made me happy. We've got enough committee red tape as it is."

"So your reactor's up to snuff—adequate cooling, proper ventilation?"

Mr. Gladiolus nodded and then droned on about how expensive the system safeguards were, especially when you considered that, after a decade, the plant was far from turning a profit.

Leach seemed oblivious to the man's reply. He tugged at his ear, sniffed a few times, and cut it short with, "What about security?"

"What about it?"

"Certainly you realize the damage that might be done should this plant be occupied by . . . radicals."

Mr. Gladiolus said, "I don't think there's much chance of that. But why don't I get Mr. Corbin in here? He's in charge of plant security." He buzzed his secretary and got her working on that task.

"How long has Mr. Corbin been security chief, Mr. Gladiolus?" Suze asked. Leach glared at her.

"A little over a year. The last man we had, well, he developed some . . . took ill. He's retired now."

Leach raised an eyebrow. "Took ill? How long had he worked here, and was he exposed to the waste that your machines produce?"

Mr. Gladiolus seemed to be reeling. "His problem was psychological, not . . . physical."

Corbin bustled into the office, a large, blustering man wearing a white short-sleeved shirt, dark cotton trousers, and a hard hat on which the words *Spy Guy* had been stenciled. He'd been summoned by a beeper hooked to his belt.

Once again, we were all introduced. This time Gran did not even bother to lean forward. She looked deathly. She had dropped the empty water glass to the carpet. I moved beside her and took her hand.

Corbin frowned at her. "Ma'am, you seem a bit under the weather, if you'll excuse my saying it."

She shook her head. "Just a bit tired. I'm fine."

Mr. Gladiolus explained to Mr. Corbin that the professor had brought up the subject of plant security. Mr. Corbin turned to Leach and began a long, rambling explanation of how complete and technically state-of-the-art his systems were.

"But," Leach asked, "suppose a genuine terrorist did somehow get through all of your intricate mazes and wound up racing for the control room. What would you do?"

"Notify the control room and have the guy on duty hit the switch that seals the room off. We got an air-lock system that can't be penetrated."

"But let's say the duty man is too late at the switch, and a terrorist enters the control room and puts his finger on the button that can cause a meltdown. What do you do then?"

Mr. Corbin's face relaxed into a smile. "Professor, you don't want to know."

"Oh, but I do."

"Well," Mr. Corbin said. "We would terminate him with extreme prejudice, to use some of the double-talk of my previous profession."

"But how would you do that?"

"Well, assuming he was in the control room with his hand on the switch, I suppose we'd have to shoot him."

"That's if the control room were accessible to your men."

"It would be."

"How?"

"Through the doors, of course."

"But you just said the room could be sealed."

Mr. Corbin began to look uneasy. "That would mean that your terrorist would have to know how to seal the room, and that's not likely. As I was telling Lydia only last week, it's not common knowledge."

Mr. Gladiolus said, "Corbin, why don't you show the professor, Miss Van Dine, and the others the area and how it's set up." He faced Leach. "You won't be able to go into the control room, of course. But it's surrounded by windows. A regular goldfish bowl. You'll be able to watch the engineers and techs at work."

"Wonderful," Leach said, standing and reaching out his hand to shake Mr. Gladiolus's.

Mr. Corbin said, "I think you folks will find this interesting."

Leach told him, "I'm sure we *all* will."

2. Until Chernobyl I had not given a great deal of thought to nuclear power. I'd heard brief, very facile arguments pro and con, but the only fact that had hit home was that, regardless of the amount of good that nuclear power achieved, science had not come up with an acceptable way to rid the earth of its terribly harmful waste. Plutonium garbage is not something you want piling up in your backyard.

So when Leach took over the control of the reactor and began making his demands, I was not totally unsympathetic to the tone of his opening remarks to the press.

But first things first.

Mr. Corbin led us to the control area, where we were allowed to look through windows while two men in white doctor's coats sat before a wraparound panel filled with buttons and levers and blinking lights and a total of ten television monitors, displaying views of the plant. We could actually see ourselves looking through the window. Three other white coats bustled about the room, pausing to examine the information on rolls of paper flowing continuously from a row of computer printers.

Mr. Corbin said, "As far as the standard ops go, the engineers stand four-hour shifts, monitoring the controls, making sure that all systems and safety systems are A-OK."

"What would happen," Leach asked, "if one of us should try to break into the control room right now?"

Mr. Corbin pointed to a long bright-red metal switch about two feet from the ceiling. "There's one of those every hundred feet throughout the building. At the first sign of any trouble you punch one of those and alert the engineers, who immediately close off the control room. It's got its own life-support system."

"But what if you don't get to push one of those switches?"

"The engineers are monitoring the screens, which give them a view of just about every nook and cranny in this building."

Hannah placed a hand on Mr. Corbin's arm and asked innocently, "What's it like in the control room?"

He grinned down at her. "Just like it is out here, only with more lights."

"But in there you'd be right on top of all the power. The raw power. I find that . . . extremely exciting."

And then Hannah did an extraordinary thing. She reached up and placed her hands on either side of Mr. Corbin's face. He was surprised, but not enough to pull away. Not even when she stood on her tiptoes and kissed him full on the lips.

It took Mr. Corbin a second or two before he broke her embrace. And then he seemed confused, disoriented, a red lipstick smear on his mouth. Leach said softly, "Now I think you owe Hannah a trip inside the control room, don't you?"

Mr. Corbin was not a brilliant man, but he was beginning to sense something was awry. He took a tentative step toward the red switch. But Leach, his back to the TV camera, showed Mr. Corbin the revolver he had removed from his bag during the kiss. He said, "We'd all like to see the control room." Lydia Dorland let out a squeak, but Leach didn't even turn to look at her.

"What the hell do you think you're doing?" Mr. Corbin growled.

"Visiting the control room."

"Not today, bub."

Leach smiled. "I love being called 'bub' by an ex-C.I.A. spook with a fat gut. It makes me want to cooperate fully. You walk us to the entrance to the control room now, or I'll blow your plump little tummy all over the window and take my chances on getting inside there before those engineers know what hit them. Or you. Do we do this the clean way, or, to use your parlance, the wet way?"

Mr. Corbin stared at Leach for a beat and realized that he was not being bluffed. He led us down a corridor to a dark blue door that was made of metal and had a small, wire-enforced window about five and a half feet from its bottom.

One of the security monitors was aimed right at us. Leach said to Corbin, "Put a nice happy smile on your face, *bub*."

Corbin did as he was told.

"Now," Leach said, "the question is: Is this door open or not?"

He turned the knob and it opened. He said to Mr. Corbin, "After you."

There were two doors, actually. We had to walk through a small space barely big enough for two people, and then through another metal door into the control room.

Gran and I were right behind Mr. Corbin and in front of Leach and his crew. One of the engineers looked up from his computer print-outs and stared at the security officer with a puzzled expression. He grew even more confused when the rest of us wandered in.

Leach, for some reason still in character as the professor, ordered the engineers and Lydia Dorland out of the control room. They did not want to go, but he and Suze waved their guns and they went. Mr. Corbin started to leave with them, but Leach said, "Oh, not you, *bub*. You're going to show me how I seal this room off."

Mr. Corbin pointed to an unmarked button on the far left of the wrap-around panel. Smiling, Leach moved to the far right and pushed a button there. There was a soft hiss as the pressure locks were activated. "*We* are not the amateurs here," Leach bragged to Mr. Corbin.

Gran made a soft whimpering sound and slipped into a chair at the right of the console. "Oh, Gran," I cried out, holding her.

"I'm all right, child," she said.

Suze and Hannah began wandering around, looking at the dials and monitors and the blinking buttons.

"Now," Leach demanded from Mr. Corbin, "what's the fastest way to get Gladiolus out of his office?"

Mr. Corbin said, "The people who just left will have him here in a minute."

"And we talk to him how?"

Mr. Corbin showed him a switch for the microphone that was attached to the control panel. Leach nodded and pointed to four digital displays marked COOLING PUMP ALPHA, COOLING PUMP BAKER, COOLING PUMP CHARLIE, COOLING PUMP DELTA.

"These are what's keeping the core nice and cool?" Leach asked, and Mr. Corbin nodded.

"And what about this?" He indicated a display on which green numerals kept changing by tenths of a point. "Is this the water temperature?"

Mr. Corbin looked at him, glassy-eyed. Leach pointed the gun at his stomach. Mr. Corbin nodded again.

Leach threw his satchel to Suze. He said to Mr. Corbin, "You've been so helpful, *bub*, I'm giving you a choice. Would you rather take a pill or get hit on the head?"

"Why don't you just let me go?"

"Because I want you over here rather than over there, where they might find some use for you."

"I'll take the pill."

Suze found a bottle in the bag, shook out a white pill, and handed it to Mr. Corbin. There was a coffee cup on the console with the words *Nuke Man* baked onto it. Leach picked it up, sniffed it, and handed it to Mr. Corbin. "You'd better hope Nuke Man doesn't have any communicable diseases," he said.

While the security officer ingested the pill, Suze and Hannah kept us apprised of Mr. Gladiolus's progress on the monitors as he raced toward us.

"Coming down the main hall now," Suze said. "Jumping to Monitor Number Three."

Leach watched Mr. Corbin intently. "Feeling sleepy?"

Mr. Corbin nodded.

"You just took poison," Leach told him.

Mr. Corbin's eyes widened. Then he hurled himself forward. Leach moved amazingly fast, and the bigger man missed him entirely and fell onto the floor with a thud.

Leach leaned over and lifted Mr. Corbin's now-unconscious head. "Suze," he called, "find some rope or wire and secure this oaf."

"So it wasn't poison," I said.

"Why should I kill him? I'm the one who's pissing on *his* parade. I only kill people who try to piss on mine. How're you doing, Edith?"

"She's very sick," I said.

"She'll be all right," Leach said.

Suddenly the room was filled with the amplified voice of Mr. Gladiolus, who was standing at the middle window, surrounded by security guards who looked about as helpless as I felt. "Why are you doing this, Professor?" Gladiolus asked.

"To teach you a lesson," Leach replied into the desk mike. "To warn the world of the danger of nuclear terrorism. And also, not incidentally, to make a few bucks."

42

1. "Amigo," Cugie whispered to me. "She is one wild woman, eh?"

We were on the backseat of Chief Gillory's black-and-white Chrysler patrol car. We were not in custody. A thick glass window separated us from the chief, who was driving, and Gwen, who was sitting beside him, smiling prettily and placing her hand on his shoulder every now and then to emphasize some point.

The chief shook his head and began to laugh. Gwen laughed with him. Was she purposely avoiding eye contact with me?

Cugie said, "It was damn nice of the chief to go along with us on this."

"Nice? He's just trying to stick it to those Feds. As soon as I told him who the guy in the plant was and explained how we might just take him, what else could he do? Turn us over to Tobak?"

There was more laughter from up front.

"Damnit!" I muttered.

"She's a hot one, huh?" Cugie asked.

I glared at him.

"I mean, she likes her men, right?"

"I don't know," I said. "How the hell am I supposed to answer that?"

He shrugged. "I'm sorry if I was offensive, amigo. But I have eyes."

Gwen had shifted on the seat so that she was more or less against the chief.

I rapped on the window.

The chief shouted, "Yeah?"

"How're we doing on time?"

"There's the plant over there."

We'd been driving on the far edge of the ten acres owned by the Raven's Point Nuclear Power Company, following a twenty-foot-high chain-link fence topped with barbed wire that seemed to go all the way to the ocean.

Before we got there, Gillory brought his Chrysler to a sharp stop and we all got out. Somebody had cut a gate in the fence where no gate should have been.

I ran a finger over the bright, recently sheared links, and stared at the tire tracks in the high grass that headed in the direction of the plant.

I said, "What do you think, Chief? Fed sharpshooters looking for a back way in?"

He shrugged. "Let's go see."

He started back for the car, but I headed him off. "Let's walk a few miles," I said, "and see if we can sneak up on whoever did this."

"Let me get my binocs."

Gwen took a look at the knee-high, unattended grass and vines and shot me a venomous glance. I shrugged. "Good thing you've got your low-heel kicks on, huh, Gwen?"

"Good thing," she said bitterly.

She stepped gingerly into a clump of grass, teetered, then took another step. The chief joined us, unwinding his binocular straps just in time to offer Gwen his strong arm for support. She took it and rubbed up against the guy, looking at me over his shoulder and sticking out her tongue before returning to conversation with him.

Cugie was beside me. I looked at him. He shrugged and said, "They were put on this earth to teach man humility."

"*Es verdad,*" I mumbled.

2. Looking like a combination pointer and Crest toothpaste ad, the chief stared through his binoculars and spotted Leach's limousine parked fifty feet or so from a cliff. We were still a few miles from the plant and separated from it by what looked like a wilderness forest.

There was no sign of human life near the vehicle, which probably meant that somebody was inside it. Sleeping? Reading? Watching us try to sneak up?

The plan we developed was boneheaded in its simplicity. Leach's tough-guy chauffeur would probably have recognized me from our brief meeting at the airport, and the chief was, well, the chief, complete with uniform and sidearm. So it was up to Gwen and Cugie to try to lure the occupant(s) of the limo out into the open.

So they gave us their guns and began strolling, hand in hand, along the edge of the cliff, looking down at the surf a couple hundred yards below. When they reached the limo, they walked around it, staring in through the front window.

When that failed to bring about any response from within, Cugie tapped on the side window near the driver's seat. The door was thrown open suddenly, knocking Cugie back against Gwen.

Leach's chauffeur emerged from the car pointing a large pistol at both of them.

Gillory tensed beside me. Slowly, he removed his weapon from its holster. It was a very long shot. "Too much green," I whispered.

We edged closer.

The chauffeur had requested that Cugie and Gwen lean forward against the car. He began to search Cugie, running his hands over the cop's pastel posterior. Gwen shifted slightly against the car.

I put my hand out and stopped Gillory. He wouldn't be needing his gun.

Finished with Cugat, the chauffeur took a side step and reached forward, placing his hand between Gwen's legs. He had barely touched her upper thigh when her right leg went up, pistoned, and sent her foot into the chauffeur's mug. The sound of his nose breaking was like a twig snapping.

3. By the time we got there, Cugie had checked the interior of the limo and Gwen had the chauffeur's gun, wallet, and car keys.

"Well," she said, "what kept you guys?"

The chief said, "That was some show, ma'am. Some show."

Cugie looked at the chauffeur's bloody, bashed nose, the shattered dark glasses. He winced and looked at me. "You sure you know what you're doing, Hound?" he asked.

"Who's sure about anything?"

Gwen said, "He's probably got the climbing gear in the trunk."

She went to the rear of the car, popped the trunk, and called out, "Not your lucky day, Hound. It's a skimpy rope ladder. I don't even know if it'll hold a guy of your girth."

I held up the ladder, testing the rope fiber. "I never heard you complain of my girth before."

"I never had to follow you down a rope ladder before."

"And you won't now. Cugie and I are going in by ourselves. It's gonna be real tricky. There are TV cameras all over that place. Besides, we don't have any idea where this tunnel will come up."

"You men aren't going, Bloodworth," the chief said. "That's my job."

I looked at Cugat. "What about you, Mr. Cervantes? Another experience to add to that book?"

Cugie stepped to the edge of the cliff, looked down. He shrugged. "I am as big a fool as you, amigo, as we both know."

Gillory took a look down himself. "What makes you think the tunnel is right here? I don't see anything but sheer cliff."

"This is where Sleepy back there was parked, waiting to pull up Leach and his cohorts. He must have had some idea where the tunnel was."

"It's too bad that Stillwell blacked out before he could tell us," Gillory said, still looking down. "Maybe I could radio the hospital to see if he's come to."

"That's a good idea, Chief."

"The hell it is. I got you pegged, Bloodworth. As soon as I'm out of sight, you'll go grandstanding over that cliff."

Cugie took a few steps back from the edge. I asked Gillory, "Have you ever been inside the plant before?"

"Nope. This'll be very educational."

Cugie bent over and picked up a rock. I shrugged. He dropped the rock and began poking around in the limo trunk. Gwen looked at us with some curiosity.

I said, "Chief, here's the situation. Lieutenant Cugat and I were partners for a long time and we know we work pretty well together. So I think we're going to go down and leave you and Gwen to take care of the sleeping giant and to back us up if we fail."

He shook his head. "That's unacceptable, Bloodworth. I'm going down alone."

Cugat was wrapping a blanket around a crowbar.

"I don't suppose there's anything I can say that'd change your mind?"

He shook his head.

When he stopped, Cugie hit him with the crowbar.

I caught him before he fell and laid him out.

Gwen said, "While you boys save the world, I shall minister to this man." She sat down on the grass beside Gillory and pressed her fingers against the side of his neck. "Pulse is fine. Breathing is fine. He'll have a sore head."

"Give him a fighting chance, huh?" I told her. "Wait until he's conscious before you attack him."

She smiled. "If I didn't attack the unconscious, Leo, dear, you and I would still be strangers."

Cugie began humming another of his Latin melodies.

I said, "Might as well get started. Gwen, give us an hour, and then you and the chief go see if you can get anybody to listen to you about the tunnel."

Cugie hooked the ladder onto the rear bumper of the limo, and I started down over the cliff. My last sight of Gwen, she looked a little worried for me. At least I like to think she did.

43

1. For two hours Leach reveled in the limelight, posturing, stating his philosophies on art and life and in general, chewing the scenery. I'd seen better performances in school plays.

But the people outside of the control room had a bit too much on their minds to consider that he might be hamming it up. The crowd of spectators had definitely increased. In addition to Mr. Gladiolus and Mr. Corbin's assistant, a fellow named Grimes, there were Mr. Wheeler, the CEO of the Raven's Point Nuclear Power Company, a lean, slightly rodent-faced man, and two FBI agents named Gildcrest and Tobak.

Agent Gildcrest wanted to be Leach's pal. He kept calling him "Barnaby," and at one point asked, "Would you rather I call you 'Barney'?"

Leach was enjoying himself immensely. " 'Barnaby' is fine. What's your name?"

"Milo."

"Well, Milo, do you think you could do me a favor?"

"Sure, Barnaby."

"Would you let some reporters in, so that I can have a few words with them?"

"I don't think we can do that, Barnaby. But we could set up a press conference for you outside. We could do it now, if you like."

Leach shook his head. He pointed to a button on the panel. "Milo, what do you think will happen if I press this button?"

The FBI agent didn't reply.

"I'll tell you, Milo. If I press this button, it will open a relief valve, and the system's cooling water will drain off. In approximately sixteen seconds the

364

metal holding the core will start to melt like butter. In thirty minutes *voilà:* a meltdown! The core—all three hundred tons of bubbling, deadly, radioactive elements—will sink slowly into the soil.

"As soon as this corrosive, glowing plutonium-uranium combo comes into contact with ground water, great ghostly mists of steam will rise up from the earth to create a billowy cloud of irrevocable, painful death. Assuming the wind is still blowing in from the ocean these days, the whole state could be feeling a warm radioactive glow by tomorrow.

"So, my new best friend, unless you want to knock over that rather dangerous first domino, get the fucking press in here in fifteen minutes. Okay?"

Agent Gildcrest turned off his mike. All of us could see him talking animatedly with Mr. Gladiolus, who kept shaking his head.

"Thirteen minutes and closing, Milo, old buddy."

Hannah shouted, "One of the monitors just went dark, Archie."

Leach said calmly into the mike. "Milo, old pal. It looks like a monitor broke. So watch what happens now."

Leach pushed the button. An irritating Klaxon blared, and the men outside the window gaped at us. A supercilious mechanical voice filled the room. "Attention," it said, "warning. This is not a drill. Repeat: not a drill. Evacuate immediately. Evacuate immed—"

Leach pushed another button, and both the voice and the Klaxon buzzer ceased immediately. He said, "Now that I have your attention, what say you turn the monitor back on."

He stood up from the console and did a sort of peacock strut around the room. He paused beside Mr. Corbin, who was propped up against a large pipe to which his tied hands had been secured. "I'd threaten to kill Corbin here, if I thought that'd make you guys move faster. But as he and I both know, he's not that big a hole card. My best bet would be to destroy the plant, including that twenty-two-million-dollar reactor, and at the same time deliver the kiss of death to the whole nuclear industry in the U.S. How's that sound?"

The monitor blinked on. We could see men with guns backing down a hall, away from the control room.

Leach shook his head. "What a bunch of rubes."

Then he seemed to remember something. He cut off the microphone and took two steps to where Hannah was standing. He drew back his arm and slapped her across the face, spinning her around.

She staggered and managed to remain upright. He hissed at her, "If you make another mistake, I'll throw you to them."

"What . . . ?"

"You used my name, you dumb bitch. Not that it really matters. But we must be professional."

Gran's eyes grew alert for a moment, then softened and clouded. She called, "Sehr?"

I moved to her.

Leach watched us carefully.

"Sehr, I'm afraid it's my heart."

Leach looked honestly concerned. "What's the matter?"

"Gran has a heart condition. It hasn't been that serious, but with the lack of sleep and all this . . ."

"Damnit!" Leach grabbed his bag. "Maybe something to mellow her a little."

"No!" I said. "She's got all these allergies to drugs."

"Then let's make her more comfortable."

"I . . . I'm fine right here," Gran said, resting her head on the console in front of her.

Leach grabbed the mike, "All right, where the hell are the media? Our time here is getting short. Miss Van Dine is ill. I don't want her to be put through any more than she has to be."

Agent Gildcrest replied, "Miss Van Dine, if you're ill, just give yourself up and we'll get you the finest medical care . . ."

"Give herself up?" I screamed. "You don't think we're here voluntarily?"

Leach said to me, "You just shut up, little girl.

"Milo, Milo, Milo, what am I to do with you? I tell you what: Get out of our sight. You're beginning to disgust us."

"Professor, if you want to get things done . . ."

"Let me make myself clear: GET THE FUCK OUT OF MY FACE, MILO, BEFORE I PUSH THE BUTTON AGAIN. Wheeler, you and Gladiolus see if you can find a spokesman who has at least an ounce of intelligence. I don't care if he's with the FBI just as long as he isn't an idiot, assuming the two are not synonymous."

2. Mr. Wheeler took over as spokesman. He was definitely not an idiot. Within minutes the press began to set up. A pool video camera was aimed at us through the glass window, and technicians hopped about positioning wires and mikes.

Finally, a very handsome couple took their place at a side window, both wearing hard hats, the effectiveness of which eluded me. They introduced themselves and gave us their names and network affiliations, both of which I promptly forgot, mainly because I was more interested in how Gran was faring. She looked much worse. She smiled up at me wanly. "I'll be fine," she said.

The middle window was now filled with plant personnel, fascinated by the unfolding tableau. From time to time Wheeler would cut off his mike and send some of the engineers off, presumably to try to shift the power source away from the control panel. Leach obviously guessed what they were doing and he didn't object, which made me suspect that he knew more about the workings of the plant than anyone outside.

Gildcrest stayed away. But his associate, Tobak, returned with two other men in dark suits.

The male newsman, in his mid-forties, tanned or made up to look tanned, asked Leach why he and his "band" had taken over the plant.

Leach, nodding his head like the old professor he wasn't, waited until the silence was total. Then he began:

"Before this morality play has run its course, you will be hearing many things about us. Do not believe what you hear, and only half of what you see. These women and myself, not exactly a band of hardened terrorists, have taken control of a nuclear power plant.

"We could, at our whim, destroy this plant, sending enough poison into the atmosphere to be carried into every far corner of the continent of North America. The fact that we have arrived at this stage in our plan is some indication of the inadequate safety conditions that are rampant in the nuclear industry. I would not begin to say that every one of the one hundred–odd plants sprinkled across our largely unsuspecting landscape is this woefully open to terrorist attack, or to some sudden malfunction that would achieve the same result as a terrorist attack. But . . ."

He stopped suddenly and frowned. "You fools," he said.

Then he turned back to the control board and pushed that button again.

Again, the Klaxon, the voice intoning its repetitious warning.

The plant employees were suddenly gone from their window, probably taking off for home and then points northeast. The male newscaster, starting to sweat under his hard hat, shouted over the mechanical voice, "Professor, I don't understand why . . ."

Leach pressed the button, securing the relief valve again. He broke the silence by yelling, "Wheeler! I didn't take you for a fool. Don't make that mistake with me. If there's a meltdown, I'm in the safest spot in this whole damned area. And we both know it."

Mr. Wheeler moved toward the front of the window, pushing Lydia Dorland and the others aside. He said, "The plant won't take much more, Fulton."

"Then don't behave like a jackass. It's not enough to merely turn on those cameras. I want them to broadcast my message to the outside world."

"All right, Fulton. You win."

Leach smiled triumphantly.

The newsman asked again why the professor and his band had taken over the plant. And Leach, without so much as a pause, repeated his opening paragraphs, almost word for word.

He prattled on, providing a brief summary of the most awful milestones in the history of nuclear power. The fire at Browns Ferry. The horror of Three Mile Island. And the worst of all, the meltdown at Chernobyl. He railed against the industry, citing examples of ignorance, inadequate training of employees, the sacrifice of safety "on the altar of greed." He actually used that moldy reference.

Then, finally winding down, he stopped midsentence and turned to Hannah and Suze and said, "Now."

The three of them made elaborate bows. Then Suze immediately returned her attention to Gran and myself, as if she suspected we might be up to something.

Leach bowed again and began removing his makeup. "What you have just seen has been an elaborate bit of guerrilla theater. I am not a professor. I am an actor. The two young ladies and myself are part of a group of players, the New Mummers, who believe that only through the arts can we bring about societal change.

"We Americans have been so bombarded by visual imagery and hype that we have lost the ability to absorb any concept that takes longer than thirty seconds to explain. Important issues of the day are distilled into video bytes —political popcorn that passes through our system as soon as it is devoured. But we will sit, entranced, for hours, absorbed in drama, and during that time we are remarkably open to all ideas and concepts.

"And so, the New Mummers are presenting their drama *Meltdown,* with the thought of keeping you entertained but also to enlighten you to the dangers of nuclear folly. And bear in mind: This is live. This is real. But it is also theater.

"Now to get back to our story. I shall now make our demands. Number One: The government must immediately appoint a nonpartisan committee to supersede the Nuclear Regulatory Commission, a committee that will watchdog all nuclear activity in the U.S. or its possessions, a committee powerful enough to close down any facility that fails to meet existing safety and security specifications. Is that too much to ask? Of course not.

"Number Two: There must be total and irrevocable amnesty for myself and all the New Mummers, including Mr. Wallace Barclay, Mr. Gregory

Desidero, Mr. Tony Wharton, three anti-nuke freedom fighters now wrong-fully detained in a Southern California prison."

"Demand Number Three: We shall need a clear and unhindered exit from the plant."

Thus far, he seemed to be doing all right. But then he went over the line.

"Demand Number Four: I am sure that everyone knows that actors should be paid for their performances. Sylvester Stallone gets an average of ten million dollars per wretched film. Eddie Murphy gets nearly that same amount. And this is for making the same dreary movies over and over again. Considering the uniqueness and the dramatic quality of our presentation, I feel we are not being unreasonable in requesting fifteen million dollars in Swiss francs for our efforts."

He bowed again.

There was silence outside the control room. The newsman momentarily forgot that there was dead air to be filled. The newswoman mumbled something about the state of the Swiss franc.

Wheeler glared at Leach.

He didn't say yes, but then again, he didn't say no.

44

The first time I climbed down the flimsy ladder, I discovered we were about a hundred yards too far north.

I hauled myself back up, and we locked the chauffeur in the limo's trunk and draped the chief along its backseat. Then Gwen moved the vehicle closer to the spot where we were going over.

Less than an hour later Cugie and I were halfway down the cliff, standing at the lip of a tunnel that had been built to carry nuclear waste to where it could be illegally dumped into the Pacific Ocean with no one the wiser.

The tunnel was about seven feet high, shored with heavy timbers. It looked to be rock-solid. A narrow set of rails had been laid along the ground, but they were rusted and overgrown with weeds. The walls were damp, and spiders had worked their little web-spinners to the bone. But the worst thing was the noise. The echo from the breakers below formed a weird earsplitting sound that filled my head and made me dizzy. The walls seemed to be closing in. Cugie felt it, too. He said, "Amigo, I'm not sure I can make this."

I figured he was a better man for having said it. "Let's just see how much we can take."

The tunnel took a dogleg to the right, and as we made the turn, the sound softened. But we lost the light. We faced a blank wall of shadows. "I suppose we might have considered a flash," I said.

I heard the rasp of a cigarette lighter and briefly saw a long, straight path to a solid wall of dirt.

Cugie must have shaken off his spooked feeling, because he passed me, walking quicker.

Then there was a clang and a curse. And his lighter flicked on and he was standing beside a rusty sidecar. A heavy drum, just as rusted, lay in the sidecar. He tapped it. It was not hollow.

"Don't touch that goddamn thing," I told him. "It's gotta be full of toxic waste. They say it stays potent for hundreds of years."

He hopped back from it. "I thought Stillwell said they never used this tunnel."

"Maybe he didn't know they did. Maybe he preferred to believe they didn't."

The lighter went out and he ignited it again. An iron ladder was attached to a metal square, approximately three feet by three feet, built into the roof of the tunnel.

With Chief Gillory's .357 Magnum digging into my stomach, I started up the ladder. Though its edges were rough with jagged rust, the rungs were smooth, as if they'd just been sanded. At the top I asked Cugie for his lighter.

"Don't drop it," he said. It was the kind of advice my mother used to give me.

It took me only one flick to find the slot for the plastic key. The rest of the area was covered with a black-green slime, but the slot was bright and shiny.

"What are you doing up there, Hound?"

I didn't bother to answer him.

I pushed the card into the slot. It fit well. I heard a click, a flat buzz, and the card popped out again. I pushed up on the metal square. But it was definitely not to be raised.

So I reversed the plastic key and tried again. This time, after the click, there was a mellifluous ping, and as the key popped out, the metal square was released. I pushed it up and poked my head through the opening. Then I climbed up.

I was in a narrow passageway, lighted by bare bulbs at eye level. A sign on the wall read: WARNING: RADIATION MAY BE PRESENT. I tried to ignore it while I studied the light bulbs.

"This suit is ruined," Cugie said disgustedly as he joined me, slapping at dirt stains.

"Somebody's been fixing up a little escape route," I said. "New bulbs."

"Where the hell are we, amigo?" He winced at the warning sign.

I put my ear to the wall. I could hear the even hum of machinery. A generator or a turbine or both. "Nearer the guts of this operation than I care to be. Who knows what kind of death rays are bombarding us right now."

"Thanks for sharing that with me, amigo. By the way, did you notice what we got on the floor?"

The green tile was covered with a silty dust that might have been untouched for nearly a decade, except for tracks caused by whoever was getting the tunnel ready for Leach and his gang. "Looks like somebody's left us a trail," I said.

It led to another locked door that my key opened. As we moved quietly to the next corridor, I could hear the sound of a television set. Cugie looked at me questioningly as he drew his gun. I slipped Gillory's Magnum from my belt.

Round a corner was a small, pea-green, windowless room in which a blond woman sat smoking a cigarette and squinting at a small portable TV with lousy reception. She leaned back in her chair, and I entered the room on tiptoe.

Archie Leach was the featured performer on the small screen. He was prowling a glass booth that he was occupying with Sarah, her grandmother, Hannah Reynes, and a blond woman I eventually recognized as Suze Stillwell by adding ten hard years to my memory of her yearbook photo. Leach was demanding fifteen million dollars or he was going to blow up the plant.

The blond sitting in the chair brought her cigarette to her lips, extending her little finger as she did so. I moved close enough to touch her neck with my gun. "Hello, Miss Doolittle," I whispered. "I just knew our paths would cross again."

She stiffened.

I moved back and she rose from the chair. She was wearing a slack outfit and her hair was a mousy blond, but she was definitely Lannie Doolittle. She looked from me to Cugie, her eyes narrowing.

"You in charge of the escape route, darling?"

She didn't say a word. I bent forward to get a look at the ID that was pinned to her chest. "So now you're Lydia Dorland," I said. "Where'd you pick that moniker? From an old childhood playmate, or somebody in one of your classes? Don't you Mummers have enough imagination to come up with original characters?"

She moved her hand quickly toward her jacket pocket. Cugat said, "Hound!" Without a second thought I tapped her on the head with my gun.

She staggered dizzily, but didn't drop. As she brushed against me, I pulled the gun from her jacket. Then I helped her to the chair.

I used my tie for her hands and, over his protests, Cugat's cravat for her feet. We stuck his display handkerchief in her mouth. Then we went off in search of the glass room where all the action was.

45

Mr. Wheeler eventually agreed to meet most of the demands, including the Swiss francs. He was awaiting word from Los Angeles on the release of the prisoners. Leach was still not satisfied. He suspected a trick, he said. I realized then that no matter what, he intended to bring his drama to a flamboyant close by causing the meltdown. Maybe he thought he could get away in time. Maybe he didn't care.

Suze continued to keep a watchful eye on Gran and myself, and that was proving to be a problem.

What made it worse was that Mr. Bloodworth suddenly showed up on a monitor. He was moving cautiously down a corridor. Hannah was supposed to be checking the screens, but she'd grown bored with that, preferring to gaze longingly at the wolfish Leach.

But she was reluctantly turning her head, ready to give the screens another scan. And by this time Mr. B. was sharing a monitor with Lieutenant Cugat.

I was trying to think of something that I could do, when Gran slipped slowly from her chair to the floor, gasping for breath. I was at her side in seconds. There was a rattle from deep inside her chest. "Please?" I begged Leach. "Can't you help?"

Leach rushed to his satchel and began rooting around in it. He said, "Get away from her and give her room."

He broke some sort of ampule and waved it under Gran's nose. She coughed and then fell back. Suze and Hannah watched the two of them, fascinated.

I leaned against the console and pressed the button that unlocked the door seals. The ensuing hiss sounded like a scream to me, but the others did not seem to have heard it. Except for the recovered Mr. Corbin, who looked at me anxiously, then smiled.

I moved toward Leach, who was pulling other drug stuff from his bag.

"That won't help," I said. "She needs her own medicine."

"Damnit. Why didn't she tell me she had a heart condition?"

"Let us go. I'll get her to a doctor."

"That's impossible," he said, standing. "I'm sorry."

He turned and saw Hannah and Suze scrutinizing his every move. "Well, have we forgotten our chores?"

Hannah turned and surveyed the monitors. She gave a little yip and said, "Ar . . . I mean, oh, hell, somebody's near the door. It looks like Bloodworth!"

The metal door flew open, and Mr. Bloodworth charged into the control room like a knight of old, weapon at the ready.

Leach reached into his satchel, and Mr. Bloodworth's voice rumbled across the room, "You're not that lucky."

And Leach realized that was the truth. He dropped the bag. Turning his back on Mr. B., he raced for the console, intent on carrying out his plans for a meltdown. I stood fast in his path.

He tried to shove me aside and, I am ashamed to say, I bit his hand. Then Mr. Bloodworth grabbed him by the neck in what I believe is called a hammerlock.

Lieutenant Cugat was in the room now, too. And security guards were streaming in, eager to be in on the kill. I helped Gran as she hopped to her feet.

Leach twisted in Mr. Bloodworth's arms, stared at her like a goggle-eyed fish. "Edith, you're not ill at all!"

She replied, "No, you wretched little worm." And bending gracefully to dust off her knees, she added, "It's called *acting*."

46

1. Terry Manion wasn't exactly on top of the world, but he was definitely on the mend. His hair had been cut and his face was smoothly shaven. He was better-groomed than I was, thanks to my excuse for a barber, Singh.

When the FBI no longer needed Manion for their case against Leach and Barclay, he'd wound up on the ward. But Sarah had phoned his former sister-in-law, who arranged to move him to a nice, sunny private room that was further brightened by a few bowls of flowers, two of which had been brought by me and the kid.

She stared at him intently as he sat in the bed being monitored by a machine with an orange screen. Evidently satisfied, the nurse unhooked him and unplugged the device and wheeled it out.

Sarah and I had filled him in on all the wild angles of our misadventure, including the fact that a Free the Mummers movement had begun in a big way, consisting mainly of young people with too much time on their hands.

I told Manion that he looked like he would be on his feet before too long. He nodded. "Maybe, but I really went under this time. This was a hell of a lot rougher than my booze blackouts. I was totally gone. Fantasies. In a state of cold sobriety the idea of Gil and me ever getting back together seems exactly what it was. A fever dream. But she was as real to me as you both are."

I looked at the kid. "Sarah, would you mind leaving us alone for a few minutes?"

"Yes."

"But you'll do it?"

"I can't imagine what you could possibly have to say to Terry . . . yes, I will."

She walked to the door and went through it. "Could you shut the door, too?"

The door was closed. I supposed she was standing right outside it, but I'd done what I could.

I said, "The thing about these Mummers: Their method of acting was to imitate people that they'd come in contact with. Or, in Leach's case, characters from the movies."

"I don't see what you're getting at."

"I think your wife did spend time with you."

He shook his head no. "That's impossible. She was on another continent."

"I'm not making myself clear. I think that someone visited you who looked like your wife and sounded like her and knew a lot about her. That's the way the Mummers operated."

"Are you saying they know Gil?"

"One of 'em does. Your niece, Cece."

"But she's dead. Leach said so. Everybody did."

"Well, Leach wasn't speaking literally. He meant that he had made a new woman of her, a woman who looked and acted remarkably like the most exciting member of her family, her globe-trotting aunt.

"Barclay's private plastic surgeon did the work on her. It didn't take much, I understand. Just some kind of filler to pump up the cheekbones, and a little nip here and a tuck there. She's not the spitting image of Gillian Duplessix, but to a guy with a snootful of dope and a head full of memories, she'd certainly fill the bill."

"You're telling me I slept with a fifteen-year-old girl?"

"I'm telling you you slept with a woman who now claims to be a twenty-year-old woman named Hannah Reyne.

"Cece's mother is on her way out here with medical X-rays and dental records. And maybe she might even be able to recognize her own daughter. She didn't bother to make the trip for her husband, just arranged for him to be transported back to New Orleans."

"She's a very hard woman, and I was surprised she agreed to put me in this room."

"Sarah can be very persuasive."

"My God, I met this Hannah Reyne. While I was waiting for a policeman named Hilbert."

"She was his mistress. As well as Archie Leach's mistress."

"There *was* something about her that reminded me of Gil, but that's a far cry . . ."

I'd brought a photo with me that'd been snapped by a newspaper photographer of Leach, Hannah Reyne, Lannie Doolittle (née Sharon Whittiker), and Suze Stillwell being led from the nuclear base in handcuffs.

Manion stared at the picture. "With that hair and the eye makeup, I guess maybe . . ."

I stood up. "I just thought it might help if you knew you hadn't really flipped out on those nights. You were with someone who strongly resembled your wife."

"Ex-wife."

"Yeah," I said, smiling at him. "Ex-wife."

"What will happen to Cece?"

I shrugged. "She's only fifteen years old. . . . Some sort of juvenile detention, unless she did her roommate in, which is a remote possibility."

He shook his head again and said, "Thanks, Bloodworth. I put you through one goddamn lot of trouble. I hope you're going to send Margee MacElroy a bill."

"Hell, I've been paid," I told him. The lawyer Marr had presented me with an acceptable check and the promise of future work. La Mornay's check had been slightly smaller, but I was surprised she sent one at all.

I headed for the door. "Are you going to be around for a while?" I asked.

He shook his head. "They're transferring me to a Louisiana hospital next week."

We looked at one another. Manion shifted his attention to the photo. He stared at it for a beat, then crumpled it in his hand and tossed it into the corner of the room. "Next case," he said.

I nodded and left him.

2. Sarah was waiting outside in the hall. "You going back in?" I asked her. "Or do you want a lift?"

"I'll come back later," she said, walking beside me. "There's something we should talk about."

In the car she asked, "Is there a chance for me, Mr. Bloodworth?"

I stared at her. Oh, Christ. The idea of Hannah Reyne being a fifteen-year-old girl had already sent chills up my spine. Now this!

"Chance for you how, kid?" Playing dumb is often the best reaction.

"You know: Is it silly for me to keep hoping that this thing will happen, dreaming that it will happen? Is it possible? I mean, the sight of you coming through that door, braving all sorts of dangers to save us. I realized once and for all that it's the only thing I'll ever really want."

"Uh." My throat felt dry. I didn't know what to say.

And then Sarah added, "Is it foolish for me to think I have a future in criminology?"

I put the car in gear and told her that I didn't think it was foolish at all.

EPILOGUE

Leo Bloodworth settled back in his office chair, put his oxfords on his desk, adjusted his glasses, and read:

> McGurk, the evil master of disguises, the human chameleon, scuttled along the floor of the nuclear plant, laughing insanely. I knew it was only a matter of time before this maniacal evildoer would sabotage the plant, destroying it and most of the southwestern United States. Worse yet, destroying *me*.
>
> Where was my faithful assistant, Blood, the powerful black man who had once been my police partner, but who had chosen to leave the force to do whatever he could to clean up the ghetto where he had been born? Off sleeping, probably.

Bloodworth took off his glasses, found the bottle in his drawer, and allowed himself a good healthy swig.

He handed the bottle to the man sitting across from him. But the man, Lieutenant Rudy Cugat, shook his head no.

"Well?" he asked with hope in his voice.

Bloodworth closed the paperback and stared at the cover illustration of an idealized version of Cugat, dressed in what appeared to be a white Spandex suit and white hat, using a cable to swing near a bright red, glowing turbine, holding a beautiful half-clad woman in his free arm, while beneath them, a horde of slavering, deformed ghouls chased them with guns and knives.

The book's title read: "Rudy Cugat's *BAY CITY HEAT*."

"It's terrific, Cugie," Bloodworth said. "I hope it's the first of many."

Lieutenant Cugat's face broke into a huge smile. He brushed an imaginary speck from the knee of his mango-tinted trousers. "You don't think the cover is too exploitative?"

"Hey, you want to sell a few books, don't you?"

"They printed three hundred thousand."

Bloodworth felt a pang of envy. "And who did you say helped you with it?"

"None other than Bentley Dwyer."

"Who does he pitch for?"

"Hound, you really don't know who Bentley Dwyer is? Only the creator of the Avenging Gourmet, the hottest paperback hero in the world."

"Hotter than Spillane?"

"Spillane? Damnit, Hound, welcome to the eighties. The Avenging Gourmet. His family was wiped out in a Mafia shooting in a Little Italy spaghetti joint. So he has dedicated his life to destroying the Mafia's entire food arm. Under the guise of a mild-mannered restaurant critic named Andrew Kolmar, he travels around the country, and when he finds a Syndicate joint, whammo. The books are great. *Baltimore Clam House Blitz, Dallas Tostado Stand Takeover, Philly Pizzeria Massacre.* They've sold over twenty million copies."

"How many books are in the series?"

"Nearly a hundred."

Bloodworth shrugged. "Well, anyway, Cugie, I'll be sure to take this home and read it tonight."

"How's your collaboration coming?"

"There's no collaboration," Bloodworth said testily. "My editor assures me they'll be publishing my book just like I wrote it. I don't know what plans they have for the kid's book."

Cugat frowned. "You ought to get an agent, Hound. They take care of you. That way you'll be sure nobody screws around with your words. Words are precious, amigo."

"I don't need an agent. I can take care of myself."

"Just a suggestion. Ah, you might want to take a look at this."

Cugat slid a folded piece of pink paper across Bloodworth's desk.

Bloodworth unfolded it. It was a check, made out to Rudy Cugat and signed by one Lacey Dubin. It was for $225,000. Bloodworth blinked, put his glasses back on, and checked the figure again.

"What the hell is this?"

"From my agent. You see, she gets the check for a quarter million and then makes out a check to me minus her commission. It's the best way, Hound. Believe me. Get an agent."

"A quarter of a million bucks." Bloodworth couldn't quite believe it. "Who? What?"

"UBC-TV. They're gonna make a mini out of my book. Then maybe follow that up with a series. Lacey worked out a very sweet deal for me. I don't have to do a goddamn thing except deposit this check. Which I better do now, to make sure I get today's interest."

Cugat put the check back into his pocket and headed out of the office. "Drinks are on me in an hour at the Rusty Swing."

"I'll be there," Bloodworth said glumly.

"Bring the redhead, if she's in town."

"Next weekend."

Cugat shook his head. "So I'll take you both to dinner then, too. Hell, Hound. If it hadn't been for your first book, I'd never have hopped aboard this gravy train."

Bloodworth stared at the door for a minute after Cugat closed it. Then he flipped open *Bay City Heat* and started in on another page.

"Diamonds are ice, and ice cools most tempers, Miss Devery," I told her. Suddenly she was no longer angry. Her passion began to mount and so did I.

Bloodworth said, "Jeez!" and flipped further.

The spike went into his side like a hot knife through lard. Ruby-colored lifeblood spurted from the wound like an untapped geyser.

As the hoodlum slipped to the ground, as dead as an extinguished cigar, Mavis picked up the bottle of champagne and poured some into a glass. She said, "To the victor belongs the spoils." I took the glass from her and drained it. I told her, "Like old Cole Porter once said, 'I get a kick from champagne.' "

Bloodworth slammed the book. "*No* kick!" he shouted. "*No* kick from champagne, you illiterate son-of-a . . ."

He stood up and raised his arms over his head. Then he walked slowly to the window that did not face the Cobra Lounge mural and stared out over downtown Los Angeles. There was a bright green park in the distance and, even further, snow-capped mountains that were turning purple in the setting sunlight.

"Two hundred and fifty grand and the peckerwood can't even write a ten-dollar parking ticket," he mumbled to himself. Then, as if he'd just heard the funniest joke in years, Leo Bloodworth began to laugh.